"If you liked *The Naturalist*, you're sure to be captivated by *Jerningham*. Carefully researched and emotionally alive, it is an all-absorbing journey to the founding of Wellington. In this debut novel, Cristina Sanders charts the tensions and triumphs of the historical era that shaped modern New Zealand. Don't even bother trying to put it down until the end!"
— Thom Conroy, author of *The Naturalist*

"A spectacular debut that brings us an immersive, intelligent and well-researched insight into the early days of New Zealand's European settlement. Cristina Sanders announces herself as a writer to watch. Highly recommended."
— Mandy Hager, author of *Heloise*

JERNINGHAM

To Shannon

CRISTINA SANDERS

thanks for coming.
Happy Jerningham's
200th birthday

love Cris.
x

THE CUBA
PRESS

Edited by Mary McCallum.
Cover art by Rakai Karaitiana.
Cover image: 'Part of Lambton Harbour, in Port Nicholson,
New Zealand', 1841, by Major Charles Heaphy vc.
Te Papa (1992-0035-1917)
Typesetting and book design by Sarah Bolland.

A catalogue record for this book is available from
the National Library of New Zealand.
Kei te pātengi raraunga o Te Puna Mātauranga o Aotearoa
te whakarārangi o tēnei pukapuka.
ISBN 978-1-98-859513-9

Printed on Eco100 paper, an environmentally responsible offset paper
produced using FSC certified, 100% post-consumer, recycled PCF pulp.

RECYCLED
Paper made from
recycled material
FSC
www.fsc.org   FSC® C102086

Printing sponsored by Wakefields Digital, Aotearoa New Zealand.
www.wakefields.co.nz

THE CUBA PRESS
Level 6, 138 Wakefield Street, Te Aro
Box 9321 Wellington 6141
Aotearoa New Zealand

To Paul

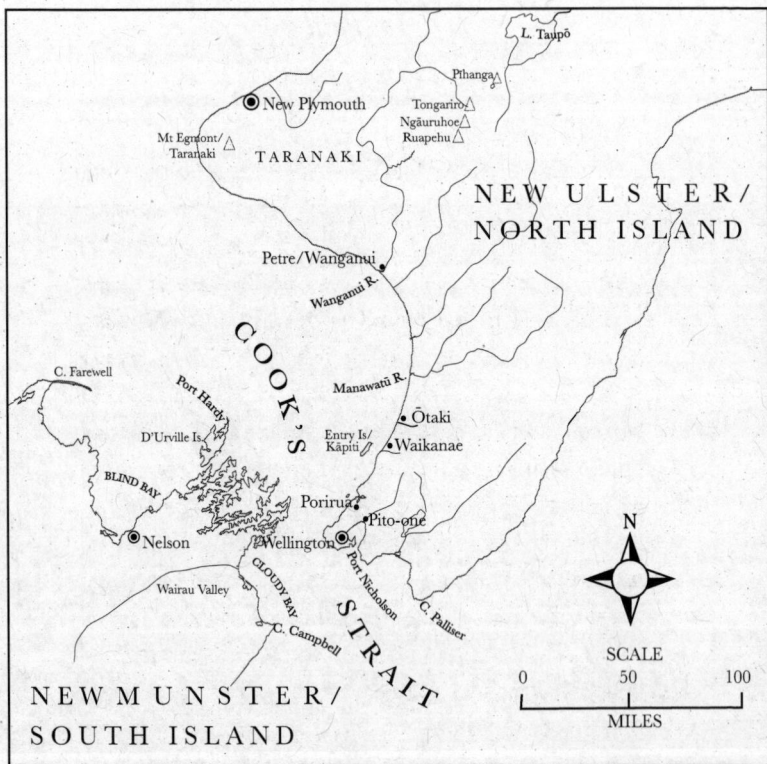

Jerningham Wakefield's journeys in 1841

ARRIVAL

A WHALE-BOAT pushed up onto the shore and a man leapt from the bow into the shallows. I was some distance away, but everything about his movements suggested he was laughing as he took his bag from a sailor and passed it to a boy waiting on the beach. Within minutes onlookers gathered and he stood within a circle of welcome, hands reaching forward, calls of greeting. Men stepped up to help hold the boat steady while their women remained hidden behind wide-brimmed bonnets, lifting hems of dresses well used to the wet. Children, both Māori and European, hopped close, elbowing for attention. With a wave of the man's hand the children flung themselves to their knees and scrabbled for treasures strewn in the sand.

Jerningham Wakefield had returned from the north.

He looked younger than I'd imagined—angular and boyish in his movements. He wore a battered cap over a growth of dark hair and was unshaven and probably unwashed.

The sailors handed across crates and barrels and Jerningham pointed directions: this there, these over here, these to the canvas tents on the tussock. Someone indicated a reed hut on the foreshore and they all laughed and crates were lifted and carried away. The boat emptied and was returned to the tide, and Jerningham reached out to clasp hands with each of the sailors, waving goodbye, shouting his thanks.

Behind him, Port Nicholson dazzled in the sunshine. In the lee of the island, the *Cuba* and the *Aurora* were peacefully anchored, sails tight against yards, flags listless in the still air. Closer in, the newly arrived *Tory* was active with sailors, and laden row-boats carried men and goods, drawing long wakes on the inky blue water from ship to shore.

Jerningham peeled away from his supporters and came up the path, a fast man with a jaunty stride, but he paused, aware of the boy who followed with his bag. He crouched down. *Is it too heavy?* I imagined him saying, and the boy, staunch and proud, declaring, *No! I can carry ten bags.*

Jerningham took off his cap and perched it on the child's head and sent him away along the track.

He looked towards the sky and combed his fingers through his hair, shoulders stretching back and lungs expanding. He scanned the circle of high hills above the settlement. It seemed young Wakefield was filling himself up, ready for whatever was to come next. Then he gave a shake like a dog waking up and strode away up the path through the fern.

I first met Jerningham later that day, when he walked out of a stormy meeting with his uncle. I was sitting at a desk in an alcove that extended off a primitive warehouse, the office of the New Zealand Company.

Though the door to the colonel's office was pulled to, the walls of the warehouse were made of raupō, through which sound travelled virtually unimpeded, and I heard most of what was being said in the next room.

"Civilise the natives. Do you understand what that means?" Colonel Wakefield's voice had lost its usual languid tone and took on a sharp edge with his nephew. "Dicky

Barrett is a foul and uncouth man and not your playmate, Jerningham. Use him to translate as necessary, but do not engage socially with him and for God's sake stay away from his wife and all her grass-skirted relations. Dancing, were you? I heard it from Dorset. Dancing with the natives?"

In my mind, I saw the colonel prodding Jerningham with a stick, a bullying housemaster with an exuberant young charge he would bring into line.

I'd heard of Jerningham's reputation for wildness. He was the son of Edward Gibbon Wakefield, our mercurial colonial mastermind, and he seemed determined on adventures to outshine his father's. In the four months since his arrival in New Zealand he had written the deeds for the Port Nicholson purchase, visited whaling stations across Cook's Strait and met with the warrior Te Rauparaha on Entry Island. He'd sailed as far north as Kaipara where his uncle had left him to refloat the stranded *Tory* and he'd organised expeditions and surveys into the interior on the journey home. He was just back from negotiating land sales in Taranaki and Wanganui. The lad was only nineteen. He probably expected praise. He was getting none from his uncle.

"Fraternising with all orders of the Māori, playing war games and sticking out your tongue as if you would waltz off into the hills with a tribe of savages. And further- more, Jerningham, you took the liberty of exploring with Dieffenbach, who is on a scientific expedition, not a rollick- ing picnic. We have so little time and so much to achieve. Do you not realise how much is at stake? Your dancing humiliates us all. Dorset wrote it all down, you know."

There was a rustle of papers, a frustrated slap of a hand on the desk.

Jerningham's voice was cool and his reply blithe. "I am a free agent, Uncle, and I will dance where and when the situation warrants it. I happen to think a dance extends the hand of friendship better than Dorset's disapproving whisker-twitching."

A chair scraped. Jerningham pulled back the door of my little office and his shadow fell over the desk. I had my back to the door, head down in my papers. The invisible, deaf man.

Behind him his uncle shouted, "You are an acting agent of the Company and by God you will behave like one!"

"Who the devil are you?" were Jerningham's first words to me. This was followed immediately, as I turned my head and raised my eyes, by a more friendly: "Never mind. You're sitting in my chair but I forgive you."

He had washed and shaved, and trimmed his glossy moustache. Like his uncle the colonel, he was elegant and tall. Straight shouldered. He peered at me intently, his eyes slightly narrowed as if he were trying to see below my surface.

"Well, get up! We can't both sit there. Though I can't imagine why either of us should sit at a desk when there is a new grog shop opened on the beach. Come on."

He jerked his head towards the door. I stood hesitantly. There was no comment from the colonel next door. I swept my papers into the upturned box that served as a filing cabinet. Jerningham was poised by the desk and watching as I put things away. He had an intimidating stillness.

"Leave that," he said impatiently, and so I followed him to Pito-one beach, out across the shingle and sand to where music and lights and laughter tumbled from the makeshift shack at the edge of the water.

━

I had arrived in Port Nicholson, the hastily contrived destination for our colony, a few weeks before. We had sailed along a rocky coastline on the North Island of New Zealand and through a channel to find a large pocket of harbour tucked away from the blustery Cook's Strait. Within a day I had been summoned by Colonel William Wakefield.

There were few options for accommodation ashore other than a damp calico tent, so I had retained my cabin on the *Aurora* through a week of wind and choppy water while a temporary hut was built for me. As a result, when rowed ashore I staggered unceremoniously on my sea legs in the doorway of the flimsy warehouse. A carpenter crouched, laying roughly cut planks underfoot. It was as well the floor was raised to allow the rain to flow underneath.

We were in the rudimentary stages of colonisation and like many of the settlers I wondered why we had immigrated so hastily, before any accommodation had been built and with town and country plots yet to be surveyed. If there existed fresh pastures they lay well concealed under swamp and forest. Still, in those early days, we were spiritedly optimistic; we trusted in Colonel Wakefield and were cheerfully unaware of the race for land that drove the Company forward at such precarious speed.

The carpenter paused in his hammering as I swayed across to the desk, a plank placed on two sawhorses, behind which sat the great man himself.

"Colonel Wakefield. You sent for me."

"Arthur Lugg, is it? Do sit down. You are an educated man and a bookkeeper?"

"I was a bookkeeper, sir, yes."

"And I understand you have languages?"

"Latin and French, sir. Passable German. Some Russian."

"None of which form the basis of Māori."

"Ah, no, sir. I imagine not."

"Shame. We could use a proper linguist. There's many a man says he can talk to the natives, but none with the kind of education we need for negotiations. And we can't trust the missionaries to be neutral."

He stretched his long legs under the desk and tapped his pencil on the copybook open in front of him. He was in his late thirties, trim and pleasant-looking, with an open face suggesting decency. He looked slightly careworn, but in no way overwhelmed by his extraordinary responsibilities. I admired dedication in a man and felt predisposed to like him.

"We need things, Lugg. You think you come prepared for a venture like this, but until one arrives one really doesn't know what is required. We could use someone who can keep track of what we need and source it, or better still, persuade someone else to source it for us. You will be our procurement officer."

"Thank you, Colonel," I replied. "But I am not in need of a job."

"It's a 'role', Lugg. I won't insult you by paying you much, but we all have a part to play in building the colony. I hope you were not intending just to watch? There it is. You can make it up as you go along, like we all do here. The title is irrelevant, though we can't call you quartermaster, obviously. No military service." He said this as though it were a character flaw. "Just muck in. What happened to your hand?"

My thumb was strapped and tied against my right hand. I had lost its tip, sliced clean off by a rope on board the ship a week out from landing. It didn't bother me particularly, and I expected it to heal over in time. I explained this to Colonel Wakefield, who looked at me dubiously, as if doubting I was fit for the proposed role because of my new disability. Actually, it is surprisingly inconvenient to lose the tip of one's thumb. God gave us opposable thumbs for a reason, and I had lost the ability to pinch. I was slow and clumsy with simple things, like fastening buttons or picking up small items. Writing ledgers though, I could do perfectly well. In fact, I rather liked the idea of being employed by the Company, on the inside, as it were. I had expected to be a man of leisure, but perhaps I did have a contribution to make.

"Does it affect you?" he asked, still worried about my thumb.

"Well," I replied, "I'll never play the harp."

"You are a musician, Lugg?"

There was an uncomfortable silence and he looked at me quizzically. I realised that perhaps we had a different way of engaging with words.

"I spoke in jest, sir."

He frowned slightly and turned away.

I followed him across the floor-in-progress to a hole in the wall, which opened into a dirt-floored alcove. The door itself was propped up against the wall. It looked too narrow to fit the frame. Wakefield gestured inside.

"That'll be your office. You may have to share when Jerningham returns until we build something more suitable. Your first job is to procure a desk. Telford's is having an auction tomorrow morning, west end of the beach. See if you can find something sturdy for under a pound."

And with that, I was employed and dismissed.

—

I spent a week with Jerningham organising food and accommodation. He took me to the Māori settlement, he called it a pā, under the western hill, and we passed with our guide through the poled enclosure to a disorganised collection of mud and raupō huts, open fires and smouldering cooking pits. Healthy-looking brown children ran up to gawp rudely at us, wide smiles showing good teeth, bare skin shining in the sun. Jerningham reached behind the ear of a pretty girl and pulled forth a penny that he held high as she jumped for it. He spun around leaving a scattering of trinkets: beads and buttons and ribbons. Bright English treasures that the children dived for like birds.

"Hat off and nose forward, Lugg," he told me, and I found myself sharing breath with a line of cloaked natives, who, one after the other, nudged their soft noses against mine in a friendly way. I was introduced to chief Te Puni, his nephew chief Wharepōuri and all their relations, with long names that flew fast past my English ears. We sat on mats on the ground in front of a low grass-covered hovel and the activity of the settlement went on around us: men passed with a catch of fish to hang on a drying frame, children rolled in the dirt, a group of blanketed women came to peer at us and strolled away again, laughing.

There was much talk from the chief, and then the others, and Jerningham asked many questions. From their laughter I gathered he spoke their language with more confidence than accuracy. Most of the conversation was lost on me, though Jerningham translated occasionally.

"Pigeons and duck," he said, "so tame you can get within twenty yards of them. The Māori trap them, but we'll send a couple of guns out tomorrow."

A man watched us from the shadow of a hut, behind Jerningham's back. His hair had been cut into a short English style fairly recently, and he wore a decent jacket over a dress shirt that had faded to a dirty grey and was tucked into a straw mat tied around his waist. He pulled back when he caught my gaze.

Chief Te Puni was drawing pictures in the air, his expressive hands undulating. He knotted his fingers loosely. Something swimming, caught in a net. "Upokororo!" he said, and then repeated it more loudly and slowly as if that would aid our understanding. Jerningham turned to me and shrugged.

"A kind of river fish, I think, caught in baskets. What do you think, Lugg? Shall we get some? We have so much fresh sea fish and no facility yet to preserve it properly. I think not." He shook his head. "And no more cockles. Nasty, slimy things." He drew his finger across his mouth and screwed up his face and shook his head. The men laughed uproariously.

Jerningham asked for more labourers and Wharepōuri offered many men, as many as we needed, to build temporary barracks and huts to house our settlers until the town was established. It seemed we would be camping for some time yet.

We stood, and Jerningham turned quickly as if he had felt the eyes on his back. The watching man disappeared into the shadow.

"Ngaiti? I know you are there. Be civilised and come out, there's a good man." He stepped forward but the man peeled out from the side of the hut, his greeting to Jerningham a drop of his head and a half-raised hand as he turned his back and walked sullenly away, bare feet slapping the dirt.

"Leave him," said Te Puni. "Ngaiti goes home his people, now."

"He is a disappointment to me," said Jerningham, loudly enough so the departing man would hear.

We shook hands with our friends and agreed to send a shooting party out the following day, and to regular deliveries of pigs and fish, potatoes and greens.

The women came forward to watch us leave. They had dropped their blankets and their uncovered breasts were presented to us as God made them, in all their variety, lined up like a garden at the gate. I had only ever known one pair of pale nipples on white skin and here were dozens of dark pink roses on firm brown skin in the open air. I breathed in the smell of smoke on a summer breeze and thought I had never seen anything so beautiful. Keeping my eyes ahead, I struggled to remain unaffected but Jerningham slowed and fell behind to greet them all.

We walked along the beach for some distance from the pā as I regained my composure. I could sense that Jerningham knew my struggle and was amused by it. He whistled a tune and bent occasionally to pick up a flat stone that he sent skimming out on the water.

As we neared the settlement I joined his game and we stood for a while like boys, throwing stones and counting the bounces.

The sand had spent the morning sucking the heat from the sun and now gave it back in waves that baked in pockets between jacket and shirt and cravat and trousers. I thought with envy of the loose woven skirts the Māori men wore, their naked torsos. I hadn't exposed my shoulders to the sun since childhood.

"Who is that man Ngaiti?" I asked.

"He is a waste of a good education." Jerningham shrugged, as if he could be rid of a man with a shake of his shoulders. "He lived in England in my father's house for over a year. He came off a French whaler, and we took him home to Chelsea, dressed and civilised him. He was quite the favourite of many of our friends. He claimed to be a chief, but of course he was nothing of the sort and was greeted with ridicule by his people here."

"But he taught you his language."

"Oh, yes. Partially. Though he proved a most unreliable translator in our negotiations. He spent more time apologising for the squalid appearance of his relations than putting forward our case. He called himself an 'ariki', but his people call him an 'ariki nono'."

"I am sure you are going to translate that for me."

"An expression you may find useful, Lugg. Not a chief, but a chief's arse. Oh, look, there's my uncle. How timely."

Jerningham scooped a couple of gull's feathers from the beach and threaded them up into his sideboards. They fluttered decoratively at his chin. "Just because I promised to be sensible today," he said.

We put our hats back on and went to make our report to the colonel.

———

By the end of February, a month after my arrival, four of the initial settler ships were in. The *Aurora* had been first, fast behind the officials in the *Tory* and the *Cuba*. I'm not especially competitive, but I admit that being among the first settlers of the colony did thrill me and I intended to feel superior to all who came after for the rest of my life.

The *Oriental*, with over a hundred settlers, had left three days before us and we cheered her arrival nine days after we made shore, a close-run thing. The *Duke of Roxburgh* made a fast passage of 126 days, matching our time. The *Bengal Merchant* had arrived next with sheep and pigs and chickens, but her passengers were swamped on arrival and one long-boat sank, ditching many families' entire possessions irretrievably into the deep water of the harbour. We awaited the *Adelaide*, which had left Gravesend with us and was now overdue. We'd not seen or heard of her since our departure.

I was kept busy by the colonel and entertained by Jerningham and was grateful for the distraction from a matter that kept me awake at night and out early in the morning, looking across the changeable water of the harbour to the southern shore. Somewhere under those hills was a woman I loved.

Ada Malloy. Every morning I stood on the Pito-one beach, turning my face to where she lived with her brother and his wife, and I laid my hand on my heart to hear its beat, touched my lips to feel their heat. We had kissed only once, Ada and I, in the shadow below the *Aurora*'s mast on that long and wonderful journey across the world. It was a kiss that had shocked us both. Too impulsive, too charged with physicality. It sustained me through those weeks on board and continued to penetrate my dreams, and it changed my compass to point towards her constantly.

Meanwhile I had finally acquired my own hut—a miserable slap-up of reed and mud but surprisingly watertight—and I brought ashore my bed and mattress, making me the envy of the settlers still under canvas. I closed my eyes to its baseness and dreamed of the house I would build for Ada. My solitary ownership lasted under a week before I was obliged to offer a billet to a young man whose own straw hut had blown down. Charles Heaphy was slim, bright-eyed and neatly bearded.

"Is that all you have?" I asked when he moved into my hut with little baggage other than a few books, a blanket roll and his drawing tools. "We can get you a cot at least. And Telford's is selling pillows, Mr Heaphy, along with all sorts of linen and comforters. We won't live like heathens under my roof."

His shy smile suggested mine were the first kind words said to him for a long time. We shook hands, a warmth exchanged.

"Please call me Charles. A pillow," he said dreamily, as if such a luxury was far down his list of essentials, "yes, why not?"

He was the Company draftsman, part of the original *Tory* crew and they were lucky to own such a loyal man. He believed everything he was told, saw what he was told to see and painted wonderful pictures of ships nestling in calm harbours with peaceful natives resting by the water's edge.

Charles did other sketches too—fast, visceral and real—of the boggy swamps and dark hills of Port Nicholson, wild-eyed native men and bare-breasted women with blue lips and tattooed chins, naked children and the impoverished shacks of the Māori settlements, but these sketches were not worked up and distributed. I don't know what he did with them. He certainly never showed them to the colonel. For the Company, Charles made the sun shine on the settlement every day. I am sure during those early days that some of his unrelenting goodness rubbed off on me.

In the evenings, Charles and I often walked three or four miles to the eastern end of the beach, along a path cut between palms and through flax and fern. We were punted across the shifting shingle of the river by an old Māori man for a penny apiece, and on to where the shore ended abruptly under a steep hill. The scrubby bushes had already been cut back and collected for firewood, the fast-burning mānuka bush a staple for settlement fires. I hardly noticed its strong astringent smell now.

I looked up at the towering hills, layers of blue folding back against the sky.

Colony. In England the word, to me at least, meant a community. I had imagined a cluster of houses in a gently undulating land, with men working open fields, ploughing straight rows for crops. A corner of parochial England under cleaner sunshine.

This was not that place. There was no farmland. This was a raw, sharply edged world.

"Missing home yet?" I asked Charles lightly. I noticed he was smiling as if those hills called to him in a way they did not speak to me. "Family? Friends?"

He laughed and shook his head. "I'm an orphan and the youngest of five. My life was always going to be out in the world, though I never imagined it would take me quite this far. I don't think we can afford that sort of indulgence, to look back and pine for England. No regrets, Arthur! This has to be home now."

There were sea-smoothed logs washed up where the crumbly sand met the shingle, and we sat and smoked a pipe as the day disappeared and the sweet air settled across the land. Charles studied, with satisfaction, the sweeping view past the harbour island to the far hills, the strange, moody colour of the water. He was a Londoner and used to life through a layer of smog. Here he blinked often, as if he couldn't believe his luck, as though someone had wiped the soot from his windows to leave a sparkling view.

"Fifteen thousand miles from home in a land without maps." Charles pointed his beard to the darkening sky. "Isn't it wonderful?"

The next weeks were filled with frantic activity. I wrote endless lists for the colonel and calculated the temporary shelters we would need until the town was surveyed and permanent houses could be built. We had brought an extraordinary amount of equipment with us, carried ashore and immediately put to use: ovens and anvils, paper and pianos. An entire printing press came off the overdue *Adelaide* that blew through the heads in early March, after a delay at Falmouth and a long voyage. The printer, a Mr Revans, swore like a sailor when his press was left just above the high tide mark, covered by a tarpaulin while it, like everything else, waited for a home.

The colonel rallied everyone around to clear and build, and Jerningham's Māori friends supplied food in huge quantities. We distributed pork and fish and potatoes among the workers. Many families had never eaten so well and that, at least, balanced the discomfort for those still sleeping under a bush.

One evening when the long light stretched over the valley, Charles brought a chess set from his battered travel bag and we sat outside to play. It was an elegant set, the pieces small but heavy—ebony and boxwood. They came packed in a velvet pouch.

Charles positioned his men neatly in their squares and sat back, stroking his beard. My injured thumb had not healed over and I used my clumsier left hand to set up. As I accidentally bumped his pieces he realigned them, each to the very centre and facing forward. He was a meticulous man.

I tapped his hand and took black, and he turned the board, so our men were in front of us.

"You are obviously a dedicated player," I said, "to carry the game all around the world in that small bag of yours."

"I'm very much a novice," he said, and I must have looked relieved because he smiled at my expression. "Jerningham gave the set to me when we landed."

"Really?" I said. I didn't imagine Jerningham was much of a man for gifts and he and Charles were not easy companions. A chess set was a precious possession in a country without shops.

"It was compensation for a malicious deed. It's the only time I have known Jerningham contrite, though the colonel probably prompted the gift. He magnetised me, you know. Twice. We were so very bored on the journey out and while Dieffenbach and I read and studied, Jerningham got up to his pranks. He'd come across some fellow in France who'd taught him to calm a person into a somnolent state using magnetism. You've heard of this procedure?"

"I've heard of magnetism," I said, "but it's a dangerous prank. Did he put you in some kind of a trance? I can't imagine he knew what he was doing."

"I shouldn't have let him," said Charles, "but there are only so many evenings you can discuss gull skeletons with a German. He tried to magnetise Ngaiti first but Māori are such superstitious creatures the poor man ran away to hide in his bunk. I was interested in the efficacy of the thing for pain relief. The Orientals do something similar with focus and chanting. So I agreed."

People passed down the path and we nodded a good evening, not rushing into our game, savouring the anticipation between setting up the board and embarking on the first move. Charles looked out across the fires of the settlement, relaxed and unhurried. I could see why Jerningham would select him for an experiment requiring a calm mind.

"I have no memory of it," he said, "other than letting Jerningham's voice soothe me. I felt heavy. I woke up confused. The colonel suggested we try again. Dieffenbach reported that I grew extremely violent. Possessed, he called it. I was uncharacteristically angry for several days. It took a long time to shake it off."

"The colonel should never have let it go ahead."

"Well, no. But I did earn us a pretty chess set."

I expected a standard king's pawn opening from Charles but he surprised me with an aggressive claim to the centre, setting his queen's pawn evenly on its square. "The set was wasted on Jerningham anyway. He's far too impulsive for chess."

I frowned at the pawn in the middle of the field and resisted the urge to nudge it askew.

Later, after Charles had beaten me twice and we called it a night, I remained outside under the vastness of heaven and wondered if anyone was looking down on us, and what they would make of it all. Here, at the end of God's broad oceans, on a scrap of land between empty mountains and sea, a few men scratched away at a patch of bush. It felt like civilisation would be a long time coming to this place.

—

Our immigrants continued to arrive, newly ashore and land-fragile.

As I had done, they tended first to stand on solid ground and sway to an internal ocean. After months on water, the new arrivals were reluctant to lose sight of the sea. They walked up and down the long strand with packed sand underfoot, not knowing where to start or how to move on. They scowled at the high hills and dense bush and wrinkled their noses at the earthy smell, complicated and wholesome after brine and bilge water. They smiled hesitantly at fellow colonists and flinched from the inquisitive natives who ran forward to offer vigorous handshakes of welcome.

For the first week or so most did little more than adjust to the fact of arrival, eyes stretched in awe at the lonely emptiness of the place and realising, perhaps for the first time, that we were camping, and that this was the extent of it. The row of tents along the shore *was* the colony.

In the beginning, the Company was the only employer in our world and all our expectations came through Colonel Wakefield. I read through passenger lists and found people for him as required. He gave immediate positions to carpenters, thatchers and sawyers. Bricklayers, until we found useable clay, were designated to the labouring pool. I worked with the surveyor, Mr Mein Smith, who had arrived in early January on the *Cuba* with the timber-fellers, builders, carpenters and gardeners. I found him men with mathematics and accounting. Men, like me, who fast realised that we couldn't sit around and observe the building of the settlement, because there was, as yet, nowhere to sit.

Our colony sank its claws into the land, with fires and clearings; our insubstantial wooden huts had a tenuous hold.

"At least we have good labourers in the Māori," said the colonel as he, Jerningham and I stood in the early afternoon, watching the strong, lean men expertly thatch our office roof with their native ferns. "Employment will soon civilise the race. Keep them busy."

"I can't imagine what they did with themselves before you arrived, Uncle," said Jerningham, but Colonel Wakefield either didn't hear or understand the sarcasm.

The view beyond the office was a clutter of construction stretching from where we stood all along the waterfront and up the river. The colonel puffed on his cigar and shook his head, tutting at the groups of men who looked so small against the backdrop of the valley, labouring to shovel a channel in the river or spread shingle on a soft track.

"My father will have expected a town of grand stone buildings by now," said Jerningham. "With horses dashing up the paved streets, carriages to carry the gentry." He cast a quick look at his uncle and then waved his hand over the shambles of Britannia. "We're getting on very slowly."

"What would you have us do?" said the colonel. "Shall I call the labourers off the wharf there and get them started on stables for your horses instead?"

"I think a gentleman's club, first. Set back, but with a view of the harbour. Stabling has certain prerequisites that we lack, Uncle. You know. Horses. And grass. But a club we could enjoy immediately."

The colonel ignored Jerningham like he would a prattling child. He pointed with his cigar to where the river was already undermining the bank by the wharf construction. "Look there, Lugg. There's more evidence that we are building in the wrong place. The whole plain is unstable."

We watched the workers climb down from the wharf and scramble back onto the bank, waiting to see what the river would do. Our town followed designs laid out by Edward Gibbon Wakefield and his New Zealand Company planners a world away in London. Men with great vision but no local knowledge. Their settlement was mapped out on imaginary, flat, dry land, built in a grid formation on either side of a deep river with access to the sea. London, in effect. To this design the surveyors knocked pegs across the shingle banks of the shifting Hutt River and over its flood-prone flanks, and the colonel watched his settlers leave for more solid ground in Thorndon.

"We should burn the forest, sell this entire valley as pasture and build our town across the harbour," the colonel said. "You see, don't you, Lugg? Mein Smith is simply wasting our time surveying this swamp. We will meet this afternoon. Call them for me. I want Mein Smith and his men. All the surveyors. And send a boat for Evans—I'll need him on my side. Five o'clock. We'll have this out."

My sympathies were with the colonel in his increasingly fraught arguments with the pedantic surveyors, who followed their instructions from home like the Bible and would build the town as directed, though it took a thousand men and a hundred years.

"Have you finished?" Colonel Wakefield shouted up to the labourers on the roof, who smiled and waved back with shouted greetings: *hello, mister; good day; thank you, sir!* Jerningham laughed as the colonel frowned and lifted his hands in exasperation, but getting no further sense from the men he pulled on his cigar, blew the smoke like an expletive and turned to go back into the office. A wisp of straw fell from the roof and stuck in his hair, lodging upright like a feather. We said nothing. It seemed an appropriate decoration for the circumstances.

Jerningham took me by the shoulders and turned me towards the road. "Get your tallywags moving, Lugg, and call the men. Finally we are getting some action. It's taken him long enough to realise Britannia has beached. Don't let's lose the momentum. There's Mein Smith coming down to the wharf now."

I walked down to intercept the surveyor, Jerningham on my heels, muttering. "He should command him to move the town to Thorndon! Why such reticence to lead? Mein Smith is a servant of the Company. He is there to serve. Who's giving the orders here?"

While the future of the colony was battled out between the officers, I concentrated on our immediate requirements for shelter. We still had families huddled under bivouacs in the scrub. Māori workers would build a fair hut, big enough for two or three families, in exchange for a pair of blankets and some tobacco. Settlers came ashore and I arranged temporary shelters for them anywhere there was space. Mushroom-like, the camps appeared almost overnight, grouped with little distinction for rank or wealth. We were all savages, sitting around our open fires in the evenings like our Māori neighbours.

—

The surveying paused at Britannia, but the needs of the settlement continued to grow.

"I need a rope-maker," said Colonel Wakefield. "There was a man on the *Oriental*. Send him to the missionary over in Waikanae, Hadfield's his name. They treat flax. Get him to bring a couple of the natives back to show us how it's done. It's *Phormium tenax*—the swamp here is full of the stuff, may as well exploit it. Are you writing this down, Lugg?"

"I have it, sir."

"And talk to Dudley Sinclair about bricks—he's on the passenger lists. Find what he needs to set up. There's clay up the valley. Molesworth might know, he's been there exploring. See if it's suitable for brick or plate. We'll meet with the blacksmiths at noon tomorrow. Round them up."

"Sir."

Jerningham's initial requirement was for wine. He predicted a stable trade for a merchant. He handed me details of a retired military man with a vineyard on the Hokianga Harbour, easily accessible for passing ships.

"Find a trader to bring a decent supply in for the settlement, Lugg, and get me an angel's share. The introduction is worth that at least."

I nodded. I knew of a wine merchant who would be glad to begin trade.

"And find me a pretty woman."

"I beg your pardon?"

"You're a procurement officer, aren't you?" Jerningham flashed his sideways glance at me, haughty and amused at the same time. He laughed at my shocked face.

"Oh, come on, Lugg! Procure me a warm woman, why don't you? Smooth skin. Soft. Willing." He held his hands in front of his chest and bounced them slowly as if they cupped heavy breasts. "With big white bouncing bubbies. What do we pay you for, anyway?"

"I didn't notice 'bubbies' on your uncle's list. I'll add them, shall I? Sail cloth, brass latches, and a pair of bouncing bubbies for Jerningham?"

He raised his eyebrows at me and then nodded. "Yes. Go on."

Within a week, Jerningham was in trouble with his uncle again. It seemed that this would be a regular occurrence and I wondered at the sense of putting the pair of them together on this expedition.

I was on the beach with Charles. It was twilight, and we had come to welcome a new settler ship anchored off Somes Island. The breeze was onshore and waves thudded unusually close, dragging the water around unpredictably. All day an inconsistent wind had stirred the choppy surface and now the tide was spring-full and heavy along the sloping beach. Colonel Wakefield had advised to wait for morning to disembark, but the call of land was strong and a brave gang of enthusiasts was being rowed ashore.

An alarm went off, a warning blast into the air.

Screams and cries and gunshots from the boat bounced over the water and set a cascade off across the ships in harbour, as if the marauding armies of the legendary Te Rauparaha himself were advancing over the hills. As flares lit the sky, men scrambled from their tents with whatever weapons they had and came running to the beach. A Māori canoe was being pushed into the surf by a dozen bare-chested and tattooed natives, who leaped aboard and plunged into the white water, shouting loud welcoming cries as they battled out through the waves to greet the settlers' overladen boat. They looked magnificent and Charles and I cheered them on, until we realised the confusion on board the newly arrived ship and the terror of the settlers in the dinghy.

In the chaos, the sailors turned their clumsy boat and dug their oars in as they scampered unsteadily back across the water. I laughed, but then Charles nudged me and pointed behind, up on the bank. Jerningham stood with Te Puni surrounded by all his men from the pā. The pair were doubled over with laughter, the small cloaked Māori with his arm on Jerningham's shoulder, pointing at the panic they had caused. They both knew how the welcome would appear to settlers arriving in near dark on an unknown beach.

It was a cruel prank.

In punishment, Colonel Wakefield set Jerningham cutting trenches through the Pito-one swamp. His concern was not at all for the terror of the settlers—publicly he laughed the incident off and told them not to behave like a pack of frightened geese—but he was outraged at Jerningham's encouragement of Te Puni's joke.

"You will undo all my work here," he told Jerningham. "I must have respect."

Jerningham curled his lip and tossed his head and his uncle's words were ignored.

———

One evening there was a stomping and a slapping on the reeds of my hut, followed by an impatient shaking of the flimsy door.

A gruff voice said, "How's a man to knock when there is no bloody wood on which to smack his knuckles?"

I looked at Charles.

"Sam Revans," he said. The owner of the press.

A shadow appeared at the calico window, a hand raised, trying to peer through the thin cloth.

We were playing chess and I was about to attack the back row, but then I replaced my piece to a frown of irritation from Charles. As I stood to open the door I noticed his knight was paused to fork my queen and bishop. Clever. Not this time.

"Mr Revans, sir." I opened the door and shook the big man's hand. He had greasy greying hair, a florid complexion and deep intelligent eyes. "I shall purchase a door knocker from Telford's first thing. We should have been disappointed to have missed such an honoured guest. Do come in."

He scowled at me. Young pup, he said, without opening his mouth. He was about five years older than I was, but seemed a man who had lived a much fuller life.

Charles introduced us, although the newspaperman knew who I was as he'd passed me sitting in Wakefield's office often enough.

"I'm interrupting. I can come back."

"If it's private business I can leave," I said. "I usually take a walk before turning in." Revans narrowed his eyes, taking my measure, weighing up what he knew of me and making a judgement whether to approve of me or not. His eyes flicked to the table.

"White, are you? Heaphy would never forgive me for sending you away when he has you speared."

"Well, I don't think he's quite at that stage just yet—"

Revans reached out a heavy hand, pointed not to the fork, which I had seen, but to Charles's pawn placed to cover an attack from his queen. Obviously now, there was the checkmate.

"Do stay, Mr Lugg. Perhaps your conversation is more intelligent than your chess."

I was still looking at the chessboard. That made three to Charles, though I wasn't sure it counted if Revans made the move for him. His twitching beard suggested it did.

Revans stepped across the small space and sat heavily on the cot, dropping the leather satchel he carried. It was stuffed with a spray of papers: some printed, some inked, many covered in smudges and ripped at the edges.

"Copy for my newspaper," he said to me, his eyes shadowed under bushy brows. "We're going to print our first Port Nicholson edition on 18 April, God willing. Advertisements coming at me from all quarters, they all need to be costed and checked, you know." He pulled out a loose sheet of paper and read: "*Wanted, sections with town acres, between numbers 50 and 100. Apply at the* Gazette *office*. And d'you know, Mr Lugg, our readers will discover there is no *Gazette* office. Of course there is not! Wakefield has neglected to supply me with one. My beautiful press sits in boxes on the sand, the flotsam of an ambitious civilisation. And what's more—we have no town acre numbers between 50 and 100. The clerk in the land office is innumerate. He can't count the men licking his buttered bun, and yet that dollymop has proved she can count to well over a hundred. I should give her the job. Eh? And dear Captain Chaffers is in charge of our shipping intelligence report and he's spent the week with his main-brace so well spliced he can't lie down without holding on. Listen to this one: *Sam McDonnell has tools for sale* and states his address as *Last tent, west end of the beach.* I ask you, is the man a crab?"

I took my cue from Charles, who was smiling sympathetically, and so I was ready to laugh when Revans slapped his thigh and let out a shout, "Oh, but it's the life, is it not? Would you rather be anywhere else?"

"I would not," said Charles. "Indeed I would not."

"It will all change soon enough, my boy, and you best be prepared. They will rake up the debris and divide the shiny settlers from the rough, and order will be imposed. We'll have structure, don't you think, Mr Lugg? Laws and protocols and busybodies telling us how to, and what to, and when not to, and who to. I was in Montreal, you know. Now there's a town where administration runs rampant as the curse of Venus. Everybody vying to dip their pen in the government's ink." He pushed the papers roughly into the satchel and shook his head. "We think we can make a difference here, build something liberal, something truly democratic—you *are* a democrat, Mr Lugg?"

"Most assuredly, Mr Revans."

"It will all go to hell. Mark me. Proclamations and declarations and treaties soggy with the piss of self-important men." He looked around our little hut in the fading light, over the upended crate that held the lamp and wicks and past the reed screen of my sleeping area, turning his head slightly at the glint of a bottle in a box. It was one of Jerningham's store, left with me for safe-keeping. I fetched it, and poured a good slug into our two china teacups and Charles's leather mug. I would replace it when the ship came back. We drank.

"William Mein Smith wants to engage you," Revans told Charles. "I heard it from Wakefield himself. I know you yearn to go off exploring with Dieffenbach, but your time will come for all of that, and meanwhile I very much hope you will join the surveyors, at least until we have our town marked out, wherever we decide to place it. He is a good man Mein Smith—doesn't always see eye-to-eye with Wakefield, but you'll learn valuable skills from him. We need you, Heaphy. That's it. That's what I came here to say to you. When the call comes, I would encourage you to step up." He stuffed his papers away and rested his big hands on the satchel.

"And if I may speak plainly, we have need of your diplomacy as a buffer between Wakefield and Mein Smith. They are two men who don't belong in the same room. He has a very high regard for you—Wakefield, that is—and you would be doing the colony a service in many ways."

Charles dropped his head, clearly embarrassed. "Mr Revans, I am a servant of the Company. I take the roles I am assigned. If Colonel Wakefield tells me to survey, I shall certainly join Mr Mein Smith and offer my very best service."

"Of course you will, my boy, no doubt about it. Just a forewarning, eh? Mein Smith is a pragmatist, he likes a straight line and a straight command, and Wakefield's confused wand-waving leaves him bewildered. Come on now, Mr Lugg, drink up, there's a drop more in that bottle."

Revans didn't leave until the bottle was empty and we three had mellowed into each other's company. An odd collection: one gruff, one upright and me. I thought about my contribution. Before I embarked on the *Aurora*, I might have said "one dull". But I looked around at my new friends and thought now "one steady".

BEFRIENDING JERNINGHAM

OUR ILL-FITTED office door was slightly ajar and I paused before I knocked, listening for voices. After a few weeks of overhearing slightly too much, I was wary of stumbling in on Jerningham up to some mischief. He seemed genuinely fond of me and rather too eager to include me in his schemes. Already, against his uncle's express permission, he'd wasted my time sourcing a non-existent racing horse from a breeder in the Bay of Islands, and had used my account to hide his substantial rum purchases.

"Medicinal," he told me, as my account at John Healy's store rose steadily. It was considerably more than one man could consume and I did wonder if the rum was used in bribes, something explicitly against Company regulations. Jerningham never admitted to giving bribes. Gifts, though, he dispensed widely.

Unusually, Jerningham appeared to be in the office before me. A movement caught my eye through the door, an edge of a woman's navy skirt against the wooden floor, so I backed away.

Jerningham was talking quietly. "I don't think you are being absolutely truthful with me, are you?"

I heard a fast intake of breath through pinched nostrils.

"But look, I'll find you a husband. It's what we agreed."

The outer door opened and Colonel Wakefield entered.

It was always dramatic with him—his high boots, long stride and head lifted as if to say: Here I am! Applause!

"Jerningham in?" he asked.

"He has someone with him, sir. A woman."

"Why is the door pushed to?" He shook his head and tutted and didn't pause as he walked in. I left them to their business, whatever it involved, and went out into the blustery day.

It was a couple of days after this that Colonel Wakefield asked me if I was married. We were across the harbour in Thorndon, checking the feasibility of relocating the town. Mein Smith should have accompanied him but the pair of them were still in angry dispute over whose responsibility it was to determine the town's location. My money was on the colonel winning the argument. He tended to get his way, despite Jerningham's accusations of leniency.

Out in the bay loaded dinghies peeled away from an Australian schooner and began the pull against the tide into the makeshift wharf at Lambton. A towering Māori man walked past us down the beach, watching the incoming boats. He was dressed in nothing more than a short blanket wrapped around his waist and he stood with his hands on staunch hips, perhaps hoping for a job unloading. Unused to such nakedness, I regarded the shape and tone of him. The colonel looked too, head tilted, the way one would admire a statue.

"I'm widowed, sir," I said to the colonel's enquiry of my status. "My wife died of pneumonia back in '37. We were only married a year. No children."

"We'll have to find you a wife to keep you happy here," he said, his eyes still on the well-formed torso in front of us. Perhaps he, too, was comparing the strength of his puny arms against this Hercules.

"I find I'm getting along very well as I am," I said.

"There's a young woman off the *Oriental*. Name of Dorothy Lewis. Pretty thing. She has a rather lovely mole, here, right above the curve of her lip. You could do a lot worse." The Emperor Wakefield, not content with engineering his colony, was now taking it upon himself to matchmake his subjects.

I was aware of Dorothy Lewis. Charles had introduced us at one of our outdoor church services, not knowing I had interests elsewhere. When her bonnet blew away down the beach there was a bit of a scrimmage to retrieve it, and I was happy enough to be the man to scoop it up for her, though she offered no word of thanks. She did have a pretty face, though I thought it would be more appealing if it lifted in a smile occasionally.

It seemed odd that the colonel would mention Miss Lewis to me. She had come over as a nurse or governess, but I heard the family had moved on to Sydney and left her behind, which wasn't much of a referral. I was sure the colonel was aware of this. I was being manipulated and was unsure why. Dorothy Lewis was fine enough to look at, but had nothing to recommend her to me as a wife.

"Well, then?"

"As I say, I am not looking for a wife, sir."

"How many settlers will be here by March, Lugg?"

"Just shy of a thousand sir, on the first fleet, and the few dozen from Sydney and round about."

"How many of the fair sex? Not including the matrons."

"About a hundred single women. Still fewer of marriage age."

"Don't think you are the only man in the colony able to do mathematics, Lugg."

We went to the wharf as the dinghies came alongside. A flat-bottomed punt held cages of livestock: small black pigs, dogs, chickens and little birds—quails, perhaps—and our Hercules stepped forward to receive them. A crowd gathered as one dinghy unloaded tea chests and bolts of cloth and canvas wrapped in calico. More native men came forward. Once unloaded, the men pulled the tops off the chests, admiring the contents as they emptied them onto the jetty—wrapped loaf sugar and slabs of hard cheese, boxes of tobacco and an assortment of candles, ironmongery and cutlery.

"Hey! Hey!"

The storekeeper came running down the beach waving his arms and the natives scarpered, grabbing what they could and leaping sideways into the crowd and away. The onlookers shrieked and cheered, laughing at the cheek while Mr Pierce, the storekeeper, frantically spun around gathering his belongings and shouting for assistance.

Colonel Wakefield was inspecting the stock on the punt. "Find out where those pig dogs came from and who brought them in," he told me. "I want to know what he paid for them. If you can get 'em under three pounds pick me up a dozen. I need gifts for Te Rauparaha."

"Yes, sir."

"And get me a cock and a few hens in lay for Mein Smith's wife—don't pay more than thirty shillings, mind. A peace offering over this whole Thorndon business." He shook his head in frustration, and I felt for the burden he carried: the juggling of people and politics and the complications of geography. "We will move the town to this side of the harbour, you know, whatever the surveyors think. I just can't abide the resentment."

"Sir."

"And look, Lugg, I will have Jerningham search out Miss Lewis's references for you and arrange something. I'd like to see you settled."

"My father said the same thing."

"Your father?"

"Yes, sir. It's why I ran away to New Zealand."

Wakefield didn't laugh. He gave me a rather bewildered look. He had no idea why he shouldn't organise the colony including my marriage to Miss Lewis. The one with the pretty mole. I didn't dislike Miss Lewis, but my ambitions for marriage were far higher.

I couldn't yet tell the colonel.

Back from the water's edge, up a narrow path, was a cleared rise that gave us a good view of the land, and Colonel Wakefield pointed out his imaginary town. "I shall live here," he said, of the knoll on which we stood. He pointed to a track where labourers cut a path up the winding hill. "That terrace will be lined with houses, both sides, built on levels on the slope. We'll have wharves there, and there, and the business district can stretch all the way to the swamp at Te Aro. Do you see?"

I saw a stream that ran down to the water's edge where a palisade of sun-bleached poles marked out the Māori settlement of Pipitea. It was the best flat land in the area, slightly raised and with good drainage. Was this where he planned his town? I saw the scruffy thatched roofs of the native shacks and a spiral of smoke from an open fire. Gardens. Further around the bay was another cluster of miserable huts and further again, on the swampy flat by an inland basin, was the Te Aro settlement. It didn't look a promising place on which to build a town. I wondered if perhaps Mein Smith was right about leaving Te Aro to the Māori.

I said nothing. I waited for him to go off to his meeting with the committee so I could go looking for Ada. I walked the waterfront, passing strolling settlers out exploring the territory, but there was no sign of my darling. It occurred to me I didn't know how Ada moved on solid ground. She had always been Ada on the sea to me. Of course she would not have taken ashore the rolling sashay I had loved so much on the *Aurora*.

We'd met in Gravesend and from the beginning, on the gangplank of the ship when Ada had turned to see me beside her, I had felt a recognition between us that this was something worth noting: an acknowledgement that one liked the look of the other. Straight away, there on the cusp of shore and ship, we were two pieces of a jigsaw that fitted just so.

Every day for over four months we were together, under the watchful eyes of Ada's brother and his wife. Malloy had been friendly enough to me, though aloof. Perhaps he could tell I wasn't born to money. I didn't imagine ours was a friendship that would continue onshore.

It was Malloy's amiable wife, Catherine, who often asked me to join them, allowing me to be close to Ada. We discussed education, society, history. She showed interest in such academic subjects without embarrassment.

It was Ada's face that captivated me; it had a mobility that flicked from surprise to delight to worry to pensiveness in a blink, and she listened with a quizzical expression that said: Go on, I want to know more, everything you say fascinates me.

We played draughts and backgammon and swapped books and stories during the long enclosed evenings. Occasionally, when the immigrants from below decks got up a party, we danced.

Our intimacy grew as we talked our way across the world's oceans and learned the other's moods on calm days and through raging storms. In the North Atlantic we filled our lungs with dizzingly fresh air, in the hot tropics we shed jackets and formality, and we braced ourselves against frozen railings as we raced past icebergs through the

Southern Ocean, every day more exhilarated by the distance from home. The widening gap between here and there we measured in more than miles and days; it was freedom itself that grew in our long tumbling wake. And over the days, the weeks, the months, our hearts began to beat, off-balance with the pitch and roll of our growing desire. The girl who had smiled at me on the gangplank became Miss Malloy, then Ada, and then, as our inhibitions fell away in waves, she became—my love.

We declared ourselves one evening as the Southern Cross floated above the rigging and shimmered in the glassy sea below. A glow shone on her cheeks from the lantern light, and strands of her curly brown hair slipped from her bonnet in wisps in the salty air, escaping confinement, like Ada.

"But will your brother approve of me?" I had asked her, as we twirled away from Malloy and Catherine, dancing to the drums and fiddles, face-to-face with our backs to the wild nothingness of the sea.

"He must," Ada had said firmly. "You are my choice, Arthur! I love you and I choose you."

Oh! To be chosen! To be chosen by the remarkable Ada Malloy and to have such domestic happiness promised before we even arrived in the new land. I was a lucky man.

I knew a proposal relied on my good establishment into colonial society. I would do nothing to jeopardise that.

I stopped my distracted wandering, pulled myself together and summoned a small boat to take the colonel back across to Pito-one.

━

I was at my desk working on the question of piggeries when Jerningham breezed in, with a curt, "Good morning, Uncle William," as he passed the colonel in the outer office.

His face was animated, and he was twitching to tell me something, but he pulled himself up with difficulty to pretend an interest in hogs and breeding sows and the need for better fencing.

Eventually the colonel left the office and we heard him calling for Mein Smith to walk with him up the valley.

Jerningham reached out and grabbed me by the shoulders and laughed as he shook me, his eyes so bright I wondered if he had been drinking.

"Do you know, I have slaves, Lugg!"

I wondered what great scheme he was planning. I didn't like the sound of slaves.

"Slavery was abolished, Jerningham," I replied, pushing him away. "I think you may have a bit of resistance if you try to re-establish the practice in the colony."

"No really. They are a gift. From Te Rangiwhakarurua of Ngāti Hau."

The Māori words rolled off his tongue. I thought sometimes he made them up, just for the fun of the pantomime, like the feathers he stuck in his whiskers to irritate his uncle.

"I have no idea what you are talking about, but if someone has made you a gift of slaves you must set them free. What are you thinking?"

But to Jerningham the exchange was a marvellous gesture of cultural goodwill. "He is a chief of an inland Wanganui tribe. We gave him a gun, you see. A handsome gesture surely! He now fancies we are great friends and he has sent me eight boys so I can travel back to see him again."

"They're not slaves, then. Call them porters. Guides."

"They are spoils of war, you pedant. They're lucky he didn't eat them. Why get so hung up on the language?"

"And are you going?"

"Certainly. At least to Wanganui, as soon as I can. We're

planning a town there, an overflow. There's simply not enough flat land here."

"They're keeping the name Wanganui, then? Has the decision been made?" I asked.

"There's some nonsense about calling the town Petre to stop little Henry's moaning," said Jerningham, "but there must be a limit to what his father's money can buy. They've licked the baron's balls already by naming Thorndon after the estate. That's more than sufficient, I think, for that lecherous old inebriate. He'll never visit and my town has a name already. Wanganui. It means 'big bay'."

"*Your* town?"

"Why not? I negotiated the sale. I'm thinking of being the first colonial to settle there."

"Call the place Jerningham then."

"I told you. It has a name. If natives call it Wanganui that's what I shall call it. Anyway, I am already on the map. The committee have decided on Point Jerningham for the outcrop at the end of Oriental Bay. Though I'd rather they gave *me* the bay and the ship could have the point, but the way my uncle treats me I'm lucky to get anything."

He pulled his box from the shelf and started rummaging around, removing papers. He dumped a stack of his journals on my desk and pulled out a crumpled watercolour sketch, which he flattened before me. It showed a blue line of coast, split by a sinuous river. Sandbars and shingle lined the entrance, white and red pines were drawn on terraces to the north. Anchors were sketched in two places along the river, and dotted lines marked the small Māori settlement.

Wanganui. With that piece of paper suddenly the place became real to me. A creek running through a shingle bank. A pattern of reeds along the thin line that marked the southern edge of the water. A scribbled patch of green with the word "scrub" pencilled over. It was a rough field sketch but those few sparse lines brought a vibrant landscape to my mind. In the east the blue lines faded out and dropped off the page like a waterfall over the edge of the known world. With my finger I traced the line as far as it went.

"What's beyond here?"

Jerningham shrugged. "We'll have to go and find out. It's a wild place up the river. The tribes from the interior regularly bring war parties down to cannibalise and enslave the coastal dwellers and drag them back towards the mountain."

I pushed the map back towards him. "You'd better not put that in your reports to your father. It will hardly help with recruiting."

"I don't care! You can't cover all this stuff up."

"You can select the truths to tell."

"Well, you can do it for me, Lugg. I give you the task of going through my journals. Make them fit for publication. I'm going to gather them into a book—they'll love all this stuff in London. You can take out the bits that compromise English decency. There. That's something to do with yourself while I'm gone."

I had seen him scribbling in his journals, eyes narrowed and sometimes his face creased in a happy grin as if every adventure was well remembered. He led a life that made the very writing of it an entertainment and he had an extraordinary fluency with storytelling, if an ambivalent regard for truth. I had the sense to know that someone needed to look over how these stories would read back home. We were selling a secure and stable colony, law and order in Christian settlements. We wanted words for what Charles was painting—civilisation among gentle groups of noble natives. Slaves and cannibalism were no part of the picture. Jerningham was bored with me and stood up to go.

"Here you are," he said, putting the journals back into

the box and pushing the whole lot towards me. "Clean them up. But I'll keep the originals. My father will enjoy them."

He met Charles in the doorway.

"I've come to persuade Arthur out across the harbour," Charles said, "to look at that model house we discussed."

I expected Jerningham to make some sarcastic comment, habitually impatient with Charles's mild manner, but his mood brightened and he shook the proffered hand warmly.

"Good man. Here he is now. Lugg! Off with you. Heaphy's come to take you to Thorndon."

I viewed them standing in the doorway together, Jerningham fizzing and flashing—his hot blood making him look like a horse at a race, and Charles with his soft eyes and incongruously bushy black beard, like some sort of rare, plumed bird peering out from its nest. The pair of them seemed to pull and repel at the same time.

"I can't just leave my desk," I said. "I have some accounts I need to prepare for the colonel. I'll be at least an hour."

"Make it an hour, then. Heaphy can wait. Look, he has his sketching papers with him. He can draw your likeness while he waits and you can send it home to your father."

Jerningham waved his hand and was gone.

—

Charles placed a chair in my doorway and made himself comfortable, folding his leg across his knee to make a platform for his sketch block, and started to draw. I pushed Jerningham's journals aside and totted up the latest batch of surveyor's quantities, double-checking each before signing them off.

"He's off to Wanganui, then? I can't say I'll miss him," said Charles. "Are they his journals he's left you? I hope there is not too much truth in them."

"Is the truth too strange?"

He took a minute to answer, concentrating on the broad sweeps of his charcoal. "If he's writing for his father it may not be strange enough. If the intended audience is the London investors the truth will need tempering."

"I hear so much about his father, most of it contradictory." I looked quickly over a paper, noted some figures and moved on. "He's a political genius one day, a manipulative schemer the next. My father called him damned, though my father sees sin everywhere and calls many people damned. His favourite lesson is Edward Gibbon Wakefield and the abduction of the child heiress. The false marriage. The imprisonment. I can't understand how he was forgiven, why the scandal didn't ruin him."

"He redeemed himself in prison. He paid his penance in devising a colonial system to raise up the poor."

"Do you believe that, Charles? Did he bring us here to build a better world for the poor or to provide a grand platform for the Wakefields' wealth and glory?"

He looked up sharply but saw my expression and smiled in return. "I'm here for adventures, Arthur. As, I'm beginning to think, are you, though you pretend it's not so. And so is Jerningham, though his adventures are of a different character."

"From what I have observed," I said, "your adventures involve walking, examining and recording. Jerningham is greedy. He wants to be the hero of his adventures, to do everything, touch everything, drink it all in."

"It's what his father would do. His journals will not surprise you then."

I went back to my papers, frustrated by the innumeracy of some of the contractors. Charles sketched.

"Where are we going this afternoon?" I asked him without looking up.

My friend had never attempted to draw me before but I wasn't at all self-conscious. I trusted him to see me truly. It wouldn't be beautiful but it would be honest. I would send it home; I hadn't been a good correspondent to my father and a Heaphy portrait would make amends.

"There's a model home on the hill above Pipitea Point," Charles said. "It's one of Manning's prefabricated ones, an enterprising young Australian fellow is selling them. I thought we might have a look."

I worked my way down a line of figures and checked my addition. "For you?"

"Me? No. I don't have that kind of money, and what would I want with a town house? But you should buy one. They're very good." I was aware of his stopping then to observe me. His hand started again with fast strokes. "I'll be your lodger."

I smiled. "I can think of nothing I would like better."

"Don't smile."

"And where will this town be? Do I have my house delivered here to Pito-one or to Thorndon?"

He didn't reply. He'd stopped drawing and was looking at his paper with dissatisfaction.

"Not handsome enough for you?"

He shook his head and folded away his papers. "Sorry, Arthur. It's not good. I just can't seem able to pin you down."

I wrote a quick note for the colonel on a document and put it on top of the file.

"I've been working on a series of Māori portraits," said Charles. "Those proud noble faces with their organic, primitive tattoos gives one such a deep sense of the man—" Pink flushed over the pale skin above his whiskers. "Oh my dear fellow, I didn't for a moment mean—gracious Arthur, I wasn't implying at all that your face hasn't nobility! Oh dear, that came out quite the wrong way. I'm terribly sorry. Stiff finger joints probably." He rubbed his hands together.

"I've almost finished here, Charles," I said, both amused at his discomfort, and disappointed he could find nothing in me to draw. I didn't spend much time worrying about my appearance and hadn't looked in a glass since leaving home, but imagined there would be some spark in my face for an artist to capture. "Perhaps this afternoon I'll ask Wharepōuri to carve me a tattoo to add some nobility to my countenance."

"There are white men who do such things. I don't know that it helps, particularly."

"I imagine that's the reason for your beard?"

"To hide my chin tattoo? I am unmasked!"

We packed up and went down to the beach, where sailing boats were plying trade, and picked up a light ketch to cross the harbour. It was steered by a sailor with a large tattoo on his right arm. Charles and I tutted and frowned to each other. After the symbolic Māori tattoos, we agreed without words that this perkily breasted mermaid would not do.

—

Every week there was more activity on the Thorndon hills. A father and son hung kettles and pots outside their well-stocked ironmongery and a butcher in a bloody apron hung strings of sausages. Charles and I walked past a set of wooden commercial buildings nearing completion, and so on to the prefabricated home, perched on a patch of even ground, where the fern had been hastily flattened all around. There was a large and cheerful young man in a timber shed at the gate, with his plans and books laid out on a long table. He was taking orders.

It was a town house, two up, two down, with a deep, wrap-around balcony and large lean-to for the kitchen and scullery behind. I thought it would do me rather well. There were twenty homes expected on a stores ship, so I put in my order for the house immediately and paid a deposit. The surveying for the town would be complete and balloted within a couple of months. I could be in my own home by the mid-winter.

Charles suggested a final look around, so we returned to the front sitting room, where a woman and a young boy stood with their backs to us, admiring the fireplace. When they turned around, I recognised Dorothy Lewis.

Her eyes flicked quickly from Charles, to me, to the doorway, with the panicked look of a cornered animal deciding whether to crouch or run.

She gave a nervous nod to Charles, who fluttered his hands in return.

He collected himself. "Miss Lewis. Master Tom. Good afternoon to you. You will remember my friend, Mr Arthur Lugg?"

I had the distinct feeling that our meeting there was not a coincidence. Miss Lewis dipped her head to me with her eyes down. Would there be a smile? I gave her my most engaging greeting, but, no. The smile was not returned.

At that moment a friend of Charles's appeared in the doorway and said in a stilted voice, "Oh, I do apologise, I didn't know you had company. Charles, you must come straight away. Wharepōuri is here to see you."

And Charles, apologising profusely, begged me to keep Miss Lewis company for a few minutes, excused himself and dashed out the door with his friend. Young Tom wandered into the hallway to watch them go, leaving me alone with Dorothy Lewis. As it had been pointed out to me, I studied the mole above her lip. I didn't really think anything of it at all.

"Goodness. I think he's after …"

"He mentioned Wharepōuri …

"Organising a painting, perhaps …"

"An interesting subject …"

We stood for a long moment, she resuming the position she had on my arrival, quite still, looking at the fireplace.

It had an adequate grate with a flue of folded iron and a lining of clay. The surrounding walls were timber covered with white canvas, ready for paper. There wasn't much to say about them.

"Are you—"

"Have you—"

"Oh, I'm sorry—"

"No, please, after you—"

Her question when it came was dull.

"Do you like the house?" she asked in a flat voice.

"Yes. It's very nice."

It didn't seem necessary to explain to Miss Lewis I had purchased a house not half an hour before. We looked around at the prefabricated windows with blue cotton curtains and white-painted shutters. To a man who had been living in a mud hut for weeks, it seemed extraordinarily smart, but it was an obvious thing to say, so I remained quiet.

"Did you come on the *Aurora*?" she asked me eventually.

"Yes, that's right. And you?"

"I was on the *Duke of Roxburgh*." She gave me rather a piercing look then, but I knew nothing of the *Roxburgh*.

Then I remembered. "Your captain was washed overboard, I believe. That must have been very frightening for you all."

She seemed to relax, as if something had been dodged.

"It was a terrible gale. We thought we would all be lost. Then Colonel Wakefield came on board and took us into port. We were carried ashore by naked Maoris."

I smiled at that. She said it matter-of-factly but the

Roxburgh ladies had been the talk of the town for a while. We'd all heard talk of "naked savages" before leaving England, of course, but it was quite another thing when one took you in his arms.

She seemed shy of me, though I didn't know why she should be, and she nervously slid her fingers over her gloves, as if trying to rub them off her hands.

I wondered about the family that had moved on to Australia, but felt it would be unkind to ask. She wore loneliness like a veil. I didn't know with whom she was billeted, perhaps the family of the boy.

I went to the window, looking out for something on which to comment. Charles was at the corner of the house, talking and smoking with his friend. I caught his eye and glared at him, tipping my head sharply to summon him back.

"What the devil was that all about?" I asked later, after we had extricated ourselves and were walking down the hill looking for a boat to take us back across the harbour.

"I thought you'd be pleased!"

"What on earth gave you that idea? I have absolutely no interest in Dorothy Lewis. Is there some sort of conspiracy going on?"

"I imagined … that is, Jerningham said …"

"Jerningham! Next time Jerningham wants to introduce me to a woman, please let him know that I am quite capable of organising my own affairs."

"I am sorry, Arthur. I really am. I didn't mean any offence. He told me you would welcome the meeting."

"No."

I couldn't stay angry at Charles for long. He had an uneasy relationship with Jerningham. They were close in age and people naturally assumed they were friends, but Charles was a modest and reserved man and couldn't seem to understand the other's moods at all. Perhaps Jerningham bullied him a bit. He certainly enjoyed baiting him. And now me, it seemed.

Charles ran alongside me until I slowed my pace as we reached the waterfront. The tide was pulling and sucking at the rocks but there were no boats going back to Pito-one, so we scrambled along the long harbour shoreline to camp. Chief Wharepōuri's men carried us over the flooded streams at Ngāūranga for sixpence a man. They were fully clothed.

———

In the evening we went to the grog shop on the beach as the clear night air picked the first stars out of the charcoal sky. All the walking and physical labour since landing had made me strong, a far cry from the jellied man who'd struggled off the ship those few months ago. I felt a new vitality walking across the beach on our harbour at the edge of the world.

Tents and raupō bivouacs were scattered in the sand hummocks above the high-water mark, surrounded by piles of goods from a recent ship: tin baths and buckets, cooking equipment, barrels and chests, tools and spinning wheels and dumps of English brick. I ran my new procurement eyes over the debris to see if there was anything to answer an immediate need, but it was all domestic stuff for the families who sat around their outdoor fires.

We passed a group of Māori walking slowly home. They were singing and their voices carried out across the water.

Under canvas, rowdy settlers drank and gossiped, their backs turned against the darkening harbour to the lanterns of the bar. We were slow to import grass seed and carpentry tools to Britannia, but fast money went into grog. Neither Charles nor I was much of a drinker but we went to the place as a change from our confined hut. A pint of Hodgson's Pale Ale each would last us the evening.

We found Jerningham in discussion with Wharepōuri. The chief was imposingly tall, with a tattooed face, straight jaw and bright eyes, though without the calm grace of his uncle Te Puni. Both Wharepōuri and Jerningham were drinking rum in large tumblers.

"Have you been to Karori, yet?" Jerningham asked Charles, as he pulled up a bench for us. "We must get that valley surveyed—there's good flat land. I was there with a man called Malloy earlier. You must know him, Lugg?"

"I was with him on the *Aurora*," I replied over my shoulder as I went to buy our drinks. And then, to prevent any more of his stupid matchmaking, I added, "I am very fond of his sister."

Jerningham laughed nastily. "Malloy's plain little sister? She's a bit of a scrawny thing!"

My anger flushed bright as blood and I steadied myself against the bar. Jerningham had no right to an opinion about Ada. His taste in ladies started with their "bubbies". Through the din I heard him ask Charles, "Dorothy has a rival?"

And Charles's reply, "Oh, leave him alone, Jerningham!"

I filled our glasses from the jug and clattered the coins onto the long plank of native wood that formed the bar. It was polished to a rich yellow shine and tightly lashed to casks at each end, and as such was one of the more solid pieces of new furniture in the colony.

For an hour Wharepōuri and Jerningham were a whirling mix of languages, gestures and argument while Charles and I watched, excluded, though I could pick up a word here and there. The chief looked less dignified as the drink hit him, and he slumped, sliding on a well-muscled buttock off the chair and down to the floor.

Jerningham called for a group of Māori women to take him back to the pā. They had been waiting outside. Perhaps this was a regular thing.

Jerningham communicated mostly with the natives in their own language, though many of them, Wharepōuri included, had a bit of English from contact with whalers and traders. For all my skill with languages, I found the transition difficult. The pronunciation was easy enough, but as it was traditionally an oral language Māori didn't follow any linguistic rules I knew and there was no structure in place to teach it. The missionaries had a dictionary, but I hadn't seen it or been asked to procure one for the Company. I envied the way Jerningham picked up conversation so easily and playfully.

Charles didn't approve. "You're doing them no favours," he told Jerningham, his crisp voice cutting through the drunken babble in the hut. "Don't you agree, Arthur?"

He turned to me for assurance, but by then I was on the brandy and slightly dazzled by Jerningham's easy friendship with Wharepōuri. I couldn't disapprove of his efforts to engage with the natives in their language. We needed to learn about them or how were we to get on?

"Really, you're as bad as the missionaries," Charles said, and Jerningham scowled at him through glazed eyes and looked around, perhaps for better company. "You should be encouraging them to speak English. They will have to learn soon enough and it's a kindness to give our friends here a head start. The settlers and traders are not going to communicate in Māori and those who can't speak English will be left behind."

Jerningham scowled and called him an arrogant stiff-neck, but Charles was persistent and I could see he was working up for an argument.

"Theirs is a meagre language," he said. "It's repetitive, poorly structured, with little concept of the abstract. It sounds like poetry—smooth enough, but useless for getting things done. They are wonderful orators, I grant you.

Imagine how powerful they will be with the vocabulary and complexity of ideas that English will give them."

"And when they lose their language?" said Jerningham.

"What?"

"Thinking is shackled to language, you know. When we enforce English, will they lose their own way of thinking? We're imposing ourselves all over them: our language, our religion, our culture. Our so-called 'civilising influence'."

"Well, not yours, obviously, Jerningham," I said.

Charles laughed at that.

On balance, I thought Charles was probably right. The language of communication in this new colony wouldn't default to the best language but to that spoken by the more powerful. Jerningham was doing his friends a disservice if he didn't credit them with the ability to master English. And of course, grog and mischief didn't civilise anyone.

"Perhaps, after they learn our ways, the Māori will continue to use their language for ceremonial occasions," I suggested. "The way we tend to use Latin."

They both looked at me dismissively. They were arguing for the devil in it—the pair of them bickered constantly. They weren't wanting compromise. They could equally take opposing sides tomorrow.

—

Jerningham left early the next morning, bright as a chattering bird, on his adventure up the coast to Wanganui.

"You will call the town Petre," said the colonel. Jerningham smiled and stuck his pipe in his mouth.

It was the middle of March, the end of summer not signalled with the turning of the leaves; indeed the climate was such we were promised the leaves wouldn't fall at all. Winter would inevitably mean shorter days and faster weather, and perhaps a dusting of snow high on the hills.

The "slaves" carried Jerningham's large bundles, mostly of items for trade: tobacco and pipes, blankets, tin pots, fish hooks and nails. The boys wrapped bottles of spirits in flax and strapped them to the baggage, whether for trade or consumption I didn't ask. They had the easy, wide smiles of youth and spontaneous outbursts of laughter that characterised their race. They joked with Jerningham in their fluid language. He carried his own pistol and there were guns rolled in canvas. I wondered who he was arming.

Jerningham raised his hand as he sauntered off along the track with his companions, the consummate explorer in a battered manila hat. I thought of that meandering blue line on his map and the adventurous spirit in me almost wished I was going with him.

Colonel Wakefield waited in the office until the party had disappeared and the settlers who had come out to stare had dispersed. "I should have sent you along to keep an eye on him, Lugg."

My adventurous spirit went into hiding and I returned to my desk.

I left Jerningham's journals unopened in a box for a few days while I chased up requests from Colonel Wakefield, who had won his dispute with Mein Smith. Britannia was not to be our main settlement; we were moving across the harbour to Thorndon. It was a huge logistical exercise and caused a line of people to form outside my office with enquiries about transport. The men seemed to think that because I shared an office with the Wakefields I had some sort of insight into the colonel's mind. That was far from the truth.

The colonel was not a man for small talk. He gave me set tasks: to make a list of boats and their capacities, to obtain tide tables from Captain Chaffers, to find a wheelwright and make a list of settlers who owned hand-carts, though we soon learned wheels were of no practical use on boggy trails and sand. We needed roads. He wanted telescopes, pencils and mosquito nets from Sydney. All this we discussed, but we didn't chat, and I certainly wasn't privy to Company plans. I had no idea how we were to move everyone around the shore.

It was a few days before I got a quiet morning to sit down with Jerningham's journals.

Tucked into the front of the first one I opened, undated and in Jerningham's scrawl, were some notes. There was no indication they were private.

I scanned them, and read them properly again.

I was astonished they had been placed in my hands. The pages contained a summary of the months spent organising the expedition to New Zealand, though "organised" was not the word. It seemed the Company had gambled with us in a most extraordinary way.

In their haste to secure the colony, the New Zealand Company had sold thousands of acres of land and sent settlers off on ships before they even knew there was appropriate land available for purchase. It was an extremely risky venture, with ships full of settlers despatched in the wake of the survey ship, giving Colonel Wakefield no time and little option but to purchase the first available land he found. If anything had happened to the *Tory* there would have been several shiploads of settlers without a destination or leader, floating off the coast of New Zealand, waving useless certificates of sale.

I sat for a moment considering this, then pulled the door against interruptions and settled in for a day of reading the journals themselves.

Jerningham had an informal and easy writing style. Unconcerned with the responsibilities of the Company's mission and the work to be done in establishing a reception for the incoming colonists, he began with stories of delicious weather and adventures. He wrote of Māori canoes that shot over thundering rollers through the surf, of morning bird song and the curl of the palm fronds. He described early light on water so pale the blue almost disappeared, a translucent reflection of a high sky. There was information on the layout of whalers' boats and intimacies from the lives of the intrepid men who sailed them. He wrote evocatively of the beauty of Kāpiti Island—Entry Island, the whalers called it—the strategic stronghold of the mighty chief Te Rauparaha. He described negotiations with the warrior himself, directly following a brutal battle he had inflamed among his erstwhile allies.

I slowed in my reading.

This was a story I hadn't been told. The colonel and Jerningham had sat with a man, blood not yet dry on his hands, and poured spirits freely as they exchanged land for what? It wasn't clear. Jerningham wrote that Te Rauparaha demanded two-barrelled guns, muskets, lead, powder, shot. The company offered blankets, soap, tools and iron pots. I flicked forward in the journal but the outcome of that transaction was far from clear. This was a purchase in addition to the one drawn up in Port Nicholson, with our friends Te Puni and Wharepōuri and the chiefs from the pā across the harbour. Te Rauparaha, Jerningham claimed, had reneged on their deal just days after he had signed, demanding more guns or he would sell our land to prospectors from Port Jackson instead.

Then further on, a comment, in passing, in a discussion of a feast at a funeral. Te Rauparaha had cooked and eaten a slave. A *salve*, I thought at first. Some sort of herbal remedy. I blinked at the writing knowing that however hard I stared at the ink on the page, the word would not change.

I dropped the journal to my lap with shaking hands

and bile rose in my throat. Was this the truth of it? The colonel would share a smoke and drink and negotiate with unmitigated evil if it meant profit for the Company?

From outside came a sound that roused me, an ordinary noise that I didn't know I was missing. I blinked, and for an instant that sound was more real to me than the journals and the office and desk at which I sat. It came as a deep stab of Somerset: a scuffle and trample and the lowing of cows. The *Lady Lilford* had arrived from Sydney, bringing livestock. I reminded myself that this was a colony of England, we were Englishmen, and we were here to make this place a better version of home.

I thought of my father, of his appeals to me. He had tried to insist that if I must go to the colonies, I should go as a missionary rather than a colonist. We had argued. I had explained Edward Gibbon Wakefield's theories of systematic colonisation to alleviate poverty in England, to transplant the best of our civilisation onto a foreign soil, but these good intentions fell on deaf ears.

"They are godless miscreants," Father had said of the Wakefield brothers. "They breed scandal. Driven by the twin evils of power and profit. Whatever it takes."

I had no calling to follow my father into the church. But I had no desire, either, to sit at the table with a cannibal. The journal in my lap had no more on Te Rauparaha, and I hoped that was the last we would hear of him.

I read on, disturbed now by pages of vitriol Jerningham poured on the missionaries. He wrote they were slippery, obnoxious men who moved ceaselessly from tribe to tribe to poison Māori people against the colonists. Missionaries, he claimed, encouraged chiefs to renege on deals, dispute sales and demand additional payments after agreements had been struck.

It was troubling reading.

Equally worrying, though, were Jerningham's scathing comments regarding the Queen's representative, a Captain Hobson, who had landed in the Bay of Islands shortly after the *Aurora* made land in Port Nicholson.

My assumption had always been that this man would look favourably on our enterprise and, together with the missionaries, we would form a unified presence in the country and the Queen's rule would quickly follow.

But no. Jerningham suggested that Hobson might not automatically recognise our rights to land purchased, hastily, to be sure, but presumably in good faith from the Māori. It seemed Captain Hobson's vision for New Zealand was quite different to the Wakefields'.

On this point Jerningham was fierce and his pen pressed hard into the page. Hobson had made some kind of sovereign agreement in the north in February and intended to take his treaty around the country, but had suffered a paralytic fit and got no further.

We were still neglected and ungoverned in the south and obliged to make our own way as best we could, though it appeared our land purchases could now, possibly, be in doubt.

Jerningham's blistering opinions of Hobson ran over several pages.

There was not a lot I could do with these journals and I hesitated to put my hand to them. News of this discord would certainly do nothing to help recruit new settlers. I copied out a couple of the more light-hearted adventures, thinking Jerningham might give them to Mr Revans to publish in his paper. But much of the rest was incendiary. As well as political instability there were flippant remarks and tall tales that were better not recorded in print. Jerningham seemed to make himself at home everywhere and had bribed his way into the hearts of lawless men with booze and stories. He wrote of bargains struck, where native chiefs supplied slave women—and on occasion their own wives and daughters—to the whalers and traders in return for guns and allegiances. It was a horrible business that Jerningham should be stopping, but instead there followed stories in which he appeared far from disinterested. I learned more than I needed on the softness of the dusky female breast.

I found the journals confusing and disturbing and wanted no part of their anti-missionary and anti-crown sentiments. I hid them under some ledgers in a box and pushed it into a dark space for his return.

THE NURSE

CHARLES HAD BEEN selected for an expedition to the Chatham Islands and I would, again, be alone in my hut.

I was used to his quiet companionship and would miss having another soul alongside. He was easy company and occasionally we passed whole evenings without a word; I with my reading and Charles with his sketches and journals. We kept up our chess challenges. I was wise now to his methodical style and usually won, and he would study the board afterwards before asking for a rematch. It wasn't that he was competitive; he just couldn't understand how I broke through his well-laid plans. One random move was all it took. He assumed I would behave sensibly and sometimes, I didn't.

Occasionally we struck up a conversation, usually on scientific topics. Charles was no gossip and we tended not to discuss the settlement's people, though he had now been commandeered by Mein Smith as a surveyor, which kept me abreast of the town's progress across the harbour. It was Charles who told me they were measuring disputed ground in Thorndon and the Māori came at night to pull out the survey pegs.

In the dark, Charles's steady breathing on the other side of our little dividing screen kept loneliness at bay and my thoughts from wandering out around the unfamiliar stars that wheeled through the foreign nights.

After his ship left there was a run of foul weather. For almost a week a cold southerly whipped across the harbour and bumped things about our fragile town. For sure I wasn't the only one thinking of the stone buildings and thick walls of home and wondering if I had given away too much too hastily. Once in a while, misery came in on a cold wet wind and I was damp with inconsolable loss.

I missed unimportant little things, poignant details of a life never particularly cherished, but somehow the cumulative magnitude of everything I would never see or smell or touch again turned my head to ice. It didn't happen often, but it was something I saw in others and learned was homesickness. Even habitually cheerful people would, sometimes, turn to the north (though they could equally have faced west or east, half a world is the same in any direction) and they would wear such a desolate look, before gathering themselves together and calling their energy back to the settlement.

It was always "the settlement" or "the colony". Few called the place Britannia. No one called it "home".

I wrote to my brother and father on those days, forcing the cheerful optimism with which we probably all spiced our letters. Strangely enough, this did raise my spirits. My descriptions of the more industrious among us compelled me to look on the bright side of things. I wrote of the growing camaraderie among settlers, who had been selected across the classes for their different skills and aspirations to ensure a balance of landowners and workers, traders and labourers. Many came as large families that, once they were housed and employed, were sure to add a homely feel to the place. I wrote of land clearing and exploration, and lived vicariously through the adventures of my friends Jerningham, Charles and our resident scientist, Dr Ernst Dieffenbach, a taciturn man who was making discoveries every day. I would not admit so soon to my flagging enthusiasm for our wind-battered, bush-covered hills.

My furniture was held in a storehouse close to the river and twice the Hutt broke its banks and washed through the wooden building, which was raised on optimistically low stilts, flooding my possessions. I hated to think of the damp state of my books.

I wanted to get on with the business of settling, to get my house built, furniture installed and garden dug before the winter came. I had anticipated a flat, dry section surveyed and ready for building. The fact that we might need to clear the land for settlement first had never occurred to me.

I saw little of Ada during this time and never to talk to. I made an effort to be in Thorndon when I could on a Sunday, so we would pass smiles at church service, and once we waved as I arrived at the dock and she was in a whale-boat, pulling away with her friends for a cross-harbour jaunt. The Malloys were lodged in a substantial wooden hut on the quay at Lambton and kept company with Dr Evans, Mr Mein Smith, Mr Revans and other prominent colonists. She seemed very attached to Hannah, the daughter of the Reverend Butler. The pair came arm in arm to service and their heads were often together in conversation.

I wondered if Ada had told her friend about our promise. She hadn't told her brother. I ran into Malloy occasionally. He was exploring Karori as a possible site for his cattle and horses and had petitioned the Company to get a road built up the hill. If I asked after Ada he gave no acknowledgement that I meant anything special to his sister, saying only that she was much in the company of other young friends and he was pleased to see her settling well. I waited and watched for an opportunity to see Ada alone.

Meanwhile my thumb, where the tip had sliced off so painlessly on the ship and had appeared to heal well, began to throb in the damp weather. When I wasn't working at my desk I took to holding it up in a kind of sling to ease the discomfort, but the pain grew fierce enough to keep me awake at night, and eventually the thing became red and swollen and the skin burst around the base of the reduced nail.

Colonel Wakefield insisted on bringing Dr Dorset in to see me one morning at work, though I was reluctant to drag him away from more serious matters. He reassured me that, other than a couple of silly buggers cutting their toes with an axe and the occasional spear thrust from an aggrieved native, all he had to deal with was bringing babies in the world, a state that pleased him very much indeed.

"It's the fresh air and exercise," he told me as he unwound the pus-covered handkerchief from my thumb. "It's keeping you all healthy. There's not been so much as a runny nose since arrival."

"I'm sure that is a fine report to send home," I replied.

Colonel Wakefield looked up from his desk at my comment. "Are you interested in our reports, Lugg?" he asked, and I blushed, memories of Jerningham's colourful writing close in my mind. He didn't notice my unease. "We need people writing to the English newspapers. The personal voice, outside of the Company. We're recruiting for the New Plymouth and Nelson settlements, you see." His smile focused directly on me. "Perhaps we should draft a letter to send off under your name."

The fact that this wasn't even posed as a question I found deeply offensive. Dr Dorset rubbed some powder into my thumb and strapped it firmly.

"Do you have someone who can change this bandage?" he asked.

"I'm sure I can manage."

"You don't appear to have three hands, Mr Lugg."

"You're the doctor. I'd expect you to spot a thing like that straight away."

He wasn't to be put off. "I suggest you arrange a woman to attend to this. Bathe it in salt water for fifteen minutes in the evening, give it a rub of powder and then have it wrapped in a clean dressing."

The colonel shook his hand. "We'll find someone for him, Dorset. Thank you for coming, I can't have Lugg incapacitated. My invaluable right-hand man without a working right hand? That won't do!"

It was kind of him to say so and I admit I softened towards him from the praise. I was hardly indispensable but did think I gave value with my services and hoped I'd earned his high regard.

We worked through the morning. The colonel consulted Dr Evans on the logistics of our move and the lawyer, a small man bursting with big words, strained my thumb's pain threshold as he dictated page after page of instructions, much of the work falling to me in the ongoing absence of Jerningham.

In the mid-afternoon we broke from our close quarters to watch the clumsy unloading of a sawmill from a barge at the Hutt River dock. Colonel Wakefield took the opportunity to mingle among the settlers, a casual walk around with his cigar in his hand, cheerfully joining in with the encouraging shouts as several Māori men swam around and under the vessel with ropes. They were to add ballast to the off-side of the awkwardly tilting boat.

"We must be more ambitious than this," Dr Evans said, *sotto voce*, to me. He swung out his arm, encompassing the wretched shacks, inadequate dock, men stumbling across the shingle. "This is a travesty of civilisation. We'll have a deep-water wharf at Lambton Harbour by next year, mark that, Lugg."

After much straining and cheering and the snapping of several ropes, the machinery was brought ashore and lifted, seemingly effortlessly, by a gang of natives onto a flat cart. I was amused by the expressions of the Englishmen—and their ladies—as the Māori worked, their brown and tattooed arms and muscle-packed legs swelling as they moved. Each took the load of two Pākehā (as they called us weaker white men) with dazzling ease, and the cart was carried over the stones and off into the bush.

We were lucky to have been welcomed so hospitably by these men.

I thought of Jerningham travelling through Māori territory, stepping into their lives as he did at our Pito-one pā, always with his friendly, inquisitive chatter and quick smile, learning their language and their ways. Far from being the "young wastrel" the colonel complained of to Dr Evans, I wondered if Jerningham's forays into their world might stand us in good stead in the future, when their first excitement of having white men among them had worn off and they wanted more than a thrown sixpence for their brawn.

I hoped Jerningham's patronage wasn't carelessly given and he would use his knowledge of these new friends well.

Dr Evans and the colonel were called to a meeting and I returned to the office. I worked until the evening. We were short of tents and had fewer houses. Our sawmills were inadequate, quite unable to provide planking for even half the existing settlers' needs. And, as I was constantly reminded, more ships were on the way.

—

I took a pie for my evening meal at the long tables that were set in the open air behind the bakery. I knew several of the patrons but didn't seek to join them. I was tired and content with my own company.

The gales, thankfully, had blown over and left the valley magically still, the open fires across the river turned from smoke to golden flame as the sky faded and darkness emerged from the shadows and the earth. The sky shone silver-bright long after the sun had gone.

There was no lack of food in Britannia. Pork and potatoes were cheap and plentiful, and the native kūmara—a fibrous, yellow sweet potato—was a staple. Tonight, a large basket of grayling caught in the Hutt River was on offer, the fish shovelled with blackened edges from grill to board, where the men picked hot flesh off the bones with fingers wrapped in watercress. Seagulls hovered to snatch the scraps.

I joined in for a while, but as my hunger was satisfied I became aware again of my throbbing thumb and imagined the pus seeping out into the bandage from where the doctor had lanced it. I borrowed a tankard from the bakery and went to the shore, skipping back and forward like a child in the waves to get the cupful of briny water, bathing not only my thumb but soaking my shoes and trousers to the knee. I walked gingerly from the beach, carrying my tankard carefully.

I met Malloy on the road. My thoughts immediately were of Ada. If Malloy was here at night, perhaps Ada was nearby, perhaps they had moved to Britannia, perhaps …

"Mr Lugg! We were looking for you. We've been to your house. What a surprise we found!"

He looked me up and down, frowning at my damp trousers and slopping tankard. He was with a group of friends I vaguely recognised from across the harbour. This was a male excursion. There was no Ada.

"We were going to ask you to join us."

That seemed unlikely. Malloy had never once sought me out before. But the men were tipsy and perhaps hoping for fresh entertainment.

"But not now—no, no, oh my goodness no!" "Better plans ..." "Prettier, haha, yes, prettier plans to be sure ..." "Hurry home, you lucky man ..."

This ramble came in a stream from the friends behind.

Incredibly, Malloy lunged forward to shake me by the hand, which was bandaged and wrapped around the tankard. I probably appeared as drunk as they were when I sheltered the tankard and reached my left hand forward to waggle his fingers.

"Well done, Mr Lugg!" shouted Malloy loudly, and they passed me in the street in a cloud of lewd laughter. "Congratulations. Well, get on home, man. *What* a woman!"

I took me a moment to register his comment amid their jeers and laughter.

"Woman?" I called to their retreating backs. "What woman?" and then louder and defensively, as if my reputation depended on the truth: "*What woman?*"

I turned and ran up the path through the muddy swamp in front of the huts, ignoring the calls of the men I bumped as I passed.

"Hey, what's the hurry? House on fire?"

Woman?

A glow of lamplight showed in the cracks around my door.

I prised it open.

And it was true. There was a woman sitting in the chair by Charles's desk. Her head was down and a white bonnet that partly covered her dark hair hid her face in the amber light. She wore a drab blue dress, but pretty white hands protruded from the cuffs. In her hands was a roll of bandage that she twisted around her fingers.

Dorothy Lewis looked up angrily, her face a pale heart.

"I am here as a nurse, not a prostitute," she said.

My shock at seeing her grew on the back of the misunderstanding of the visiting men. It was like a dunk in the cold sea. I felt shamed by Malloy's louche assumption, and nothing but compassion for a poor woman so compromised. Men could be so odious to defenceless women. I felt ashamed of my sex.

"I am so dreadfully sorry, Miss Lewis," I said. "I just passed the men in the street. I had no idea they would visit, and no idea you had been sent." I shut the door but did not step forward towards her, instead I dropped my hands to my side and stood passively. She looked on the verge of tears, big eyes in her sullen face, and her lower lip jutted forward, the challenge of a powerless creature.

"Dr Dorset told me to change your bandage in the evenings and mornings. I didn't want to stand outside your house in the dark, so I came in. I promise I haven't touched anything."

"Miss Lewis, I am sure you have behaved entirely properly, and I completely understand you have been sent to attend to my hand. The doctor said he would send someone. I am sorry I made you wait, I wasn't expecting such prompt service."

"Your friend asked if I lived here or was just visiting for the night. I told him I was a nurse."

There was an air to Dorothy Lewis that suggested misunderstanding. The sulk that seemed to be her constant companion gave the impression she was in the wrong in some way and had been caught out and asked to explain. With her sitting at my table in the lamplight, comely and plump, waiting for me with her long lashes and pretty mole, of course Malloy had jumped to the wrong conclusion. I needed to find him and clear my name before the scene was replayed to Ada or his wife, Catherine.

"I will explain the truth to the men tomorrow, Miss Lewis, you have my word. And now, look, if you will, I have brought salt water and I see you have a bandage. It is not a pretty sight and just a slight wound but rather difficult to manage one-handed. If you would …"

She was competent enough at cleaning and bandaging and didn't flinch at washing away the pus that had gathered again under the nail. I deliberately held my head up and looked away across the room, rather than at her cheek and long white neck as she bent over to attend me. It was a surprisingly intimate sensation, having my hand taken and cared for. For the first time in a long while I felt the loss of my wife, who seemed to have faded so fast from my mind. She had also been a brunette and pale-skinned and had held my hand in much the same way as she had tended to cuts and grazes, though her hair had not been as shiny as Miss Lewis's nor skin so white. I let the memory of her wash over me and go.

"Dr Dorset said you would give me a shilling," she said when she was done and was packing her scissors, bandages and little bottle of powder away in a neat cloth bag.

"Yes, of course." I was careful to give the money into her hand rather than put it on the table, which seemed a dismissive gesture. "Thank you, Miss Lewis. Perhaps you might come to the office in the daytime tomorrow to change the dressing?"

"No, I won't go to your office," she replied swiftly. "I will wait at the end of the track in the morning and not come down until I see you are about."

The subterfuge seemed worse than having her walk in, but I wanted her to leave. I nodded.

"The doctor also suggested I undress you."

For a moment I completely misunderstood and I blinked rapidly in confusion. The doctor told her ... what?

She didn't hide the sneer on her face and spoke in a monotone, "Can you manage your buttons with one hand?"

I didn't care for the knowing expression in her voice.

"I'm sorry, of course, thank you, yes. I'm sure I can manage very well. Perhaps just my jacket?"

I cradled my damaged hand and she helped me shrug off my jacket. She unbuttoned my waistcoat. I lifted my chin so she could remove my cravat and collar, her hands cool against my neck, and I meekly accepted her help with cuffs and the top few of my shirt studs. I stopped her there.

"Thank you, Miss Lewis, I can manage the rest."

She nodded and stepped back. "Can I take these to the laundry woman?"

"No. That will be all."

She gave a curt nod, picked up her bag and left. I was feeling rather disconcerted. It occurred to me she hadn't called me by my name, or the more deferential "sir", or anything at all. There was an air of detachment in her I found disagreeable and I wished the doctor had sent me a less provocative nurse.

━━━

Within the month, Jerningham was back, regaling us with stories of escaped convicts from Australia, whaling stations, Māori companions and wild men in the bush. The colonel put him to work but he didn't settle easily, and spent more time talking and smoking with Te Puni in the pā and fishing with Wharepōuri than at his desk in the office.

"How did you get on with your slaves?" I asked, when finally I got him to myself as we made our way home around the harbour. We'd had a day of trouble over at the Thorndon site, where the Māori were still openly disputing the sale of their land and complaining we were building on their gardens and burial grounds.

His head flew back in one of his encompassing laughs, bringing me, the hills, the harbour and all the birds in the sky into the absurdity of it all. "Do you know, the perfidious little rascals left me after a few days. They saw better money back here so they paddled off before I got to Kāpiti. Some slaves! And don't give me that self-righteous look, Lugg. Of course I paid them."

Jerningham had a nickname now among the Māori—Tīraweke, the name of a chattering and inquisitive bird. They ran up to him as we passed the small settlements, calling out to him like noisy birds themselves, vying to be the one to carry him across the streams. He recognised many of these friends and greeted them by name and with delight, and asked after their families.

"There are missionaries up the coast now," he told me. "Mihanere, they call them. They have no love for us, openly speaking against us to the chiefs, telling them we will take their land and chase them into the hills, insidiously poisoning our Māori against us while they quietly take land for themselves."

He spoke angrily of Hadfield and Williams, so-called men of faith active all the way up to Taranaki, frightening the natives with their talk of a righteous god, one who abhorred their customs and scorned their ways.

"Many of them are converting to Christianity, but they simply layer it on top of their ancient superstitions and rituals."

Jerningham pulled a switch from the bush at the side of the track and slashed at the undergrowth like an explorer in virgin jungle. "And rather than sit with them and learn from them and help them come to God through love, Williams rants and shouts and despises all he sees."

"The word is he's taken some land around Te Aro," I told Jerningham.

"The devil he has! He came last year, slipped in like a shadow as soon as we had left for the north, and convinced the chiefs that our land deal was not valid and they should sell a chunk to him. On what grounds is our agreement not valid? Tell me that! There is no law in place to prevent us buying land from the chiefs. This is their country. Who is Williams to tell them how to dispose of their own lands? Oh! What are they supposed to think, Lugg? They like us and trust us and want us to live amongst them, but they are frightened of this austere missionary and the power of his god."

Jerningham threw the switch out into the water as we clambered around an outcrop of rock above the high-tide mark. In the distance, the settlement of Britannia sprawled along the coast, past the fragile palisade of Te Puni's pā, the white tents and mud huts and a shambles of wooden buildings marking where the river ran into the sea. And towering behind, the dark sweep of bleak hills.

We came in after dark and headed for the pie shop. We'd not eaten all day and I'd kept our spirits warm with talk of the fresh fish dinner waiting for us. But it wasn't to be, not for Jerningham at least.

Colonel Wakefield intercepted us as we came through town.

"I expected you back on the afternoon boat," was his greeting.

"We were held up," said Jerningham. I'd stopped as we drew alongside the colonel, but Jerningham brushed past and continued without pausing.

Colonel Wakefield fell into step, military in manner, his voice sharp at his nephew, and Jerningham brusque with his replies. I watched them walk off, veering away from the grilled fish, back towards the waterfront and the office.

I ate alone, and went home at the appointed hour for Miss Lewis to change my bandage. Despite her care, Dorset's magic powder and regular clean dressings, the wound wouldn't heal. I couldn't avoid bumping the thumb and because dirt was everywhere, the bandage was always black by day's end.

I appointed a girl to sweep, and keep my clothes in order, a feline thing from Cornwall of around ten years old. She fetched water, emptied my soil bucket and brought me tea in the morning so I could rest my hand from menial chores, but there were few days when my activities did not involve scrabbling around in the mud somewhere or other. I could write neatly enough with a pen wedged between my fingers and would have been happy with my desk job, but I was constantly called out to oversee this or that and wasn't a good patient who would remember to put my hand in a sling every time. In Thorndon I'd had a horse take a chomp on the bandage and the skin had broken again, the clipped remnant of nail squashed deep into the swollen flesh. The salt water was soothing, but the thing throbbed annoyingly through the night.

The next day there arrived another invalid in need of Dorothy's care. Charles returned from the Chatham Islands with a gaping wound in his leg. He'd been caught in the middle of some inter-tribal conflict—an innocent bystander, he admitted eventually, after joking he'd taken twenty down before they caught him. The ship's doctor laid him out, slightly feverish, on his cot. I sent a boy to catch Dorothy on her way home and she returned immediately, watched as the doctor showed her how to clean and wrap the wound. Her face was unresponsive as Charles smiled up at her and apologised for the bother.

"You'll not make her love you," I said to Charles after

they left us alone. "I've not had a smile or kind word from her yet."

Charles gingerly adjusted his pillow and rolled to move the pressure off his leg. I had offered him my bed, which was higher and more comfortable, but for all his mild manners he had a tough constitution and said he preferred his cot.

"Don't fuss," he told me. "It's a minor wound."

"There's good soup at Coglan's, some strong stout, too. Can I fetch you some?"

"Don't fuss, Arthur! You can sit and talk to me."

I had been fussing about, I realised, back and forward across the little hut, trying to stay out of the way of the doctor and Dorothy. I lit a pipe for each of us, poured a slug of medicinal brandy and sat back in his chair, eyeing him in the mellow lamplight, pleased at his return.

"You're not in pain?"

"A bit. But there's no long-term damage and the pain will pass, faster if I don't dwell on it. Tell me what's been happening here. Jerningham's back?"

"He is. Back from his barefoot wandering. He lost both slaves and shoes along the way."

"Did he really?"

"He did. Very careless of him. But he's come back totally enamoured of his friends up in Wanganui. The way the colonel treats him I wouldn't be at all surprised if he takes off and stays up there. Although Henry Williams might object, he was waving around some agreement saying he had already purchased the whole of Wanganui for the tribes in perpetuity."

"Did Jerningham settle the matter?"

This was a question I had asked. I thought Jerningham had been cunning, though the colonel wasn't as generous and accused him of gadding about.

"The tribes wanted confirmation that their sale was to

Wide-awake," I said, "and that his people will come and live among them. That's what they call Colonel Wakefield now—Wide-awake—which I think is charming."

"It's certainly hard to catch him napping."

"But Jerningham didn't complete the transaction. He noted their belief that nothing was sold to Williams but didn't press the Company's claim. He told them he just came as a friend, to meet them and give gifts. They needed to wait for Wide-awake to complete the sale of their land."

Charles nodded. "That was a clever move. Building trust."

"Oh, and he brought us back presents!"

Rolled in the dark corner were two porera, woven flax mats of creamy white and tan, Charles's with a zigzag pattern of parallel lines and mine with triangles around the border. They were primitive weavings but had a certain charm and would keep back the damp. I laid them out on the floor, both in Charles's bare section of the hut. I had my English rug to step on in the mornings.

"We're slowly going native," I said to Charles, but when I looked over to him, he was asleep.

——

Two things happened in the following month that were to change our lives in the colony dramatically.

Colonel Wakefield had received some warning, and I suppose it is to his credit that we hadn't all packed off to a new colony in South America in panic. But the colonel remained outwardly calm, maintaining order in the settlement and shielding us from the storm that was brewing as our growing activities drew the attention of the Crown. The first thing seemed relatively small at the time, but lit a fuse for a later explosion.

We had been abandoned to our own devices in Port Nicholson. Captain, now Lieutenant Governor, Hobson had not visited or sent any representative and there was no law in the settlement other than that which we organised ourselves. Indeed, it was written into our immigration agreement that we would elect a committee and govern ourselves until either the British government stepped up (or the French we joked) or, failing any country taking possession of the land, I supposed we would eventually have become a republic within the land of the united chiefs. So it was that the committee appointed two constables and a magistrate and we had a little jail, mainly for drunks and brawlers. We had town stocks, too, which served effective justice. The Māori thought them a grand invention and always joined the noisy crowd baying at the poor delinquents.

The trouble came when a ship's captain was brought in front of the magistrate on a brawling charge and refused to recognise the court's authority. I had gone with Revans and Mein Smith to watch the entertainment. We weren't disappointed. It was good theatre. Captain Pearson, master of the *Integrity* from Hobart Town, had been in an argument with his charterer and had punched him. The charterer had him arrested for assault.

There was Captain Pearson, a thin man with the sallow face of a drinker, in the dock—which was no more than a chair and bench—shouting hysterically that this was not a court, and that we were treasonous subversives and Wakefield was a demagogue and he refused to be bound by our mutinous justice.

Amid the jeering and clapping of the crowd, I turned to Revans and Mein Smith, who were both on the committee. Far from joining the excitement, they looked bewildered and rather worried.

"We do have authority to pass justice here in our own colony, don't we?" I asked them.

But neither man gave the fast affirmative I expected. They

sat in thoughtful silence for a while, and as the constables were gathering Pearson's flailing limbs to take him off to jail, Revans and Mein Smith slipped out of the courtroom.

"Where's Wakefield?" Revans asked me as they left.

But I didn't know.

The next day we learned that Captain Pearson had escaped custody and was back on his ship, from which we were unable to extract him. He sailed north.

The second bit of excitement followed swiftly behind Pearson, who was soon forgotten with the sighting of the schooner *Ariel* out at the heads, and the arrival of Reverend Henry Williams to town.

The missionary was received into Colonel Wakefield's new house, but this was the only courtesy given him. The colonel and his committee kept Williams and his captain waiting over an hour and we learned later their meeting was acrimonious. Jerningham stayed away and paced around our office, drinking heavily and occasionally peering out of the door, waiting to see the delegation back to their ship.

"It's this treaty, Lugg. Williams has been charged with taking it around the country and getting the chiefs to agree to British sovereignty. We knew it would happen eventually—that, and the pre-emption of land sales—and my father instructed us to agree to all of it. But Hobson has frozen all further sales and declared all our existing purchases invalid under investigation. And Wide-awake just walks around with his eyes closed! He should have been up at Wanganui already. At Taranaki too. He's too slow, we could have signed off those purchases months ago. He should have given me the authority."

He had come to my alcove doorway now and was leaning in, glittering with agitation. He looked slightly mad with his intense flare-eyed stare, as if he had taken lessons from his Māori friends in intimidation. I fully expected him to stick out his tongue.

I refused to be bullied.

"Well, Jerningham, I welcome British sovereignty and the settlers will be relieved to know we are, once again, subjects of Queen Victoria and ruled by her government."

He pulled his lips back into a snarl and roared through closed teeth, like an animal or feral child in the street. "Don't you understand, you blinkered bye-blow? This land," he stomped his feet, *bang bang* on the floor, "if we haven't bought it, sure as a bobtail's fart you don't own your town and country section now."

"If it was bought illegally I don't want to own it."

"Listen to me, Lugg. Get it into your head. *It wasn't illegal when we bought it.* God's truth! That overbearing land-shark Williams resents all the protection we are offering the Māori, all the benefits our association will bring them. He wants to enrich the church. He wants personal gain. Nothing more. He has no interest in your welfare, or the welfare of the natives. Strutting around the place like an aristocrat, Hobson is a fool to side with him."

I didn't want to hear any more of this. I didn't like Jerningham when he was drunk and I didn't believe for a moment our land would be taken away. My reservations about Te Rauparaha aside, I believed the colonel to have acted in good faith with the local Māori, and that men of the calibre of Mein Smith, Dr Evans, Revans and the others on the committee would find an easy compromise with the government. Our government. The Crown was on our side, Reverend Williams was merely an agent, a distraction.

Possession was nine-tenths of the law and we were here now, in a well-formed and ordered settlement in good harmony with our natives. The Queen was hardly going to send us back to sea.

For a week the Reverend Williams stalked around the district on his long legs, peering through his little round glasses and talking to the chiefs, calling the tribes together. The colonel and the committee left him to go about his business and he made no attempt to bring them onside. Williams was competent in the Māori language and the chiefs held him in high regard, although Jerningham continued to bluster about and call into the pā as soon as the missionary left, questioning his friends on what had passed and warning them not to trust him.

I was at my desk a few days later when it all blew up. Mein Smith and Dr Evans were calming the colonel as he swore and cursed and smashed about his office. The door to my alcove had never been fixed and was propped half off its hinges. As usual, I kept my back to the men and head down in my books, assuming the men would forget I was there. Jerningham called me the invisible man.

The colonel raged. "I have sent Jerningham to find Wharepōuri to tell him not to sign. I'll send him around them all. They are gathering down at the Taranaki pā today doing their kōrero kōrero, with Williams in the middle telling them God knows what. It's a poor document, Hobson's treaty, sloppy and ambiguous, and we have not even been consulted. Jerningham can advise against it, they will listen to him."

"I strongly advise against that course, Colonel." Dr Evans was talking quietly, bringing the fever pitch down. "We knew this was coming. We can accept it in principle. 'Sovereignty' is an important concept though heaven knows what the Māori make of it. We can't stop this."

"What about our land?"

"We can take the retrospective land claims to Sydney. Hobson is incapacitated—he's a very sick man. We'll go directly to Governor Gipps." Dr Evans steepled his hands and tapped his fingers together. "He must validate our land. They want an easy colony. For all that Gipps is jealous of our success, he, of all people, must want to avoid the mistakes they made in Australia. And here it is—voilà! A model colony, with eight more ships poised to leave England and three more towns in the planning. We have given them exactly what they want, their working ideal."

"Yet we put up the finance, take all the risk and they get the credit," shouted Colonel Wakefield. "And what about this repugnant little side deal for Williams? Forty acres, right on Lambton Harbour? The man is a rapacious hypocrite!"

"My town is at Lambton Harbour," said Mein Smith. It was the first time I had heard his voice raised. "Williams gets no part of it! Our purchase pre-dates whatever deal he thinks he's negotiated on that land."

"He claims to have bought it for the natives," Dr Evans said, his voice still low and clear. I was slightly alarmed at unwillingly becoming part of their conspiracy, though I had long since ceased my paperwork and was avidly following the discussion.

"Listen. I advise we do a deal with Williams. He doesn't seem to understand that we reserve a tenth of all town sections for the Māori as policy. I suspect the chiefs don't properly understand this themselves—Dicky Barrett translated and it is unlikely that fat uneducated whaler understands fractions in English. We can present this to Williams as a compromise: this tenth—the tenth we are already committed to—this becomes his forty acres, set aside as a Māori reserve in perpetuity. And we sweeten the deal with a prime acre of town land as a gift for him, personally."

"No gifts!" shouted Mein Smith.

"No, no, really, this is good," Colonel Wakefield broke in, his voice suddenly quiet and controlled. "Don't you see?

It compromises him. This is good, George. Yes. We'll taint him with his greed. We'll do just that."

I heard him hit the desk with a satisfactory slap. The sudden switch in his voice chilled me. It was as if Evans had put a knife in his hand and he was already baring the chest of the missionary.

AMPUTATION AND TREATY

ANOTHER IMMIGRANT SHIP arrived in April, the *Bolton*, and with a festive spirit I went with a large party of settlers and gathered to greet them, together with our Māori friends. They provided a welcome reassurance that recruitment had gone well at home amongst strong and healthy English families, the type we laughingly called "good stock" for our new country. They had developed a camaraderie on the voyage across and blew in with the sunshine on a full tide, spirits high on fresh air and nothing but praise for the look of the new settlement and optimism for the colony.

For all the shadow of uncertainty hanging over Colonel Wakefield at the time, he gave them an exuberant welcome. Perhaps the *Bolton* had brought good news in the home despatches, Edward Gibbon Wakefield swinging parliament behind the Company and battling his way through London's political morass.

Wherever the Reverend Williams was lurking about the harbour, he could not fail to be impressed with the arrival of such a shipload and the ability of the New Zealand Company to pull off such colonial success.

There were barracks now for incoming settlers, finished huts for some, and a generous display of hospitality was turned on at Pito-one beach in the evening. We feasted and cheered, there were speeches and news and letters, and many settlers welcomed family and friends into our growing community.

By the end of the evening, though, after a long day of being slightly under the weather, I started to feel feverish and dizzy. I sat apart from the crowd, on the edge of a group of friends whose faces began to swim confusingly out of focus. Sam Revans was there and generous with the wine; he sloshed it around our cups and when I covered mine he nudged my hand aside. One of the last things I remember clearly was the wine pouring over my hand and the spirit spreading into my bandage with a fierce burn. I had an urge to pull off the cloth and plunge my thumb, with its itching and chafing, pus and all, down into my cup.

"Whattya doing, Lugg? You're wasting good wine! Give me your cup, I don' see why you can' drink to their good health like everyone elshis … everyone elsh, elsh is— hahaha!"

Revans turned away and didn't see me topple off the bench to the floor. There were others lying there, but they were drunk. I wasn't drunk. I felt cold and clammy and it was with great difficulty and through a dark fog that I got to my knees and crawled away, cradling a firecracker of pain in my hand, up the path, eventually getting to my feet to stagger home.

Charles wasn't there. He enjoyed his daily nursing by Dorothy, so fascinated by her feminine figure he hardly took his eyes off her as she moved about him, but he wouldn't rest and had gone to the celebrations. Charles usually hobbled around on a makeshift crutch but tonight he had left the crutch leaning on the door frame and I used it to steady myself across the room. I dropped into bed. My thumb was flaming, the bone singed away and the fire from my burning hand lit up the hut. Dorothy was there …

I think I screamed when she pulled the bandage and exposed the burning torch she held in her hand, but it was my thumb she held, and she was standing in the doorway shouting and then her face was a Māori face, wild eyes and tattooed cheeks, but it was Dorothy's voice that shouted: "Hold his arm. Keep him still. Take the cloth." I tried to sit up and release my hand, but I was pinned and a cold wet cloth slopped into my eyes. Hours later, after a frenzied fight against the man who held me down, I collapsed shaking and pathetic into a pool of bubbling golden pus, hovering away from them all as Dr Dorset cut my thumb from my body and Dorothy caught my blood in a cup.

—

"She probably saved your life, Arthur," Charles said, our roles reversed again. He was spooning soup into me as I lay propped up in bed, tightly bandaged and strapped. "I would have left you for drunk. She got a fat Māori to sit on you and cool your head while she ran for the doctor. If she hadn't stopped by, you might well have woken up dead."

"Where's my thumb?"

"We kept it in a jar so you could bury it later," said Jerningham, arriving in the doorway. He waggled a bottle aloft and set some glasses out on the table.

He looked bulky, and as he came close I saw he wore some animal pelt over his jacket.

"I don't want brandy."

"You aren't getting any. It's to offer your guests, dear boy. Heaphy and I need it to bear the smell in here. But I did bring you a smoke."

He stuck a lit pipe between my teeth and I pulled the bitter plume deeply into my lungs and held it until the room started to go black. It helped ease the pain. Every movement sent a nervous clash down my right side.

I lay still.

"You haven't commented on my robe, Lugg. It's the one I had you procure from the Sydney trader. Possum skin. Do you like it?"

"It's hideous. Take it off."

"I won't."

The two of them talked over me, the words draining away like blood.

"What?" I asked after a while.

"Which what?" said Jerningham. "Heaphy's trip to find the source of the Hutt River or the fact that our natives have finally signed Hobson's blasted treaty?"

"I thought you mentioned Ada." I was confused again. Had someone said Ada? Or in my fever had I slipped back to our time on the ship, with all this ahead of us? "Does she know I am here?"

"Who?"

"Probably Ada Malloy. They are friends. I think he's sweet on her."

"Oh, Malloy's sister." This was Jerningham. "I think I've sorted that one out."

I wanted to tell him to bite his tongue and not mention Ada in my presence, but the corner of the room dissolved and the light from the doorway played tricks on the shadows and the men loomed large and small and I was confused as to why we were talking about Ada at all and determined to keep my mouth shut until I had a clearer head. I pulled on the pipe still clenched in my teeth but the baccy was dead.

Jerningham reached forward to re-light it for me.

"Heaphy is going on an expedition with Dieffenbach," he said, lightly. "We're hoping the Hutt Valley opens out into the Wairarapa. We'll need that farm land."

I wondered how long I'd been feverish. "What did he cut off?" I asked. I felt queasy again and pulled on the pipe.

"Your thumb, Arthur."

"My thumb?"

"At the joint. The tip went black."

This had already been explained to me. I was having trouble keeping thoughts in my head. Dorothy had found me in my bed and, extraordinarily, realised I wasn't drunk but feverish. She had run for the doctor and pulled him from his revelries, screaming that I would die if he didn't come. She had caused quite a stir, but the doctor had heard her and responded.

Dr Dorset had amputated my thumb. He'd saved my life and crippled me forever.

I felt my eyes filling with tears, fast, scalding, and I was unable to move as they gathered on my lashes and slipped down my cheeks, full of salt and self-pity. With no defence, I lifted my chin and stared at the ceiling. The tears seeped into my collar, and my friends stumbled in their talk and were quiet.

Then Jerningham got out his handkerchief and held it gently to my cheeks, dabbing away the shame. His kindness was unexpected, and I was grateful for it.

———

I was a bored invalid. I had strict instructions to keep to my bed until my temperature steadied but I was in considerable pain and longed to get up and walk around. Dorothy came twice daily to check my dressings and she rather bossed my little housemaid, Lucy, but they were shy on conversation and couldn't tell me what was happening over at Lambton Quay and Thorndon. Charles had gone on the expedition up the river with Dieffenbach, and Jerningham was mostly locked away with his uncle, who was preparing to send him on a dash up the coast, a step ahead of Reverend Williams with Hobson's treaty. Until the Māori signed, his reasoning was that every petty tribe in New Zealand was still an independent foreign power, and therefore free to trade and negotiate as they would. The colonel was gambling that Hobson's pre-emptive land laws could not be applied retrospectively, and he was appealing this to Governor Gipps in Australia, while his brother Edward Gibbon Wakefield pleaded the case back home.

Jerningham sat with me some evenings to discuss the day's affairs and keep me up with the politics, always waiting until after Dorothy had left, and always with brandy and a smoke. He was a challenging companion, not at all soothing, but animated and talkative and a much better gossip than Charles. He suited his Māori nickname, the chattering tīraweke, very well.

"Hobson will have to bring his capital here to Port Nicholson. He's a fool to alienate us all," said Jerningham. "All trade passes through the strait. Every colonist will want to come here. It's the obvious choice for the capital, ready made. Who does he think he's lieutenant governor of, anyway? A feeble bunch of missionaries, some whoring whalers and a handful of scattered northern tribes? We are here! Old Wide-awake is going to build him a government house, and we will welcome him to Port Nicholson and watch him squirm as our colonists ask him: 'Well, Hobson, tell me plain, is this my land?'"

"And what is this journey you are going on now?"

He stretched out his long legs in their shiny boots, a young mirror of his uncle, and pulled on his pipe, the smoke filtering past his fashionable, newly curled moustache and up to mingle in the raupō thatch, causing the insects to stupefy and drop like pennies onto my bed.

"I'm off on the *Surprise* in the morning to complete the Wanganui purchase. They're loading her up now. We signed the deeds at Kāpiti last year, so I'm to pay for the district and receive confirmation from the chiefs. Get in before they sign away their rights to Hobson."

I wondered that the colonel entrusted Jerningham with such a mission. He was certainly a canny negotiator, but still only twenty years old and reckless. He was in way over his head and I feared for his safety.

"Aren't you afraid?" I asked him.

"Afraid, Lugg? Of what?"

Māori, I wanted to say. Shipwreck and storms. Rolling surf and treacherous rivers. Getting it all wrong. Being too slow, too late, too impulsive, too familiar, getting a spear through the heart. *Cannibals*—the last a cruel whisper in my head.

"It's a big responsibility," I said.

He leaned forward with his eyes glittering in the light of lamp. "I was born for this, Lugg."

I had never had a friend like Jerningham before, so nonchalant at the thought of danger and so sure that the world was made for his enjoyment. As if the journey halfway around the world was only the beginning and life without danger was only half a life. I was in awe of this man and his adventures, but by now I'd had my fill of unpredictable living and was ready for a quiet, settled life.

—

Sam Revans came to visit me. He was surprisingly sympathetic for such a gruff man and he insisted on seeing my wound as Dorothy cleaned and wrapped it. There was a neatly stitched vertical laceration where Dorset had folded the skin over the removed bone and an ugly knob at the joint, but the skin showed no sign of infection and the swelling was beginning to ease. I hated the sight of it.

My friend had brought me a large cake from Mrs Mein Smith, which he proceeded to eat himself, dropping crumbs all over my floor. He broke off a big chunk and wrapped it in paper for Dorothy to take home for her children.

"Children?" I asked in confusion. I admit I had never bothered to question Dorothy on her domestic arrangements. She had become slightly less surly over time, but our conversations were limited to bandages and pain and buttons.

"She has two wards from Australia in her care, and a younger child recently orphaned. The wards will go into domestic service and the young boy for adoption. Miss Lewis is a useful pair of hands when children are dumped on us. And a fine-looking woman."

"I suppose so, yes." I was pleased to hear she had decent employment and it wasn't only my shillings keeping a roof over her head.

"Many men would chop off their right thumbs to be so intimately nursed by Dorothy Lewis," he said with a raised eyebrow, but the comment was distasteful to me and I didn't engage in his banter.

He had brought me a copy of his latest *Gazette* and passed an hour reading snippets out to me.

"Mr Pierce has opened a hotel and has Westphalia hams for sale, you'll be excited to hear, Arthur." He smacked his lips dramatically. "Mr Telford announces he has marmalade and pickles, though not, one would hope, in the same jar. And there are lots of people advertising to buy and sell country acres. The filthy speculators."

He looked up at me, sharp eyes under bushy eyebrows.

"You've not bought your land to lie idle, Arthur?

"Certainly not. Down with the speculators. A man should put his feet on the land he owns." I spoke with conviction, though I had not thought at all beyond my town acre to the additional country section. I knew nothing about farming.

"Well said. Though don't give up the town, we may need

you here. If you weren't a cripple I'd give you the editor's job. You managed to turn Jerningham's fantasies into popular pulp." The carefully edited versions of the Wanganui adventures had run as a series and proved popular. "They brought glass on the *Bolton*, did you know? It says here." He tapped the paper. "You can get a window in this nasty little shack of yours."

I told him I had a prefabricated house on order with glass windows and cloth curtains included, and he looked suitably impressed.

"Here's one for the diary, Arthur." Revans pulled his chair closer and leaned in conspiratorially. "Wakefield is planning a public celebration to mark the naming of the town. It doesn't say here, but I know, and I'll tell you, if you can keep a secret. They're intending to call it Wellington. That's hush for now. I suppose we do have to wait for instruction from London. More than he deserves, old Wooden Head, and I don't suppose he'll ever visit. I was hoping for Revansville. I suppose Luggtown has a ring to it too, do you think? Though God knows you'll need to do more than give the doctor some chopping practice to deserve naming rights. Celebrations followed by a dance for the gentry at the Exchange."

I was tired now, and had almost asked Revans to leave me to sleep, but this last notice caught my attention. I had been spending much of my convalescence thinking about Ada. I had had no contact with her and she'd sent no word that she knew of my affliction. I had been so busy with the colonel and Jerningham's work that she had not been constant in my mind where I'd promised I would hold her. Perhaps it was time. I would take her to the dance.

"Sam, can you take a message for me?"

"For publication?"

"Not for publication, no. A personal message. To a lady."

"My dear fellow, don't you know I am the worst gossip in town? And absolutely the most trustworthy, if I may say both with complete sincerity. To whom is your message directed?"

"Miss Ada Malloy." Her name came easily to my lips and I could feel the familiar pull at the corners as I thought of her, my shipboard darling. "I can't write, you know, all bandaged up like this, but you can carry my message for me. Please tell her ..."

He interrupted me. "Stop, Arthur." He held up his finger in a call for silence.

I waited as he blinked away and down. He rubbed his head and pushed his fingers into the back of his neck to release tension, looking troubled. I had a sudden dreadful thought.

"Is she dead?" A pain worse than the cutting stabbed behind my eyes.

"Dead? Ada Malloy? Of course she's not dead! Why would she be dead? She's engaged to be married, man. She's certainly not dead."

The pain drained away. Thank God. She wasn't dead. The breath I had been holding released from my lungs.

"Engaged?" I asked. Who had told Revans?

"Yes. To a chap called John Bently. Filthy rich, came on the *Oriental*. Bently is the godson of the colonel's brother, Captain Arthur Wakefield. His father and Malloy's father were great friends. I probably wouldn't be sending her messages, if I were you. Not the right thing to do."

"I don't think that can be true," I protested. "Ada Malloy is promised to me."

But I remembered her brother's dislike of me, and the smirk on his face when I had explained to him that the woman in my room that night, the moody woman with the hostile eyes and the pretty mole above her mouth, was my nurse. What had he told Ada? Surely Ada, my Ada, would not have thrown me over on a piece of her brother's nasty gossip.

I thought I had done the right thing by keeping my distance until I had my house and property and could ask for her formally. I had made no approach to her, though God knows there were times when I could have swum across the harbour and made my way, dripping, to her door. Had I neglected her?

Should I have been bolder?

"Can you get a message to her for me, though, Sam?" I asked. "Can you tell her I have done no wrong and would see her?"

Revans pursed his lips and shook his head as if to say it was a bad business and he wanted nothing to do with it. "No good will come of it, Arthur. The engagement was announced last week."

"There has been a mistake."

"I tend to find not, in situations like this."

"This is not a 'situation like this'. We promised each other. It's very simple."

The newspaperman was rubbing his head again and he stood up, looking scruffy and big in the small room.

He was leaving. "Please, Sam!"

"Yes, yes," he said angrily, as he collected his heavy coat from the back of the chair and turned to look at me disapprovingly. "I will try to give your message to Ada Malloy when, if, I get a chance. But I say you are better to let it go. She has a good match with Bently. Why confuse things?"

"She is confused."

"Probably not, my friend. Probably not."

His departure left a cold draught in the room, with clammy fingers that circled my neck and seeped past my collar like winter rain. I manoeuvred myself inelegantly from bed to desk, my stitched wound sending a slow-moving pulse of pain up my arm. I gathered writing implements with the thought of penning something to Ada myself and clumsily jerked the cork from the ink bottle with my teeth, but the nasty black fluid spilled into my mouth. I sprayed globules of foul, metallic-tainted spit onto the white paper, which formed dots of strange symmetry, and as I blinked the dots connected into pictures of seaweed and driftwood, flotsam and jetsam. Debris washed up on a desolate shore.

FIRE AND EARTHQUAKE

REVANS'S VISIT left me disturbed and unhappy. I was unsurprised when the wind picked up and whipped against the walls; it seemed natural that the elements would reflect my mood and shatter the world around my house and my life, causing pain in its erratic destruction. By midnight I could hear the waves smashing on the beach and the crash of falling trees around the settlement. I feared for my hut as strong air pressure lifted the thatch and the roof strained horribly against the lashings. I almost wished it to rip off into the sky and take me with it, to let me fall crippled and alone on a bleak rock somewhere, abandoned. God could point his finger and choose—this one, or not.

Sometime during the long, sleepless night a commotion drew me to the doorway. Runners in the lane were shouting, carrying beaters and dragging carts, panicked voices turning to screams and cries for help.

The wind was still buffeting the huts and the settlement crawled with figures, all heading away from me, silhouetted by a conflagration on the rise above the river. It was as if someone had put a torch to all the little houses at once so they burned in the dark like a bonfire on Guy Fawkes night. I left my thoughts of Ada lying in my bed, threw my hand in the sling and a jacket over my nightshirt and ran into the wild night.

Cornish Row was ablaze. A fire had taken the houses by their guts and was feeding in a frenzy, with smoke billowing from the damp walls and the interiors roaring in an astonishingly luscious gold. The storm pulled curls of flame and soot wind-spinning high into the air and drove fierce gusts to light the trees and sheds behind the houses.

Colonel Wakefield grabbed me as I raced along the path and turned me around, directing me back to the waterfront, calm and efficient in the chaos around him.

"Lugg!" he said firmly, his voice clear above the melee. "Find Pierce at the Britannia, tell him we need his hotel as a hospital tonight. Arrange for Dorset to attend there. Fifteen families. They'll have burns and one at least needs a leg setting. We'll bring them down in carts. Get Dorset whatever he needs. Go!"

He was already calling to the man behind me with the clanking buckets, sending him to join the chain gang by the river, and then he turned smartly back to the blaze.

An eddy of smoke caught me in the lungs. Coughing and temporarily blinded, I stumbled back into the wind, but within fifteen minutes I had woken Pierce and we had flung open the hotel and lit the lamps. We cleared the shack's big main room and, as a steady rain began to fall, the first victims arrived, carried by neighbours—pathetic, damp, burned scarecrow-like bundles that we helped onto cots. Dr Dorset was hard on my heels, bringing with him our other doctors, Featherston and Fitzgerald, and together they gave me a list of items and requirements that had me running through the night as the weather stormed over the hills and dawn broke slowly over the scarred town.

"Make sure they all have accommodation, Lugg, and see that whatever remains of their possessions is safe until they can reclaim them."

The colonel looked weary when I reported back at the

office the next day, but he was surrounded by his coterie and snapping out instructions. My disability meant a replacement at my desk, a man with a working right hand. I didn't resist. I was determined this time to keep my hand strapped and slung until it had fully healed. Another infection and Dorset would take my whole arm. But, writing aside, I could make myself useful by carrying messages and organising the things Colonel Wakefield commanded to happen.

"Get a team of workers to clear that whole row and see what they can salvage. They're the most impoverished of our immigrants, they live cheek by jowl in those nasty little huts, it's a damn shame. A very bad business."

He rubbed his eyes, his fingers still covered with soot. It smeared across his eyebrows, giving him a theatrical look.

"We must legislate on suitable building materials in the new town, we can't have these huts made of straw. If you see Evans tell him I want to see him. And, Lugg, get Pierce to collect donations for the families and have Revans put something to that effect in the *Gazette*."

I paused outside the office and looked southward towards the heads. Slate-grey slabs of coast pinched the harbour entrance under layers of heavy cloud and the water slapped in a high choppy churn. There would be no boat service today. The breeze came in gusts, snapping and fingering my hair and bringing the smell of winter cold, while the rain fell in haphazard showers. A bleak season was coming and my outlook was dismal. I was stinking of smoke and in pain—tired of the failure of this place with its disappointments and relentless squalor. I'd arrived with Ada, full of love and optimism, a complete man, with my heart intact and body unamputated, but in four months I'd planted nothing, built nothing, achieved nothing.

If Ada didn't want me, perhaps I should simply go home. I had nothing here.

The settlement reflected my misery.

Trails of soot, carried down the paths on many footsteps, trickled like dirty tears to the river, which ran high alongside fragile banks. The wind carried a smell of dead fire and despair. I stopped to look at the charred remains of the huts, like stumps of rotten teeth, the edges still steaming in the rain.

Dr Evans was on site, and together we organised carts to take whatever could be salvaged to one of the warehouses on the river. I got a scribe to note down, as far as we could ascertain, which goods came from which property and the names of the householders. Families came in to claim what they could, and we confirmed they had a neighbour or friend with whom to lodge. It was a long and distressing afternoon.

By evening most of the Cornish families had been rehoused. There was a generosity in the lower orders that I hoped would be matched when donations arrived from the rest. My housemaid, Lucy, came in, dirty in a soot-encrusted dress. She stood flat-footed, addled, chewing her scrawny colourless plait. Dr Evans had found her wandering around the town. He gently pushed her forward.

"This one will need a place to stay."

"Where's your mother, Lucy?" I asked her. Her father had drowned off the ship on the voyage out.

She raised her head when she heard my voice. "Ma's with the doctor, Mr Lugg," she said in her quiet, reedy voice. Everything about her was thin. "She took the smoke bad. She's bleedin' with the coughin', sir."

"Lucy can stay with me," I told Evans.

I packed up, we closed the warehouse and I took Lucy home. Dorothy arrived and together we got the girl cleaned up and fed, and into an old smock of mine that reached to her ankles. We put her into Charles's cot and she slept immediately, her head peacefully nestled on the pillow, as if she hadn't just had her home burned to the ground around her and her mother left choking blood.

"I'll check on her in the morning," said Dorothy.

"I'm grateful. Thank you."

Dorothy gave me a half-smile then, a lift of the cheekbones, perhaps a concession that she wasn't working for me, but with me, on something shared. Something that didn't require self-defence.

I lay awake a long time, listening to the scratching of bugs in the thatch, thinking of fire and poverty and wondering what to do with Lucy if her mother didn't recover. Perhaps Dorothy would take her in. Once I had a vision of my future with Ada in it and might have pictured us offering the girl a home. But if I couldn't let that domestic vision go I also couldn't imagine it with any clarity.

———

I was up early, long before dawn, and went along the waterfront to wait with the baker for his fresh bread. He slid his trays from the ovens with a sharp pull, the hut smelling of yeast and homeliness, and he wrapped a loaf in paper for me, adding some buns and a pot of sugary jam from his pantry for Lucy.

"With my love to the poor wee thing," he said, a big man with glassy eyes.

It was just as I stepped out of his pool of light that the land lurched, as if someone had jerked a rug under my feet.

I heard the baker shout when it happened again, and then I was thrown to the ground by a distinct back-and-forth shake of the earth.

The baker's bag pitched from my hands. I reached for the buns as they jumped about on the moving ground.

"Maoris!" In the dark, panicked people were staggering

out of their huts as the shaking started again. The baker cried "Earthquake!" and I heard his pans clattering from the shelves to the bench and floor.

I gathered my bread and ran along the moving path, where lamps were being lit as people tumbled about, some with guns and knives, looking wildly for an enemy who could make the ground rock.

I found Lucy cowering on the path outside my hut, an angular shadow like a long-legged insect in the dirt, calling for her ma. I put my arm around her shoulders and led her back inside and sat her on the cot.

"It's an earthquake, Lucy. You are safe here with me," I said calmly, even as the earth bucked again. We sat side by side in the dark until the rocking subsided and the land was still. Not knowing what else to do, I tucked her in and went back to bed and I must have fallen fast and deeply asleep.

I missed the several aftershocks and excited noises of the settlement, and when I woke up much later in the morning Dorothy had been and gone, and Lucy was dressed and breakfasted and laying out my clothes. I was disconcerted to think Dorothy had been in the room while I slept.

Later in the day, I took Lucy to visit her mother. The doctor told Lucy she was sleeping, but to me she appeared unconscious. It was the doctor off the *Oriental*, Fitzgerald, in attendance, and Pierce, the publican, clearly wanted his room back.

"I'm going to take her across to Thorndon," Fitzgerald told me. "She needs a bed and warm blankets. My infirmary is still nothing more than a mud hut, but cleaner than this pigsty and there is a nurse on hand. Where is the daughter staying?"

"I have her with me for now, but I share with Charles Heaphy and he will want his bed back shortly."

"I have no room for the girl. And you'll need to find something long term for the mother. Her lungs have been badly burned and she will be an invalid—if she recovers."

I wondered when the settlement's problems all became mine to solve.

"May I bring Lucy to visit when you move her mother?"

"Best not."

There was an evening meeting of the settlers and we gathered under a thatch cover in the drizzly rain, ostensibly to discuss our new militia, but people turned out to share their experiences of the fire and earthquake. The colonel called us to order. Our Māori had suffered in some scrapes with the Wairarapa tribes over the hill, he told us, and there was some bad blood with a tribe in Ōtaki. The committee had decided we should have protective measures in place to defend ourselves should the need arise. All men between eighteen and sixty would drill and be available if required. Māori included. The notice was in the paper.

Colonel Wakefield looked around the assembly, but no one had any argument on the topic and the talk passed quickly back to the earthquakes and what they might mean. There had been further jolts during the day, none so shocking or long as in the morning, but frightening in their rumbling mystery. We missed Dieffenbach, our scientist. He might have been able to explain what was causing the tremors and how long they might continue, but he was away with Charles on the hills beyond the Hutt Valley.

Dr Evans suggested the mountains to the north could be the cause. There were huge active volcanoes in the centre of the island and an explosion there would cause tremors all across the land. I added exploding volcanoes to my list of fears for Jerningham on his travels.

—

I needn't have worried. Jerningham stepped ashore from a whale-boat the following morning. He seemed to have grown taller and certainly he was leaner. He looked fierce and had a wildness in his expression as if he had been through great danger and didn't think much of it. His hair was long and loose and his untrimmed beard thick and dark. He swung a canvas bag from his shoulder and pulled out scrolls wrapped in wax paper, which he brought up the beach to present to his uncle.

"Your deeds to Wanganui." He gave the colonel a bow and flashed him a dazzling smile.

"Lugg!" he said. "Find me a barber and a clean set of clothes. I need dry boots and breakfast, and then I will join you in the office, Uncle William, and tell you all I have achieved."

The colonel pursed his lips but nodded to me. "Take him to my house and clean him up," he said.

I waited for the "welcome home" or some kind expression of greeting to his nephew, but it didn't come.

"Well?" I asked Jerningham, after he had eaten, bathed and dressed and the barber was styling his trimmed hair. We sat in the front room of the colonel's wooden-framed house, looking through glass windows to where immigrant workers were putting a fence around his garden and a couple of native boys were digging a flower bed.

Jerningham sprawled back in his chair, a thick crust of the baker's best smeared with lard in his hand, closing his eyes and enjoying the sensual pleasure as the man rubbed oil into his scalp.

"Did you get there ahead of the missionaries and their treaty?"

His sharp chin, free now of the beard, nodded up and down. "Williams and Hadfield arrived the day after I sailed in. They walked in overland. But it wasn't a race, you know.

The chiefs were honouring an agreement we made last year, Lugg. I wasn't negotiating anything new, just confirming and paying to seal our existing bargain. My friends hadn't wavered. They are building houses for us all the way up the river, and waiting for us to come and live among them."

"But Williams got his document signed?"

"Apparently so, though he was quick and secretive about it and the Māori have no concept of what it means. *Sovereignty*—there is no word for it in Māori. Even Williams can't begin to translate something where the concept doesn't exist. One chief told me the Queen had given him a blanket, and he'd signed a cross beside his name to say he'd received it."

"Surely not!"

"You have no idea of the malfeasance of that missionary. When I told the chief that it meant Queen Victoria was now chief over him, he laughed uproariously but then got very angry. I fear Williams's duplicity will come back to haunt us all."

"And your dealings? The Māori understood what they meant?"

Jerningham sat up and shot me a hard look. He waved the barber away.

"I went around all the villages, Lugg, Captain Chaffers with me, and the crew as witnesses. I used an interpreter. I gathered the natives together in one place, so all the chiefs could debate the transaction between themselves. I sat with thirty of their superior chiefs and they each had their men about them—we counted several hundred of them, naked and painted and carrying their weapons. The chiefs said they had been discussing the sale for months with their people and all agreed and considered their land sold to us. They were satisfied with the goods, and we brought the stuff ashore in huge piles and they scrambled over them, as the

– 103 –

Māori do, and divided them in their own way."

I could feel my face tighten, eyes narrowing as I tried to visualise this scene and understand its significance. I knew I should let it go, but it disturbed me that Jerningham, in undermining Hobson's agreement, had been hasty. "But they signed your agreement *after* Williams had already left with his treaty?"

"For God's sake, Lugg—what would you have me do?"

He stood up, pushed the chair away and grabbed a jacket that the colonel's man had laid out on a divan and, without hat or necktie, strode out the door. He shouted over his shoulder, "You don't listen, Lugg. This was merely a confirmation. Our agreement dated from last year."

That afternoon the wind picked up again. The blasting evening southerly blew a ship fast by the nose directly into the harbour. By morning it had been identified as the return of the *Integrity*, and word from a sailor was that it was packed with government troops sent to charge us all with treason and take us in chains to Hobson at the Bay of Islands.

Dear God. After earthquake and fire and flood, we should expect a ship of our own soldiers, at least, to be on our side. I looked over the untamed hills and empty land, knowing the nearest civilisation was a thousand miles away, and I struggled to understand how it was possible to fall foul of the law here.

THE QUEEN'S
LOYAL SUBJECTS

IN THE PEARLY LIGHT of a wet dawn a Union Jack, newly raised on the pole near the colonel's Pito-one residence, clattered sharply in the blustery rain. I was up early and walking the beach to work. A boat pushed off from shore and scurried fast across the harbour to the *Integrity*, carrying a uniformed constable and armed guard.

Dr Evans and Revans were with Colonel Wakefield and Jerningham in his office, along with another committee member, Mr Hanson, a man of strong opinions. They were laughing loudly at the departed constable, and I was sure they'd made their derision clear to him as he'd executed his duties and raised the Jack.

"It's too rich!" I heard Hanson shout, clearly enough to be heard by the settlers, who had gathered under cover in the lee of the hut.

The baker was there, and the men I had recently seen tending the colonel's garden, and a labourer and his family, and more, all come to discover whether their leaders were to be arrested and they abandoned. Their smiles were nervous as they glanced from face to face, slightly reassured, perhaps, by the guffaws from inside. Hooded eyes, shady with sleep, peered from doorways, children tucked away behind skirts as if soldiers were already storming up the path. Word travelled fast in our small settlement.

"Mr Lugg," called Dr Evans, as I entered the hut, "have you heard? Our escaped Captain Pearson has told the lieutenant governor that we are a self-governing colony of renegades and turncoats and he has sent his magistrate, Shortland, to rout us out. Tell me, sir, is it you leading us in rebellion against Her Majesty?"

They all swung their attention to me hovering in the doorway, their ruthless laughter demanding that I join in their game for which I felt ill-equipped and reluctant. I needed to pick up my documents regarding the fire settlements, but I had no desire to cross the room to my alcove, so I stepped no further.

"I am the Queen's loyal subject." I spoke emphatically and with deep seriousness. I felt the need to make my position absolutely clear. If it were true that Hobson had sent a regiment to suppress the colony, I had no place in that room.

"As are we all! The Queen's loyal subjects!" Again, Hanson shouted for the benefit of those gathering outside.

I abandoned any hope of retrieving my papers and stepped back out into the crowd.

We milled around for a while, immigrants and settlers, sharing what little we knew, as the leading men of the settlement gathered and debated and were joined by the remaining committee members on a fast sail over from Thorndon. Eventually, Dr Evans was put on a row-boat and sent out to the *Integrity* for clarification, and the *Tory*'s captain was rowed back.

"What news, Captain Chaffers?" I asked the harbour master as I helped him ashore.

"It's *Mr* Chaffers now, Mr Lugg," he said. "And your harbour master no more." He turned his face into the driving rain for a moment until he appeared to be blinded by it. "Are they meeting?"

"They're in the colonel's office now. The full committee is there."

He didn't turn immediately, but took the rain on his face, stretching his neck so the drips could ease past his collar and roll down into his skin, as if he found the irritation a welcome distraction. After a deep sigh, he left me and went off up the beach, ripping his hat off and fiercely rubbing his head, muttering low words as he crossed the sand.

Out by Somes Island, the *Integrity* bounced low in the water. I could see soldiers on her deck. Dr Evans looked like a small fish in his boat, swimming gallantly across the swell to the whale. Suddenly Lucy was at my side, pulling at my hand.

"You need to come, Mr Lugg. It's Dorothy, sir. She ain't well. She's fallen." The girl tugged my confused thoughts and the rest of me off the beach and up into a side track, where a small group of people clustered over a bundle on the ground. It was Dorothy, clutching at her stomach with her knees bent up to her chest, her dark hair loosely draped across the mud and the rain falling on her agonised face. I could hear deep moans. An old woman had grabbed her arm and was pulling her sideways and another tried to raise her to a sitting position, but I could see her body was curled tight as a millstone and they were hurting her.

"Clear away, you. All of you. Let go of her. What are you doing? Get away, stand back." I bent over the wretched Dorothy, who turned her face away when she heard my voice. The sight of her in the mud crushed me with pity.

"Go away," she whispered, and then cried out sharply and tucked her face down into her knees.

"What is it?" I asked the women around her. "Stomach cramp? What's she been eating?" But no one replied. They faded back and let me take charge. I knelt in the mud and scooped my damaged hand carefully behind her neck, ignoring her as she attempted to roll away and push me off. I tried to be gentle.

"Tuck her dress under," I told Lucy as I wrenched Dorothy from the puddle and staggered to my feet. Her tense body made her awkward to lift and she was surprisingly heavy with her clothes full of rain and mud. There was a small crowd around now, watching as crowds do, waiting to see if catastrophe would follow. The old woman patted Dorothy's arm, as if patting would help.

"Lucy, find Dr Dorset. He was in the square here earlier. I'll take her to my hut." But Dorothy writhed and banged her head against my chest and I felt my damaged right hand slipping in its grip. I shouted at her, "Will you stop that!"

Through ferociously clenched teeth she pleaded, "Take me home."

"You need a doctor, Dorothy. Let me help you."

"I want to go to my hut. Please. Please!" And she convulsed again and dropped her head, sobbing into my jacket, hidden from the gaze of the gaping onlookers as I stood flat-footed and leaned in to try to shield her head from the rain. Although she had nursed me for weeks, it was the first time I had ever touched her and she felt oddly precious to me.

"Go," I said to Lucy. "Bring the doctor to her hut."

Like the Pied Piper, I led a party of rats along the road, hem-soaked and grey, people coming from their houses to look. "See there. It's Dorothy Lewis ..." "Will you look? It's Mr Lugg carrying her ..." "I always thought ..." "What's wrong with her?" "It's them herbs she got from Mrs Knowles." "Oh, the poor lamb, who's to look after her?" "What's she gone and done?" "He's never taking her home?" "She's not, is she? We've been landed near four months …" "I'll get a kettle on …" "Does she have another dress?"

Their gossip pattered down like rain into puddles until we arrived at the far end of the settlement, under the stinking charred remains of the burnt Cornish huts, to a low hovel. One of Dorothy's wards, a stocky girl of about twelve years of age, was playing with a boy who dragged a ball of woven flax on a thread, bouncing it across the floor. The place was cold and smelled damp. Three little box pallets stood with their ends against the wall and there was a bench with a water jug and pots. It was bleak but cleanly swept, and there was a prettily stitched cotton cover on each bed, neatly folded.

I was reluctant to cross the threshold but Dorothy was exhausted, shivering and moaning and still clenched tightly in on herself. I ducked my head under the lintel, leaving our followers outside.

"Your guardian has stomach cramps and I have sent for the doctor," I told the girl, who snatched the toddler from underfoot and held him to her skirts.

I laid Dorothy clumsily on the bed furthest from the draughty door and she turned away from me, pulling up her knees and turning her face to the wall.

"Go away, Mr Lugg!" Her harsh voice peeled from layers of rasping breath.

Unnerved by her tone, I backed out and went to hurry the doctor.

Lucy met me outside the office, slapping her hands on her dress in agitation. "The doctor is in there but I daren't go in."

The door to the hut opened and Jerningham stepped out into the rain. He came quickly across to me. "What is it, why's the girl crying for the doctor?"

I had no reason to expect help from Jerningham, but

there he was, his forehead crumpled in worry and his attention undivided.

"It's Dorothy Lewis. She's collapsed with stomach cramps. She needs a doctor urgently."

Jerningham's expression froze for a heartbeat and I felt a cold blast of despair that he would turn his back—this was no attacking war party, merely a sick woman—but my fear was misplaced. He crouched quickly down to Lucy.

"You know Mrs Knowles? Tell her I sent you to fetch her for Miss Lewis. Tell her she has the cramps. Go!" He watched the girl run away up the path and turned to me. "Fitzgerald's over at Thorndon and Dorset is addressing the committee now. You won't get him out."

He shook his head and droplets flew off in long chains. "Mrs Knowles will know what to do. You'll need to pay her … here …" He pushed a clutch of coins from his pocket into my hand without looking down, folding my fingers over them as if enclosing a secret. "Best thing you can do to help is get her warm and dry—there's nobody with dry clothes in this wretched town—you'll have to buy things, go to Telford's, get a smock, towels, bedding for the poor creature. Put it on my account."

He had taken my arm and was directing me along the track towards the shop. "Let your girl run the messages for Mrs Knowles, Lugg. You deliver the linen and then stay clear. There's nothing you can do."

And he left me, ducking his head against the rain. I watched him wrench open the door of the hut to join our leaders discussing the warship in the harbour and the soldiers in her hold.

—

Lucy came back in the evening. I had recently added a fireplace and chimney to my hut, and she came in gratefully out of the rain to the warmth of the flames, her little cat face turning side to side to warm both flanks. I reassured her she could stay until I found a billet for her, knowing gentle-natured Charles would not disapprove. The good girl laid my muddy jacket on the clothes-horse to dry and set to mending a shirt I left out for her.

I asked after Dorothy.

"It were something nasty she ate," she said, solemnly. "Mrs Knowles fixed her. She said to thank you for the dry things and said she will return them as soon as they's cleaned."

"Oh, she is not to worry about that. I was just the messenger. Mr Wakefield paid for them. He doesn't expect them back." I waved my hand, noticing the wet bandage I had forgotten to change all day. I unravelled it and let my ugly, thumbless hand dry in the muggy air.

"Mr Lugg?" She had her head down over her stitching.

"Yes, Lucy?"

"Are we in trouble with the Queen? It's what Mrs Knowles and they's all saying."

Her pale face was pinched with worry and I recognised her powerlessness and her fear. She, together with her drowned father and burned mother and their hardy neighbours, friends and fellow labourers, had risked everything they owned and everything they knew to cross the wild seas for these new pastures. It was a horrible gamble; more than the Wakefields and their committees and the magistrate in his warship on the dark harbour could ever possibly understand. The better life for the working classes wasn't a universal promise; more it was a sweeping statement that would be proved true, or not, by future generations of little Lucys looking back.

She herself had lost everything that kept her safe.

I wanted to tell her that it would be all fine, that this was a friendly visit from the government, that the troops on board were on our side, that the colony was in no trouble, that her mother would come home and the rain would stop and the sun would shine in the morning.

"Leave that shirt, Lucy," I said. "Get some sleep and in the morning you can go to the baker's for hot buns."

I stayed awake through the night, with a sense of deep unease.

I must have slept at some point, as you do even when you feel your eyes haven't closed all the long hours, because I roused myself late the following day and noticed a folded letter propped on the table, an arm's reach from the door.

Lucy, small in even Charles's modest cot, slept like a girl who has been woken at dawn every day since she could lift a broom and then one day is left to nature's course. I took the letter and went outside. It was addressed to "Mr Arthur Lugg" in a woman's hand. *Ada*.

Crossing the silver harbour to Thorndon, the *Integrity* was close-hauled into the wind, and there were troops alongside the sailors on deck. Two boats had pulled out from the Pito-one shore in chase, with the settlement's strongest oarsmen ferrying the committee in pursuit.

Yesterday's drubbing rain had finally blown over, though the grey sky was streaked with vertical pillars of white as showers came over the hills, and the wind continued to charge around like so many horses. There would be no news until the boats returned.

I took Ada's letter to the office and sat at my desk, then moved restlessly out to the colonel's desk and finally stood in the doorway. With her message in my hand, I was anxious of the content. If I never opened it, it would always declare love.

Our long voyage out seemed a fantasy now, a ribbon that linked one life with another, over which we had walked precariously together with hands touching. I had felt so sure, during those months on board, that being loved and having a purpose everything would simply fall into place. But, once ashore, I had to admit Ada had not been in my thoughts as a lover should be. I was not some fop who would hide for hours for a glimpse of my beloved's face, or send hourly tokens of love, or embarrass her with too-forward advances. I showed my love through my work to establish a position for myself in the colony, so when I went to her brother he would welcome my suit. Ada would not respect an idle man.

I pulled her to my mind now—my earnest-looking Ada with her intelligent eyes. Exactly the girl Arthur Lugg of Somerset had wanted as a life's companion. Not at all the sort to tempt the likes of Jerningham—he had dismissed her as plain—but for those four months at sea she had engaged me fully.

I didn't want to lose that.

With my clumsy hands I broke the seal and jerked the letter open.

> *Dear Mr Lugg,*
>
> *I thank you for your kind regards, which were conveyed to me by Mr Revans, Secretary to the Committee.*
>
> *I was distressed to hear of your medical procedure and subsequent disability. God grant you a speedy recovery to robust health. I understand you have been very busy with colonial affairs and I wish you well with your employment. My brother, Catherine and I are all well.*
>
> *You are aware that I am recently engaged to be married to Mr John Bently. My brother entered into this agreement on my behalf with my full consent and we will be married in the spring.*

I must now broach a rather delicate matter. I ask that the brief shipboard "amour" that entertained us on our outbound journey be consigned to the past, and not referred to again. It is not something I have mentioned to anyone and I would be grateful if I may call on your word of honour as a gentleman to remember only a young and impressionable girl's excitement at the romance of travel. Nothing more.

I trust in your confidence.

Sincerely,

Ada Malloy

DRUNK AND DROWNED

I SPENT much of that winter drunk.

I don't know how I slid so fast into hopelessness. I suppose it passed the time. There were soldiers in town now and Shortland had taken control of the settlement on behalf of the Crown to suppress our treasonous rebellion. I might have welcomed the security of a recognised government but, along with many of the settlers, I felt slighted by the arrogant Hobson, stamping his heavy boot on the young neck of our enterprise, with not even a visit himself to view our achievements. He shunned us and rejected Port Nicholson as his capital, proposing instead an unpopulated northern wasteland at Waitematā.

I was unemployed again. The colonel had gone north with a petition to settle the land issues and Mr Hanson, his deputy, didn't want or need my services. Jerningham was back and forward to his hideout in Wanganui. Sam Revans was busy stirring up sentiment against the injustices of Hobson and had no time for me. Charles and Dieffenbach had returned from the failed mission up the valley—there were no hidden expanses of flat land—and then Dieffenbach had gone exploring again and Charles had crossed to Thorndon and rented a house with a new friend. He was surveying the town with Mein Smith, so it was natural for him to base himself on that side of the harbour, but all the same, I couldn't help feeling abandoned. And I was lonely.

Lucy kept my hut and clothing tidy and fetched water for me when I woke blind and stupid in the afternoon and then staggered around until the fog lifted. I sent her to live with Dorothy. Looking back, I am ashamed to say I don't know when her mother died. I gave them money.

My town section had been allotted in Thorndon but, in the typical haste that characterised our colony, the map was incorrectly drawn and when it was amended my section became a Māori plot. I made the trip across the harbour once to view the survey, but the settler ship *Coromandel* had arrived and was chaotically spewing ship-sick settlers and stock onto the beach. I went ashore amidst a herd of bullocks bellowing their distress in outpourings of steam into the cold air, and turned straight back for the relative quiet of Pito-one.

The whole thing was hopeless, anyway, until the government recognised our land purchase. I wasn't such a fool to build my house on land that might be stolen from under me. Some settlers were again discussing packing the whole thing up and moving to Chile. I heard all this through a curtain of alcohol and let others do the thinking.

The storms came on incessantly, winds blown directly from the southern ice continent, whistling up through the heads of the harbour and over the town, keeping everything and everyone damp and raw. With nothing to occupy me, and no skills of use to anyone, I simply got up at midday and went through the rain to Pierce's hotel to take my place by the fire and let my clothes dry onto my cold body. I drank whatever came to hand, with whoever was there. Captain Chaffers welcomed my company—despite his demotion he remained "Captain" to us all, but he had no work while Shortland and the colonel wrangled over his position and duties, so he drank to pass the time. I helped him get blind drunk on several occasions. He was one of the quiet ones who slipped into a stupor. Other days I drank with Wharepōuri and the Māori from Te Puni's village, who shouted and raged as they drowned themselves in nasty spirits bought from the whalers. I didn't care either way.

Jerningham returned from an adventure and came to find me, blazing with injustice. He'd been a week on a whaling station at Kāpiti, barefoot and bearded as they hauled in their catch, and had walked back over the hills from Porirua in the morning to an ambush by the committee. I was alone in my usual spot by the fire in the Britannia when he slumped into the chair opposite, loosened his dirty cravat and called for wine.

"And something strong for my men outside. What do you have, Pierce?"

If Jerningham noticed my dishevelled appearance in the middle of the afternoon, he made no comment. He sent a bottle of imported rum to the Māori gathered around the open fire with instructions to "look after them well!" and picked up the nearly empty wine bottle at my elbow to sniff the contents.

"God, Lugg, that's nasty stuff. Pierce! Have you got any of the Hokianga red? I've had a foul day and my good friend here is trying to poison me."

He kicked a log on the fire, scowled at a patron who came to greet him and turned his back on the room. He drank.

"Did your uncle not give you a warm reception?" I asked, after the first glass had revived him and the second was well in hand.

It took a while to get the story from him. It unravelled from a tight and angry ball of abuse. I was already two bottles ahead and slow to piece together that the "fat-faced buttock clencher" was Dr Evans and "piss-proud round-mouth" was his uncle, the colonel.

He had been harshly chastised by Dr Evans, unfairly, he claimed, for a private speculation he had made during the Wanganui purchase, which Evans said had sullied the clarity of the Company's deal.

"As if anyone would mistake a gift of a few pigs for a land settlement agreement!" he said. "If afterwards—*afterwards*, I say, Lugg—I did a bit of speculating on my own account, what business is it of that verbose lobcock Evans?"

The *missionaries*—how he spat the word—also dared accuse him of unscrupulous dealings. When according to him they were the biggest land-sharks in the country, dishonestly exchanging land for God.

"At least we give them blankets, Lugg. What's a Māori going to do with God?"

I was in no state to analyse the rights or wrongs of Jerningham's activities, though perhaps there was a little niggle of warning in the back of my wet brain. But he was a friend to me and so I stood by him, buried my doubts and joined in the loud cursing against the missionaries.

Jerningham and I crossed the harbour to get away from my dull misery at Britannia, and spent three days in Dicky Barrett's new hotel on the quay at Lambton, never sober. The last night we slept under a table. Barrett threw blankets over us. There was no kindness in the old sea-dog's heart, but he valued a paying customer.

The third morning, after a heavy breakfast of eggs, sausage and thick porridge, Jerningham pulled on his boots and said he was going to find a woman.

"You know," he said, and I held his bloodshot eyes as the only steady points in a moving world, "this is the only port in the whole world without a proper brothel." He waved his arms about as he tried to wrap a cravat around his neck.

"There is no brothel," he said. "In all the world, how did I end up here?"

I looked at the uneaten remains of fried eggs on my plate, their whites grey and lined with grease and the yolks skimmed with a light gauze. My stomach couldn't take it. I imagined my eyes looked like that egg.

"But don't worry, Lugg." Jerningham tapped the side of his nose. "I know a place we will find a warm welcome." He nodded encouragingly, but I wasn't about to join him. Even in my derelict state I knew I was too much my father's son for a brothel to offer me anything but sin. Besides, I felt disgusting and sick and in no state for a woman.

"Not a virgin, still, Lugg?"

I looked around for my coat. I couldn't remember if, days ago, I had arrived with one. No coat?

"You know I was married," I replied, snapping at his challenge. "My conquests have all been in a marriage bed." My tongue was thick in my mouth and I pushed it through my teeth a couple of times to scrape off the fur. When he laughed I added to annoy him, "Sanctified by God."

Jerningham's eyes flared and he whispered, conspiratorially, "Does he make your cock bigger?"

He slapped me on the shoulder and I followed him out, leaving Dicky a generous tip on the bar.

Jerningham thrust his hands deep in his pockets and lifted his head into the sharp air. His face was creased but he looked well on it, handsome and rugged, and I trotted alongside knowing that I was as crumpled and grey as a damp rag.

I didn't want to meet anyone, so I followed Jerningham through the back of Te Aro behind the pā, alongside some scratchy bushes and up to where a row of rough huts and lean-tos sat outside the town boundary. There was a scurry in the undergrowth and a barefoot girl ran ahead into a hut. As we neared, the door opened quickly and a woman reached her hand out for Jerningham and pulled him inside.

"You, too, Lugg," he said over his shoulder. "Come on. Betty's game." But I shook my head.

"His was amputated," I heard him say to the woman as the door closed on their laughter. The young girl slipped out and back down the lane to her watching post.

I walked on with my eyes down, kicking the dirt on the unformed road. A bottle of spirits from a waterfront whare and I was drunk again, cradling the bottle in my wretched hand, when the whale-boat crossed the harbour.

———

The wind picked up strength on the crossing and hit gale force on our approach into Pito-one. How stupid to be on an open stretch of water on a day like this. I should have looked at the sky, heeded the warning of the clouds driven low over the water on relentless winds. We were running side-on to the surf and it was obvious the craft was steered by an inexperienced hand. The boat, overladen with passengers, rolled horribly on the swell and panicked screams broke above the roar of the wind. The nose turned towards the shore, worsening the angle, and I gripped my seat. We over-corrected and the boat rolled again. Drunk as I was, I sent a prayer to my neglected god for forgiveness as the port-side gunwale cut the water and slowly, inevitably, my body fell backwards and the weight of an invisible hand tipped me into the churning water.

It was brutally cold.

Much colder than the air.

The freeze come smoothly over my face and my head. In my shock I didn't struggle, my heavy clothes pulling me down. Numbness came like bubbles through layers of fabric and into my skin, fast at my collar and biting at my crotch and slowly, slowly seeping into my boots. Under the water there is no weather and dead quiet replaces all the chaos of the world above. It is instant. One second there is the full cacophony of a capsizing boat with screams and shouts and the ghastly, heavy splash of bodies dropping into the sea and the next, an absolute absence of sound.

I had never felt so alone.

Nine men died that night.

I was one of God's small mercies.

Chief Te Puni himself found me under the water, dragged me ashore and turned me over. He thumped the water from my lungs and pummelled me until my breath came back in an astonishing suck of pure life.

And the noise came back in a rush. The crunch of heavy bare feet on thick sand, the drag of bodies across stones. My eye was prised open and I heard Colonel Wakefield's voice up close.

"It's Arthur Lugg. Dorset, over here—he's alive. Men! Carry this one to the house."

And, with the breath, suddenly everything came back. Everything. All the horror and confusion and strife of this one life we are given, the chaos that tags us at birth and plagues us all our days, shaking us away from complacency and comfort, throwing punches from left and right until we stagger into the grave. I was carried, horribly alive, and laid in the back room of the colonel's house, where Dr Dorset stayed with me all night.

———

When I woke with the new light, the good doctor took my pulse, nodded, and gave me a pat on the shoulder. There was a set of dry clothes laid out for me, and Dorset helped me with the buttons. Colonel Wakefield had left a message that I should join him later for breakfast.

Until that moment I wasn't sure I had wanted to be saved, that I wouldn't walk straight back into the waves, but their kindness undid me.

Slowly, step by shaking step, I returned to the beach.

It was cold and peaceful, the storm over, and the watery sun ran a pale spear of light across the harbour, where the raging waves had done their destructive work the night before. There was no evidence of the harrowing event, the tide had come and gone and the churn of footprints in the sand had disappeared, along with the screams of the drowning and the wailing of the Māori, all the evidence of our distress dispersed by waves and wind. Nature tidying with her fast efficiency.

A light wind whipped the Jack about on the flagpole— the Queen's handkerchief fluttering over us all. Shame crept up on me. It percolated into the cracks that had been cut in my mind by brandy and beer, little nicks rent in my fabric, until I hung my head like a bad child. I heard my father's stern voice frightening me as a boy with the dangers of straying from the moral path and the special hell awaiting those who abandoned virtue for hedonism. Although I had left my father behind, his teachings were harder to shake. Under the righteousness, I believed they were simple truths. I put one foot in front of the other until I was back at the house. Colonel Wakefield gave me a quick look over and declared me recovered. Back from the dead.

"I understand you've been indisposed for much of the winter," he said diplomatically, as we sat in his dining room to a breakfast of mutton chops and tea. We ate off china with silver cutlery and I sat ramrod-backed to compensate for the fact that I held my knife in my fist like a monkey. My instant sobriety caused a kind of patchy blindness in my mind as I searched for appropriate words, but he continued. "It has been a difficult time, I won't deny it, but we mustn't give up, mustn't lose our way. I want you over in Thorndon, Lugg, and I want to see a house on your section by the year's end. You will set an example to the other settlers. We will advance this colony on our founding principles: civilisation to the barbarians, Christianity to the heathen, and order to replace lawlessness. We are under siege, but we are fighting a just and a noble cause and I will not see all our work overturned by the unmitigated malevolence of Hobson. I need all my men with me on this. Heads up!"

I was one of the colonel's men again. With food and warmth came clarity and I felt pathetically grateful for the opportunity of a sober conversation. I asked him, "What of the debacle over the town survey while you were away? The map has to be redrawn and there are fights over the allocations. Perhaps I could help?"

"Administration. That's all." He lifted his haughty chin. "It's just administration, Lugg. People should do their damn jobs properly. Mein Smith is as big a fool as ever walked this earth to go public before his plans were checked. I'll have his job for this mess."

I let his energy and ambition rouse me. Colonel Wakefield was a fighter. While I slumped and lost myself in grog, the colonel hit back with punches.

"Yes, sir."

"We need the place to look like a town. I have my new residence going up in Thorndon, the site's drained and fenced already and I have a frame house being set up. I understand you made a similar purchase. Clear your plot and start building. Just get on with it. As soon as you're over in Thorndon and ready, your old job will be waiting for you. And don't you worry about the land business. I'll sort it out if I have to cut off Hobson's tail and whip him with it."

He came to the door to see me off, checking that I turned right to my hut to start organising my move back to civility rather than left, down the path to the hotel.

—

On a clear spring day in September, with the long and shameful winter behind me, I went to find Charles Heaphy. I had followed the colonel's instructions: left the grog in Pito-one and had set about clearing my newly allocated plot in Thorndon. The house was half erected. My builders, despite the tree-covered hills, couldn't obtain enough cut timber for the front-room floors, but the back section was roofed and waterproof, and I piled my furniture, mouldy from storage, into the one finished room. I fenced, and dug a front path. It was strenuous work for which I was out of condition, but it gave me a reason to get up in the morning.

Ada had married, without my so much as catching a glimpse of her. I heard nothing but good of her husband, John Bently. He had a fine house right across town on the elevated ground of Majoribanks Street, and every ship from Sydney brought luxury furnishings to his door. He and Ada entertained generously and instigated Māori Monday, where one chief or another from the local tribes would dine at their table. I heard Bently spent his days with Ada's brother, Malloy, walking the forests in Karori, following the country surveying closely with an eye on allocation. He was the model settler and I hated the sound of his name.

Charles was surprised the morning I arrived on my visit. Over the winter, while I drank away my days, he had been sober and diligent, and on the odd occasion when our paths had crossed his disapproval of my state was clear. This time he seemed pleased to see me dressed and respectable and welcomed me warmly.

"I'm so glad you are building on your plot, Arthur," he said.

We sat on the porch of his home in Thorndon, a worker's cottage at the foot of the Tinakori hill, and talked for a while about events in the settlement over the last few months, developments to which I had been mostly oblivious. Always a Company man, Charles spoke harshly of the incompetence of Hobson.

"He claims we have usurped his power and he commands our allegiance. How can this be? There was no power here to usurp until he sent Shortland. And, frankly, Shortland was a poor choice of representative. They laugh at him, Arthur. The Māori know pomposity when they see it. They follow him up the road with feathers in their hats and chests stuck out, hands clasped behind their backs. They're fair mimics. People come running to applaud the parade."

"And yet Shortland is the Crown representative and Hobson our appointed governor."

"*Lieutenant* governor," he said. "He has no power. It all comes through Gipps in Sydney. And he turned his back on us most clearly when he named Auckland as his capital, that uninhabited swamp, when the majority of the population he's to govern is here, four hundred miles distant. Revans is getting a petition together to have Hobson removed. I will add my voice to it."

I was uneasy with this growing divide between the Company and government and this pressure to take sides. "We're British subjects, Charles. Temporarily we were under the jurisdiction of the New Zealand Company, in the same way that at sea we would obey a ship's captain. But the government has now arrived."

"The government should not run roughshod over us like an invading force."

"It's hardly that!" I would have laughed if it weren't for

the seriousness of his expression. He glared at me as if I was the one spoiling for a fight.

"The Colonial Office must recognise the Company as a government instrument of colonisation," he said. "We broke no laws settling here. If Hobson won't recognise us and continues to subjugate us unfairly we must go to a higher authority."

Charles and I seldom disagreed but I couldn't understand his insistence. He had no land to lose if Hobson ruled against our purchases. He was merely an employee of the Company. And I realised that was the crux of it, his good name was tied to the New Zealand Company. He worked in the field with Mein Smith, away from the company offices, and was unaware of the duplicity of some of the dealings done in the Company's name. But a petition to overthrow the appointed Crown representative was mutiny and I would have none of it.

"What does Jerningham say?" I asked.

"Too much, as usual, all of it unhelpfully rude. He has no diplomacy. We need to shut him up before he inflames the situation beyond repair. The colonel will send him off on another adventure soon to get him out of the way." And with a laugh that lightened the mood, he added, "Much in the same way one would distract an infant to keep it quiet."

I stayed while Charles brewed some of his nasty kawakawa tea and admired the sketches he had made of ships at anchor. He suggested a walk the following Sunday and I readily agreed.

⸺

We set off early, winding up into the steep hills above the harbour, following the Kaiwharawhara valley past a native village, where we stopped briefly to greet Dog's Ear, the truculent chief.

"You! Pigs!" he shouted angrily as we drew near. "Pigs!"

But he took our hands and drew us inside his pā, offering us his seat by the fire, where his people sat around idly, sleeping or staring. Children played with sticks in the dirt. A recent slip had brought down trees that lay awkwardly across the path, but there was no evidence of industry to clear the blockage away.

"You pigs in potatoes!" Dog's Ear pointed up to a small terrace where we could see scars in the earth from the rutting of pigs that had no doubt escaped from a settler's enclosure. An easy day's fence-building would solve the problem, but the natives showed no inclination for the task, playing and pulling faces instead with the children at the hearth.

Charles promised to report back to the colonel, and with much hand-shaking we thanked him for his hospitality and left, taking the narrow track up through thick bush. We walked without pause; there was no natural resting place on the overgrown path and the expanding view behind us was frustratingly hidden by the trees. Several times we thought we were about to broach the top, only to find a lip of hill and another climb ahead.

"Why do the paths in this country always lead straight up?" I complained to Charles. "Why don't they meander around the ridges, so we can take in the scenery and make easier work of it?"

"Because they are not leisure tracks for the gentry to stroll and admire the country. They are routes to get from A to B, and always take the most direct line. Have you ever walked with Māori on a trail, Arthur? They make nothing of the hills. They are marvellously economic travellers."

I grumbled a bit more but was content with his reply. I determined to walk more on the hills and become as fast and fit as a Māori.

We climbed above the harbour, and although we walked away from civilisation, with every step I felt I was coming back to it.

Charles, of course, made no comment as my pace slowed. Perhaps he realised I was returning from the lost. He was a perceptive man and over these last months he might have recognised in me the loneliness of the drunkard. If he did judge my struggle I knew, as always, it would be with compassion.

Life was clearer up in the sky. I had spent the winter sick for loss of England, but with the return of spring the push I had felt to abandon colonial life now disappeared. Perhaps, like Charles, I was ready to make a commitment to the country. I had land, legally bought. To own it, I needed to begin pushing roots down into the soil.

I realised as we walked that the date was 18 September, a year to the day since I had boarded the *Aurora*. A year so full of challenges and events its magnitude seemed equal to all my previous life. Those on the other side of the divide felt distant and grey, they fell away in importance next to my companions in this enterprise: Jerningham, Colonel Wakefield, Revans, Dorset, Dieffenbach and Heaphy, all so full of industry and life. I had chosen these men as my people and this was my place and I wanted to get on now and be part of it.

I thought with gratitude of the two people who had saved my life: Dorothy, from the black poison of gangrene; and Te Puni, from the waves in the dark harbour. I felt I needed to repay them in some way. With my loyalty. My industry. Something. After a steep scramble, we rose up to where the tall vegetation had been burnt off to leave a low covering of scrub, and we stepped out of the forest into the light, high in the sky upon a knoll, the hilltop the Māori called Kaukau. It felt like God's platform.

We didn't speak much, but I had something on my mind and it rankled so much that when we finally sat, side by side and in a natural state for conversation, I almost blurted it out.

"You know, Charles, I have been thinking about Dorothy Lewis. I feel something should be done about her. She needs to be settled. She deserves a chance, I think, and she was very good to me."

That much I had planned to say. It was partly the reason I had gone to find him, to enable a natural lead-in to this. It was a discussion that needed to happen before I took this path or that.

I was close to picking up something I should offer Charles before taking it for myself: a semi-precious stone or something useful, like a new lens for a telescope. Perhaps he would smile and take it with gratitude. Or he would say—no, I don't want it, you should take it.

Strangely, I had no idea where to go next and was not at all sure what I wanted to hear from him. Charles, always one to let a silence hang for slightly too long, waited for me to go on.

I struggled. "You see, I rather thought that you ... well, I thought perhaps I might speak to her, but should mention it to you first, because ... because you might ..."

I stopped. I had made myself clear enough. It was up to Charles, now, to fill in the gaps if he wanted to. My breathing stilled as I waited on his reply.

"Dorothy Lewis is not my type, Arthur." He sounded rather strained as he said it. I think I felt relief. A lightness, anyway, as if loneliness might not be my lot forever. Charles had his pipe in his hands and he fussed with the tobacco. He looked a bit embarrassed. "Generally speaking, I mean."

He got his pipe lit and we sat in silence for a while, looking down through the sky to the heads, where the pale grey water of the harbour spilled out into the dark blue of the strait. I pointed to a large winged bird swooping below us, soaring with splendour over the tops of the dense foliage.

"Some sort of harrier. That's a wingspan of what, five or six foot?"

"Make a note for Dieffenbach."

We ate our meagre lunch, a cold potato and scrap of salt pork and while Charles got out his sketching paper and took readings and made accurate maps and fast, accomplished drawings, I entertained myself by throwing stones down into the valley.

We lingered too long on the hilltop and were late coming down. In the forest the darkness gathered between the trees, and the roots and vines had disappeared into a complex layering of shadows. Charles, in the lead, rather than cautiously feeling his way along the track, gave himself with alacrity to the darkness and I followed. We whooped and hollered and charged down the treacherous path at breakneck speed, with a recklessness even Jerningham would admire, and somehow arrived back in the valley without broken necks, just as Dog's Ear and his men came up looking for us.

"Thank you, Te Kāeaea," I said, suddenly remembering his proper name, and I shook his hand heartily. From the delighted smile that stretched across his haggard face I learned a gracious lesson.

—

My house felt different that evening, like early morning in summer just before the light comes up. Full of promise.

I sat at my desk and imagined Dorothy sitting across the room by the fire, with her long white hands occupied with some stitching, perhaps, or turning the page of a book. In my mind there were flowers on the table and objects on the mantelpiece, shadowy, feminine things that I couldn't imagine, the sort of things Dorothy would collect and arrange.

I had grown up in a household of men and my previous marriage, through youth, inexperience and a certain timidity on both sides, had been more dutiful than romantic. I knew little of how women expressed themselves and I was confused by Dorothy. If I conjured her image, she wasn't smiling at me. I wasn't under the illusion that she loved me, yet.

I turned the lamp up brightly, took some good white paper from the drawer and wrote a careful proposal. After several false starts and much crossing out, I removed any passionate declaration that might frighten her and appealed to her good sense.

Dear Miss Lewis,

I am generally a reserved and steady man, but please believe me when I say I have no such composure in writing these words to you—a fast-beating heart guides my pen. My solitary existence has become a burden to me and I have prayed for guidance. God ordains a man should take a wife as a help-meet and a companion through life's trials. He has placed your image before me and I believe he guides my steps to your bosom. It is clear a bond has grown between us and I am grateful for your past care of me and recognise your many merits. Perhaps, in time, you may come to love me.

Therefore, I am emboldened to beg your indulgence and lay before you a proposal of marriage.

I am a widower; I admit to no children or dependents, debts or claims on my person whatsoever and my fortune

*is such to be able to support a lady well beyond your
present expectations, being the unimpeded owner of
an acre of town land, with a residence, one hundred
country acres, plus the wherewithal to support a
gentleman's life and needs in the colony. I have no
expectations of you other than your feminine modesty
and gentle companionship in the years ahead.*

*Should you do me the honour of accepting this anxious
proposal, I believe we will live a comfortable and
contented life together. May God grant us children.*

*That you may consent to our union is the sincere wish of
your very sincerely attached,*

Arthur Lugg

ADA AND MARRIAGE

THE FOLLOWING AFTERNOON I ran into Ada Malloy.

She was heading to town from the far end of Oriental Bay, striding purposefully along the stones above the high waterline, with her head up and arms swinging confidently, looking neither right nor left. Her bonnet was pushed back by the wind, and long curls lifted from her forehead and bounced behind her as she walked. She was alone.

I had come out of a gully onto the beach after a long contemplative walk across the hill behind and there she was, half a dozen steps away. I don't know who was the more surprised.

She spun around with the wariness of a man about to put his fists up. Then she recognised who it was coming toward her and looked relieved as if I had saved her from, well, I don't know what. She certainly didn't look particularly as if she needed rescuing, with her face all feisty and strong. And then, in a trice, there was something else, an angry flare that flushed her cheeks, already coloured from her exertion, an even brighter red.

"Ada! What are you doing out here all alone?"

She nodded curtly to me, and her pace, which had slowed at my approach, picked up again and she was past me without stopping. I fell into step alongside her, across the sloping shingle.

"You probably shouldn't be this far from the settlement on your own, you know. At least let me escort you home."

Delight at finding her alone overrode the hurt and disappointment that had accompanied my recent thoughts of her. There were conversations begun on the *Aurora* and cut off mid-conceit without concern, for we'd had the certainty that we could pick them up again and continue the topic through the years ahead. They lay like a ragged hem along the edge of my mind, threads I'd pulled on sometimes while my life unravelled.

She slowed her pace slightly and angled her head as if agreeing that yes, since I was here and was walking in the same direction, I might accompany her.

"Miss Butler lost her shoes," she said, by way of explanation.

"Did she?"

"We were paddling at Point Jerningham, and a wave took them out to sea."

"And Miss Butler is … where?"

Ada waved her hand back the way she had come, but all I saw was a receding tide and the glassy harbour. "I'm going to fetch her another pair, she can't walk home in her bare feet. Oh, don't worry, I haven't left her on a rock with the tide coming in! She is waiting with Catherine in a little cove, out of sight. I'll send a runner back."

We walked at a fast clip, our boots crunching noisily on the unstable ground. It occurred to me I had never before walked with her for more than ten paces without changing direction. On the boat our gait had been unsteady, too. I sighed. There were gulls on the shore and small running birds with long piping beaks pushing about in the shingly sand. Ada was deliberately silent.

We didn't speak for a long time. I wanted her to introduce a conversation. But as we passed the stink where the fishing boats pulled in I had to fight the urge to pick her up in my arms and carry her over the guts and slime on the rocks. Instead I walked helplessly alongside as her dainty feet marched straight through the muck, knowing I had no right to touch her.

"Ada—"

She cut me off instantly, sharp as a knife. "It's Mrs Bently, now."

"Yes, of course. I know. I knew. May I offer you my congratulations."

And we walked on again in silence for a while.

"I understand you are also married, Mr Lugg."

"What? No. That's not correct."

"Well. Whatever passes for marriage in the colonies. I understand some people are more relaxed about the details here."

"Ada." I grabbed her arm and pulled her to a stop and swung her around to face me. Her dear, intelligent face was pulled in a sneer.

"How dare you?" I shouted at her, my eyes, like those of a misunderstood child, filling with angry tears.

Doubt swept across her and she looked at me in horror. There was a terrible realisation that swept down that beach as we read the truth on the face of the other. Around us the gulls screeched and squabbled over scraps of discarded fish.

"How dare you believe that of me?" I said again.

Her expression broke like a wave. She looked as though she were caught red-handed in a deep shame as she realised she had been deceived. The implications swirled around her. She was reading my eyes, scanning one to the other, looking for truth which—of course, for it was the truth— she found. "He lied to me," she said at last. It was not a question. She was not a stupid woman.

"You should have trusted me, not listened to your brother. Of course I had no other liaison. I was promised to you."

Her bastard brother had lied to her. I had visited Malloy, the morning after his false assumption that Dorothy was my mistress, and he had heard me out. My mistake, I realised, was to stress that Ada should hear nothing of the nurse in my room. Thus, I had revealed my intentions towards his sister. His retaliation had been fast.

"He said you had a woman living with you. He found her waiting by your bed."

"Colonel Wakefield sent a nurse to my hut to bandage my hand. That's what your brother saw."

And, as if in supplication, I removed my glove and presented my thumbless right hand to her, the long gash of my disfigurement offered as a gift.

Her hands flew to her mouth in horror, not, surely, at my deformity but at the truth it proved.

By now there were people close by. Dr Evans and his wife, out for a stroll, shouted a *hallo!* and clambered down from the path and across the beach to join us, and Ada explained to them about the shoes and the ladies waiting at Jerningham Point, and Evans offered to go for the women and Mrs Evans said she would go home with Ada, and a boy would run to meet him with shoes, and through it all I stood aside and realised it was over.

When there was no one left on the beach with me, I walked down to the place where the wet sand meets the dry and trudged along in that littoral space, where things are not one thing nor the other, life is not of the sea nor the shore, creatures are washed in from the oceans and away off the land, and a curled piece of seaweed, part submerged and part baked by the sun, like me, could go either way.

I couldn't tell if the tide was going in or out.

I picked up a long stretch of the inky black weed, a pretty thing with a scalloped top and string of little pompoms like lace on a woman's sleeve, and I ran it through my fingers as I walked, bursting the balls open with my one remaining thumb. The slime dripped out of the torn pods and over my hands.

On the way home I stopped at Mr Telford's haberdashery to buy new sheets for my wedding night. The good man folded and tied them carefully with a ribbon, and I had to turn away from his pleasant chatter and shake my head to dispel the imagine of Ada and her unpinned curls, lying on the smooth, cool, cotton.

———

Dorothy Lewis and I were married on a sunny morning in December by the Reverend Butler, the same minister who recently married Ada to Bently. Charles stood as best man and Lucy held flowers for Dorothy. Sam Revans came to witness the marriage, and afterwards we had a picnic on the beach, the gulls flying high above like so many grains of thrown rice. Dorothy was nervous throughout the day, but she smiled at me and, in her happiness, she was the prettiest girl in Pito-one.

I hadn't mentioned the event to Jerningham or the colonel. I didn't expect Ada knew.

In the evening we took the boat across to Thorndon with Dorothy's few possessions and walked the road up to my house. Our home.

When I took her to bed, it was still light. I didn't watch her put her nightdress on and I didn't play with her. It had been so long and my anticipation was so high that she hardly had time to pull back the covers before I discharged my duty. Her eyes were shut and she bit her lip. I watched her face carefully and wasn't rough. I don't think I hurt her.

She was warm and soft beside me when I woke the next morning and I felt such gratitude when I asked her, "May I?" and she replied that yes, I was her husband and she knew what to expect.

Then she dressed me, helping me with my buttons.

I took a day off from my fencing and we spent it indoors, familiarising ourselves with the change in our lives, politely learning how one might fit around the other. She was neat, Dorothy, and went about her business with competence, but I knew that already from the way she had nursed me. She explained to me her previous charge had a skin complaint and she had learned to bandage the poor boy's hands and arms. I wanted to ask her why the family had moved on to Australia and left her behind but the question sounded accusatory, so I said nothing.

Lucy came to live with us. I set up a box-bed for her in the warm scullery off the kitchen and the girl was grateful for a corner of her own.

It was with a contented, perhaps even smug, expression that I went back to work in the Company's new wooden building on the quay at Lambton, but neither Jerningham nor the colonel noticed my new face. They waved me towards a stack of inventory papers and set me to update the Company's accounts. As before, I shared Jerningham's desk, now facing him across mahogany like a partner.

Far from being marginalised by the government's take-over of the colony the committee was as busy as ever, working on the assumption that the sheer scale of the enterprise would protect us.

"My father is sorting this nonsense out with the land purchases in London," Jerningham told me. "Hobson is irrelevant. We've had a letter to say the Queen's ministers are with us on this. Hobson will regret setting himself against us."

Shortland bustled in and out of the office occasionally, but Jerningham soon found a way to be rid of him. "That ship," he'd say to Revans, or me, or whoever was there and would play his game. "The small one behind the Australian brig. What's that?"

"That's Shortland's little *Integrity*."

"Shortland's little *Integrity*? So it is. She's smartly rigged but bit small for the buffeting she'll get in Wellington's winds."

The first time, Shortland's hand went to his hip and I feared Jerningham had pushed him too far, but he turned on his heel and left the office. After that, word spread that to get rid of the man, one just had to go to the window, look out at the ships and say "that ship ..." and he'd leave the room.

The *London* arrived in port with another two hundred and fifty immigrants. They were temporarily lodged in barracks and in tents on the shore, and the beach was strung like bunting with the usual bewildered souls. With them was the surveyor for the promised town of New Plymouth, asking for the pre-purchased fifty thousand flat and fertile acres. The colonel assured him this land existed north, in Taranaki. In addition to the Plymouth immigrants, three more ships had been purchased in London and recruiting was steady for a proposed settlement called Nelson, to be championed by another of Jerningham's uncles: Captain Arthur Wakefield. The fact that neither New Plymouth nor Nelson even existed yet perhaps wasn't made absolutely clear to the settlers and speculators who eagerly invested in the Wakefields' schemes.

We'd set a match to a little corner of kindling and I did wonder if we should stop piling on the wood before the thing blew up like a wildfire.

My wedding was announced in the weekly paper and the colonel pointed it out to Jerningham. They seemed to have forgotten their hand in the matchmaking, and both appeared surprised at the news. They pulled the paper from one to another as if making sure of the content. After a bit of coughing and a shuffle Jerningham gave me a hearty handshake and the brightest of smiles.

"Congratulations, Lugg, you sly old fox! Have we a drop to toast the newlyweds, Uncle, a dram of something in your cupboard?"

"Glad to see you settled, Mr Lugg." The colonel also shook me by the hand and brought out a bottle of good brandy and, although it was well before noon, he called Revans, Mein Smith and Dr Evans in from an adjoining room. We had a cheerful celebration and the men toasted my health and that of Dorothy, and then we drank to the future of the colony and all the settlers. Mein Smith eventually toasted the Queen—rather as an afterthought— and we raised our glasses and cheered loudly, loyal subjects of Her Majesty on the wrong side of the world.

I was back at my desk later when Te Puni came looking for Jerningham. He shuffled in with his habitual flax blanket wrapped around his shoulders, worn over wool trousers and bare feet. He didn't notice me at first, and was confused when I rose and bowed deeply, but as I shook his hand recognition lit up his face.

"The drowned man!" he cried with delight.

"You saved my life, Te Puni. I am in your debt."

"I fish you from the waves and you breathe." He laughed as if it was the funniest thing that I should be drowned one minute and gasping for air the next. As if life was a pre-determined thing and it was everyday work to drag a man from the water and pump his lungs and then wait to see what the gods would do with him.

Jerningham had told me that with the very sick the Māori took them outside and left them. The strong recovered and the weak died. This was their interpretation of God's will and I wondered what the missionaries made of it.

"My life would have ended there, in those waves, if you had not heard our calls and come so quickly to save us."

He looked down at the stump where my thumb had been, clenched in his strong grip.

"Shark?" he asked me. I had the feeling I would have risen in his estimation if I had said yes, that I had beaten off the brute, who swam away with nothing more than my thumb in his jaws. I imagined Te Puni would admire that sort of man.

"Infection," I told him. "The doctor cut it."

He gave me a half smile, patted my shoulder affectionately and went off to look for Jerningham. I heard them outside, talking loudly and sharing stories in pidgin English and Māori, Te Puni's voice deep and expressive, pulling laughter from Jerningham like a cork from a bottle, spilling that richness into the midday air.

"You have a fireplace, don't you, Lugg?" Jerningham came back inside and dropped some papers on my desk. "Burn these, would you mind? Keep them close." He raised his eyebrows at my suspicious look. "Hobson will be coming after us for taxes soon, you know. He's practically bankrupt. Let's not make it too easy for him."

We had a bit of a purge over the next couple of days. I put my foot down and refused to alter or falsify any papers, but saw no reason why some records of profits on imports mightn't be lost, especially those written by my replacement when I was incapacitated over the winter and Hanson's man was in charge. He hadn't my filing skills and it was common knowledge that many boxes ended up in the depths as they moved across the harbour in small unstable craft.

We were called to the window by a shout and a challenge. Shortland stood on the stony road in his puffed-up finery, enlarged by his tall hat. His face was red and agitated. He was pointing his cane at a bullock driver, commanding him to stop, shouting loudly over the man's calls to his beast.

A group was forming, young lads leaping around at the confrontation, calling friends to watch the humiliation.

"I'll whip you, Shortland!" shouted the bullock driver in a loud, guttural voice, looking around and leering at the onlookers. He was a crude man, coarsely dressed, and he shambled along on flapping boots. "Get on with you, you dirty beast!"

Jerningham was out the door in an instant, but he wasn't running to Shortland's aid. Revans, too, was on the street, his usually stern face alight with fun. He grabbed Jerningham by the arm and the pair roared with laughter.

The bullock driver's voice swelled to reach his growing audience. "I'll kick you in the liver if you don't move on, Shortland, you shitty, black-faced mudrake!"

Shortland strode forward and seized the man by his collar, his cane raised to strike. The driver swung around as if startled, as if he hadn't noticed the colonial magistrate standing there. I flinched as the cane hovered above the sloven's ruddy face.

"I'm talking to my bullock! You can't strike me! A man has a right to chastise his bullock!"

"That ship," someone shouted from the audience and the derisive laughter followed the collective reply: "It's Shortland's little *Integrity*!"

It was fine entertainment. Shortland was on his own. Even had his constable been with him, I suspected the man would have slunk quietly away. The disagreeable bullock driver had scored one for the immigrants and Jerningham went back inside to report the fun in a letter to his father, always delighted by the absurdities of colonial life.

For a few weeks life seemed to settle. The colonel was away on expeditions to the Manawatū and Taranaki and, despite the uncertainty of our lands, settlers with spring fever continued to fence and dig and build. More ships arrived, filled with workers wanting labour.

Dorothy was proving better company than I had expected. When I came home in the evening she always pointed out some little task she had done during the day that might please me—a collection of flowers on the sideboard, or a new way of arranging her hair or dress. I'll admit I was a bit apprehensive when she hovered expectantly and I didn't immediately see the change—I'd comment on a new ribbon (but she'd worn it when we married) or some new digging in the garden (which she'd already shown me). She had taken over looking after my clothing and I was well turned out every day, and when she read aloud to me in the evenings her voice was even and clear.

"You should go out, sometimes, Dorothy, and make some friends."

We were sitting at the bay window of our tidy front room, looking out to the street in that sweet evening moment after Lucy had retired to the scullery and Dorothy laid out the teacups. We were forming our domestic habits and I liked them.

I had never seen Dorothy with a girlfriend. Even in Pito-one, she had been always with her charges or alone. She was rather hard to place, and I wondered if she didn't really fit, something I knew could happen with a governess. They were the in-betweens in a family.

I wondered about inviting some friends for tea, but my companions were all single men. Charles would be kind to her but terribly shy, Revans would terrify her and

Jerningham ... I wasn't sure how Jerningham would behave. I imagined I wouldn't like the way he looked at her pretty mole. We needed some new friends.

"Some of the merchants' wives would make suitable companions for you, my dear," I suggested. "Or the solicitor's daughter is about your age, she's attached to young Dr Fitzgerald. She has a book club with Mrs Telford, wouldn't that be fun?"

Dorothy poured the tea without replying but her lips were pursed.

Intellectually Dorothy was the equal of any of them, and certainly better educated than Mrs Telford. I decided to be a bit more bold. "Tell me about your parents and your family life, before you went into service."

She handed my cup to me, slowly. "I had an ordinary upbringing, Arthur. I've told you before."

"In Putney."

"Yes. My father had a shop. Antiques."

That was new. I had heard her father sold bric-a-brac and I had imagined a cart.

"My sister and I were taught at home by my mother."

"She was educated, then, your mother?"

Dorothy regarded me steadily, her chin raised slightly. It was almost a haughty look. "My mother was a Wittinger," she said. I didn't know the name, but from the tone it was clear I should. Perhaps my wife was better born than I was. "She was very accomplished. She was cut off when she married my father. I never met the family."

It was almost accusatory the way she said it, as if I had slighted her by not recognising this superiority in her background.

"But she died when you were young?"

"No, she didn't. I was fifteen. The fever took my father, mother and sister in a week."

I didn't know why I hadn't asked before, during those tedious hours when Dorothy had visited my hut and wrapped my rotten thumb and I had sat dumb. I should have talked to her, asked her about her life. Like many men, I had made the assumption that a woman's life held little interest.

"And what happened to your father's little shop?" I asked her.

"This is all in the past, Arthur. Do you really want to know every detail of my life?"

"Yes, yes I do. I enjoy our conversations. What happened?"

She folded her hands in her lap and stared blankly out the window. She spoke quietly. "It wasn't a little shop. Lewis's of Putney covered two floors and specialised in French furniture and silverware. The Wittingers were clients until my father eloped with their daughter. We supplied all the best families in London."

I didn't know my wife's history at all.

"And when your parents died?"

Dorothy shrugged. "My father had a son from a previous marriage. After the funeral that son sold the shop to pay his debts. I can see from your look you wonder why my father hadn't made provision for me, but he didn't expect to die. None of us expects to die."

"So you went into service."

She nodded curtly and I could see she was upset. She often had a guarded look and it was back now, a blank stare that promised a monosyllabic answer to any future questions. I pictured a younger Dorothy, with a very different future ahead of her from the hovel in the mud from which I had removed her. There was a story there, but I took my cue from her sulky look.

"Shall we go up? I have an early start in the morning."

In bed she turned from me to face away and I lay for a

long time looking into the darkness, needing her to release me, wanting to roll her over and touch her but not finding the courage.

WANGANUI

"I NEED YOU to go with Jerningham to Petre," the colonel said, barely raising his head from the papers on his desk. It was already littered with letters, spread for the ink to dry, though the sun had only just appeared over the eastern hills.

"To Wanganui, sir?"

He waved me out. "The town is named Petre. Leaving Thursday. We'll meet in an hour to discuss it."

It was a week before Christmas. I was about to invite Sam Revans, William Mein Smith and his wife for a supper on Christmas Eve. Dorothy would not be sorry for the delay in her first role as hostess, though I was nervous of telling her I would not be with her at Christmas.

I went looking for Jerningham and found him sauntering along the waterfront to the office, followed by a shaggy brown dog. He picked up a stick and threw it, and the dog chased the high arc across the beach to the water.

"Hello, Lugg," he called, and he pulled me behind a cart until the dog, finding his playmate gone, shook himself and went off to chase seagulls.

"Nice dog," I said.

"He's Dicky's," said Jerningham. "I should never have encouraged him. He'll find his way home."

I told him about Wanganui. He seemed surprised by my news and not particularly pleased.

"I have no idea why Wide-awake's sending a cripple like you with me. What use are you?"

"That's kind of you to say."

"I am taking Wellington Carrington up to start the surveying. And I'm picking up some horses. What can you do, monkey-fist?"

I wasn't an experienced rider, but I was insulted by his tone. "I've lost my thumb, Jerningham, not my wits. Perhaps the colonel wants me to keep an eye on you."

"What a splendid idea, there is so much you could learn."

We passed workers running a new wharf out from the beach, the clink of hammers and crunch of gravel a constant river of noise. "There is a Māori war dance Para promised to teach me," Jerningham said. "I thought of teaching you, though you hardly have the chest for it." He poked my front with his finger and I batted him off, but he ducked away. A moment later he flicked my hat from my head. I caught him with a backhand and we ended up running up the steps to the office slapping like boys.

The colonel looked up when we came laughing through the door and I sobered immediately. Jerningham removed his hat and lobbed it across the room where it teetered for a second on the coat rack before tumbling to the ground.

"Damn," he said, retrieving it for a second try.

"Put your hat on, Jerningham, and go and meet Carrington at Barrett's. I've called for labourers—select them between you and take half a dozen. See what else Carrington needs for his survey and let Lugg know." The colonel had a tight voice he used solely for Jerningham: long-suffering, as if he held his contempt in check only because the boy was a member of his family. "Go on. I need a word with Lugg."

Jerningham raised his eyebrows at me as he left.

"I want a report on his activities," said the colonel, without preamble. "I have heard some accounts up the coast that make me uneasy, Lugg. Just tell me what you find there."

"I am to act in what capacity, sir?" I asked, puzzled by the lack of trust between the two. "An informer?"

His chin lifted and he gave me an affronted look. "You are a procurement officer, Lugg. You will report back on requirements for the town and the likely outlay in costs. You know how things escalated here. You will assist Carrington as required for his survey, but you will also stay close and watch my nephew's behaviour and let me know how the situation stands."

I knew Carrington by sight, one of Mein Smith's coterie of serious theodolite-carriers who rarely came to town and never to socialise. I had just escorted his brother and family from the newly arrived *London* to the dark back room of the Thistle Inn where they were to stay until a house became available. The brother was chief surveyor for the Plymouth Company. I sensed a connection with the Wanganui trip.

"May I ask, Colonel, is the Plymouth settlement planned for Wanganui? I hadn't realised the choice had been made." I didn't imagine that would please Jerningham, who seemed to consider the place his personal playground.

"Is this information that concerns you? You have been asked to accompany a surveying party. That's all." He tapped his pencil against his table, a sign I was dismissed. I bowed my head to him and turned to go.

"And the town, Mr Lugg, is called Petre."

I had no desire to go with the party. I was enjoying my new marriage bed too much to want an adventure up-country and felt resentful that my role was as much babysitter to Jerningham as assistant to the survey. It seemed that being a Company servant meant I could be deployed anywhere at any time with little notice. I packed a change of clothes, my shaving gear and bought a new travelling hat.

On the eve of Christmas I said goodbye to Dorothy and boarded the schooner, the *Jane*, for Wanganui.

—

The *Jane* was the first ship I had been aboard since I came off the *Aurora* nearly a year ago, and my sea legs were weak. My body flopped uneasily on the rocking deck like a spineless thing.

Once on the water and aweigh, though, I felt a change come over me and some of the old spirit that had prompted this whole adventure came pumping back into my blood. Jerningham was delighted with everything—the sun and the wind and the freedom of the water—as the town disappeared behind us. He didn't give it a backward glance. He slapped me on the back when we raced through the heads, the ship's swift momentum scattering a fountain of diving seabirds, with a pod of dolphins leaping joyously under the bow wave in flashes of slippery pewter.

"Get us close enough to throw a biscuit!" Jerningham shouted to the stern-faced captain as we cleared Barrett's Reef, hanging wide out over the water, his arm outstretched as if he were dashing alongside the boat with the wind held taunt in his own invisible sail. I recognised the slap of the waves and zing of the rigging; it was every bit as musical as it had been on my first voyage, when I had fancied myself in love and so happy with Ada Malloy.

The captain and his rude-looking crew took us expertly through the strait on a dependable southerly, racing lightly over the water, with wild hills on the north and rows of gleaming, snow-capped mountains to the south. The *Jane* ran up the coast with full sails and sun sparkled off the sea.

We came up to Kāpiti late in the afternoon and, before we had dropped anchor in the channel, the whale-boats had put out from the island, looking for trade or news.

Burly, unkempt men in dirty smocks and unwashed hair, their headsman a toothless fierce-looking old tar with bulging, yellow eyes, the whalers were delighted to see Jerningham on board.

"I knew yer'd be back, Mr Wakefield—we've kept ye a place in the boat." The headsman's voice was thick Yorkshire and phlegm. He stood on ham legs in the rocking dinghy, holding up an arm as if to drag Jerningham aboard. "Skinny Nick's gone, took a harpoon through the eye last week, so we'll be missing a boat-steer. Perhaps you'll join us!"

"You're a good man, George, and it's a tempting offer! You know I spent the best days of my life with you."

They swapped ribbing and gossip, their language coarse and heavy. Jerningham appeared to have an encyclopedic memory for ships' names and their captains, and the monikers of all the crews.

"Slapping Jack and Fatman went south with the Sydney speculators and good luck to them." The whaler shook his mangy head in disgust. "Those crafty Ngāi Tahu sold the entire Middle Island to the Australians and then turned around and signed Hobson's treaty, promising it to him. And Billy O went with Te Ariki, Pale Parata and his tribe to Kākāpō Bay. You remember Te Ariki? Face like a mutton-bird."

"And lazy! He would have been sacked but for the softness of his skin!" countered Jerningham to the laughter of the men. "Geordie Bolts will be a harder master to him than you ever were!"

The men handed across a gift of fragile gull's eggs and Jerningham passed back a bottle. "You must come to Wellington to celebrate the naming of the town," he said.

"Best grog in the country." The men cheered and waved as they pulled away, back to their station, their drink and their dissolute lives.

"They're an ugly bunch of scoundrels," I said, as we climbed down into our own sturdy row-boat, but Jerningham frowned at me.

"Don't judge them," he said. "They do what they do with skill and courage. It's not for you to approve or disapprove."

Still, I was relieved when our boat proceeded in the other direction, away from Kāpiti's small islands, towards the mainland. Carrington remained with the captain on board, two dour men looking in opposite directions.

"I'm going to introduce you to a missionary, Lugg. Octavius Hadfield."

This sounded like trouble, but it seemed in this, also, I was mistaken.

"There are not many missionaries I would pull from a burning wreck," Jerningham said, and I knew there was truth in that, "but Mr Hadfield is one of them."

We headed towards the shore. I hadn't realised the small ribbon of white seen from the ship was a tall barrier of breaking surf.

"There was a battle here last year," said Jerningham as the men pulled us closer to the breakers and the spray flew in long white plumes towards us, lacy and delicate. "We arrived here on the *Tory* and the sand was still slimy with blood. Bodies everywhere."

Perhaps it missed Jerningham's attention entirely that I was clasping the gunwales with white knuckles as we neared the crashing waves, bigger by far than the small surf that had tipped me to near drowning at Pito-one just four months before. Or perhaps he told his story to distract me and knew full well why the colour had fallen from my face.

"That villain Te Rauparaha had invited all the local

– 152 –

warring tribes to the funeral of his sister. Of course they couldn't refuse. If you ever meet him, Lugg, you must put on your most arrogant face, as if you can't be bothered with him. Never directly challenge him. If you are obsequious, you're lost."

We were close on the edge of the surf. Water slapped the boat without rhythm, a drunk's confused clapping, and the plunging oars ripped the waves like paper. I tried to focus on Jerningham's voice. "He's a force, to be sure, but we are Englishmen. Even Te Rauparaha must know God has granted us superiority."

The churning of the surf was upon us now, the boat rocking like a see-saw as the crew waited their chance to ride the waves into the beach.

"They had served up a slave at the funeral, Lugg. Cooked him in their earth oven. Te Rauparaha's treat for his guests, the old cannibal. Then he roused up a couple of local tribes, got them so riled they fought each other viciously on the way home. He brilliantly reduced the power of both his rivals and stirred up hostilities that will last for generations."

On a shout, we ploughed forward and shot above the sea, driving towards the beach on the crest of a high roller. I closed my eyes in terror and gripped tightly. Jerningham whooped and yelled his excitement. The wave's immense power drove us on, our boat held straight by the strength of the helmsman, and then slowly, frightfully, we dropped down the face of the wall. The wave broke and the bright foaming mass gathered behind us, swallowing us whole and spitting us out into the shallows, where the men all leapt ashore and cheered.

I staggered away to the humiliating laughter of the sailors, up the wide beach towards the sand dunes, an admission that I was no adventurous hero. The men could pull the boat up out of the sea.

I preferred my ships to come in to a wharf and lower a gangplank. I wanted to sleep in a bed at night. I wanted civilised company, not sailors and whalers and reckless young daredevils too much in love with danger.

I looked north and south along the endless expanse of grey sand and spiky grass-covered dunes. There was nothing. It appeared our little collection of mud huts around the harbour in Wellington was the only civilisation this country had to offer.

And then ...

No. I was mistaken.

But it came again. On the wind. Voices of angels blowing out of the wild.

I walked towards the hills and there were people singing. It was glorious, melodic. I didn't understand the words but it was a tune I knew as well as my own heartbeat. "Abide with Me". Sung with Māori words, more beautifully than I had ever heard it sung before, floating on the air in this lonely place. *Abide with me.*

—

Octavius Hadfield's congregation was in the open air, a wide, invisible chapel filled with light, between the forest and the sea. There were thirty or so native faces before the slim, dapper missionary, all turned upwards and open to the sky, and they sang with such intuitive harmony my heart pounded in my chest. I felt the glory of God, right there.

His love poured out of the ground, through the channel of the minister, and was held in a glimmering pocket of lustre around his people, in a church built of faith and air.

There were tears in my eyes as the service ended. The natives, trained to wait until dismissed like a classroom of diligent children, swarmed us with over-excited greetings, all hugs and handshakes.

"My dear friend," Mr Hadfield greeted Jerningham, and the two men warmly embraced. This was the same missionary who had accompanied Reverend Williams as they chased Jerningham around the country, getting Hobson's treaty signed with devious means and unscrupulous bribes.

Yet the friendship these men exhibited towards each other was undeniable, Jerningham's enthusiasm clearly authentic. It was another of his many inconsistencies that I struggled to reconcile.

We followed the entourage across the open space, and Jerningham reached into his pockets and dispensed trinkets to the congregation: painted wooden buttons, Jew's harps and beads, and a white handkerchief to a rather beautiful young woman who held back behind her brothers, smiling shyly. They called his attention constantly—"Tīraweke! Look! Tīraweke, me, me!"

I hoped for conversation with the missionary, but there was no privacy to be had. Hadfield took us to his house, a clean and spacious whare, and the Te Āti Awa people followed us in, crowding through the doors and windows, sitting on the floor and the few scattered chairs. Talk was loud and open and constantly interrupted.

I was pressed between two of our hosts, who fingered the stuff of my jacket and the scar of my amputation, one actually sniffing my sleeve. They explored my face with keen dark eyes as if assessing my mettle through absorption. I felt overwhelmingly observed.

I asked one of the fellows how they got along with their quarrelsome neighbour, the fearsome Te Rauparaha, and the Māori around me pretended to quake at the mention of his name, making wild faces and undulating calls.

"Don't let him catch you!" one of them told me. "He take fine slave, make beautiful tattoo, and look, your white skin, so soft! So painful for you, ta moko." He stroked his own tattooed cheeks proudly, as if for him the pain of skin-chiselling was nothing. "And then cut your head!" This was accompanied with a gruesome drama. "Your tattooed head good trade!"

"Is this true?" I asked Hadfield, horrified. "Te Rauparaha trades in tattooed heads?"

Hadfield, suddenly aware of the turn of our conversation, rebuked the man. "Enough, Hine! That is no conversation for a guest."

But he nodded to me, honesty on his earnest face. "I'm afraid it was true, Mr Lugg, though the trade was banned in '31 and the practice has died now. There was a demand for heads from Sydney traders that Te Rauparaha was only too happy to fill for a clutch of muskets."

"He must be a difficult man to live alongside."

"He can be unpredictable,' Hadfield said, "but, for now, Te Rauparaha and I seem to get along. I don't imagine I'll ever make a Christian of him, but he approves of my bringing faith to his people and is helping to build our church. He wants peace. There has been war among the tribes forever, you know, but the escalation the muskets brought was devastating. Was it avoidable?"

"The muskets?"

"The muskets, the escalation, the whole horror of it. We can't undo it and we haven't the right to tell Te Rauparaha or anyone else to change the way he lives. We can only encourage peace and lead by example."

An evening meal was brought for us and we sat at a long table without linen but with cutlery and plates for guests. Even then the constant press of bodies continued as the natives milled in and out of the whare. I had two children at my feet pressing their hands on my boots and occasionally another would lean against me affectionately. He began sorting through the potatoes on my plate with his fingers, selecting the best morsel for me to put on my fork. Jerningham and Hadfield didn't appear to think it strange, and both carried on conversations in Māori to their right and left while continuing to talk between themselves.

"Your uncle the colonel visited us recently, bringing his Manawatū settlers. He has not softened his stance towards the governor."

"No indeed," said Jerningham, "nor have any of us in Wellington. Shortland has been recalled now, and to a man we cheered to see him go. There is no sign of a Hobson visit. But tell me how the settlers fare?"

Hadfield gently removed a child who was attempting to climb on his lap to poke at the wilted greens on his plate. "Well enough. They are sturdy and industrious and should thrive here. They've cleared the bush where the river comes out of the hills and employed labourers from the marae. They plant summer crops this week."

I studied Jerningham's relaxed face. His expression was open and friendly, his habitual arrogance wiped away entirely, and he looked handsome and fine, a man others would follow. For an hour he and Hadfield talked of crops and timber, of the doings of the local tribes and the peace that the missionary intended for the region. They shared a mission that had nothing to do with God or profit, but was simply the joy of achievement, of making a difference, of making things better. An elderly woman stood beside Jerningham, her grey hair wrapped in flax and feathers, her lips tattooed blue, and while he talked she laid her hand lightly on his shoulder. He reached across and held it there. It was a tender gesture.

"You seem to know Mr Hadfield very well," I said to Jerningham. We'd said our evening prayers and left him for the night. We walked the perimeter of the mission, pausing to look at the sky, feel the weather.

"Surprised you, did I?"

"It's a bit of a leap from your normal stance on missionaries."

I expected banter, but the quiet of the evening service had stayed with him.

"Mr Hadfield is a deeply compassionate man," he said. "Not your usual missionary. He doesn't impose himself on the natives or rearrange their system of aristocracy."

It was to Jerningham's credit that, so fast, he had re-examined and abandoned his prejudice, and I wondered what the trigger had been.

"Oh, and he did save my life a few months ago," he said. "Now I make a point of stopping by for a day or two whenever I can and take an interest in his mission."

"He saved your life?"

"That's a story for another time, and not one I want relayed to my uncle. It concerns a party of drunken whalers, an ill-advised spot for defecation and a Māori warrior with a tomahawk. My scalp would have been cleaved and I would have died with my trousers at my ankles had not Mr Hadfield intervened with his clever diplomacy."

"Te Rauparaha?" It seemed this chief was never far from my mind.

"Worse. His nephew, Te Rangihaeata. A man with a ferocious appetite for war and no mercy. I sincerely hope you never meet him."

Amen, I thought.

We slept all together, our crew and the natives lying on mats in the sleeping whare, though Mr Hadfield absented himself to a private space.

I had laid my blanket out with the men, but when I returned from my ablutions I found it knotted with twine, two of our crew sniggering as I tried to untangle it with my crippled hand. There was a nasty smell to it, as if they'd wiped their arses on it. I suppose I was an easy victim for a sailor with a cruel streak. Jerningham used his knife on the knots and relaid my bed for me, before scooping the blankets off the two men and throwing them out the window.

"Outside, you dogs!" He was laughing as he said it, but the men accepted the punishment without a word and went out to sleep under the stars.

It was a warm night and I tried to be at ease, but despite the friendly welcome from Hadfield and the fact that Jerningham seemed very much at home with these people, I was reluctant to relax, the very foreignness of the situation keeping me on edge. I felt vulnerable and unprotected on this lawless strip between coast and hills, where tribal war was a constant and Hadfield's peace a tenuous thing. We were in a house made of straw and there were warring forces out there that could come this night, tomorrow night, or any other night and tear it to the ground.

Fierce men with tomahawks. Cannibals.

Jerningham had his pistol rolled with him under his blanket and each crew member was inconspicuously armed. Until then, I had never felt the need for a weapon, nor could I hold one with my thumbless hand. But for the first time I was conscious of how my injury unmanned me and as I lay awake on the uncomfortable mat, I determined to learn to shoot left-handed.

———

Sleep wouldn't come. I disliked the press of bodies. The men had a distinctive odour of wet earth and sweat and their snores ran around the hut like snuffling, rooting animals. Waking dreams came in snatches through the long night, vivid with digging pigs, shrunken heads, and gleaming eyes in tattooed faces.

I rose at dawn and climbed over the tumble of bodies into the relief of the cool air and followed a path away from the mission towards a strip of raised ground where gardens had been cut from the surrounding bush.

The morning threw a wholly new complexion onto my fears of the night. Te Rauparaha, Rangihaeata and their warriors melted in the daylight. The shadows of a fresh sun threw crisp patterns on the path, and the bush, with leaves so varied in size and shape and texture, sparkled with every possible hue of green.

Mr Hadfield had his sleeves rolled up and was already busy in the garden, a group of near-naked Māori children holding the sides of a woven screen he was attempting to tie onto a frame. I got the sense of too many helpful little hands, pulling the screen this way and that, but Hadfield seemed unperturbed.

"Good morning, Mr Lugg. If you wouldn't mind taking the edge from Kahurangi, we're trying to fix it to the top of the frame ... he can't quite reach, yes, thank you. Ātaahua will pass you the rope, and Mr Lugg can tie ... oh, I do apologise, you'll have difficulty with knots, wait a minute while I tie this off here ... very good, and Kahurangi if you would take over from me here while I tie the other side, more rope, please, Irihapeti, thank you, my dear ..."

And with much cheerful chatter and help from the children, the screen was fixed.

We left the young workers digging a pea trench below the frame, enthusiastic and clumsy with the wooden trowels, and walked to the edge of the raised bank to look down onto the neat fences and whare of Hadfield's mission. Other than an elderly woman tending a fire, there was no one else up. It was a scene of quiet domesticity, like one of Charles's paintings: *Peaceful Native Village*. An illustration to sell tickets.

"How did you sleep in the wharemoe, Mr Lugg?" Hadfield asked me.

"Very well, thank you," I lied.

He gave me a sympathetic glance. Perhaps my face betrayed how unsuited I was to adventure.

"Jerningham tells me you are his nanny on this trip, commissioned by his uncle to keep him in check. Is that a reasonable charge?"

It was a direct question and I stumbled a bit in my reply. "Nanny? Well, not really, that's not quite ... I, ah, Colonel Wakefield does have some concerns, yes. You, perhaps, see a different side to Jerningham. There are aspects to his behaviour ..."

"I think I understand Jerningham Wakefield very well. We were adversaries before we became friends."

"Yes, of course."

Mr Hadfield was a few years younger than me, and a few years older than Jerningham. I liked his quiet directness.

"I think I am a good judge of character and I like you, Mr Lugg. I am glad our friend has your companionship. I, too, have heard rumours from Wanganui that have caused me concern and I am relieved Colonel Wakefield has seen fit to appoint a guardian, if, indeed, that is one of your roles. You are, I imagine, a good choice. When he is here, among these people, it is clear Jerningham is a good man with a generous heart. But he is under pressure to be his father's son. There is an expectation of recklessness and wild living that goes with that."

I couldn't help but comment, "Yours is an unlikely friendship."

It seemed an obvious thing to say, but Hadfield looked surprised. "I don't see it that way. Intellectually, we have much in common."

There were ships in the channel now, in the deep blue

water between Kāpiti and the shore. A tall-masted vessel that had been invisible against the dark of Te Rauparaha's island was moving slowly south on a cross-wind. Possibly it had moored in the roadstead. Two smaller whalers and fishing vessels were in the channel, close to shore.

Looking northward, the coastline was a lace-edged ribbon that disappeared into an appealing summer haze, promising a day of calm, warm weather. Yesterday's surf had reduced to low waves. Far away on the land's horizon rose the perfect cone and full skirt of Mount Taranaki.

We left Waikanae and sailed on up the coast, but the wind turned north and we had to tack far out to sea to get any distance ahead at all. The mountain remained tantalisingly distant for another two days until the wind turned again and blew us on a strengthening westerly back towards shore, and finally the *Jane* rolled on a heavy swell over the bar and into the mouth of the Wanganui River.

There was a dirty sheen on the water and the mean riverside huts looked bleak and unwelcoming, but the surly crew brightened as we dropped anchor. I couldn't imagine what they saw in the place. Jerningham, too, peered eagerly upriver, tapping his feet on the deck, impatient to get ashore to whatever awaited him there.

━━

My first day in Wanganui I spent in a large, wooden whare, where Jerningham left me in charge of a disputes tribunal.

"I have no qualifications for this," I said, but Jerningham pressed me, saying it made no difference. There was a problem that needed sorting before it escalated into tribal warfare, and the nearest magistrate was at least two months away. He lent me a jacket with a braided collar and put me behind a table, with chair for me and one for a translator. This immediately raised us above our petitioners, two aggrieved families who sat on mats on the floor.

"You are not claiming to be anything other than a mediator," he said. "They have agreed to let a sensible Englishman arbitrate their grievance and you are the nearest thing we have."

Although I had lived around Māori for nearly a year, I knew nothing of their ceremonies and little of how they behaved among themselves. The case was against an old woman living on disputed land. It could have been stated fairly quickly but lasted nearly the whole day. Both sides brought the entire family along, and each elder stood and spoke for long periods, beginning with naming all their ancestors going back for generations.

It was marvellous theatre for the first couple of hours, and I gave up trying to follow the gentle voice of my translator the more to enjoy the spectacle and the gestures that accompanied the oration. Eventually, my translator explained that the old woman's son had sold some of the land to an Australian whaler in exchange for a small vessel. The land was not theirs to sell, said the other party—a claim that was familiar to my Wellington ears. It was a gift from a chief some four generations back, but of course there was no written evidence of this and the only proof was contained in the seemingly extraordinary feats of memory, stories passed down from father to son.

Both families seemed to agree on the facts, but they got more excited as the orations of the descendants continued all day, eventually raging like a child banging up and down the scales on a piano. After much vitriol and fist-shaking and back-turning and face-pulling, the contesting party decided they didn't want the vessel anyway, or the land, but they wanted their rights acknowledged.

Jerningham returned late in the afternoon and called a halt, and we retired to a small room where, finally, I was given a plate of food, the inevitable pork and potatoes.

"Where would we be without the foresight of Captain Cook, eh?" asked Jerningham, who was bright-eyed and in the best of spirits. "He threw a few little piggies out into the bush and tossed a couple of potatoes onto the fertile soil of this place and voilà! Seventy years later Arthur Lugg gets his dinner."

I looked around for cutlery, but there was none.

"Send someone, Jerningham," I said. "I won't eat with my fingers."

My translator was tucking in and dragging his meat around the plate, but I was tired by then and the ignominy of eating like a native felt like the last straw. Jerningham clapped his hands and sent a boy on the errand. "And a starched white napkin and a silver platter!" he shouted after, but the boy was gone. He poured wine while we waited, and we drank while my food grew cold. Jerningham ate a potato from my plate.

"Though I shouldn't be hungry," he said. "Para made me a fine lunch of pigeon and pūhā. We ate it from the pan."

The boy didn't come back. I ate with my fingers.

The pork was sweet and salty and delicious. Restored by the food and wine, I accepted Jerningham's handkerchief to wipe my greasy fingers and felt slightly ashamed for my outburst.

"There," I told him, handing back his handkerchief, which he dropped on the floor. "To hell with the linen."

I gave him as comprehensive a summary of the dispute as I could, the gist of it being a misunderstanding never acknowledged that rankled and festered.

"All they want is a resolution," said Jerningham, serious and decisive now. "We are encouraging mediation rather than utu—their revenge can go back and forward forever until a dull little crime is sharpened by so much storytelling that it's as keen as a blade. Let me handle this now, your job was to look important and listen—which you have done admirably, my dear Lugg."

Jerningham settled the dispute with payment of pigs in lieu of the vessel on one side and an agreement on the other that the old woman could remain on the land for her lifetime. He claimed we had averted a conflict that would have been fought to extermination across families. I didn't know the truth of that, but it was well done, and I was pleased to have played a part in the proceedings, however small.

I was back on the ship that evening, and, as he had done the previous night, Jerningham slipped away. Over the following days, as Carrington and his men were out in the field and had no requirements of me, I assisted Jerningham. There were tribunals and meetings and disputes to resolve, nothing that required a magistrate necessarily, just a witness to the stories being told. Jerningham would set me up and I would turn to him to find him gone, leaving me in charge.

I mediated a case where a Māori woman had left her husband for another man. The husband agreed to let her go but wanted payment, to which her new husband agreed. And there was an ex-whaler who thought he had purchased a woman for a year but found that she went back to her family after a few months.

"You cannot buy a woman," I told the dirty little man. "Have some dignity. Marry her legally or let her go. We follow English law now."

Jerningham came back late that afternoon, sauntering into the meeting house exuberant from all-day adventuring.

"Where do you keep going off to, Jerningham?" I was hungry and tired and this wasn't the work I had been sent to do. "You can't leave me here as some kind of proxy judge. What if they challenge my authority?"

"Yes, I know," he said. "The whole situation is absurd. Hobson has claimed sovereignty for the Crown but has neglected to send any kind of authority to Wanganui. Or anywhere else. We have English law, but no one to enforce it. I do what I can, Lugg, whenever I am in town. They trust me, and you, obviously, as my agent. We are setting an example of how it could be, and when we eventually do get a magistrate he can sort it all out. We can't *convict* anyone. Though God knows a set of stocks would bring swift justice."

"You are not the sheriff and I am not your agent."

"Fair enough, and well said. We'll call it a day, shall we? You can go out with Carrington on the survey tomorrow if you are bored here."

I was bored, obviously, after three days of enforced listening to translated oratory, the constant repetition of the tribal history over and over. I wondered if the advent of writing would change the need of these people to tell their histories constantly, and how much their uncanny ability to recall long past events in such detail would remain after events were recorded on paper. If a written version became the only truth, dispute resolution would be faster and easier, though it would be a stretch to say the English system of justice was fairer. There was a catharsis in these long hearings from which I thought we might learn.

They were a highly excitable race, the Māori, and easily angered, with revenge usually fast and brutal. They needed laws if they were to live among Englishmen, or, more correctly I supposed, if Englishmen were to live among them. But it was hardly my responsibility to mediate all the petty squabbles of the town. Or Jerningham's. Or even his uncle's, who had no recognised authority and was little more than a land agent, gambling on the sale of disputed land.

I opted to check the surveying progress across the river. I noticed Jerningham hadn't included himself in the survey party.

"What have you been up to, Jerningham?"

His eyes shifted away, and back. "I went looking for the horses today. The *Broughton* anchored off the coast and dropped some men but took the horses to a richer sale in the Waikato." He shrugged off the loss and I wondered if it had been his money at stake and without the colonel's knowledge.

"And then?"

"Is this the Inquisition? I have been with one of the local chiefs, Kuru is his name. His men are building huts for our settlers when they come."

"We haven't even surveyed the town, yet."

"That will come later. Carrington is marking out some hundred country plots for the Wellington overflow, though I've a hunch he's putting his own name on the best of them. Our people can rent huts on Māori land until the town is established. Kuru sees the benefit of that."

"Kuru owns the Māori land here? I thought you had purchased the district. Surely the Māori, having taken our payment, are now renting on Company land?"

Jerningham clicked his tongue at me. "It's not quite that simple, Lugg. Wanganui is not Somerset. There is still a bit of work for my uncle to do on the detail."

The detail seemed always to follow a few steps behind Jerningham. I had no feel for the district yet, having been enclosed indoors with the disputes, and I had a desire to get out and explore.

"I'd like to go up and see the Māori settlement." There were two pā, one on either side of the river, but I had not set foot in either. "Is that where you stay, where you spend your nights?"

He jumped up without answering. "Let's get you in some shooting practice this evening. You're more useful to me armed than not. Pistol or musket? I've a fowling piece given to Kuru, which I have been cleaning here, or we can use my musket. Let's see if a cack-handed cripple can hit a large tree at five yards."

Diverted, I followed him away from the whare and we walked above the high watermark of the river towards the sea, past some small fields of wheat and barley to a scrappy piece of flat land where a group of spiky-topped cabbage palms stood sentinel on a bank of grey clay.

Jerningham handed me the pistol and I took it in my left hand. I had only held a gun once before and never fired. It was heavier than expected and my fingers were not dexterous.

I thought Jerningham would be frustrated, but he was surprisingly patient with me.

"Try the right hand, grip with your little stump thing. Support with your left."

My damaged right hand did feel more useful than the left. Jerningham pulled a lump of the firm clay from the bank.

"Show me how hard you can squeeze it," he said, and we played with squeezing balls of clay for a while, left and right while he looked carefully at the indentations and declared my right had the stronger grip.

He handed back the gun and I squeezed and shot. After a while, I hit the tree. Jerningham had lined my misshapen balls of clay on the bank to dry. "Art from disfigurement," he joked.

We ate an evening meal on board the ship. Shortly after I went below to get tobacco, and when I returned, Jerningham had gone.

"Where does he go?" I asked one of our sailors.

I communicated as little as possible with the ill-mannered crew, and this coarse man I particularly avoided, but he often rowed Jerningham upriver and had the eyes of someone who didn't miss much. His sneer deepened my unease.

"Whare Wikitoria," he said with a Māori accent but none of their song in his voice, and I held my face steady as his nasty eyes judged my reaction.

It was the first I had heard of the place. Whare Wikitoria: Victoria's house. From the look on the man's face, it seemed unlikely to be a house of which our Queen would approve.

WHARE WIKITORIA
AND A STORM

CARRINGTON HAD taken a shack near the pā at
Putiki, on the south bank of the Wanganui River, slightly
downstream from where we moored. I joined him for
breakfast, hoping for eggs and bread with butter, but there
was none. He served a small bowl of sugared porridge with
water. Carrington had a thin blond beard and receding
hair line that made his face seem exceptionally long, and
heavily lidded eyes. It was hard to gauge his mood and I
had discovered he was not a man for chat. He poured good
coffee, not the thin stuff we got in Wellington.

"My brother brought it for me," he said. "He guessed I'd
be missing it."

He and his team had spent two laborious days cutting
lines through the high, tough fern on this bank, and his
men had now crossed, pushing surveying pegs into the
ground across the raised flat, where a river bend formed
two sides of the proposed town's rectangle. The site of the
Wanganui township, clearly named Petre on the purchase
deeds, included a Māori pā on the river's edge.

Carrington had added several Māori to his team of
workers, missionary-educated young men with good English
and a willingness to learn. They waited impatiently as we
finished our breakfast, studying the surveying instruments
and taking reckonings with Carrington's compass.

He sent one of the men to buy tobacco from the store, which I was surprised to hear was owned by Jerningham.

"He has a trading ship, the *Sandfly*," said Carrington, "that runs up and down the coast. It's currently loading flax in Porirua. He also picks up deals from Wellington and Sydney. The *Jewess* came in to Purua this morning with some trade. Mr Wakefield is offloading several crates of wine as we speak."

"Why have I heard nothing about this before?" I couldn't imagine Jerningham as a shopkeeper.

"Well, I think our friend is rather good at compartmentalising his activities. You are here in the role of his uncle's spy, he tells me."

"Oh, that's nonsense!" It was a thoroughly offensive suggestion. Jerningham had called me his "nanny" to Hadfield, but "spy" was an altogether more unpleasant word. "What's the secret, anyway? A shop! Is he trading in guns, in slaves?"

"No, it's all fairly innocuous, as far as I know. Pencils, planks, ropes. I bought some spades as gifts for my native workers. He sells tea, sugar, flour. And grog, of course— he is trying to civilise the place. I imagine the income is undeclared and illegal." It appeared Carrington didn't think particularly highly of Jerningham. "Or perhaps," he continued, "he is planning to put down roots. I spoke to his father in London before we sailed and he expected him home by return ship. But he has no intention of returning to England, has he?"

"I've not heard so, no."

"Well, I wonder what our good colonel will make of that?" Carrington said. "Jerningham is a difficult boy to keep on a leash. Unstable. Bright enough, to be sure, but likely to go off like a firework in any direction."

We packed up the plans and walked down to the river,

where we hailed a waka to take us across, as one would hail a hansom cab in London.

"Do you know a place called Whare Wikitoria?" I asked as the surveyor and I crossed the brown, sluggish water.

"It's Jerningham's house," he replied, and pointed out a large raupō hut among a collection of whare upstream. There were a couple of row boats unloading crates on the shore in front. "It has quite a reputation. I have not been invited to step inside. For which I am very grateful."

Jerningham had both a shop and a house and hadn't thought to mention either to me. I don't know why this hurt. It wasn't as if I was particularly interested in his personal affairs, but this felt like a deliberate omission, a lack of trust. It was behaviour that had occasionally surfaced in Wellington; he would treat me like his dearest friend one day, argue with me like a precocious younger brother another, but he'd never fully take me into his confidence. I was beginning to learn he had many dearest friends and didn't mix them. He seemed to believe I really was spying for the colonel.

We pulled up at a wharf, a flimsy affair of planks stacked on the bank, and the natives immediately gathered around. One old man's bare feet were black with mud, and the trousers of his English workday suit were rolled to the knee. Instead of a hat he wore feathers in his topknot. "Mr Carrington, why do you come here? You take your men and go away."

Our workers clambered ashore and we passed out the equipment to them before accepting a hand across the planks. One of the young men stopped to argue with the man in the suit, but Carrington walked past the group without stopping.

We followed the men through the fern to a trampled patch of land, and they made a pile of their chains and axes and spades. "They've pulled them again, Mr Carrington," said a worker, and I could see along the surveyed line where pegs had been dug out and thrown aside.

"Then we'll put them back," said Carrington, and the men took up their hammers and spades and began again.

As the survey progressed the natives gathered around to watch and quarrel. The man in the suit stood in front Carrington on the path, waving his arms as he spoke. "Mr Wakefield did not pay for this land. Why do you make your survey? Where is my payment?"

Carrington looked at the protestor and blinked, his expression saying, *who on earth is he talking to?* He stepped around him and continued on his way.

As I stood to one side observing the activity, a Māori man came and stood next to me. He wore English clothing—a good shirt but without tie or jacket, decent duck trousers and boots. We watched for a while in silence as the protesters pulled out the pegs Carrington's men had laid in. They stamped their feet at the surveyors and rolled their eyes threateningly.

"My name is Para," my companion said eventually. "Mr Wakefield's friend. Do you need help?" He held out his hand for me to shake.

"Mr Wakefield has mentioned you. I am Arthur Lugg. Pleased to make your acquaintance." It felt reassuring to have a man with a brown face standing with me. "Can you tell me, Para, what they are arguing about?"

He *hmmm'd* and pursed his lips, frowning slightly, as if it was a most difficult question with no simple answer. Instead of a direct reply, he translated snatches of conversation for me. His English was basic but the gist was clear.

The Māori disputed that the land being surveyed had ever been paid for, or that the sellers had the right to sell. They said they didn't understand what they had signed, the payment was not sufficient, or they didn't get their share, or their share had been stolen from them, or that this or that wasn't included in the purchase.

Meanwhile, another group arrived from a cluster of huts by the river. They were poorly dressed English working men, who strode up and seemed to think I was in charge. They complained to me that they had purchased subdivided plots from absentee landlords and had walked from Wellington with their families expecting land ready for them. They were impatient to work it and had waited too long already for possession. How were they to feed their children? The season was passing; there was no seed planted. They wrote their names on wooden stakes and beat them back into the disputed ground. The Māori took them out. Carrington measured and drew up his plan and ignored them all.

I stood with Para and listened to the arguments from both sides as the surveyors worked their trade, heavy with chains and axes and spades. At the end of the afternoon, Para shook my hand and went away with his Māori companions and I returned across the river, exhausted.

I ate a meat stew with Carrington at his lodging but he was in a surly mood and shared no conversation. I returned to the ship dispirited with the whole muddled business. And perhaps it was not just Wanganui. The Company claimed to have bought almost half of the island now. It was entirely possible all their other claims were as tenuous and disputed as Wanganui.

Jerningham came on board late, as I was preparing to turn in. He didn't look tired. His breeches and rough smock hung on his sparse frame with more elegance than I had ever mustered for a dining room and his hair fell forward over his high forehead as if the barber had laid it so. He shone with his customary energy and the sense that there was great excitement going on somewhere around a corner, somewhere I hadn't been. He clapped his hands when he saw me, with eyes so bright I wondered if he was drunk.

"Forget the surveying tomorrow, Lugg!" he cried. "Carrington and his men can do all that. We're going paddling up the river in a waka for a few days, sightseeing. You've been far too serious and it's about time we had some fun. I'm going to show you the country. Be ready on the shore by nine o'clock sharp."

And just like that I was back under Jerningham's spell. I stepped away from the surveying and my report for the colonel and Carrington's tribulations with the Māori and the settlers. They weren't my responsibilities.

—

I slept well, woke early and put on my travel hat. It was a deliciously fresh summer morning when we set off in a long waka upriver and into the interior, the onshore breeze catching the sail and making it easy going for our half-dozen paddlers. I was pleased to find Para was one of our guides, and we were joined by a pair of Australian speculators off the *Jewess*, well-dressed, middle-aged men with money to spend. Off a farm up behind Melbourne, they told us, looking for a bit of land at a better price than could be found in Australia. Jerningham, perhaps sensing a sale where a cut might go his way, was at his most entertaining and charming. He had stocked the waka with items to trade, baskets of food, bottles of brandy, and beer that cooled in the water puddling at our feet.

I have never been as happy as I was on that trip. No matter what came after, those days with Jerningham on the river were glorious, especially that sense of abandonment as we left all trappings of civilisation and all our responsibilities behind. I happily slept wrapped in a blanket on fern crawling with woodlice and wētā, I took my turn clumsily at the paddle so our Māori friends could rest, I helped pole and drag the waka through the gentle rapids and I lay back against the mats through the quiet stretches, smoking, day dreaming, watching the blue sky framed by the curtains of exotic trees as the banks grew steeper and the land more mountainous. The scenery was untamed and dramatic.

We passed large river terraces cleared of fern, with neat whare fronting the river. It looked an idyllic lifestyle. Family groups clustered in pockets along the navigable water, with access to the sea and the mountains. They came down to the shore as we paddled by, calling out their friendly "Tēnā koutou!" and offering melons and sweet berries from their gardens, sometimes cooked delicacies. I ate parrot wrapped in rangiora leaves and a sweet baked tree root that tasted like gingerbread. Many of the villagers seemed to know Jerningham, or know of him, and he lifted his Panama hat with a wide smile as we came alongside and swapped small gifts and gossip.

"They call me the Pākehā who purchased Wanganui," he explained to the two Australians, who were scanning the fertile fingers of valleys with investors' eyes and questioning Jerningham about the land and its owners and development prospects. They were canny and fast with their reckonings and I found it hard to place them, behind the Australian twang of their words was something else. A touch of London in the background, perhaps, though they'd clearly not had a proper English education. Like many colonials, their life stories began with the here and now.

I left them to Jerningham, being more interested in the words and phrases of Māori I was learning from Para, my patient teacher. I began to pass small pleasantries and entertained myself during the monotonous stretches of paddling by singing songs in Māori with our guides. I left behind my need for grammatical structure and verb tables and found conversation wasn't as difficult as I had supposed.

"This word, taua," I asked Jerningham. It was a word several of the riversiders had used, with a look of concern. "What does this mean?"

He turned towards the river, out of earshot of our Australian companions, but his voice was unworried. "Oh, there is a rumour of a war party coming down the river. From Taupō."

"Are we in danger of running into them?"

"I shouldn't think so. Kuru is up the river. He would have sent word of any gathering. Anyway, their grievances are not with us. It's a tribal thing."

"Even so, I wouldn't want to run into—"

"Oh, hush, Lugg! You're such an old woman! Look at these boys now on the riverbank, shall we give them a race?"

"I don't see how concern for our safety makes me an old woman," I said. "I know the reputation of the Taupō tribes. They're ruthless cannibals."

Jerningham ignored me and the Australians were paying no attention, calling out to the dozen children who had appeared on the bank. They pushed a small bark canoe into the river, shouting challenges and throwing flowers and grass. Our paddlers slowed to allow them to catch up and then we let them chase us along the water, pausing so they were almost on us before surging off again.

Jerningham threw hard biscuits, which the children leapt into air to catch and splashed into the water, rising spluttering in triumph with a soggy treasure held high and grins as wide as the country.

We all took the paddles to push up through a stretch of faster water, the Australians dropping their reserve with their jackets and showing us they were strong and confident labourers. I thought it a thrill to be a man, on the water, working in a company of other men, using brute strength to fight the river and to explode, exhilarated, out of the fast run into the calmer waters above. Old woman be damned, I thought, and lifted my paddle in glory.

Jerningham was the first to strip off and plunge in when the afternoon grew hot as a Māori oven. I splashed in the shallows while the others swam in a deep pool into which the water plunged with the crash of cymbals from the rapids above, and the walls of the natural theatre magnified our voices and laughter and threw them around the gorge. As the Australians' familiarity with us grew their speech patterns changed, the London accent stronger now. Jerningham whispered to me, "How remote is remote enough, do you think?"

It took me a while to understand. The roughness beneath the patina of purchased quality had a story. How long had Jerningham known? Stripped of their clean shirts and tailored jackets, the scars showed on their backs.

"Convicts," he said. "Mark my words."

I wanted to ask more, but Jerningham disappeared again under the water, he and Para on a challenge to pull a rock from the deepest part of the pool. Our Australians had stopped their games and now floated on their backs, nothing above them but wide blue sky. Escaped or freed? We'd had Australians arrive in Wellington over the year, mostly chancers who took labouring work, or retired military men with pockets of cash buying speculative properties. Dr Evans insisted we welcome them and no doubt he benefited well from the inflation of the Wellington market. But these two were neither military nor labourers. They were rich and looking for a place to hide, and to me, that branded them felons as clearly as the scars on their backs.

Whether that was true or not, the men were good company and I followed Jerningham's lead. We asked no questions and allowed them their enjoyment of the day's beautiful freedom. We pulled the waka onto a stretch of gravel and lay in the sun to dry off, and ate a meal of soft cold kūmara and chewy dried fish, spitting out the bones together. Afterwards, they brought out pouches of Australian tobacco to share, filling the pipes of the Māori and leaving them some spare. One of the pair picked up a quiet song, and the fact that they might or might not have escaped hard labour in a penal colony and stolen their fine clothes merely added to the excitement of the day.

Jerningham stood first, his hand up to still our chatter.

From around a corner and above the rapids came voices on the air, flowing downstream above the water, strong with numbers, singing and chanting.

It grew louder. Rhythmic. A rousing paddle chant. There were a great many voices and they were fierce and deep.

I chilled, suddenly, the sun and warmth gone.

We all slowly stood, the calls above the roar of the rapids echoing and magnifying down the gorge until it sounded like there were hundreds of disembodied voices rushing fast and inexorably towards us.

I resigned my senses in fear. Couldn't see, couldn't hear. Even my sense of smell left me as I was gripped in a white panic. There were no options. I had no skills to resolve whatever it was that was coming upon us as assuredly as the flow of the river. If this was a war party sweeping down to murder their coastal cousins, we had nowhere to go. If they recognised Jerningham as the thief of their ancestral lands, we were already dead men. I'd heard a tomahawk could cleave a scalp down to a man's shoulders.

Jerningham reached over and pulled the swag from the waka and dropped it at his feet. There was no time to load his gun. I stood still, shirtless and barefoot on the stones, and I heard one of the Australians backing off towards the cliff walls and scrambling for a foothold in the fern. A man who survived transportation and hard labour would not die easily on a Māori spear.

I shot a quick look at the cliff behind. It was steep and crumbling. There was no climbing that.

The singing changed to war cries that bounced off the unpredictable water as the waka shot the rapids. They plunged into the pool before us, one after another, dark boats with swirling carvings and dark-skinned warriors with the same patterns carved into their skin.

More waka. Seven, eight, a whole fleet. I looked for guidance from Para but his face, usually so animated, was expressionless. The warriors drifted past us, looking curiously but without apparent hostility. Their waka gathered in the back-eddy of the pool.

"Tīraweke!"

Had I heard it?

And again. "Tīraweke!" There were many calling now, the sound of birds chirping, and the men began turning into the bank.

The last waka plunged into the pool. There was a great cry from the water, and Jerningham, beside me, let out a long sigh of tightly held breath.

"Kuru."

I felt my knees give, like crutches kicked away, and I dropped to the stones heavily, sucking the air in gulps.

The chief stood in the stern of the last waka and his commanding voice carried down the river. The whole fleet had gathered on the bank now. Jerningham stepped forward to greet his friend.

Stand up, I told myself. For God's sake, get up! But my knees were stuck to the stones. I looked over the fierce faces and the powerful, proud bearing of these men and wondered—*how are we to know?*

"I was coming to see you, Kuru!" Jerningham said,

pulling his shirt on over his head. He took the outstretched hand of the chief and performed the hongi—pressing nose to nose. He went down the line, shaking hands and greeting all the hands that reached out for him.

"Tīraweke!"

"I bring my cousins back," Kuru explained in English. "We make a journey to the coast."

He gathered all the chief men of the party together on the stones and lined them up for formal introduction. Jerningham yanked me to my feet, and I was sure to look carefully into each face to read the expression there as I spoke my few words of Māori greeting and made the hongi, touching noses, sharing breath. They didn't seem interested in me at all. Perhaps they sensed that I was a man of little importance, standing as I was nervously behind Jerningham. A small-framed man with blistered skin.

"These are chiefs from Ngāti Apa tribe." Kuru indicated the hills upstream and behind us, in a huge sweep south of the river. "They look on your town plan. They do not sign your purchase but have interest in this land. Tīraweke, you ride with us!"

We left Para and his men to go on up towards the mountains, and we returned downriver, on a fast current, the holiday over, no more a relaxing jaunt but part of a Māori fleet. The Australians and I were baggage, forgotten, in the last of the waka. The Ngāti Apa warriors sang and chanted and handled their boats fast and fearlessly through the rapids, and all the while Jerningham sat in their midst with Kuru.

"He looks like their king," one of the Australians said. The pair of them were again buttoned into their jackets and looked every inch the gentlemen. They were right about Jerningham. The finest clothing in the world could not match the air of the young King Wakefield as he was carried down the river in the midst of a Māori war party, completely at his ease, his Panama hat pushed back on his head and his face tilted up to the sun, untouchable and transcendent.

That evening, after Jerningham deposited me back aboard the schooner, I waited until it was fully dark, slipped ashore and walked along the riverbank to Whare Wikitoria.

—

On the flat shelf above the river a crowd had gathered around tables and benches set out as a public house. They were a typical colonial mix of men: traders and whalers, settlers and Māori, all smoking and drinking and talking. They funnelled back to the open door of the large raupō whare.

Jerningham's Whare Wikitoria.

I drifted closer, keeping in the shadow of the surrounding huts. I recognised some of the Māori from Kuru's party, less impressive out of their waka and on dry land, arguing with sailors, all heavy with drink.

I sidled up to a window and looked in.

Inside, the long room was done up like a mock baronial hall, with broad sweeping beams to a high ceiling and a table running almost the full length of it. There were casks at either end, and men, liberal with their pouring, filled cups and threw the drink down their throats.

A heavily whiskered man sat inside the window in the shadows, his arm loosely around a Māori girl in a dishevelled English dress. I couldn't see her face and didn't want to see her eyes. There were other girls, each hooked by a possessive arm. I knew this business went on, but to be confronted with it, dirty sailors with native girls, I found deeply distressing.

The crowd parted and I saw Jerningham.

He sat like Jesus at the Last Supper, candles from above him lending a halo effect to his shaggy hair, his hands out in a gesture of generosity, surrounded by his disciples. He was telling a story but there were men and noise between us and I couldn't hear the words that held his audience so spellbound.

He wore a woven mat wrapped around his naked shoulders, with a twist of feathers and shells around his neck. I would have passed off this affectation as a dress-up game if his expression had not struck me so forcefully. I remembered his dalliances with mesmerism—my friend seemed hypnotised, as if he really believed he was a Māori chief gathering his men after an adventure on the river.

For a while I watched from my perch, worried and amused in equal measure, mindful that I was to report back to the colonel what I found, and thinking it was better if these remained capers of which I was unaware. Then I was jostled by men reaching past me to take jugs of sweet-smelling rum out the window and the crowd pulled me towards the wide open doors.

I heard my name mentioned, in a rough voice I didn't recognise. "I know 'im. Name's Arthur Lugg."

Another voice in reply: "What's he doing here then? Why's he holding up the surveying?"

I reached the scrum in the doorway and over the shoulders saw Jerningham with his hand up to placate the speaker, the lordly gesture he used so easily. "Mr Lugg has nothing to do with the survey. He is a mere lackey."

I was a lackey? I felt my anger rise. Even if Jerningham was attempting to defend me against these men, I strongly objected to being called a lackey.

"He was sent by my uncle to report back on the degradation of this town. He is here to make sure I am singing from the Company's hymn sheet."

"I know 'im," repeated the first man, his voice slurred with drink. A great bear of a man staggered past me in the doorway and I missed some of his words. "Indeed 'e came on the *Aurora*."

"He married that pretty one off the *Oriental*," said another voice. "Dorothy. Dorothy Lewis. With the curvy hips. Imagine the arse beneath them hips."

"An arse like a peach."

"A ripe peach. A peach to squeeze!"

"What'd he go an' marry her for?" shouted the first.

I needed to push inside and stop this talk. These men, at their drink, discussing my wife. Why did Jerningham not stop this? I struck out with my elbows as another man fought to come out against the flow.

"Hey," I shouted into the room, but they didn't hear me. I pushed forward.

"Exactly!" I heard Jerningham's voice, clear above the rest. "Why on earth would you marry what a man can have for free?"

I burst into the room, raging in the light, grabbed a drunk by his collar and, throwing him aside, slammed against the table where Jerningham sat with his followers.

"Damn you!"

He looked up with amusement at the interruption and then he saw that it was me rocking his table and swearing. He jumped as if burned, a sleepwalker jerked awake to find himself on the edge of a cliff, his eyes full of panic.

I reached across the table and grabbed him by the neck of the stupid blanket he wore, pulled my unmanned fist back and punched him across the face.

His head jerked back on impact but there was no blood, no satisfying crack of a broken nose.

The crowd around him peeled back.

"Oh my God, Lugg! Lugg, please. Oh my God, Lugg,

my friend, my friend, I am so sorry. Lugg, forgive me."

Both hands were up, empty palms, his head lowered like a shamed man. The native cloak was a childish affectation, its power gone.

Silence grew outwards like a pool of blood.

"I meant nothing by it, Lugg. You know I meant no offence! Not to you, nor to your good wife."

I had my hand raised again but I couldn't strike a blubbering man.

"I am a sinner, Lugg," he said. "We are all sinners here. We have vices that we can't control but you are a decent man and carry no sin. That's all I meant, Lugg. Arthur. You would not fall as we have done, as I do, but you are a moral man and obey God's laws. That's all I meant by it. I apologise. Wholeheartedly. To you and to the name of your good wife." Jerningham held his hand over his heart and he bowed deeply to me. "Mea culpa, Arthur Lugg. Forgive me my stupid words."

I shoved him back into his chair and left him there. With his drink and his women and his debauched followers and his pretentious little kingdom, his ridiculous Māori cloak and the feathers around his neck.

The next day we sailed for home on the *Jane*, leaving Carrington behind to finish his maps. On board, I turned my back on the hovering Jerningham and looked steadfastly out to sea.

———

We stopped a day and a night off Kāpiti Island.

"This is an opportunity to meet Te Rauparaha, Arthur," Jerningham said, coming to me with an appeal in his eyes and his head dipped as if the fool intended to press a hongi on me. I turned my face aside. Perhaps he thought a meeting with a cannibal was some kind of peace offering, a man with fewer scruples than himself. *Why would you marry what a man can have for free?*

"Just a courtesy visit. Will you come?"

I turned my back on his invitation and stayed aboard with the bluntly spoken captain, who suited my mood better. Jerningham was now polite and respectful towards me, with none of his usual banter, and I determined to leave our relationship just so. Mocked so cruelly by one of his faces, I looked through his kinder face as I would through glass.

We had a cargo of potatoes on board and carried a few travelling natives, who spread their blankets on the deck. I kept my back to Jerningham and spent time with a boy, practising my Māori phrases.

"Aata," he said when I asked his name. "My father is Arthur Black. He was a whaler." He said this with pride, though when I asked where his father was now he couldn't answer.

Aata was missionary-schooled, happy-faced and clumsy with adolescence, but both his spoken and written English would have graced any school at home. He had me reciting nouns and numbers and I concentrated on these lessons to keep my anger at Jerningham from spilling into a rage.

We sailed down the coast to Cape Terawhiti the next day on a gentle north-easterly, but instead of dropping in the evening, the wind swung north-west and gained strength fast, rising to gale force as we entered Cook's Strait, too late to turn back.

The captain sent our passengers below and his men furled sails, stowed and lashed gear, preparing the ship for a storm.

"Send Lugg below!" I heard Jerningham shout to the captain, but the skipper needed his men on the ropes and set me as port lookout. We raced on the wind as the darkness dropped fearfully, depriving me of sight minute by dreadful minute. My fear of the sea and the dark sank a deep cold into my belly, and broke to icy shards any courage I ever possessed. The waves grew and we dived into great mounds of water while the rain soused us wet as the sea. The ship caught the swirling winds of the strait, slapping us around while the sails, taut one minute, flailed puppet-like the next. The captain shouted, the sailors hauled and their maniacal juggling kept us from rolling over and tumbling below. I set my face to the west, staring into the void, looking for towering cliffs but seeing only the monstrous sea. The captain and Jerningham together fought the wheel to hold course and the men worked the sails tight. Waves crashed over the deck.

We abandoned hope for our planned anchorage at Sinclair Head—the surrounding water was littered with reefs and the night too dark to see our way in safely—and we drove out into the strait in the fury. The mizzen and reefed foresail strained to hold us steady on top of the waves and prevent the dreadful alternative, the cold plunge below. I had no doubt that under the water was death. Te Puni would not dive to my rescue this time.

It went on through the night. Jerningham and the captain battled the screaming ship across the dark hours. I clutched the rail and prayed and cried and stared into the waves, every movement of the water seeming to offer a looming cliff or reef.

The dawn brought no answer to our prayers but more walls of water, no less terrifying in the pewter light that filtered through the clouds. As we crested a wave, we saw smudges on the horizon that could have been land, but we fell back into a trough before the skipper could take a reckoning, and he and Jerningham argued about our position and heading. There was no sign of let up, no clarity on the horizon, no break in the clouds above.

The Māori, below decks, were keening and battering at the hatch to be freed.

"Keep the damn darkies off my deck!" the captain shouted when Jerningham went to release them, but he insisted on bringing them out, onto the open top, where they could see the sea and feel the winds.

"They travel on open waka," Jerningham cried across the hatch. "Below they feel like they're buried alive."

We dived again and a wave immediately washed over the bow and crashed down into the hold.

"Man the bilge pumps! Wash the bastards overboard if you want, Wakefield, but batten the fucking hatch!"

I was sent below when the light grew such that I could be relieved and I stumbled away from my post dragging my uselessness down with me. There were islands of floating potatoes beneath my bunk and somewhere below men were pumping and shouting, but I rolled in my bed semi-conscious and sick—the deprivation of food and water keeping me awake when I should have slept like the devil.

During the night I felt an arm around my shoulders lifting me. "Drink something," said Jerningham. He held a cup to my lips and I lapped a sweet liquid. Cold tea with sugar. The noise of bashing waves had subsided though I could hear the race of water on the hull. I drank and fell back. I must have slept soundly then. When I surfaced again it was late afternoon and the winds had dropped to gusts, but a heavy sea was running and the rain fell as if thrown.

The captain—had he slept?—was with Jerningham on the aft deck, the pair still arguing about their position.

"Look," he said, hand on Jerningham's shoulder and eyes scrunched, peering south. His beard, previously a motley black, now appeared quite grey. "If that's Cape Campbell, we're still well south!" We dropped into a trough, and the captain gripped the wheel as the wind fell from the sails and we rose again. I followed the captain's direction and could see cloud on the horizon, nothing more. We drew closer, and through the driving rain I realised the long low smudge of white that I had mistaken for a cloud was actually a line of cliff face.

"Let's get some sail up and we'll head back across for the lee of Cape Palliser," he said. "See if we can anchor up until it passes."

"We're safer out," said Jerningham.

"We haven't got the fuel or the water."

"We won't get ashore in this."

"If we stay in this rip we'll run to the Chathams. We need to get in."

I took my lookout again as they worked and argued, and we drew slowly into land, but then the tide turned against us and we lost the battle of sail, wind, rudder and tide. When the night wind came off the land we were as far away as before, blown right back across the strait.

The sea quietened somewhat and at midnight I was relieved of my watch. I collapsed again below into instant sleep, but woke in the night ravenously hungry to hear the wind had picked up and was thrashing again against the bow. We were heeled far over on a fast tack. The fear of going far out to sea paralysed me. Both the captain's bunk and Jerningham's were empty and there was a hollow cave in my stomach with the thought that they had gone overboard, the whole crew had gone overboard, and I was alone on the ship skudding across the Pacific.

I rushed out of the cabin and collapsed onto a pile of potatoes, where Aata lay curled, above him heavy hammocks. Across the cabin was the bright glow of firelight. A silhouetted sailor crouched over a steaming pot. He beckoned me over and handed me a spoon of something warm and greasy that slipped down my throat with the musky aftertaste of a long-dead animal.

In a hammock below the hatch I found Jerningham fast asleep, his cheekbones gaunt and pale, lips slightly parted in a peaceful snore, his long eyelashes fluttering as if he watched a dream and was enjoying it.

For two more days and nights we were caught in the ripping waters of the strait, fighting winds and tides, unable to find shelter, wresting the little ship away from coasts, where murderous reefs poked like spears from low water. The sea turned about several times in the course of a day so we could make no headway at all, and Jerningham and the captain argued and pointed and battled the winds and somehow kept us alive. We were out of food and firewood, and our remaining water we shared, one parched mouthful at a time.

Finally at the end of another long night we dragged ourselves north across the strait and caught a light southerly through the heads. A calm dawn lit the sea as we sailed into Port Nicholson, the homely fires of the settlement calling us to anchor. Wooden houses clustered under a circle of hills, looking comfortable in the morning sunshine. It looked a haven of peace. My knees were shaking as Aata helped me into the dinghy and then ashore onto Thorndon beach, where the rank smell of damp seaweed on the edge of the tide was as welcome as the glistening stones underfoot. I was filled with the longing to walk up the road, home to Dorothy and have her take care of me. Feed me, comfort me, put me to bed, wash and lay out my clothes, read to me. Before I walked off, I could not help but turn and shake both the captain and Jerningham by the hand.

Their courage and skill had kept us afloat.

TE ARO AND A BALL

AFTER A LARGE MEAL and a bottle of wine, I'd slept through the afternoon and night and had woken well rested in my soft bed to find clean clothes laid on the chair for me. I washed and shaved and wandered outside to discover my wife under her wide-brimmed sunhat, sorting stones.

Dorothy removed her leather gloves and laid them down, and she blushed when I commented on them, apologising for the expense. "You know you can buy what you need, Dorothy," I said. "We have credit with all the shopkeepers. And look what you've achieved."

She stood by my side as I looked around the transformation of our patch of muddy rubble to the beginnings of a well-ordered garden. I didn't think often of my father but he came to mind now, the proud expression he wore when his vegetables performed. He would approve of Dorothy and at last I had a neutral topic on which I could write.

"I've burned all the fern off the bank," Dorothy said. "Lucy and I did it together." She took my hand and led me around, pointing to where she had removed stones from the dark crumbly soil and laid them neatly between the planting rows. A patchwork of bright green lettuces grew in the rectangular bed and there was the start of a herb garden on the bank. "The lettuces were a gift from Mrs Mein Smith."

I was pleased to hear it. "Have you been out making friends?" I asked.

"She stopped by with Mrs Evans and they gave me plants and some flower seeds. I think they wanted to see what we had made of the house."

"And did you invite them in?"

"No. The house wasn't set for visitors." Dorothy had her closed face on.

"Oh, Dorothy," I said. "I don't think anyone here would mind if the chairs are not brushed or cups on the table. Has anyone else visited?" I reached out and took one of her soft white hands in my calloused broken one.

"No."

She came inside with me, unwrapping her gardening apron, which she folded neatly away in the cupboard under the stairs. She was wearing her navy blue dress, the one she had owned before we married. Perhaps Mrs Mein Smith could recommend a dressmaker.

"I didn't know when you were coming back," Dorothy said, "I would have prepared better."

"It was nice to come home yesterday and find you out in the garden. I don't expect you to be waiting by the door for me."

We ate a late breakfast together at our new dining room table, a walnut piece with fold-out wings that I had brought from Revans. It suited our little room. I wondered if Dorothy approved of it now I knew her history. It was slightly disconcerting that she had knowledge of antiques sold to the better houses of London and that she might be judging my unrefined taste.

After eggs and pork sausages there was bread with fresh butter and honey.

"This will do very well," I told her, and had Lucy bring me more coffee. "Wellington is becoming a proper town!" I sat back in my chair. "What else has been happening since I have been away? Any ships?"

"There were new faces at church on Sunday. Off the *Blenheim*. I couldn't understand a word they said. I think they're from Scotland."

I found this interesting news, not being aware the Company had been recruiting in Scotland, and I raised my eyebrows for her to continue, but she knew nothing more. Her interests were naturally domestic. I tried not to look disappointed. I could learn more when I went back to the office.

"Any other news?"

"Another earthquake. Smaller this time. Lucy was frightened, but you know how timid she is."

I asked after the weather, her embroidery, how Lucy's cooking was coming along, and what had happened to the birds that had been building a nest in the tree at the front. She answered nicely enough but asked me no questions in return.

"Do you want to hear about my trip," I said at last, "and my adventures with Jerningham?"

She looked down at her teacup. "Yes. Tell me about your trip."

And so I told her. About the voyage out and Reverend Hadfield, about the surveyors we had left in Wanganui arguing every inch with the Māori, about our trip up the Wanganui River and the extraordinary beauty of the interior. I told Dorothy about meeting Kuru's large fleet of waka and how frightened I had been thinking they were a war party sweeping down the river to kill us all. I spoke about the storm and the days at sea when I thought I was a dead man and never coming home.

I didn't mention Whare Wikitoria. I didn't mention the suggestion Jerningham had shouted to his disciples in that place, in a voice thick with drink and power, that I hadn't needed to marry what I could have had for free. Was that Dorothy, specifically? Or women, generally?

What had he meant?

"Jerningham saved all our lives on that ship," I said, and she looked directly into my eyes.

"I'm glad he did," she said, with her shy smile and a genuine warmth in her voice I hadn't heard before.

—

There was a fête and a ball planned for 22 January, our colony's anniversary day. *My* anniversary I should say—the date the *Aurora* arrived. I told Dorothy that we special ones who had come on the first ship were to receive medals and for a while she believed me. I liked to tease her.

I had reported back faithfully to Colonel Wakefield on my trip to Wanganui—the lawlessness, the surveying disputes, the debauchery. I described Jerningham dressed like a Māori chief in his whare, and his trading and shop-keeping.

The colonel nodded without looking at me, his eyes expressionless. He had his pencil poised but took no notes. It seemed I was confirming what he already knew.

Jerningham was given the arduous task of recording the disputed town sections in Wellington but within days he was bored with town life. He filled the *Sandfly* with goods for trade and then he was off back up the coast to his beloved Wanganui, leaving the job of dispute recording to me.

I took Dorothy to a dressmaker. The two recommended by Mrs Mein Smith were already fully booked for months ahead but there was a Scottish woman off the *Blenheim* with good references and bolts of fine cloth. Dorothy wanted some cheap grey stuff, as if wearing a pretty dress alarmed her, but I chose for her an elegant pink silk. We were shopping in Cuba Street, a dusty thoroughfare at the heart of the settlement where the merchants clustered. All our town streets were laid out to generous proportions, preparing for a future of bustling shops and carriages that clattered along the paving. I helped Dorothy across a drain to Mr Hornbrook's establishment, where we bought ribbons and shoes.

She was matching buckles to the shoes when I was drawn away by a commotion outside the shop. Men were running towards the police barracks.

"The Maoris are rising!"

I grabbed a man as he passed. "What is it? What's happening?"

"They have murdered Captain Daniel and thrown Revans's house into the sea."

"Who have? Where is Revans?"

But the man broke free and dashed after his fellows.

I pushed Dorothy back into the shop and told her to take shelter behind the counter. I ran to the quay. I hadn't gone a hundred paces when I came across Captain Daniel himself, looking flustered but unharmed, walking home up the empty street.

"I have been manhandled by a bunch of savages," he replied to my urgent questions. He looked aggrieved and flicked dust from his coat as if brushing the incident from his person. "They have indeed risen up and threatened me with a tomahawk. I am lucky not to have had my head split. How can we live with such primitives, who rise to war with each small provocation? These Maoris need to go, Mr Lugg, and I will tell Colonel Wakefield myself."

Daniels had the face of a man with something sour on his tongue. He was a puny character, often complaining, and I wondered why on earth he ended up here.

"Where is Revans?"

"Trying to fish his house from the sea. Yesterday the Maoris agreed he might build his house in their pā there, but today he may not." He tapped his cane on the ground, an angry man looking for something to squash. "There was some small thing, an insult. I think one of his builders called a native a slave or some such, and all hell broke out. The bullock drivers jumped in and the natives attacked the animals. The workers whipped them back and the nasty little bastards shoved Revans's house down the bank and into the drink. I tried to stop them. I told their chief this was not the way forward, but he chased me away, swinging his bloody tomahawk at my head. They are savages, Lugg. There's no reasoning with them."

I went down to the pā. The constable was restoring peace and I found Revans on the beachfront. He was hatless, his hair unbrushed, suit rumpled and his collar unbuttoned as if he'd started to get dressed that morning but thought the better of it. He stood with his hands on his hips, overlooking a section of his drawing room, wallpaper side up, floating in the shallows. Behind him the Māori from the pā picked up bits of clothing that had fallen out in the fray and held each piece up as if they were at a market stall—a grey nightshirt, a pair of tatty drawers. Some items of clothing they tried on and took away, unwanted items they dropped.

"It's just a house," Revans said to me. "Nobody died."

A chief I knew called Wī Tako came over the stones and stood with us, looking at the broken house trailing timber panels and twisted door frames over the bank and down into the water. The wallpaper lifted and floated like seaweed. We, all three, were inclined to laugh but did so quietly, chuckling to ourselves as a seagull perched on the frame and pecked at the strange raft, the inside-out house. After a while the chief called to his men to fish it out.

I fetched Dorothy while Revans collected a suitcase of his belongings, and we took him home. Lucy made up a bed for him in the little room upstairs and he became our guest while his house was rebuilt.

Rain lashed down on anniversary day, and the fête was cancelled. God would send sunshine to bless the alternative celebration organised by people of the working class for the following day in protest at their exclusion from the formal activities.

"The whole thing was nonsense anyway," said Revans gruffly, as we stood at the window and looked out on the rain. "Having two sets of celebrations. The colonel insists on enforcing this division between the gentry and the workers, but I think the popular games tomorrow will be much more fun. What do you think, eh, Mrs Lugg?"

"Perhaps they might be more jolly," said Dorothy.

"Quite right! That's why we have come across the world. To break down some of those old barriers. There was a party last night on the *London*, did you hear them? All classes of young people, all mixed up. It carried on until morning. I saw the revellers rowed ashore. I wasn't invited, of course. Jerningham and his friends, no doubt."

Dorothy looked up sharply.

"Jerningham is away," I reminded Revans. "He won't be at the ball tonight."

"Well, that's a good thing, you know! He'd dance with all the pretty women, and those of us with less obvious charms—and I include you in that category with me, of course, Arthur—we would be wallflowers all night. Which reminds me, Mrs Lugg, you have promised to dance with me. If you refuse me I will probably hunt you down with a tomahawk."

Dorothy smiled shyly at him, but didn't reply as she packed up her needlework.

In the afternoon, while Dorothy rested, Sam Revans and I talked politics, or, more accurately, he talked and I listened. I was cautious about becoming embroiled in his increasingly outspoken criticisms of the Company.

From the window I saw a Māori man in full tribal regalia come and peer over our fence to the house, and on seeing us, he lifted the latch and came barefoot up the path. With pleasure, I recognised Te Puni.

—

I had never invited a Māori chief into my house before, but Revans took it in his stride. It seemed he was the one Te Puni had come to see. Revans called the wide-eyed Lucy to make tea and invited the chief to sit at the dining room table.

I held the chair for our guest and passed him the plate of biscuits as if it were the most normal thing in the world.

Te Puni smiled happily at me. "The drowned man," he said with a laugh and shook me heartily by the hand. "This is your house."

"Yes," I said, "and you are very welcome."

We ate biscuits together in silence, the chief with perfect posture and a dignified expression. He wore a woven shift made from soft flax, and a feathered cloak neatly folded around his shoulders. I couldn't guess how old he was. It was possible he didn't know himself. His hair was turning from dark grey to white as if middle age was behind him and it was pulled back in a topknot stuck with soft feathers and combs, the look of a much younger man. Charles, I knew, had done many studies of the tattoo marks on his face; he considered the chief a fascinating subject, ageless.

"I have sent my people to help Taranaki rebuild your house," he told Revans. "I am sorry for trouble."

"They were sorely provoked by my servants," said Revans,

"for which I apologise. I have spoken to the men to keep a civil tongue."

Te Puni nodded.

I'd never heard Revans apologise to anyone before, it was not in his nature. He was always the man with the last word. I was proud of him. He spoiled it, however, by adding, "But that is no reason to throw a man's house into the sea."

Te Puni pulled out his pipe—one of the long-stemmed Webbs Jerningham gave away—and I brought a taper from the kitchen and lit it for him. Lucy followed me as far as the doorway, peering out at the strange visitor with tattooed face and woven cloak and feathers in his hair.

"I would not encroach on your cemeteries, or other tapu places," said Revans, "but you sold us that land in Te Aro. Do I not have the right to build my house on land I own?"

"You may stay there, yes. I have told them they must leave you in peace now."

Revans nodded, but I knew he would not be satisfied with this.

"Others will come," he said, "The sections on either side have been sold. Other men will build their houses there."

"It would be better if they did not."

"Will they dispute every plot of land?"

Te Puni sighed and looked out of the window. "How many? How many more Pākehā come? Is your whole tribe coming?"

Of course, there was no answer to this.

"I have seen Sydney," said Te Puni. "Many Englishmen. I did not expect so many to come here, into my home. You, Mr Revans and Mr Lugg, are welcome in my home."

It seemed ungracious to remind him that when he sold, it had become our home. There were over two and a half thousand settlers now in Wellington, more up the coast in Porirua and Wanganui, and farms reached deep into Hutt

Valley and west over the hills to Karori. New Plymouth and Nelson settlers were on the way.

"Is this your ancestral home?" I asked him. I couldn't imagine how I would feel if a foreign contingent arrived in the countryside in Somerset and spilled out endlessly over our hills, trampling over the graves of our forebears.

But Te Puni laughed. "No ancestor here. Taranaki!"

"But your pā in Pito-one, you have lived there a long time?"

Revans was shaking his head across the table.

"Pito-one, few year. I came here to Te Whanganui-a-Tara eight year."

"Who was here before you? How do you come to own the land?"

He didn't seem perturbed by my questioning, though Revans was rolling his eyes in warning.

"Ngāti Mutunga and Ngāti Tama left me these lands."

"These are other tribes? Are they still here?"

"They went to the Chatham Islands," said Revans. "They were fighting among themselves when Heaphy got in the middle and took his leg wound."

"Did you buy the lands from them, Te Puni?"

"They left." He gave me a slightly fiercer look from under his brows.

"You told Colonel Wakefield you owned all this land."

"That's right."

"You sold it to him. Now the people in Te Aro pā say the land still belongs to them."

He grunted and fixed his cloak around his shoulders.

I persisted. "The other chiefs, from Pipitea, Kumutoto, Taranaki, all these pā within our town survey. Did they all agree to sell their land?"

The chief shifted again in his chair. "They take gift. All chief want gun, blanket."

I looked in horror at Revans, but he had backed away from my questioning and was drinking his tea and gazing out of the window.

"The rain's stopping," he said. "I think it will clear up for the fête tomorrow."

"You must wish for wind," Te Puni said. "With no wind, our waka will beat your canoe every race."

With that he stood, shook us both by the hand, thanked me for the tea, and waved and smiled at little Lucy, who hovered close to her shadow in the doorway. He stopped to regard her, a little pale thing twitching like a mouse in a corner.

He rolled his eyes. She didn't move.

He gently stamped his foot forward and shot out his tongue, the whites of his eyes alarming against his dark skin.

Lucy's hands flew up and she covered her mouth, but her eyes crinkled and I could see she was giggling.

Te Puni reached up and took a long white feather from his top knot. He stepped back two paces, lifting his feet high, and laid the feather on the table behind him. He pointed to Lucy and pointed to the feather.

Then Te Puni, chief of the Te Āti Awa people, walked out of my house and strolled away into the rain.

—

"I don't feel well, Arthur. I think you should go alone."

I had engaged a young woman to put up Dorothy's glossy hair, a lady's maid who had advertised in the paper. Lucy hovered at her side, holding brushes and combs and ribbons.

My wife sat at the dresser in her beautiful dress the colour of bruised roses, a colour that glowed against her skin and picked out something bright in her complexion, a flush of blood close to the surface, a hidden heat.

And she'd wanted a grey dress!

"Oh, my dear!" I stood behind Dorothy and caught her eyes in the mirror. She smelled of bath salts and something sweet and clean. I bent over and kissed her naked shoulder. "You look exquisite." Her eyes were large dark orbs in a slender face and her mole, the mole that other men talked about among themselves, was the point of asymmetry that caught and held my gaze, the beauty spot that drew attention to her otherwise flawless skin and the tender sweep of her cheeks. "Of course you must come. You will be the belle."

I sat on the edge of the bed to observe the skill with which her long locks were plaited and twisted and gathered on her head, a mass of coils and braids that slowly lifted and exposed her elegant neck.

I noticed she didn't thank the hairdresser. I would mention that in the morning. Good manners were easy.

"They're not my people, Arthur," she said, looking at me in the mirror. "I was a governess. I don't want you to be ashamed of me."

She pulled on the long white gloves I had bought her. They hadn't been easy to obtain. "You are a lucky woman to be married to the procurement officer," I'd said when I handed them to her. "There is only one man importing gloves in the colony and I happen to know him. These were off the ship yesterday."

Now she sat with her gloved hands in her lap, looking down. "I've never danced at a ball," she said. "I don't know any of the new dances."

"Oh, Dorothy. They're not my people either, you know. The only dance I know is a waltz. We can do that. Shall we?"

She looked up at me, confused. Perhaps she had imagined me dancing through my childhood in grand country ballrooms.

"My background is not as it appears." I took her hands in mine. It wasn't a secret. "My fortune found me only recently, dear, and this is all rather new to me too. Four years ago I really was a bookkeeper. Not for amusement or as part of my education. It was my job. I grew up in a modest house. My father was a clergyman, as you know. He spent any inheritance I might have had on my education. I married a woman of similar circumstances, but she came into a great deal of money shortly before she died."

Would Dorothy think of me differently, now that she knew? I looked at her eyes, but she wasn't looking back.

I had not revealed my circumstances to anyone in the colony. It wasn't a deliberate decision. I was not hiding my past. The topic simply hadn't arisen. No one had questioned how the son of a vicar could afford colonial acres. But it was the truth: I had married, and a year later my wife had caught pneumonia. Before she died, a week, ten days, I can't remember exactly, she received an unexpected inheritance. She died without enjoying a penny of it and there I was, almost overnight, with an extreme and unexpected change of circumstances.

The scale of change in my life seemed to demand a dramatic response and I'd bought colonial land on the strength of an advertisement. It seemed more honest to take the money away rather than step up to a different life at home, out of my own circle. To the Company, my cash was as good as the next man's. I was sure Revans, Heaphy, Dieffenbach and my other friends, if they knew, wouldn't think a thing of it and would welcome any decent, educated man at their table. I wasn't sure Jerningham would be so kind.

"We're new gentry, you and I, Dorothy. By virtue of my childhood, I might as well have come here as a missionary than as a landowner. So, let's hold our heads up, behave impeccably and with you looking as beautiful as you do tonight, well, we're as good as any of them."

We went downstairs to where Revans waited. Lucy had brushed his suit and pressed his shirt and he looked well. Prosperous. He regarded Dorothy the way a man looks at a racehorse on which he might place a bet.

"Mrs Lugg, you have swept me quite away," he said, his hand pressed to his heart. She looked at him blankly.

We walked down Molesworth Street to Lambton Quay and along the waterfront, keeping to the new pavers to save the silk of Dorothy's shoes from the mud that slid across the road. The rain had stopped at noon and the wind had died and Barrett's Hotel shone brightly, with flaming rushlights lining the door and a mass of candles sending light from every window.

It was the first real glamour the town had seen. Elegance radiated from an English hall in a place that a year ago had been nowhere. It was a remarkable achievement for our little colony and a wonderful celebration to mark the anniversary. Despite all the setbacks and troubles that still plagued us, here we were, a year in, walking into a sturdy room filled with seventy or eighty of the town's prominent settlers, an excellent class of people, turned out in their best finery and shining with pleasure.

Malloy's wife, Catherine, greeted us at the door.

"Mr Revans and Mr Lugg. How delightful. I am on the organising committee, and so I have the pleasure of welcoming everyone as they arrive. How very good of you to come."

I presented my wife.

"Charmed," said Catherine, and she shook a rather startled Dorothy by the hand.

Revans turned to me as we gave our hats over at the little alcove that served as a cloakroom.

"You know Ada Malloy is bound to be here, Lugg." He took off his gloves and handed them after his hat. "Ada Bently, I should say. No nonsense."

How did he know? I had made no mention of Ada to Revans since the day I'd asked him to carry my letter to her. Could he identify my casual glances at the passing faces, read the throbbing drum at my temple? He glared at me now from under his thick brows, the sharp eyes of a fox peering from a hedgerow. I breathed quietly and looked steadily back at him and said nothing.

Returning to Dorothy I took her arm and patted her gloved hand gently. It was a warm evening, but she was rigid with cold or fright and her wide eyes flicked around rapidly, resting on nothing.

"What lovely flowers," I remarked as we passed into the main hall, but I don't think she saw them.

"Just smile at people, and nod your pretty head occasionally," I whispered to her, but her smile didn't come naturally at the best of times. She was scowling with what looked like displeasure but I was coming to recognise as fear. She was undoubtedly the most beautiful woman in the room and every head, coiffured or combed, turned towards her as we stepped forward. Perhaps the grey dress would have been the more sensible choice. Revans, half a step ahead of her, leaned across to make some comment to me, giving her some shelter from the glare of the eyes.

Ada was across the room. Her startled expression gave her away immediately. She may have known by then that I had married, but she certainly wasn't expecting a beauty like Dorothy to materialise on my arm. She stood with her brother and her handsome fair-headed husband.

I had not seen Bently at close quarters before. He wore his clothes well and had the confident air of a tall man, with a touch of arrogance like Jerningham. But where

Jerningham delighted in roughing it and blurring his edges, Bently was groomed as a king's courtier. Sleek. He looked like wealth.

Dorothy glanced around at the collective but didn't pause at Ada. Perhaps Ada didn't stand out in the crowd to others in the way she dazzled me. She was wearing a brown dress with ruffles and bows, and her hair was pulled back from her pale face. I preferred her as I remembered her on the deck of the *Aurora*, with her simple cloak and her dark frizzy curls whipping out of a bonnet too flimsy to contain them.

"Would you fetch us a glass, Arthur?" said Revans. "There's a chap with a tray of champagne by the door. I'm sure Dorothy would like a sip." He lifted my wife's hand onto his arm and began to lead her away from me. "I will introduce your charming wife to some friends. You must share, Arthur, it's only fair. Are you with me, Mrs Lugg?"

Revans took Dorothy directly across the room, pulled along the path of Ada's gaze. In panic, I reached to hold them back but it was too late, they were already across and Malloy's party was turning to Revans expectantly.

Ada's lips pursed and her eyes narrowed as she confronted my wife.

I couldn't watch. Perhaps it was better this way, getting the inevitable over with. My concern was for Ada's reaction, but when I saw Malloy notice the transformation of Dorothy from humble nurse to glamorous wife I was glad to turn my back and trip away to the corner of the room and busy myself with champagne.

Later, I waltzed with Dorothy and I felt the eyes upon us. We stepped in time to the music and moved around the room with the party. It seemed all that was required. When we rested, Malloy was beside me.

"Very nice, Lugg," he said to me, nodding towards

Dorothy as if she were a plush jacket I had put on for the night. I thought for a horrible second he would ask her to dance, but Revans stepped between them.

"Why don't I introduce you to Hannah Butler?" he said to Dorothy. "She's a charming girl and you know her father, the reverend." He led her away, speaking comfortingly. "She's about your age, I'm sure you'll have lots to talk about."

For all Sam Revans's gruffness, he was a clever and intuitive man and I was grateful to him.

Malloy stepped onto the dance floor with his wife and I found myself, suddenly, standing beside his sister. Ada Malloy. Ada Bently. Her husband was somewhere else.

I wished her face wasn't so easy to read.

"Your nurse," she said quietly.

"My wife," I corrected her.

Perhaps I had hoped to make Ada a little jealous. Perhaps that's why I had insisted on the pink dress, the gloves, the hair styler. Now I felt sorry and wished Dorothy was attracting a little less attention.

"I can well believe you fell in love when she nursed you. She's very pretty, Arthur."

"But I have already told you, Ada, that's not the way it happened."

We spoke softly, against the band. To those watching we might have been commenting on the weather. "You married Bently and only then I spoke to Dorothy. There was no overlap. I want to be clear."

"But you fell in love with her when she nursed you."

"I was grateful for her care," I said. "She saved my life, Ada. She found me staggering like a drunk man and didn't turn away. She recognised there was poison in my blood, heading for my heart. Dorset says I might have died overnight, otherwise."

"So, you fell in love with her."

"Ada! Will you cease this."

I gave a slight bow to Dr Evans and smiled at his wife as they passed by.

"When did you fall out of love with me and in love with her?"

My head reeled with the music and the noise of the crowd and the press of people on the dance floor. It reeled with the persistence of Ada, and I wanted to break free of the hole she was stuffing me into, a dark guilty space. I had committed no crime against Ada. She had been my first choice and I had promised myself to her.

"I don't know if I am in love with her."

We were interrupted again as Colonel Wakefield entered the room. The band stopped on a beat, and we—all the colonel's loyal subjects—turned as one towards the doorway and clapped and cheered loudly to the man who had brought us all safely here. He had guided us across the world to a glittering ballroom in our own colony, built with our efforts and toil. What a success he was!

He bowed, looking almost bashful, and the sleek pomade of his hair gleamed in the light of the overhead candles. The first thoroughly happy smile I had ever seen from him lit up his face.

Bently came to fetch Ada and led her into the line to greet the colonel. She looked back at me, over her shoulder, a look that anyone in the room could have read for its clarity, if in that second they had been watching her face. *Wait for me*, it said. *We haven't finished yet.*

ADA

I CAME OUT of the newspaper office, where I had dropped off an editorial to Revans. I knew he wouldn't like it. It was Dr Evans, again, in full praise of the infallible Company and extolling the virtues of the honest settlers. There was a ship bound for England and he wanted his message sent.

"I won't publish this nonsense," Revans said.

"That's your decision, my friend," I said, "but please ensure the colonel knows I passed it on."

"Here's something the colonel won't like." He picked a paper from his messy desk and flapped it at me. "The governor is advertising for mechanics again. We pay for them to immigrate here and he steals them north to work for him."

"We don't have enough paid work to keep them occupied here, Sam."

"That's because settlers like you won't develop your land and employ them."

I'd had this lecture from the colonel, too. The country land ballot in December had allocated me my hundred acres close to the Porirua Road. I had no intention of becoming a farmer. I wouldn't know where to start. I proposed to hold my land as an investment. I wasn't alone in this, most of the purchased land was bought by people who would never set foot in New Zealand. I didn't place myself in the same category as the non-immigrant speculators, though. At least I was here, contributing to the economy.

"Will you write in your editorial that Te Puni's men trounced us in the canoe races?"

"Certainly not," said Revans. "But I will mention that Molesworth fell twice in the horse race."

"It was good to see the Māori joining in, I thought."

"You know they almost didn't? Some killjoy missionary told them they weren't to compete in sports, but you can't keep a Māori from a race. Offer a challenge and they will reply."

"We should be careful of our challenges."

I left the office and wandered in shadow between two buildings, heading towards the front.

Ada appeared at my elbow in the narrow lane. It didn't seem a coincidence that she was walking there. She was buttoned up in a modest dress and the wide ruff of her bonnet shadowed her face.

"Hello, Mrs Bently," I said. "What brings you to town?"

She walked slowly and I pulled my pace in to match hers.

Ada folded her bottom lip between her teeth and slowly, sensually, dragged it out. I was watching so closely I could see the blood rush back into her lip as she let it go.

"What is it, Ada?" I found her expression difficult to read.

"My brother and Catherine are coming to town on Saturday, for the weekend," she said quietly.

We walked even more slowly. Sunlight shone on the stones at the end of the lane. I didn't want to reach the end until I knew her meaning.

"I'm going to the house tomorrow, to air the rooms before they arrive."

"I see." The end of the lane was five steps away.

"There's a problem with the latch on the back door. You

can't see it from the path. Perhaps you would come and have a look at it for me? Around noon?"

We stepped out into the sunlight. Ada's friend Hannah Butler was outside the drapery shop waiting for her, and the women waved to each other.

We slowed to a soft stop.

I was suddenly acutely aware of my breathing. I inhaled sharply to stop it racing. My shoulders felt hunched up around my ears. I forced them down.

Hannah Butler was only a few yards away. She was coming forward in the clean sunshine with her bright smile and brisk manner.

If I was in any doubt whatsoever of Ada's meaning, a quick look at her face made her suggestion absolutely clear.

My head jerked in a nod. "Good afternoon," I said, but I had to say it again because I was unsure whether the first time I had said it aloud.

I quickly walked away, almost stumbling as my knees seemed to want to turn inwards and my feet walk backward. I'm not sure if I greeted Miss Butler or pushed past her without a word.

Oh God, I thought. *Oh God.*

Ada's proposition was as unsettling as an earthquake.

I got home. I hadn't noticed the walk past the colonel's residence or the rise of Molesworth Street. Dorothy was in the garden. *Oh God.*

I went upstairs and sat at the dresser. Dorothy had laid out my clothes for dinner but I couldn't move. Despite the summer heat, I was shivering.

I looked at myself in the glass. An ordinary man. Not an adventurer or a hero. A decent man, I hoped. I studied my reflection and no other thoughts came. I stared directly, but unseeing, at my eyes in the glass, until my head buzzed and I was forced to blink. Somewhere in an unexamined corner

–

of my mind, somewhere below where rationality lived, I knew I was forcing thoughts away deliberately, because thinking is a practical thing to do if you need to make a choice, whereas I had no choice. With Ada, there were things unfinished. More than conversations.

———

The next day, at noon, I opened Malloy's back door. As Ada had said, you couldn't see it from the path. There was nothing wrong with the latch.

She wore a simple cotton dress and no bonnet, her tangle of dark hair was undone and natural and her face so full of me. I leaned forward and took her bottom lip in my teeth and gently pulled her towards me. I had thought of nothing else all night.

"This is once, Arthur. Just once. I have to know. Do you understand?"

We made love in the little box room upstairs, on a pallet on the floor. I have never felt such desire as when she arched her body into mine and called me to give myself into her. She moaned and murmured and made fierce noises, wild as weather, and we went into the storm together—she, my Ada, came with me and fused into me as the sun burst in my head and my mind evaporated. It was the most extraordinary thing I have ever experienced.

I watched Ada's face as she came back from where we had been. She drifted down, back into my arms, her body seemingly filled with love.

I lay with Ada curved into me, body and mind and soul, and knew this didn't finish anything.

———

Jerningham was back from Wanganui by the month's end and Colonel Wakefield charged us jointly with overseeing road building and reporting progress back to the committee.

The Company had employed labourers to cut a road along the waterfront from Wellington to Pito-one. "Some-one needs to employ them," the colonel said, rather bitterly.

The resulting bullock track linked the settlements and I rode it reluctantly with Jerningham. Reluctantly, partly because I had never learned to ride well and feared falling, and partly because I didn't want to be with Jerningham. I was still uncomfortable with him after his insult at Wanganui.

It was a relief to find him subdued and riding with restraint on his hired nag. He mumbled like a petulant child about the lack of decent horses in the colony but now I made no offer to follow up the breeders in Sydney for him. The next day we rode the bridal paths in progress from Kaiwharawhara to Porirua and up the hill to Karori, where Malloy and several others had built fine country houses and were quickly burning farms out of the forest.

One afternoon Jerningham invited me to dine at the Wakefield Club, an exclusive little set of about twenty men who gathered in the evenings in a small house in town. I had been invited once previously by Dr Evans but had declined. I imagined them sitting around in the panelled dining room with a well-laid table pretending that outside the club walls London society went about its business and cabs stood waiting to take them home at a fast clip through Mayfair.

"Thank you," I said. "I'll come."

An incident that morning had left me troubled, and through our day of riding and meeting with the surveyors I had not managed to shake my suspicions. I found it impossible to broach such an intimate subject in everyday conversation with Jerningham but, in the confined and face-to-face situation of a formal dining table, where good manners were assured, I decided to take him to task.

Jerningham had walked into the Exchange around breakfast time. It was an early hour for him to be up and about. I was with Dorothy, who wanted to look around the new library. We were leaving with our books when he appeared. I naturally stepped forward to introduce him to my wife, but she disappeared from my side, back into the shadow of the wall. Jerningham turned away. I fetched him and brought him over to where she hid and made the introduction.

Dorothy was rigid as he bent quickly over her hand without his usual flourish of gallantry and then went off about his business. He hardly gave her a glance.

My wife, perhaps, I could understand. She was shy. But for Jerningham to make no eye contact with a woman, particularly a woman as young and indisputably pretty as Dorothy, meant something was at play. His words at Whare Wikitoria had not left me. *Lugg is a lackey*. And, *why would you marry what a man can get for free?*

It takes an effort of will to ignore a suspicion that you do not want to entertain, that has no part in your life. But a notion that a thing is hidden is hard to ignore. I needed Jerningham to tell me there was no secret, nothing I didn't already know. In belittling me and my wife he had just been a nasty man playing to the crowd.

Had it meant nothing? In the formal setting of his club, I would make him confirm it.

When dusk came I put on my best suit, my hat and gloves, and went along Lambton Quay to the Wakefield Club. Jerningham was waiting at the reception area for me. For a second I hardly recognised him. He had shaved his heavy beard off and left a handsome moustache and long whiskers. It opened up his expressive face to give a younger, more playful appearance.

"Do you approve, Arthur?" He lifted his chin and rubbed the missing growth. "It was getting very hot under there. Like carrying around the entire Karori forest on my chin." He gave me one of his intimate smiles with a warmth that filled the small vestibule. "And it was a quick and easy way to earn my uncle's good favour again."

He shook my hand, tilted his head towards the heavy curtain that screened the door into the club and gave the laugh that said *come along with me, we'll have some fun.*

"Henry Mayhew has sent us copies of his new magazine, *Punch*," he said as he held the curtain for me. "You know Henry? He's poking fun at what he calls the London Charivari. All satire and jokes, but bound to put noses out of joint." He was flattering me to pretend I might know Henry Mayhew. Obviously it wasn't just his uncle's good favour he was trying to win.

We went through into the smoking room and I stood on proper carpet for the first time since leaving England. I felt uneasy in the place. Although I had grown up in a masculine household, our rooms had been simply furnished. They encouraged reflection. In this book-lined room the armchairs were deep, the curtains plush and the oil paintings on green walls showed hunting scenes. It was a room in which to contemplate power.

There were a few men standing by the stacked but unlit fireplace. The room was hot. The curtains, instead of keeping the summer heat out, seemed to intensify the warmth, and cigar smoke already swirled along the ceiling. Jerningham indicated I should sit. He poured whisky for us from a decanter service on a side table. They were heavy measures, soft liquid in cut glass. I drank readily and shifted in my deep chair. I found I had forgotten which way my legs crossed. Dr Evans entered but joined the standing party across the room.

"The menu looks rather good tonight," Jerningham said, his tone light and conversational as if he wasn't expecting a discussion about my wife. He looked around at the door occasionally. "The whitebait have gone, more's the pity, but there are oysters and a decent asparagus soup. And a beef and ale pie. Do you like oysters, Lugg?"

"Thank you, yes." I didn't have small talk prepared. I wondered who he was watching for. I hoped the colonel was not expected.

Jerningham refilled our glasses and pointed out the newspapers from England on the tables.

"Never less than a hundred days off the press. The old country could have fallen into the sea by now for all we know."

I drank.

"Ah, but we know you are not a political man, don't we, Lugg? You keep your opinions close to your chest."

Just one glass and I was back to being Lugg. I was Arthur when he wanted my forgiveness but it seemed that time was over and his confidence had returned. He made my name a cumbersome word, as if I were something he lugged around.

I ignored his question and looked around at the richness of the room. I hadn't come to discuss politics. I had come to ask why he had slandered my wife.

The colonial elite arrived and settled in armchairs. They lit pipes, took books or newspapers or gossiped quietly. When Ada's husband arrived I nodded to him briefly, as if he were of no consequence to me, but I allowed the corner of my lips to curl upwards. The fact that he spent his evenings at the club meant that he was not at home with Ada. I accepted a third glass of whisky and shortly after, when it was gone, I followed Jerningham unsteadily through into the dining room.

To my surprise, Dr Dorset was there and seated at our table. I didn't imagine he was a club member.

As I sat down, Dorset placed a small paper parcel on the plate in front of me.

"What's this?" I asked.

I could feel the whisky now. Seated, it had flowed down to warm my boots, but in walking across the room it appeared to have replaced my blood and was pumping through my veins to my heart and head.

Jerningham sat opposite and leaned across the table at me with a wide grin.

"It's a present."

I looked at Dorset, who returned a conceited look.

"A present?"

"Open it, Lugg."

Confused, I pulled the bow to undo the string and folded back the paper. There were others around now, men who seemed to join us by some private arrangement of which I was unaware. Dr Evans stood behind Jerningham and Mr Molesworth was with him, watching.

Something tipped out of the paper and clattered onto my plate.

It was made of wood, with a leather joint and a soft leather pad where a strap fed through a small, flat, brass buckle. The wood was richly coloured and polished and when I picked it up it felt satisfyingly heavy. This was a beautiful thing, with the dip of a fingernail carved on the surface, in a shape I instantly recognised. My thumb.

Unable to resist I slipped my fingers through the strap and Dorset reached over to pull it snug across my palm, nodding as he adjusted the fit. My stump slotted into the cavity and was held warm against the soft leather.

I moved the joint. The thumb moved. It was a new thumb. My new thumb.

I looked down at my matching hands in wonder.

I knew when I looked over at Jerningham I had tears in my eyes.

"The clay?" I asked. "That day in Wanganui when we were shooting? You kept the clay?"

He still wore his indulgent smile. In my blurred vision it appeared he was crying too.

"How is it?" he asked, and he took my hands in his and turned them over and around in front of my eyes. I felt whole again.

"Thank you, Jerningham," I said.

Around me, the men erupted in applause.

When I got home, late and flush with food and friendship, I woke Dorothy. She sat up with her heavy hair tumbling from the night scarf and leaned across the bed to reach for the lamp. I sat beside her and put my hand with its new thumb in her lap for her to admire. I could feel the heat from her warm limbs and smell her sleep perfume.

"Jerningham had Dorset make it for me," I said. "He is the best friend a man could have."

Dorothy lifted my hand and, as Jerningham had done in the club, she turned it over and around to admire the craftmanship, the leather joint and carved nail, the way it fitted. Once again, I was a fully integrated man. She stroked it and then she stroked my face. She said nothing as she helped me with my buttons, and then laid back as I pulled her gown from around her buttocks and lifted her hands so I could pull it over her head. I had not laid her out naked like this before. I was bold and hot and when I touched her breast with the tip of my new thumb she arched up. I ran the wooden tip down the length of her body from her mouth, pausing at the hollow of her throat and drifting slowly between her full breasts, tapping over the rise of her belly. She opened her legs for me.

I couldn't help myself. I dipped Jerningham's thumb into the soft part of her and watched her gasp.

My cock, when it came, was sapped of its usual vigour due to whisky and wine, but it was comfort enough to have Dorothy in the bed with me and to wake up with her in the rosy light of morning.

———

Jerningham's gift had a profound effect on me. I wore it strapped on my hand always, and removed it only at night, slipping the thumb off after I blew out the lamp and reattaching it when I was barely awake. I hadn't fully realised how my deformity had affected me until, gloved, I could shake a man by the hand again.

Of course, the thumb lacked any tactile sense, but the curved flexibility of the design was so lifelike and strapped so neatly into the knuckle that I quickly learned to compensate for lack of feeling by using the stump as a lever. I became visible again and I was able to stand up and take my place in the world.

I was indebted to Jerningham in a defining way. He had realised something about me that I hadn't even realised myself. He had fixed me. It was a precious gift.

Over the following months, the strange connection between Jerningham and Dorothy happened again, a few times, if we all met on the street or at a public meeting. The pair of them avoided each other's eyes every time. It was no crime. I ignored my suspicions.

But, inevitably, my relationship with my wife felt more complicated than before. I had taken her at face value and now I considered there might be things I didn't know about her past. I never questioned her, I didn't know what to ask and I didn't want answers that would confuse my understanding of her. I liked the Dorothy I had married and I wanted to protect that, so I ensured she didn't go out unaccompanied, and enlisted Lucy as her shadow when she went for the shopping. Occasionally, I would arrive home early and come quietly in the back door. My wife was always respectably engaged around the house.

And all the while, every second Friday, when Ada went to prepare her brother's house for his arrival from the country, I slipped through Malloy's back garden at noon and lifted the latch that wasn't broken. There was never any doubt that we would repeat our tryst. *Just once*, she had said. *Just to know*. And now we knew and we were reckless with it and just once was never going to be enough.

"Have you come to look at my entranceway?" Ada asked me on one occasion, shockingly, as she pulled me inside.

We had forgotten about the conversations we wanted to have and our unfinished talks on philosophy and politics. We barely spoke, our respective lives held no interest to the other. We always went directly to the little room upstairs and barely stripped off our clothes before falling onto the folded quilt to take possession of each other, wildly, greedily.

We weren't tender lovers, we didn't take time to learn each other's bodies, we didn't enjoy the long slow, running fuse of build-up. It was eager, fast intercourse that took us frantically to explosion and left us entangled, breathing in great flutters.

I asked nothing about her married life, and she asked nothing about Dorothy. They were things that happened in another room and we agreed we wouldn't invite them in.

Ada gave herself willingly, with no hesitation or shame, as if she belonged to me. When I was with her, I thought of nothing else, my life safely contained behind closed doors. We both knew we had no option but to accept these stolen hours as a gift. The attraction of her naked body drew me to her with the inevitability of waves crashing on a beach.

I continued to come to the door and she continued to let me in, and we were happy together in that little room. We never mentioned the fact that we should have been married to each other.

———

In May we heard that Hobson, now Governor Hobson, had read a proclamation in Auckland that freed us from Australia and established New Zealand as an independent colony of Britain. As he had done many times before, he promised to visit our settlement in Wellington, but the promise went unfulfilled.

"Hobson's coming!" people would say, meaning, *here's a blow of wind that heralds nothing*.

Revans, back now in his rebuilt house on the waterfront, continued to whip up anti-government sentiment in his newspaper and seemed to go slowly mad with frustration. The last straw for him was the announcement that Hobson had chosen the founding Legislative Council for the country, and there was not one New Zealand Company representative appointed.

"Have you heard this?" he raged to a packed congregation at Barrett's Bar, where we gathered for the news. Restless settlers stomped and jostled. "Representative government that represents a few swamp dwellers! Nothing more! Our governor still refuses to visit Wellington, where the vast majority of his subjects live. He governs a few muddy missionaries and some lawless traders in the north and the overpaid sycophants in Auckland. There's no seat for any of us on the council! What are they afraid of?"

"They're afraid of *you*, Mr Revans!" shouted some wag from the back and the crowd roared with laughter. Revans waved them down, calming the room to be heard above the noise. "They tax us and censure us, but we have no voice.

Do you know, he has renamed our islands? Hobson calls them: New Ulster, New Munster and New Leinster. When what we all would really prefer is a New Hobson!"

His audience clapped and cheered.

"Do we live in New Ulster, my friends?"

"No!"

Revans came to see me one night in May, late at night when Dorothy had retired and I was about to go up. He was already drunk but insisted I open a bottle of wine and drink with him.

I had a good supply in the cellar by then and let him choose. He wasn't a selective drinker and took the closest one I offered.

"I can't do this anymore, Arthur. Can't keep fighting with words and whipping 'em all up in meetings like I'm some kind of preacher. We're all of us thrashing around and nothing will be achieved if we don't work together, but who's to lead us, hmmm? Where's our leader, the man of strength and vision to pull all this together?"

He rubbed his bushy eyebrows with stumpy fingers and emptied his glass in gulps. I pushed the bottle across.

"For a long time I thought Wakefield could do it," he said, which rather surprised me.

"I never thought you saw eye to eye with the colonel?"

"Oh Christ, man, I don't mean William! That brainless bag of pomp. He'll never have the guts to take them on. Edward Gibbon Wakefield, though, is a man of extraordinary ability. Ever meet him?"

"The Wakefields and I moved in different circles, Sam," I said. "Back in England."

"He's a man with ideas. Too many of 'em, sometimes. He pulls solutions out of the sky when you think all is lost and hey presto, you're all back in the game. But he's easily distracted and who knows where his attention is now? He's busy with his colonies in Canada and in Australia. He should be *here*. We emigrated as a result of his considerable persuasion and he's abandoned us to be ruled by these mediocre minds."

I wasn't sure if he was referring to Hobson or Colonel Wakefield. Or both.

"Captain Arthur Wakefield is coming in a few months, of course, with the Nelson colonists," said Revans. "Gibbon preferred him for Wellington but he was serving out his army commission, so we got William instead. Arthur's a decent enough man. Disciplined. But, again, no *vision*. Not a man for these intricate negotiations with the Māori and the Crown." He waved his arm around and the wine slopped out and onto his jacket. "Jerningham's the only one with any political *brilliance* at all, but the boy's unstable, the colonel has no control over him, this place has turned his head. Oh, yes, I know you two are as thick as thieves. You need to watch him, Arthur."

I nodded, serious now. "I do watch him. I do. And I worry about him. But I can't see that I have any influence."

"He could be quite the politician if he weren't so self-absorbed. Certainly has the acumen for it. But the boy's forever showing off. Never got his father's attention as a lad, you know. His mother died in childbirth and Gibbon wouldn't have anything to do with him for a long time. Of course Gibbon was in jail during Jerningham's formative years. Probably why the boy's so reckless now."

"He's young," I said, without much conviction. "He'll settle down."

Revans's eyebrows shot up in surprise. "You think so?"

I didn't want to talk about Jerningham. The wine had made me sleepy and I was ready to go up to bed.

"What of you, Sam?" I said. "You came here tonight looking like a man with something on his mind."

Revans shifted in his chair, pushing his bulky frame back to sit straighter. He ran his hand over his springy hair a couple of times, which did nothing to improve his dishevelled appearance. "I'm running out of steam for the *Gazette*," he said. "I haven't got the energy and I can't stomach the hypocrisy. And they've stopped paying me, you know. There are several bills outstanding. I'm sure you are aware of the money issues facing the Company and there's no income here to speak of, nor likelihood of one the near future. I've got a little timber enterprise going on the side with Mein Smith, don't you know, and I plan to keep my head down, focus on business. It's enough to keep a man occupied. We're thinking of a farm too, further afield—we've got a few dairy cows due at Evans Bay to start the herd. It's a less complicated and less compromising life."

"What will happen to the paper?"

He heaved himself up even straighter and shot me a surprisingly sober look, though his glass tipped and the dregs of his wine sloshed out. "Well, my boy, I wondered if you—"

"Good heavens," I said, "that's the worst business offer I've ever heard!"

Revans coughed and muttered a bit and brushed the spilt wine from his shambolic suit.

I poured him another glass and we sat for a while in silence as the candles burned down. None of us had got what we expected in the colony. The fresh start had fooled us for less than a year before we realised it was inevitably tainted with the sourness of the past. All our inabilities had run like rats onto the ships with us.

Revans was right in saying there was no man of vision to lead us. We each carried images of how this new world should be shaped: what to exploit and what to save, who to champion and who to challenge. We squabbled and criticised and waited for some kind of sense to prevail and we lost sight of the very thing we had come here for—the better world. Our great utopia had been replaced by a place of petty fighting. Revans was exhausted from his ranting against the government, the missionaries and the Company, but each was as bad as the other, all scrabbling for power, trampling over rights and ideals, bribing the Māori for land or labour or souls, with the Māori supporting whoever would give them a fighting advantage over their blood-thirsty neighbours. The missionaries preached but no one heeded the lessons.

And yet, for all the chaos we left in our wake, the colony progressed. New settlers continued to arrive, and Revans and I continued to grumble and drink into the small hours. We never ran out of wine.

WANGANUI AND HOBSON

TO JERNINGHAM'S DELIGHT, over the winter several ships brought decent riding horses to town. A few settlers had fenced acres, and where they had burned the fern off, bright tussock grass now sprouted vividly on the hills. We visited them all.

Wellington's climate of warmth and rain ensured steady growth, but the native grasses weren't ideal feed for the horses. Like everything else that didn't quite conform to plan, this, too, became the Company's problem.

"We need English grasses. Clover," the farmers told Jerningham and he nodded to me as if he intended I should rush off immediately and source an importer of clover.

I had selected a strong bay mare for myself. Jerningham said I paid over the odds for her and no doubt I did, but she was the reliable mount I needed, and with her I grew quickly more comfortable on horseback. My new thumb helped. I couldn't grip with it but my stump levered the contraption into a holding position and to look down at proper hands holding the reins gave me much confidence.

Jerningham received notice that his shipment of horses was finally due in Wanganui, the ones that had been diverted up the coast before Christmas. Colonel Wakefield suggested I accompany him overland and gather reports from the surveyors he had out in the field. When I heard

Charles Heaphy would also be one of the party, I readily agreed.

We planned for three weeks away, but the days stretched out and, in the end, we were nearly two months from Wellington. I wrote to Dorothy and explained I was delayed on Company business, but there was nothing stopping me returning at any time as there were regular ships running along the coast. I was enjoying being back in the company of men and riding my mare through the forests and along the beaches, and when the nights came in early we had a fire and a pipe and often a song. Charles, as always, was good company. He had brought his chess set along and we played by lamplight, sitting under a tarpaulin stretched between the trees. Either he had improved considerably or I had lost my edge. Even Jerningham managed to beat me.

"That new thumb is distracting you and ruining your game," he said. "Take it off and I'll give you another shot."

"I won't," I said. "It distracts me from your smug face. You can play Charles. There's a pouch of my American leaf if you beat him." I gave my spot on the canvas to Charles, who clicked his knuckles like a boxer before setting up his men. He beat Jerningham easily.

"Uncle Arthur gave me this set," said Jerningham to Charles, immediately repositioning the pieces on the board. "I might have to borrow it back off you when he arrives. Or perhaps I can win it back. Best of three?"

Best of three turned into five and then seven and by the end of the week Jerningham had lost his horse.

"Heaphy's become a clever little bastard," Jerningham said to me, "but I don't care about the nag. There are better horses waiting for me in Wanganui."

We visited the wreck of the *Jewess* schooner, which had run onto the rocks abreast of Porirua in April, with a cargo of goods and settlers bound for Wanganui. She was a sad sight, lying with her belly exposed on the sand like a stranded whale. Some cargo had been salvaged but most had been looted by the natives and the settlers had been obliged to go on, without possessions and on foot, to their new settlement, where I knew they would find little enough to welcome them.

We stayed again with Reverend Hadfield at Waikanae. This time I came with pockets full of enamel buttons and trinkets collected from a Chinese trader, but I didn't get the same charming response as Jerningham when I handed them out. I hadn't remembered names or faces and was clumsy with greetings. The language I had learnt with Para and Aata sounded stilted.

Hadfield spoke of an important kōrero with the local tribes, and talk was of a war party coming down from Taupō to join forces with the Ngāti Raukawa tribe to revenge their defeat at Waikanae the previous year. Te Puni and Wharepōuri had brought their warriors from Port Nicholson to fight alongside their Te Āti Awa relations on the coast and the tribes were on the verge of full-scale war, but it appeared that Hadfield had stepped in with his diplomacy and clever negotiation and averted the bloodshed, for now.

Te Puni was delighted to see me, and, as always, surprised to find me still alive. Perhaps he imagined as soon as I was out of his sight I was likely to come to grief. He was pleased to be going home with all his men and his mana intact.

"Mr Hadfield, true man of peace. Everybody agree, go home, no fighting," he said, and then he smiled. "A miracle!"

We carried our weapons close to hand as we rode north through Ngāti Raukawa territory but, although Jerningham stopped to question the local chiefs he knew, we saw nothing to alarm us. The Māori we passed were working their neatly cleared garden plots, weeding vegetables and trimming branches in the orchards. Even in the winter there were cabbages and onions and rows of dark green spinach against the well-tilled earth. All was peaceful and orderly.

I enjoyed the ride, my new mare was sound and responsive, the weather cool but dry, and the light was as sharp and clear as the best of an English winter. Unlike the bare trees of England, here the winter vegetation was lush and exotic and full of green.

—

Once in Wanganui we left Jerningham to his affairs, while Charles, another surveyor and I rode out and marked the progress of the district. They updated maps and confirmed boundaries. Charles was enjoying his new horse, though he always seemed to me a man happiest on foot.

"Will you give Jerningham back his chess set?" I asked, and Charles's laugh made me realise he would never be won over. His animosity to Jerningham was not publicly admitted, but it was very real and a permanent thing.

We heard disturbing reports of angry immigrants and we stayed away from the town with our backs to the noise. Politics were Jerningham's affair, but it was hard to avoid the disquiet. One troublesome settler stirred up mischief over a piece of unallocated land and got the mihanere to protest against the Company. The entire settlement got riled and fighting broke out: loyal settlers against hostile settlers, unconverted Māori against converted, the mihanere. Māori could always find an argument to inflame that might go back generations, and immigrants whipped them up as it suited them—over land, over payment, over the prediction that the Company would steal everything they owned and chase them and their families into the hills to starve.

Jerningham gave up any pretence at bringing justice and declared he was no longer a company agent. The protesters, he said, should address their concerns to Wide-awake in Wellington.

He had other preoccupations. His trading business was booming. His little schooner, the *Sandfly*, was busy along the coast, and he juggled pigs and tobacco, grog and household equipment for the growing number of settlers that had drifted into town. He and his friend Kuru had a herd of branded pigs running on the hills behind the settlement, and together with a pack of dogs and a scruffy group of locals, they rounded them up for trade. Passing whalers dropped salt and barrels for him to fill with pork for their return.

Jerningham claimed now to be an expert in the hunting, slaughter and salting of pigs.

"I got a couple of good pig dogs off Kuru last month," he told me one evening as we sat under canvas, somewhere north of the top line of the district. "They know to go for the jowl or the ear. Dogs that take the hams spoil the meat. I had to sell my last pack, though they were good runners. Kept going for the haunches." He stretched out his legs and pulled on his pipe and blew smoke through the open tent flap up into the winter night. His beard was growing back in and his face was lean and wind burnt, white creases around his eyes. "I got a litter out of the bitch first though, and I'll get Kuru's boy to train the pups. There's money in dogs, Lugg. Every settler will need a pack for hunting or protection."

One of his mongrel companions slept outside, an Australian kangaroo dog, part mastiff and part greyhound, with a bit of bulldog thrown in. It wasn't a friendly animal, but it was fiercely loyal to Jerningham. Its night-time prowling and snarling gave me uneasy sleep but there were travelling chancers drifting along the trails now, pilfering and alarming honest settlers. There had been murders, too, of settlers by natives. I stayed close to Jerningham.

"I've got another domestic bitch littering in spring," he said. "She's a mongrel but I put her to a terrier and she'll breed smart town dogs. I'll keep a couple of pups aside for you."

Pigs and dogs and horses and trade—he had his fingers everywhere.

We returned to Wanganui the following afternoon along an old Māori trail despoiled by the trampling hooves of oxen. On a steep barren hillside we climbed over a slip where a narrow path had fallen away and saw, in the gully below, a beast with a belly swollen like a whale, stinking in a swarm of flies. The trail of hooves passed on up the hill above, a pointer to some settler's new occupation.

"I need to drop by the shop," said Jerningham, as we reached the river and the plank and canvas town came into view. "You may as well come along."

The shop was unnamed, a small trading post and one of several within the boundaries of the town but away from the river, in amongst the Māori shacks, where I seldom went. There were pans and tin buckets hanging on a rail outside, stacks of roughly cut planks stacked by the door, and inside the smells from the open barrels of pickled cabbage competed with cakes of soap.

I asked if he was keeping proper books. Wanganui was a lawless place, but no business was above the law when it came to taxes. Of course he laughed. Jerningham, like the common miscreants and thieves of the town, remained ungoverned.

"You're hardly setting a good example," I said.

He pushed a stack of paper over the table at me. There were scrawled notes of trades done: a keg of tobacco for some bushels of raupō and some sawn planks, a cask of wine for unspecified labour, tea and flour for ... it looked like a name ... *Molly*. Only the missionary, Mr Mason, paid in cash—hard silver for two kegs of tobacco.

"You sort it out then, Lugg. You're a bookkeeper."

"I *was* a bookkeeper," I said. "I might retire and paint watercolours. You could commission me to paint something for your shop, but I doubt you could afford my prices."

"Has Heaphy finished his drawing to send home?"

"The shameless advertisement? I think so, yes. He just needs to add the angels. Perhaps your father will have them embellished in gold leaf before printing."

"Oh, for heaven's sake! You are a cynic. I sometimes wonder if you want us to succeed here."

"Well," I said. "I do wonder about the wisdom of sending more settlers out when we can't house the ones we have. Shouldn't we hold off until this land-claims business is settled?"

Jerningham shook his head slowly and rolled his eyes. "You're such a small thinker, Lugg. So little ambition. I'm surprised you were ever brave enough to leave your front room."

Whenever he got nasty, the comment from Whare Wikitoria surfaced. It was never far from my mind. *Why marry what you can have for free?* Jerningham took a bottle from under the counter, poured whisky into grubby glasses and pushed one across the counter to me, shoving the paperwork aside.

I narrowed my eyes. Women, generally? Or Dorothy, specifically? The thought came and went; I had trained myself to let it go. I drank, but the grog had a muddy flavour. It tasted like Wanganui smelled, that hint of something rancid just below the surface.

"Tell Heaphy I need him tomorrow, and the other men. I'm bringing in the horses. I need all hands—even your crippled ones."

I held up my gloved hands and waggled my fingers in front of him. Ten digits, same as any man.

I walked back along the river to the lodgings and a quiet evening in with my companions, leaving Jerningham to whatever he did with his nights. Charles was intrigued with my report of Whare Wikitoria and I sent him along to poke his head around the door. He reported a den of ruffians, white savages, he called them—smoking, drinking and playing dice—and there were local women, but Jerningham was no longer dressed as a Māori chief. He was just a drunk, no different to any other.

Early the next morning, as promised, the horses came off the barge. They were thin-legged and wild-eyed, but Jerningham calmly wrapped his arm over each neck and whispered nonsense as he led them through the shallows and gently up onto solid ground. He paid with cash and small portables, and we led the skittish horses up into the hills a long way to the north of the town.

Jerningham's agent, a young Englishman called Smith off the *Adelaide*, had fenced a small plateau above a valley, where the native grasses had grown over cleared hills.

"Who owns this land?" I asked Jerningham.

"It's not on the map," he replied. "But I have an arrangement with Kuru."

"You can't just appropriate land!"

"Who knows? It's only for long enough to fatten them up. Smith has a couple of lads coming to break them in, stable hands with Somerset pig shit still on their boots—I daresay you'll recognise the smell. We'll be clear of here by spring, the boys will ride them to Wellington. I'll sell 'em to Malloy."

I looked across to Charles but he kept eyes fixed forward and didn't engage. For once he appeared not to have his charts or his pencils, those tools of the trade he took everywhere.

It was a long walk back to town and dark came early. Jerningham took us to a hot and muggy chop shop in the settlement between the canvas and driftwood shacks along the river, and we ate a tepid, greasy dinner of lamb and rice. The rice tasted like it had been boiled in river mud but the lamb was tender and fresh, if only partially cooked. We toasted the success of his horsey enterprise with mugs of strong ale and Jerningham settled the account with a small bag of tobacco and a few leather washcloths.

A few days later we got the news that the governor finally intended a visit to Wellington and so we packed up and rode south, without any particular rush. None of us believed Hobson would really materialise anywhere south of Auckland. We'd been shouting, "Hobson's coming!" into the wind for eighteen months.

—

We got back to Wellington on a Friday morning. It was the second Friday of the month, the day before one of Malloy's weekends in town. Ada would be preparing his house for their arrival. Before I went home I walked down the back lane and pushed the flax leaf into the fence. I felt a great physical need for Ada and her generous, responsive loving. At home I greeted Dorothy, gave her some little presents that I had picked up along the road and took a bath to wash off the mud.

Then I said I had some work to attend to, and I went back into town, past Malloy's. Above my folded flax, another leaf was tucked neatly into the fence.

"I thought you weren't coming back!" said Ada.

I leaned her against the wall in the scullery and ran my fingers up her soft, plump legs under rustling skirts. Her hands were everywhere, pulling my face towards her so she could press my lips open and offer me her passion. I felt her ache for me. It thrilled me to push her up against the sideboard with the foaming mass of petticoats around her hips, she all but fainting in her corsetry constraint and me tied by my trousers at the knees.

We staggered upstairs, unlacing as we climbed and came again in our little room, sticky with passion and lust and desire more powerful than anything else in my life. She was the essence of me. I planted my pole in her earth and rose above her and she threw back her head and moaned.

Afterwards, she wiped herself down with a cloth, dressed quickly and bundled her frizzy hair up under her bonnet.

"Come back here," I said. "I need you again. Get undressed. One more time, Ada."

"I mustn't. Not today."

We had agreed never to ask, or to question.

I had been away for two months and yet we hardly passed a word. We had formed a habit of minimal conversation, the very thing I used to think I needed from her. This other force pushed everything aside until it was satisfied but it seemed we could never get enough, never let anything else in. I watched her hasty movements. She was clumsy—her ribbon hung down from her hair and her skirt was bunched unevenly.

I didn't help as she struggled with petticoats and the things that trailed. I liked to look at her like this, fussing about her clothing, knowing I had just pinned her naked and shuddering beneath me.

"You'll need to go, too," she said. "I have to close the latch."

"When can we spend a night together, Ada? I want to wake up with you. To talk with you."

She fluttered her hands then, and turned away from me to hide her face. "We can't, Arthur. Please get dressed now."

So I did. I pulled on my breeches and shirt, tied my

cravat, shrugged into my jacket and laced my boots. I smoothed my ruffled hair. Then I clattered downstairs, weak at the knees.

Ada was standing by the back door and she was crying. My joy collapsed like a punched face.

I knew immediately.

I couldn't imagine why I had been so slow.

It was different for her. Of course I struggled, but I managed to put Ada and my other life in separate places so I could cope with the deception we practised. I had my love for her here, and the rest of my life, including my wife, over there. Women's emotions were more fragile.

She stood with her eyes to the floor, her crinkled hair falling over her face and her wide, unhappy mouth turned down and quivering. She wouldn't look at me.

I didn't have any words for her. My explanations crumbled. I had nothing to say that would even begin to make amends. I knew what Ada and I did together was inexcusable.

We had closed our eyes and followed our lusts and let the demons inside us twist our understanding of right and wrong until the damage, always irreversible, was blatant. We did these things upstairs in that little room so fast we couldn't stop to admit that our love was a landscape of volcanoes and storms.

I stepped towards her but saw a ripple of tension. She didn't want me to hold her.

I was tuned to every tiny movement she made, every flicker of her face. I had studied that face through so much, and in so many moods. She had no disguises. I knew Ada.

And I knew that, now, she didn't want me there. I went past her, lifted the latch, and let myself out.

I went home.

The following Thursday a little vessel came through the heads and toiled across the harbour. The telescopes came out.

"Is that our cattle?" the colonel asked Jerningham, who was at the window.

"Too far out yet to see," he said. "Too small for cattle. She's a lubber of a ship, too slow for a whaler. Ha! Probably our governor in a bucket!"

We all went to the window. The ship made its way between the barques, brigs and schooners at anchor. We had a full and impressive harbour, with traders and whalers in port and a cluster of coasters.

"That is, indeed, the *Victoria*," said Colonel Wakefield.

"What a very inferior craft." Jerningham offered his telescope around.

As she approached we could make out the red ensign at the peak and the Union Jack flying on the mainmast. We looked at each other in disbelief.

Jerningham, finally, laughed. "Well, come on then, put out a flag for him! Hobson is here!"

As the police magistrate and the postmaster rowed out to meet him—"They have to go. He pays their wages," said Jerningham—the colonel sent a boy to raise the flag at his home in recognition. It was a token gesture only. We made no other welcome for the governor's arrival and the ship bobbed, neglected, on the tide.

The next day we stood on the beach watching as Hobson and his men climbed down into the row-boat, but as he neared the beach, on Jerningham's signal, we all retreated indoors. I was at Dr Dorset's house with many others and we didn't so much as look out the window as he stepped ashore. We had decided against hissing. I, for one, would not hiss at a governor appointed by the Queen, but we agreed there would be no cheers for the man who had been so negligent toward us for so long. Jerningham, peering around from behind Dorset's curtain like some neighbourhood tittle-tattle, said there were some Māori and a few rough labourers on the beach and some lunatic on a horse by the side of the boat, splashing the governor and his party and shouting greetings.

Not one respectable colonist was there.

Dr Dorset poured wine, and we toasted the colony, the Company and the colonel, who had done so much more for our well-being than the small, lonely man on the beach.

The governor walked quietly over the sand and up to Barrett's Hotel, and once he was ensconced indoors with his entourage we all went back onto the streets.

Governor Hobson spent the weekend inside.

"Will you meet him?" I asked Charles, who had come to my house for dinner. I often invited friends for dinner now, it made the evenings more lively than long hours spent alone with Dorothy.

"I have an appointment with the surveyor-general, who is with him," he said, "but I won't meet the governor until he behaves like our representative rather than some foreign diplomat come to bleed us with taxes. You?"

"I'm invited to the gathering on Tuesday, but you know, I find it is the only day I have spare to supervise the work on my henhouse. The poor colonel has rustled up fewer than twenty men to attend, and most of those have to borrow a suit."

Tuesday was strangely quiet on Lambton Quay. Astride his horse outside the hotel, Jerningham chatted to the governor's smartly uniformed aide-de-camp, who stood on the doorstep rather forlornly trying to gather guests to greet our visitor.

"Lugg!" Jerningham called to me as I passed on the other side of the road, almost on the beach in my attempt to keep away. "Oh, come on now, a pouch of my best tobacco if you step inside and meet the governor. Our man here is at a loss for customers and I am finding it hard to help him."

I waved and smiled but didn't pause in my fast walk.

I met Te Puni and Wharepōuri sitting in the sun further along the beach front. They were smoking their long-stemmed pipes and looking out over the water.

"The drowned man," said Te Puni, who stood with great politeness to shake my hand.

"You do not meet the governor," Wharepōuri said. It wasn't a question. I shook my head but gave no reasons. "His jacket is very nice," said the chief, and brushed his hand over the shoulders of his cloak as if imagining the fringe of a golden epaulette beneath his fingers. "He has small body like a boy but face like old man. Line here, line here." Wharepōuri dragged his fingers down his cheeks. He would have been only a handful of years younger than the governor, but his skin, chiseled with its curled dark tattoo, was firm, and he stood with his chest forward as if he carried imaginary wings on his back. "He does not walk like a man of great mana," he said, and it was hard to disagree. If he was looking for an explanation of why our great chief was lacking in gravitas, I couldn't give it.

"We meet Mr Clarke," Te Puni told me, tapping his pipe out on the stones. I had a pouch of tobacco in my pocket, some of Jerningham's best American, and I brought it out and filled their pipes, though we had nothing to light them with. "He is now our protector. I take him to meet all chief. He give back our tapu ground and our pā."

I discovered later that Clarke was an agent of the Church Missionary Society, recently elevated to a newly appointed role of chief protector of the aborigines. He slunk about the pā, seeking the discontented and offering an ear for their grievances and petty hostilities. He got on the wrong side of the colonel early on by making some lewd suggestions that a payment made for land was actually payment for a woman. This was a terrible accusation to make against Colonel Wakefield, who led the settlement in propriety. Clarke was left looking entirely ridiculous. The colonel refused to have anything to do with this new busybody, and the incident shoved the wedge deeper between the Company and the Missionary Society.

Colonel Wakefield, Mr Hanson and Dr Evans escorted Governor Hobson about the settlement. He was a gaunt figure in a fine costume and wore a withdrawn, almost haunted look. They took him to the farms in the valley to meet our men of industry and commerce, impressing on Hobson what a fine settlement we had become, knowing well that his chosen capital, Auckland, was a miserable few huts bordering a wasteland.

Even though many of Wellington's colonial leaders had actively petitioned to remove him and were reluctant to engage with his assembly, over the course of the following weeks there was little we could do but accept the fact that Hobson was our administrator and the law flowed from his hands. The governor got his business done, appointing members to his government from the least resistant.

"Going over to the enemy," Revans said, when Hanson was appointed crown prosecutor and immediately took on the haughty arrogance of the Auckland men, along with his treasury payment.

"I am a magistrate," Jerningham announced one afternoon, as he returned from a meeting with the governor. The wind and rain came at a slant across the harbour and he had run down the road and burst into the office, bringing the wild weather with him.

"You jest!"

He flung his coat over the stand and stood in front of the fire, which hissed and spat as he shook himself like a wet dog. "Indeed not. I am a magistrate of Wanganui, along with three others. *And* we get a constabulary. Oh, I know, Lugg." He seemed delighted by my shocked expression, as if the trick of behaving unexpectedly outweighed all other considerations. "You didn't expect that."

"Well, no, not that. To date you have been consistently outspoken against the governor and all he embodies. Though your inconsistencies have long ceased to surprise me. Tell me what has persuaded you, so suddenly, to take Hobson's coin?"

He did one of his about-faces, throwing me into the wrong for my doubt. His laughter fell away. He turned away for a moment to stoke up the fire to a smouldering pile, clattering the irons against the grate.

"It's Wanganui. You know my efforts there. If nothing is done to bring it to order, all my work is for nothing."

"This is about ensuring a return for your investments, then?"

"No." The centre of the fire caught and flames burst behind him. "No, that was uncalled for, even from you. I don't give a fig about investments, there is nothing up there making any profit for me. I give it all away, you know, in gifts and incentives. But I love Wanganui, I have put so much into it and I see thieves and villains destroying the very fabric of the town. Without vested power there is so little I can do. I mediate, and they're at each other's throats again within days. The abuse of the law is constant. Loose characters come to town specifically to steal from honest settlers and I have no authority to bring them to justice. Someone has to promote the peace and I have accepted the commission."

"I congratulate you."

The puff went out of him then and his shoulders dropped. "I know what you think, Lugg. You think I am no better than anyone else."

I thought he was considerably worse than anyone else, but I held my tongue.

"It may well be true," he said. "Perhaps I don't have the political experience yet. But if I don't step up and do this, who will our politicians be? Shall we raise the butcher to the role? Some petty labourer? There is no line of men rushing to go over to him, you know. Mein Smith has also taken service."

"That will give him a better position from which to argue with your uncle."

"You can sit on your hands and scoff, Lugg," he said, my lack of enthusiasm obviously annoying him. "Let me know when you make your contribution."

I smiled at him then. I knew something he did not. Dorothy was carrying my contribution to the colony and he would arrive in about six months.

CRISIS AND
CONFRONTATION

THE MIDWIFE came downstairs with fat feet on the narrow treads. She gave me a grimace and nod and I unclenched my hands from the edge of the table. I had held the promise of our child for less than a week. Lucy had run to fetch first Mrs Knowles, and then me from the office. By the time I got home it was over.

As I went to the dresser to find my purse and fumbled for the money, she chatted in what she probably imagined was a reassuring way about the mechanics of what happens when a woman loses a baby.

"When it happens early on, like this one, it's not a bad thing, Mr Lugg. It's just God's way of saying this isn't the one, and it is safely and easily discarded. You mustn't think on it too much. She's cleaned up, she's resting now and I've done all the necessary. I've sent your little Lucy off to the laundry, so you've nothing to do on that score. Take Mrs Lugg up a cup of tea in an hour or so, and some soup if she fancies, or something sweet, and let her rest for a day or two. As I already said to her, she's a healthy young woman, there's no reason why she mightn't go ahead and produce a family of ten strapping boys for you."

"Well, I don't know that I—"

"Many women have one or two misses before they go on to have a family. I lost two before my twins, imagine that!"

I didn't want to. I counted the coins into her hand, and when she hesitated I added another as a bonus.

"I thank you, Mr Lugg. She'll recover much easier from this than that first one, last year, which was much further on. None of them cramps this time. It were terrible, and you carrying her through all that mud. The first was worse—it usually is."

The first? Last year?

She gave me a shrewd look, the plump little woman, almost gleeful, as she watched my expression change.

He didn't know! her triumphant look said, and I could imagine the words repeated all along the mean little row where she lived, up in one of the gullies above the town that never saw the sun. *He didn't know!*

I saw her out, speechless.

I took Dorothy tea and some sugary biscuits that Lucy had made. She was wan, her hands limp on the coverlet and the room had a sharp tang to it, of salt water and blood. I plumped her pillow and held the cup out to her.

I sat next to her and felt … nothing. How should a man feel when he finds his wife has carried and lost a baby before she made her vows to him? I was as empty of emotion as the white sheet that had replaced the one Lucy had taken away. The one soaked with her blood and my blood in the child that wasn't born. A year ago in Pito-one I had carried her through the rain and laid her on a bed and brought her new sheets—sheets Jerningham paid for—as she cramped and bled out the blood of another child, made with another man's blood. Another man's blood inside my *wife*.

Her eyes were down and her habitual closed expression back, but now instead of interpreting it as sulky I saw she was defensive. She might have looked listless and floppy, but there was a full, rigid, impenetrable wall around her.

Dorothy took the teacup without looking at me. "Thank

you, Arthur," she said quietly. And then, "I am so sorry."

I tried to make her look at me, but she wouldn't. The teacup rattled in her hand and I took it away from her. "Sorry?"

She nodded.

"What are you sorry for, Dorothy?"

She did look at me then but I didn't see guilt, only bruised eyes that spoke of excruciating sadness. "I wanted to give you a child."

"Oh. I see." I couldn't bring myself to offer her any sympathy. I dropped my eyes.

I had carried her through the mud and Jerningham had pressed coins into my hand. "Fetch Mrs Knowles," he had told me. Had I known, then, that Mrs Knowles was a midwife?

Jerningham had known.

Dorothy ran her hands over her fingers, wrist, knuckle, joint, nail, pulling off the invisible gloves.

I wanted to ask—was it Jerningham's? The first time?

Breathing was suddenly difficult, there was something in my throat and I couldn't get the words out. My face was burning and it wasn't until I felt the tears fall onto my cheeks that I realised I was crying. I turned away hastily and left her alone.

I was irritable and drunk when, late that night, Sam Revans knocked on my door.

He let himself in and slumped into an armchair, his blotched face speckled with a couple of days' grey growth and eyes unfocused. I waved a bottle at him. It was empty. Revans took it to the scullery, filled it from the flagon and poured a large tumbler for himself. Even in my shambolic haze I could tell it wasn't his first of the evening, either. His cravat was flapping and collar loose. There was something slimy on his jacket front that hadn't quite dried.

"What do you want, Sam?" I could hear my words were slurred.

"First, I have a message for you, and then I want to know why you are in such a state. Perhaps the two things are related."

He looked around the dimly lit room into the shadows. There was only the one lamp and the fire burned low. "Where is your good wife? Is she tucked in upstairs, adding beauty and allure to the warm marital bed?"

I grunted. Then in an instant of absolutely clear sobriety, I thought, he knows. Revans knew about Dorothy. My corrupt wife. He had come to mock me. Perhaps Charles also knew. And the Colonel. The Colonel was the one who had pushed me towards Dorothy at the beginning! Good God, they all knew, the whole settlement knew and had taken me for a fool, used me as the cuckold, tied me up to Jerningham's discarded slut. The room spun around me and I could hear buzzing like a bee on a windowsill, thrashing against the glass.

I pushed myself out of my chair but my knees were loose and I sank immediately, a heavy drop onto the rug. "You bastard!" I lunged forward and made a grab for Revans, got a grip of his jacket, pulled myself up and swung my fist at him. He threw his arms in the air to push me away and the wine slapped into my eyes.

"Woah! Woah! Lugg, steady on. That's enough, now. Get yourself up—come on, there's the fellow, sit yourself down. Easy now. Easy now."

I had missed my footing and fallen onto my back and I felt Revans drag me by my armpits back up into the chair.

"This is not like you, my friend," he said. "Left the bottle behind, hadn't you? Made a new start? Sit down, Arthur. You're not a man for fighting. You'll do yourself a damage the way you flail about. Here, let me get a cloth for your eyes. That's right now. There. Easy now."

"You're talking to me like I'm a horse."

Or that's what I meant to say. The sounds formed strangely on my thick tongue and my lips wouldn't move properly. The window of sobriety had firmly closed. I couldn't remember why I had tried to hit him.

"Mywife," I said. The words wouldn't separate.

"A fine-looking woman."

"Upstairs. Sheshin bed."

"Well, that's to be expected. It's late."

"Loshababy."

"Arthur? Say that again?"

"Loshaba ... losh ..." I breathed in and out slowly. "Losha baby."

"She was with child? She lost a baby and that's why she is in bed?"

I nodded. Perhaps I was crying again.

"My dear man. I am very sorry."

"Schecondtime." It was important that I looked at him when I told him this. I had lost the use of my tongue and my eyes stung with wine, but I watched his face. I could see it with exaggerated clarity in the dark room. He had frozen. "Happen lashyearswell."

Revans nodded.

"You knew."

He nodded again.

"Jerningham!"

His head cocked to the side and his heavy brows dropped. "Jerningham?"

"He had my *wife!*"

"Arthur? No, stop there. That is not true. Why bring Jerningham into it? I heard the reports from the *Roxburgh*. It was Jerningham who helped her."

My glass was empty and I held it out to Revans, who

hesitated, but only for a second, before refilling it. But I lost it somewhere on the way to my lips and I was vomiting into the coal bucket that Revans held under my chin, and sometime later Lucy was wiping my face with a cool cloth and I could hear Revans snoring on the floor.

—

"There are two things I need to say to you, Arthur."

The muck on Revans's clothes had caked and a slice of carrot was breaking away from the mess and flaking off. The morning light came through the doorway, but no one had opened the curtains in the living room, where I realised I had spent the night uncomfortably wedged into the armchair. The room smelt of spilled wine and vomit.

Revans gently levered me into a sitting position and came around to stand in front of me. "Firstly, in due course, I suggest you ask your wife why the Peabodys left her here and went on to Australia without her. And secondly, the message I came to give you was left at your office yesterday. Colonel Wakefield asked me to pass it on. It is from Ada Malloy. Mrs Bently, I mean. She says her brother and Catherine are arriving early and will be in town for the whole month."

The light was too dim to see his face and there seemed to be a black object in front of my eyes. I reached out to brush it away, but there was nothing there. I turned my head and the blackness swam back, and so I sat still for a while and waited as it slowly lifted up towards the ceiling.

"Get him some water, Lucy."

The water helped.

"Did you hear me, Lugg? One, ask Dorothy why the family left her behind. And two, the Malloys are in town for the month."

I nodded. I had heard the first time.

"Now, I'm wondering why Mrs Bently should want you to know that?"

"Need to see Malloy about a farm."

"I don't think that's true, Arthur." He turned to go, but then came back and put his head close to mine. "Truth. You may not want it, but without it you are lost."

I had Lucy make me some food, and I washed in the scullery. Then I went out, without going upstairs, without confronting Dorothy. My not-virgin bride.

Jerningham was the one who tried to help her.

Was that it? The awkwardness? Jerningham was protecting me from her shame?

——

The governor had sailed away south that afternoon on the *Victoria*. A crowd was dispersing along the harbour, an excitable lot, as if they had just won a prize and couldn't wait to tell everyone. There were fiddles and pipers playing in the bars along Lambton Quay and a scuffle had broken out between whalers and immigrants outside the brewery at the foot of The Terrace. I dodged a red-bearded sailor who took a swing at me, but before he could do more he was pushed from behind and both brawlers slipped in the heavy mud brought down the gully from recent rain. They continued their fight on the ground. The mud spewed across the quay and down to the beach and I carried it on my shoes as I went to find some distraction.

I found a party going on at Dorset's house, in celebration of the governor's backside. I went in for the wine. It seemed easier than going home.

Jerningham was there. Though it was not yet midday, he obviously had been drinking for some time. "To the governor's backside!" he called, and we charged our glasses and drank to Hobson's arse. Jerningham had sat through weeks of long frustrating meetings with the governor, and despite his new role as magistrate, he was rowdier than ever.

"He wants to site Nelson close to Auckland!" he told me. We were in the doctor's living room drinking with Revans and Mein Smith and a few of Dorset's friends. "Well, of course he does, the slimy, self-polluting jackass. He sites his capital at the wrong end of the county and expects us to provide him with subjects to rule." Jerningham was fast drunk and he fell over as he made an elaborate bow. "Oh my buggery highness! My lord! I am already on the floor. Give me your boots to lick. Please, Governor Hobson, whose backside brings such joy. Allow me to polish the dust from your boot with my tongue."

He had grabbed Dorset's foot, but the doctor kicked him aside.

"You licked his cock, not his shoes," said Revans. "You take his commission one day and then publicly humiliate him the next. Your childish outbursts get us nowhere, you young fool."

"Let me quote *you*, Revans," said Jerningham from the floor, rising onto one elbow and raising his bottle in a toast. "*Remember, Captain Hobson! You have the power of annoying us for a time, but it will not be difficult to crush you and the paltry coterie by whom you are ruled.* Your words, if memory serves, published in your paper."

"You bacchanalian sponge," said Revans. "I am a man beholden to none other. You, however, are a magistrate. And sometime secretary for your uncle. Some would call that a contradiction."

"I call it genius. I will take his coin and with it pay his passage home."

Dorset offered wine around and though I knew I had to go home and face Dorothy, I accepted one last glass. And then another.

"What's the decision on the new colony?" someone asked. "Did Hobson win? Will Nelson be situated in the north?"

"Over my dead body." Jerningham pulled himself to his feet and dashed back his hair. With his chin thrust out and shoulders straight he looked remarkably sober again, one of his best tricks. Revans, on the other hand, usually looked drunk over morning coffee. He still wore the same jacket, wine now added to the feast gathering on the lapel, and there was a bruise under his eye. I think I had hit him.

"We want to put Nelson on Middle Island," said Mein Smith the sensible. "That would place Wellington in a central position, and of course Hobson doesn't want that. There are several good deep harbours around Banks Peninsula—that's the bit that sticks out, Lugg, halfway down the east side. You've seen the maps? Good, flat, fertile plains behind. It's a prime location for Nelson."

"But Hobson won't let us buy it?"

Jerningham grabbed the back of the chair so he could lean over and talk at me, with the voice of a peevish child. "He won't, Lugg. He won't let us have it. And do you know why? Do you know why?"

"The fucking French," said Revans.

"It's the fucking French," shouted Jerningham. "He says they have a claim. First it was the Māori and now it's the French. Who cares what the fucking French want? Hobson! He'd sell it to the convict whores of Sydney before he'd let us have it. They have a claim, because what? They sailed in one day and put a flag on a hill? We have two thousand people coming to settle our Nelson colony. And Hobson sails off to talk to the fucking French!"

I went home. I had Lucy make me up a bed in the spare room. The nursery, Dorothy had called it, in the few days between telling me I was to be a father and bleeding my baby away. Perhaps she had tempted fate. A woman who had miscarried once must know it could happen again.

"How is she?"

Lucy, as always, was quiet and diligent. She had cleaned away the debris of the night before and my house was calm and neat. My silk night jacket lay over the back of the chair. I was grateful to her. I liked Lucy. I think she liked me. She had been a scrawny little ten-year-old the day she had called me to Dorothy's aid because of the cramps. Perhaps everyone in the settlement knew what the cramps were. Except me. Arthur Lugg, fool.

Perhaps worldly little Lucy imagined I knew Dorothy's state but married her anyway. Perhaps she thought I did it out of compassion and that was why she liked me, because I was a kind man. Perhaps, perhaps.

Lucy was taller now, and more confident. Healthier. At least I could look after a servant girl well. She bobbed her head to me. "She's feeling much stronger now, Mr Lugg. She was right hungry today. I gave her all the eggs. I hope you don't mind. I can fetch some from a neighbour if you're wanting an egg for your supper."

"Not at all, Lucy. I've eaten. I'm glad she has an appetite."

Perhaps the consensus in the settlement was that I knew. I knew Dorothy Lewis had fallen and I married her anyway. I took on another man's cast-off for the love of her pretty mole. For the pity of an abandoned woman. Did this make me a saint or a fool in the hooded eyes of the colony?

Could one choose? If one did something that could be called either foolish, or compassionate, without realising, could one choose afterwards which it was?

Whose was it? Oh God. That was the thing. Was there a man walking around the colony who had tasted my wife before I untied her on our wedding night? If not Jerningham, then who?

I walked quietly up the stairs, but they creaked beneath me. The door to our bedroom was closed.

I pictured her lying, waiting, with her dark hair spread out over the pillow, the withdrawn eyes staring at the door, waiting for me to turn the knob. I stood there for a long time not knowing what to say. Not having decided, yet, which man I was.

I slept in the spare room.

———

In the morning I still had not made a decision.

I took the breakfast tray from Lucy, knocked on the door and went in to see my wife.

"How are you feeling, Dorothy?" I asked as I stepped forward with the tray, bringing an atmosphere of high pressure strong enough to compress hearts and lungs.

She looked well enough. Her colour was good and her hair, unbrushed, was piled loosely on her head so shiny tendrils dropped and curled against her long throat in a becoming way. She had been reading. She looked at me with a docile expression, as if she was waiting for my permission to get up.

I thought I would look at her and understand something of what went on behind the eyes: guilt or shame. Remorse, perhaps. But there was nothing. The suspicions that had been building over the last months had made me colder to her and she was consistent in her emotional absence. But I knew, now. She had a past. I just lacked the detail. I wanted to shake it out of her. *Who? Who was it?*

"Much better, thank you. I will get up today."

She ate her breakfast without chat. If I waited long enough, perhaps she would make an attempt to break us free of this heavy climate. But no. Her power of silence was stronger than mine.

So eventually I spoke.

"I need you to tell me why the Peabodys went on to Australia and left you here."

Her eyes flared wide and met mine, flicked away again. She wasn't placid now.

I almost walked out then, away to the office where I had a pile of stock lists to check. I found this situation with Dorothy distressing. Depressing. I'd spent six months in a small mud hut with Charles Heaphy without one misunderstanding. Women would do better to be a bit plainer with their truths.

"Just tell me what happened. That's all, Dorothy. Why did the family leave you here?"

"Mrs Peabody didn't want me."

"From the beginning. There was a problem. When did it start?"

"The problem?"

I said, "Yes," as though I already knew, and merely wanted her version of events to tally. "Tell me what happened from the start like a story. I won't interrupt. But I want to know exactly what happened and why they abandoned you here."

She stared down at her hands, rubbing her thumb across the backs of her fingers as she often did. After a while there was a flutter of animation in her face. She hardly moved but it appeared that something propelled her forward. Her chest lifted and chin tilted up and she looked straight ahead.

"It started in London, when I first arrived," she said, and her voice had a determined edge. I nodded at her to go on but I needn't have. She seemed to want to tell me. "Mr Peabody said to his wife, 'There's a pretty new governess, I told them to send a pretty one.' And Mrs Peabody looked as though she was going to cry. He went on like that all the time, in front of his wife, in front of friends. He was a big man, with protruding eyes that followed me around the room. He said Mrs Peabody should do her hair like mine, and lace tightly to get a figure like mine and all the time he pretended to everyone that he was in love with me, but he was never kind to me. He just liked to make Mrs Peabody feel sad. I don't know why."

I sat still, in the eye of a storm. Dorothy never looked at me. I was invisible.

"The other servants hated me because they said I led him on but Mrs Peabody didn't say it, she knew what he was like and that it wasn't my fault. She was a good woman. Mostly, I ate in the nursery with the children but on Sundays when I went downstairs the servants made me eat in the corridor—they said I thought I was too good for them. I was primping myself for my betters, they said, and couldn't mix with them. Scotch was the only one who told them to let me in, Mr Peabody's man, but he wasn't often there. So I was pleased when Mrs Peabody said the family were leaving for the colonies and only taking me and Scotch. The others were let go, but before they left they told lies to Mrs Peabody—that I always talked about Mr Peabody and watched him all the time.

"I never talked to anyone about anything and I didn't watch Mr Peabody. *He* watched *me*. He always had lots of men friends around and in the evenings, when I brought the children down, he'd make me do a turn around the room so they could admire me. I thought he might be different away from all his friends, if he was together more with his wife. I didn't think what it meant, to be on the ship, for months like that, all jammed in together."

Dorothy spoke like she read, neatly and without much expression, leaving the words to form into pictures of my own making. I was ashamed I hadn't encouraged her to talk about more appealing subjects. I could glimpse the edge of another Dorothy, unfettered, maybe as she had been as a child, who enjoyed telling stories and being listened to.

I didn't need to pretend compassion. It was no surprise the poor woman was guarded. I knew men like Peabody, men who took pleasure from making women feel uncomfortable, and they made me cringe. I wondered if I should leave it there. She was rubbing her fingers again, slipping off the invisible gloves.

She had paused, perhaps ashamed of what came next. She flushed as she stared at the coverlet, the blush lifting from her dainty collarbones and colouring her neck. I realised I needed to know what happened on the ship.

"I want you to tell me everything, Dorothy."

She swallowed, and her vulnerability aroused me. It had been weeks since we had been together in a marital sense—the twice daily flush of our early married life hadn't lasted two months. I didn't reach for her so often now and when I did I used thoughts of Ada to excite me. Dorothy never instigated contact like Ada did, but when we were first married I had found that reticence provocative. But suspicion dulled desire.

Until now.

The pressure in the barometer rose. I leaned across and put my lips on the mole, the beauty mark that seemed to get men so excited. She was entirely still. I went further. I took her lip between my teeth as I did with Ada, but gently with Dorothy, and I sucked softly and then parted her lips and pushed in my tongue. I was aware of my breathing as I closed my eyes and absorbed her sleepy smell of bed linen and dreams; my breath became laboured and deep.

Ada would flare up when I kissed her like that, and push her cool hands up inside my shirt, and I imagined her little teeth sharp, biting me back and her hips pushing forward. But there was no such return of passion from Dorothy. Just acceptance.

I pulled slowly back from her, my trousers cutting painfully across my arousal. My eyes were half closed and my hand went to my buttons, but I fought myself back from that wave of need that almost propelled me onto the bed and on top of her. It would be so easy to roll her over and lift her covers and slip in behind her. Of course she knew. This was her story. She had put this into my head. This was what happened. How easy it was.

I was confused then. I didn't know whether to take what I wanted or to walk away and pretend it hadn't happened, that I hadn't been aroused by the thought of Dorothy on the ship, in a cabin, as if she was somebody else. Of course she knew why my tongue had darted forward into her mouth.

I wouldn't do it. Not tied up with this image. It would dirty any future we might have. But I found myself unable to rise from the chair and had no choice but to remain where I was.

"I'm sorry," I said, clumsily. "Please go on. Just tell me."

It was that look again, the sneer in her eyes. The same look she had made when, as my nurse, she had offered to help me undress and I had responded, as any man would, with desire lighting me up like a torch.

She spoke roughly now, almost as if to punish me for wanting to know.

"It was worse on the boat. There was nowhere to go. He watched me all the time and punished his wife. I was in the little cabin with the children and the Peabodys were next door and I could hear him, shouting at her, telling her to smile but complaining her smile wasn't as sweet as mine, though I can promise you he had never seen me smile. Then he started saying that he couldn't do it unless she turned her back and the noise went on and on, his grunting and struggling, her crying. He was a big man and Mrs Peabody suffered terribly and was so ashamed. She knew we could

– 257 –

hear, me and the children, and the other cabin passengers, too. Nobody said anything, but they looked suspiciously at me as if I were to blame, as if I would be involved with that man.

"He got more and more angry. He was at her the whole time and then he would slam the door and go up on deck. We were two months at sea before he started saying that she was so weak-willed she would die at sea. He said that in the dining room. He made sure I heard him. He said that people fell off ships all the time. He said if she died he would be free to marry whoever he wanted and he'd be sure this time to marry somebody pretty enough to lift his trouser front."

Dorothy held one hand in the other now, running her fingers through rhythmically as if shedding skins, over and over.

"And one day something changed. Scotch, Mr Peabody's man, told me. He was billeted down below, but he came up to me and told me that Mrs Peabody had rewritten her will and got the captain to witness and hold it. Everything was hers, in trust for her children, and she had written him out. And then Mr Peabody wept and cried and begged her to forgive her, and Mrs Peabody told me that they couldn't stay in the colony with all the other settlers and would go on to Australia. Start afresh. But I couldn't go. She said she was sorry, but I had possessed him. So they gave me notice and planned to abandon me. In a colony. On my own. When I asked for a reference, she said—as what? A corrupter? I swear I had done nothing to earn that."

I had been watching Dorothy's hands as she spoke, but I looked up now and saw the hard set of her jaw as her voice grew tighter.

"And so I asked Scotch what I should do."

"The manservant?"

Maybe I had gone ahead down the wrong path.

"He told me that, for a single woman, the colonies were no different to convict settlements. I couldn't go there alone. Women were snatched on the beach and shared between the desperate men. I begged Mrs Peabody to take me with her but she absolutely refused. By that time, the other settlers were having nothing to do with us. I spent most of the time in the cabin with the children. Mr Peabody ignored me. He was all attention on his wife and never looked at me at all. Scotch said they weren't even going ashore in New Zealand. They would just put me in a canoe with the natives and maybe the natives would take me if nobody else claimed me, and I didn't know the truth in that. How could I know? I had heard about Sydney, how the women were raped before they even reached dry land. I didn't know the truth of anything. And then Scotch ..."

Her voice faltered. The breakfast tea was cold, but I poured her a cup of water and she held it in two hands but didn't drink. It was a relief to see her hands still.

"Scotch said he would leave them, too. He said he would come ashore with me, and we could get married. He said he wouldn't get his wages from Mr Peabody, but we could find work and he would look after me. I didn't like him very much." I had to lean forward to hear her now. "Truth was I hardly knew him. He was like the other servants, he kept away from me because of Mr Peabody. So I was surprised that he would do that. And I didn't want to marry him."

"But you said yes?"

She nodded sadly.

"I said yes. I didn't know what else I could do. I heard settlers say the colony was lawless. I was afraid to go ashore alone. So I told Scotch I would marry him."

"What happened then?"

She looked at me blankly. It might have been better to let

it go. But I knew that without the end of the story I would, for eternity, have an entire kaleidoscope of images in my head with each different scenario shifting as it played out. "I want you to tell me what happened."

"I've said enough."

"No!"

I took the water cup from her hands and set it on the table with the breakfast things.

"Just tell me, Dorothy, and then it's over."

"It's never over."

"It will be for us. I will never ask you again."

"It doesn't matter. I think you know what happened. You've always known."

"Ah! Is that what you think? You think I've always known? When I found you lying on the ground in the mud with your knees clenched up to your belly? That I knew then? That I saw an unmarried woman with a stomach ache and I knew she suffered from sin? And I married you … why? Think, Dorothy. Why, if I had known, would I possibly have married you?"

"Go away, Arthur!"

"You will not tell me to go away in my own house. I tell you categorically, that I knew nothing of your previous condition until the midwife let it slip yesterday. Perhaps everyone else in the settlement knew. Perhaps they all know now. But not me, Dorothy. I was the one remaining fool. And so, you married me."

She shook her head, and her hair slipped out of the clip and tumbled over her shoulders. "Oh, you should have left it alone, Arthur. If you didn't know, it didn't happen. If we never mentioned it, it didn't happen. It had gone away."

"I will have this out, Dorothy. You married me. You swore obedience. You must tell me."

Then her head came up. The flush had spread over her

- 260 -

cheeks and her eyes flared wide at me. This wasn't a story anymore, but a dare.

"All right. I will tell you everything. That's what you want, isn't it, to know everything? Will it make you happy, do you think? Do you want me to strip naked while I tell you?"

The rawness of that comment stung me, but I was not such a fool to deny I deserved it.

"Dorothy, no, I don't want that."

"So listen. Here it is. This is my story. Before he went to Mr Peabody, Scotch made me promise we would marry. He said he wasn't going to throw away his life for me if I just ran away when we got ashore. He said he wanted it in writing. We were all up on deck. It was evening, and Mrs Peabody had taken the children to the front to look at the waves. Then Mr Peabody said she looked cold, and sent me to their cabin to fetch her shawl."

She held my eyes and there was no going back. This was Dorothy's confession and I was her priest.

"I went below. Scotch followed me and when I got to the cabin he bundled in with me, and he put his arms around me from behind and asked if I loved him and I said no, but if he treated me well maybe love might grow between us. It was dark inside, but out the window there was still light on the waves and they looked so frightening and deep. He made me promise that I would marry him and he sounded unsure—he said I was far too good for him, too beautiful and I was sure to leave him before we were married. He said again he wanted us to sign a commitment. And then he said, rather than sign with ink and paper, he would dip his nib. That would commit me."

I wanted to stop her then, but she held up her hand and went on. "Everything, Arthur. You asked for everything. I laid down on the bed and turned my head to the wall. No one would hear me if I cried out, he was bigger and much stronger than I was and I thought we would be married within the month. So that's what happened. I didn't fight him. He pulled up my skirts and did his business and I closed my eyes."

Now I knew.

"But he went on to Australia anyway, without you."

"Yes. He tried to give me a purse but I threw it in the sea."

"Did you tell Mr Peabody?"

Dorothy was miles away now, not wiping away the tears because her hands were occupied with peeling away the gloves, the skin.

"I didn't need to tell him. He watched. He came out of the shadows and held my hand while it happened."

I pushed out of the chair and my hand flung back and swept the tea tray off the side table, the cups and jugs clattered to the floor, pretty things smashed irreparably and lying broken on the ground. Hard pieces of debris. Brown tea seeped from the teapot spout to stain the wood.

"I shouldn't have asked. I'm so sorry, Dorothy, I shouldn't have made you say—"

"And then—"

"No more."

"And then—"

"I said no more!"

"Everything, Arthur!"

"No! I don't want you to talk anymore. Just nod. That's all. The man went to Australia?"

Dorothy looked dishevelled and wild, her jaw taut as if she fought to keep herself together and she nodded once with a sharp, fast dip of her chin.

"He abandoned you. Never came ashore?"

Nod.

"You carried and lost his child."

Nod.

"That's when I found you, in the mud, and carried you home? That's what was happening?"

Nod.

"Jerningham knew and he helped you."

A hesitation, and then a nod.

I pushed my hands through my hair to cool the pressure from my head. This, or that. I was angry, and disgusted, but not with Dorothy. Not with her. The filthy, filthy men, to use my wife in such a way. I kicked the teapot and watched it bounce across the floor, catching on Dorothy's neatly arranged slippers.

She was right. It would've been better had I never known.

"I need to—"

"No. You don't. You don't, Dorothy. You don't need to do anything. Enough has already been done to you." I made shush noises and touched her hair. "No more talk. No apologies. This is over. Do you understand me? This is over. We will never mention it again. You will get up and get dressed and we will go for a walk to the harbour and look at the ships and, dear God, I hope one day soon I will give you a welcome baby to hold. That is all."

I went fast out of the room and called for Lucy to bring hot water and help Dorothy dress and I waited downstairs with such rain in my head I thought I would drown. But later, when Dorothy came downstairs in her grey walking dress and white lace collar and we went out arm in arm into the winter day, it was bright and cloudless and the air sat still and languid on the glassy harbour and nothing moved.

CAPTAIN ARTHUR WAKEFIELD

THERE WERE CHEERS on the quay as Captain Arthur Wakefield sailed in on the *Whitby*, and they continued as he was rowed ashore to step in amongst us.

I asked Revans if he knew him well.

"Oh yes, reasonably." Revans shaded his eyes as he regarded the new addition to the colony. "He's everyone's favourite Wakefield, you know. Nice but dim. We've got a fine collection of Wakefields now: one corrupt, one insane, one soft. Oh, and there's another with him, the sister's son, young Charley Torlesse. Don't know him. Probably a fast buck like Jerningham, here to ride horses and notch his belt with native women."

"The captain was a navy man?"

"Sailed the world missing promotions year after year. Never makes a decision, never upsets a soul. He'll do very well here."

The *Whitby*, and two companion vessels, the *Will Watch* and *Arrow*, carried labourers and surveyors for Nelson, another town that, like Wellington, had been sold before being bought. Captain Wakefield was to lead the development, though there was still no agreement where Nelson would be placed. There were shiploads of settlers sailing in their wake with their boxes of linen and books, furniture and expectations, and somehow the combined

Wakefields were to clap their hands and make a town appear from forest-covered hills to welcome them.

Revans shook his head and went muttering off to the sawyers. He spent his days now building up his timber business and had all but abandoned the *Gazette*. The Company's views were no longer his own and his sarcastic voice rang harshly in print. The colonel would accept his anti-government and anti-missionary ravings, but Revans had begun to turn on the Company in print and that was unforgivable. The editing of the *Gazette* went to a Wakefield supporter called Wicksteed and the Company paid his salary.

An alternative newspaper appeared, critical of the ruling cohort's confrontations with Hobson, and was widely circulated. It lasted only the one issue but provided a glimpse of the growing body of settlers who were challenging the Company's anti-governmental stance. Mein Smith, too, found himself continually on the wrong side of Colonel Wakefield, his advice ignored and the surveying often now going to more loyal Company men. "Docile serfs," Mein Smith called them. He and Revans were careful not to challenge the colonel to his face, but in private they were critical of the chaotic way land was bought and sold, and they talked of long-term plans to leave the settlement and buy a sheep run together, somewhere far away.

But all of this discontent was swept aside as we gathered in the garden of Colonel Wakefield's fine residence to celebrate the arrival of his brother and young Charley.

I took Dorothy to the party, careful, this time, to let her wear the modest grey she preferred and a soft, full bonnet to cover her shining hair. She was still the prettiest there.

I was delighted to see Te Puni was present, with chief Wī Tako from the Kumutoto pā. Both were dressed impeccably in dinner suits with starched white collars and lace cravats, and they wore them well. Though both rather short, like many Māori they had impressive figures and a regal way of standing, as if any second they would be called upon to speak to the entire assembly and were gathering their breath accordingly. I took Dorothy across the lawn.

I approached, unused to seeing my friend in English regalia, and not sure whether to present my nose for the usual hongi. It seemed an odd thing to do with someone in a silk hat. Te Puni shook me firmly by the hand and kept his nose out of reach.

"Mr Lugg, the drowned man."

"Te Puni, may I present my wife, Mrs Dorothy Lugg."

He inclined his head deeply and graciously took her hand, but he never took his eyes off her face. "You must thank me," he said. He kept her hand and seemed to be reading her expression. His eyes crinkled and beard twitched. "One day I swim and pull this man from the waves. I am good swimmer or you have no husband."

To my great surprise, my quiet Dorothy answered him back. "Ah, Te Puni, I have heard this story. But you could not have saved him if I had not saved him from an earlier death by poisoned thumb."

"Ahh! Is that so? A lucky man, two friends to save him. I am glad to meet you."

Dorothy's smile was bright and genuine and I gazed at her with such relief. Perhaps, after all, she was a woman with a wit I could love.

Jerningham was on the verandah steps with the welcoming party. I knew now why Dorothy was shy of him, but I put my arm around her waist and we walked over to the group. Dorothy and I were facing them together, and I didn't care who knew her sordid story because it was the past. She was now Mrs Lugg and under my protection. We spoke to the colonel, and were introduced to Captain

Wakefield. I shook hands with Ada's husband, Bently, who I remembered was Captain Wakefield's godson, and Ada and Dorothy dropped polite nods to each other without the ground opening beneath our feet or the sky crashing down.

With Jerningham we met Charley Torlesse, his handsome young cousin, and several of their school friends who had joined the expedition as surveyors in training. Jerningham's spirits were up, delighted to have a group of new drinking mates. He amused them with the fact of my detachable thumb. "You must buy him a drink one day, and he'll show you how it works."

Then he politely took Dorothy's gloved hand. "Mrs Lugg. How charming."

She bobbed her head and didn't look at him.

The music started. It wasn't Covent Garden, but they had mustered a passable collection of strings and two flutes, and I was proud to see the new Wakefield looking around the happy company with satisfaction. For all Revans's gloomy predictions that the captain was dim, he appeared a fine, sensible, military man, with many years of good navy service under his belt. He was genial in company and it was a joyful party with an atmosphere of relief, a collective uplifting. The colony had been reinforced.

The boost of high spirits lasted until Governor Hobson returned from his trip to the south and again set himself up to lord over us from the wood-panelled room at Dicky Barrett's.

I was not party to any of the discussions during the day, but in the evenings I helped with Captain Wakefield's plans for the Nelson colony. The colonel spread out lists and documents over the desk and put an accountant and his scribes to work.

"A list of land sales in the Hutt and Porirua," the colonel dictated and others took notes. "Average prices, increases, asking and selling prices. Same for town prices, here and Petre. Give us a feel for inflation. Get me the initial New Plymouth sales too. And wages. What have we been paying the workers? By tomorrow."

He took a breath and turned to me. "Lugg, come here. Where are the papers for the sawmill? What did the looms cost, where did we get them? They'll need suppliers for twine, rope, lines—how much can Pratt and Bevan supply? Who do we have in Sydney for lamp wicks? Is there a local alternative? Get the harbour charts off Chaffers. One of the boys can make copies."

Jerningham paced outside the circle of workers, ranting about the governor again. "Greedy speculators? How dare he? Where does he imagine the money is coming from, seal blubber?"

Captain Wakefield looked up at his nephew, but the colonel ignored him and kept up his barrage of demands to me.

"Chain, Lugg? We sold some, if I remember, that we bought from an American. Do you have the records?"

"How can we be accused of buying beyond the wants of the Company when we have settlers coming by the shipload?"

"Lugg. Chains."

"Sir, I'm sorry, I don't quite recall—"

"By the shipload!"

"Well look it up, can't you? Where are the documents?"

"They may be among those that sank."

Jerningham dropped into a chair and I thought he'd finished his diatribe, but a second later he leapt up again.

"He accused us of prospecting by exploitation. You should have heard the outcry. Just who is being exploited?

Everything we bought has been agreed and paid for—"

The colonel continued as if Jerningham hadn't spoken.

"What do you mean, sank? Arty, will you need chains, do you think? What do you have with you? *Sank*, Lugg?"

"Yes, sir, we sank a few boxes of documents. We thought that some of our earlier trades might be better off—"

"—and why continue this fallacy that the Māori are children when their entire history is based on warfare and trade? They understand a bargain. They have an instinctive sense of value, and any one of them could teach Hobson a lesson in diplomacy, the pathetic, thin-arsed vaurien!"

"Jerningham! Stop that, for God's sake. What's this about sinking documents?"

"We have plenty of chain on the *Whitby*," said Captain Wakefield. "Let's break now, shall we? I think Mr Lugg has quite enough to go on with. Would you mind, Mr Lugg, searching out these few details and reporting back here in the morning? And I might ask you to introduce young Charley to Captain Chaffers, if you'd be so good. He might help with the copying. You'll find he has a reliable hand."

"Sir."

I was relieved to leave the bedlam. As usual, everything was rushed and last minute. The planning was knocked up on a scrap of paper by inexperienced men with incomplete knowledge.

Captain Arthur Wakefield was battling with the governor during the day, holding his request for land in the south while Hobson insisted the only available land was north. Now the trio of Wakefields—the captain and the colonel and the ranting Jerningham—were talking about going to Te Rauparaha behind Hobson's back to complete the sale agreed in '39, before the requirement for Government pre-emption.

Any mention of Te Rauparaha gave me a taste as if I had unwittingly bitten into something foul and only realised my mistake as I swallowed. I had heard such ill spoken of the chief I wondered that the colonel still entertained any thoughts of dealing with him. He had proved an enemy to all his friends, Māori and Pākehā, at one time or another and reneged on deal after deal. And yet they encouraged Captain Wakefield to believe he could sail over to Kāpiti with a few guns and blankets and sign a compact. As if the chief's curly scrawl would not immediately slide off the page.

"What news of Daniel?" the colonel asked his brother, as I turned with armloads of papers to take through to my desk. "Is it as bad as Gibbon says? Is he coming?"

"I'm afraid so," replied Captain Wakefield, in a low voice. "There is really no alternative. He's burned his bridges at home, that's certain."

"We'll find him something."

I came through for my hat and coat, and the conversation stopped.

"Thank you so much for your help, Mr Lugg," said Captain Wakefield. "Your knowledge is invaluable."

"Pleased to be of service, sir."

I walked up the hill and home to Dorothy, but my mind was churning and sleep was long coming.

We were back in the office early the following morning, the Wakefields hammering out their attack strategy.

"Look, Jerningham, here's a turn-up," said the colonel, waving his nephew into a chair. Despite the late night and their morning appointment with the governor, there was much still to do. Following the surveyors, the tidal wave of Nelson settlers was almost on the horizon, and still they had no land and no facilities ready. I laid the documents he had asked for on his desk. "Listen," continued the colonel, "this was delivered to my house, last evening. From Hobson." And he proceeded to read the letter in front of him.

> "To W. Wakefield, Esq.
>
> Sir, in order to enable you to fulfil the engagements which the New Zealand Company have entered into with the public, I beg to acquaint you, for your private guidance and information, that the local government will sanction any equitable arrangement you may make to induce those natives, who reside within the limits referred to in the accompanying schedule, to yield up possession of their habitations; but I beg you clearly to understand that no compulsory measures for their removal will be permitted.
>
> I have made this communication private, lest profligate or disaffected persons arriving at the knowledge of such an arrangement might prompt the native to make exorbitant demands.
>
> I have the honour to be, Sir,
>
> Your most obedient servant,
>
> W. Hobson
>
> Wellington, 6th September, 1841."

It wasn't lost on me that the communication was delivered for private guidance and information, yet the colonel read it aloud in an office that held his family members, Company officials, employees like me, and two labourers fixing a draught around a window, who stopped work to hear the news.

So here was Hobson, offering protection to the natives in public while giving the colonel express permission to clear them out of our way, so long as no mud stuck to his shoes.

I started to understand Jerningham's loathing of the man, but Jerningham, of course, was delighted. It was exactly the sort of deal he excelled in himself.

"Revans will be pleased. He can officially turf the buggers out of his garden now."

"That's rather a contradiction to his earlier message, isn't it?" suggested our newly arrived captain.

"He's a contradictory man," replied Colonel Wakefield. "He doesn't specifically forbid us from resurrecting our 1839 deal with Te Rauparaha either. But he told me, and hark this, he will be perfectly irresponsible for the consequences!"

"He says that now," said Jerningham. "But when our settlements in Middle Island are thriving he will be perfectly responsible for ensuring our taxes are collected to feather his nest."

Captain Wakefield took the folder of documents that I had prepared for him. It contained my list of suppliers in Sydney and other colonies, and the expected prices for goods and services. A growing list of traders to trust and those to cut. He flicked through the papers and I liked the way he looked up to acknowledge my work. His face held similar features to his brother the colonel, but on Captain Wakefield they combined in a friendlier countenance, perhaps tempered by a kinder nature. "Very good, Mr Lugg. Thank you. I've asked Charley to drop in to see you today. I'd be grateful if you would show him your methods. He has no training in bookkeeping and it is a useful skill he will need."

"Certainly, sir."

They left for their meeting, two diplomatic and serious men with Jerningham, the young cub, bounding around them. Charley Torlesse arrived shortly after and we had a most enjoyable day at the books and maps. He was keen and high-spirited, similar in energy to Jerningham but perhaps without the dark side of character that troubled his cousin.

Two days later the governor sailed away, beaten to an agreement by the Wakefields. Nelson was to be found across Cook's Strait, making Wellington central to the colonies, and diminishing the power of Hobson's chosen capital of Auckland. I watched the man climbing, with assistance, into the row-boat, his sallow skin stretched over thin bones: ill and tired and, I thought, rather sad.

Many colonists had softened now he had been among us, issued proclamations and held court. Sam Revans, of course, still filled the paper with unforgiving lashings of scorn but he now seemed on the wrong side of public opinion. However insubstantial, sovereignty had arrived and people went about their projects with reassurance that their purchased land would, in fact, belong to them. English law would see them right.

—

I asked Dorothy what she wanted to do with our town section. There was the opportunity of a proper English garden now, with many seed nurseries offering varieties from home. I imagined roses by the picket fence, and some flowering climbers over the verandah.

"I'd like to grow vegetables."

"Would you, Dorothy? Not flowers? For arrangements? Would you not rather we got a man in to look after the vegetables?"

"I don't mind flowers at the front. But I'd like to grow something useful as well. My lettuces grew so fast last summer. I want to learn how to make a garden that will feed us. Louisa Mein Smith has a vegetable garden. She has a Mr Ingestre to help. He advertises in the paper. Perhaps we could get him along and he could do the digging, and then teach me what to plant. I've never had a garden before."

"Splendid. Find me the advertisement, and I will arrange for Mr Ingestre to call."

"Thank you, Arthur."

I went to work. On the way home, I dropped in to see Mr Ingestre and soon the kindly gentleman was a regular visitor. We put in a picket fence and I began to like the *click-clack* of the dropped latch as he passed behind the house to find Dorothy in the back garden, waiting to talk about soil and slope and climate. They had sketches and plans they spread over the kitchen table and he lent Dorothy books on vegetable husbandry. Lucy helped weed and Mrs Mein Smith came to visit, offering her seedlings and talking to Dorothy about dibbers and trowels and the advantages of her husband's imported bamboo as a wind screen. Even Te Puni dropped by sometimes and watched the landscape progressing, making enthusiastic comments in Māori. If I didn't understand every word he said, I gathered all of the spirit behind them. He brought Dorothy a strawberry plant. I have no idea where he got it.

The weather warmed. Dorothy shed her winter shawls and I often came home late in the afternoon to find her still in her gardening gear, with her sleeves rolled and cheeks red, brushing the soil from her apron. She liked to show me how the scheme was developing: with spinach, celery and carrots in neat rows, and her peas climbing up a contraption of vines wrapped around a set of poles.

"Feel the soil, Arthur. See how it crumbles?"

My father had green fingers and my brother and I had worked in our home garden as children, but I pretended it was entirely new to me. I enjoyed her obvious delight in her new skills.

"It's rotting seaweed!" she said. "Mr Ingestre brings it in bags for me. But it doesn't smell. Not at all."

We invited William and Louisa Mein Smith for tea and they talked horticulture all afternoon. Mein Smith asked my wife earnestly about her plans for the rotation of her brassicas. Dorothy, and her vegetables, bloomed.

———

The official recognition from the governor, Captain Arthur Wakefield's presence and a delightful run of spring weather combined for an encouraging effect on the settlement. I was pleased to see settlers going about their business cheerfully; employment was up and confidence restored. The promise of a new colony across the strait, plus good news from the settlers up at New Plymouth gave the feeling that we were no longer alone. Other than the fiercely competitive Jerningham, most of us were pleased to hear reports of growth in Auckland, where Australian immigrants, soldiers and merchants took land and there were plenty of Māori labourers to hand.

Hobson was pushing growth by actively encouraging English immigration and reselling land that he had purchased from the Māori at a good profit. Their success gave us trade, and for all the workers Hobson stole from us we had many of his immigrants coming south. Revans reported that Hobson's spending was out of control and he would bankrupt the country, but we took no notice.

We built a cricket pitch on Thorndon Flat. As the days lengthened, while the worthies argued club rules and dress code, Charles Heaphy and I organised pick-up games and practices.

One Thursday, a few days before the Nelson expedition left, Jerningham and Charley Torlesse and their young friends escaped their duties and joined us on the pitch. We ran around in the spring sunshine in our shirt sleeves, playing ball as if on a village green in Somerset.

Charley was a tall lad, a strong sportsman for only sixteen years old. He was the leader of his group of boys and they stood around the pitch where he placed them. They were junior surveyors on the Nelson expedition and I fancied Revans was right when he described them as "fast young bucks". When daylight fell away from the pitch and we pulled up the stumps, Heaphy excused himself and I waved to go off home to Dorothy, but Jerningham would have none of it.

"The Southern Cross, Lugg. It's new, and they have some good wines from my man in Hokianga. You can't leave the boys to explore on their own, imagine the trouble they'll get up to. You must come with us."

It wasn't the first time he had taken his disciples off on a tour of the public houses. Captain Wakefield and the colonel would certainly not approve. The grog shops had multiplied like spongy mushrooms on damp soil in the two years since arrival and, dark and unappealing as they were, Jerningham patronised them all.

"I don't think so. Thank you."

"Oh, really—show some hospitality!" He put his arm around my shoulders and led me back along the waterfront. Charley and his friends, following hard on Jerningham's heels, vied for his attention with loud shouts of laughter. "These young men need guidance. I treat it as a moral duty. Didn't I hear you tell Uncle Arthur you would keep an eye on Charley?"

"I can't imagine how you heard that. I certainly didn't say it."

"You have a responsibility to help these young men find their feet in the new world."

I heard the boys chatting behind us.

"It's your turn—you go with him, Jackie."

"I'll go again!"

"Wills and Charley tonight."

"We can all have a turn with her."

"Charley has to go on his own, first."

I turned to Jerningham in horror. "What have you done? You surely didn't visit your lady friend with them?"

"Lady friend? My goodness, Lugg! What a delightful description for a working woman."

I pulled him ahead so the boys dropped out of earshot. "Jerningham, you mustn't do this. These young men are in your care. What are you thinking?"

But he laughed at me and continued to guide me along with him, as if I were complicit in all he did.

"They'll need to visit a brothel sometime." His voice came under his breath, conspiratorial. "Best I show them around. There are some things to look out for and I can certainly—"

I ducked out from under his arm and turned back to the boys.

"Charley Torlesse, your uncle Arthur suggested I show you around this evening. I'm on my way home now. Please join me for supper—I'm sure my wife would be delighted to see you again. We can go to the concert later in the Exchange."

All credit to the boy, his eyes gave away nothing of the disappointment that hung on the faces of his friends. He looked neither at the boys nor Jerningham and his response, though a beat late, was composed.

"Thank you, Mr Lugg. That's very civil of you. I would be delighted."

We peeled away and left them, cutting down the lane behind Malloy's house. Jerningham, disgruntled with his reduced party, muttered that the evening was spoilt and the boys might as well all go home to their billets for an early night.

Charley may even have been relieved. We walked and chatted about cricket. The lane curved as we neared Malloy's fence and I saw the tip of the flax bush, grown tall now. Charley said something about a game in England when his brother, Henry, had hit a six but had started running anyway and crashed into Frank coming the other way, but I wasn't listening. His words dissolved into sound with no more impression than bird trills as we passed along the fence line and I saw the flax leaf woven carefully between the two upright posts, the white paint beginning to peel already in the colonial sun, and my heart raced ahead of any rational reality my mind could conjure.

Ada. Friday. Tomorrow. Ada's mouth. Ada's breasts. Ada's hips. Ada's face—with the light and dark that chased over her features like wind on the harbour. It had been weeks and I thought she had given me up.

"Mr Lugg?"

"Certainly, yes, Charley."

I had no idea to what I agreed and we walked through the settlement, up Molesworth Street and into the house, where I reintroduced Charley to Dorothy. I duly sent Lucy out to buy a tidy supper from the Thistle and opened a good bottle of wine with which we toasted Queen Victoria and the New Zealand Company and the success of the Nelson expedition (but not the governor), and all the while I existed in two places and two different times. Here today, and with Ada, tomorrow. It wasn't that I was thinking about her as I ate my dinner—I was careful to keep my attention where it belonged—but I was warmer than the evening called for and I could feel my collar against the skin of my neck and was aware of the smooth cotton of my shirt on my chest.

After dinner we took Charley to the concert.

A visiting Māori choir from the Ōtaki mission sang Psalm 100 in their own language. Indeed, it was a joyful noise before the Lord, and they had come before his presence singing.

Kia hari te hāmama ki a Ihowā, e ngā whenua katoa:
Mahi atu ki a Ihowā i runga i te koa, waiata haere ki
tōna aroaro.

It was beautifully done, their rolling language well suited to such music and they sang with the sincerity of the recently converted. They were dressed in blankets and mats, some with sailor's caps; one woman wore an English jacket over a flax skirt. They would have looked most out of place in an English hall of stone but the wooden Exchange was decorated with flax hangings woven with zigzags, diamonds and symmetrical marks in gold and black and green. Our distinctive mix of native and English design flowed through the building, the congregation and the music.

Charley asked me the meaning of the woven patterns but I didn't know. Perhaps they were just patterns.

"Jerningham will know," I told him. "He's our resident Māori expert."

I was looking past Charley to Ada, sitting with her husband diagonally opposite, at the end of a line of bonnets. She turned once and smiled at me over Bentley's broad shoulder. If Dorothy noticed, it was no more than a friendly acknowledgement, a polite dip of the head.

But I fizzed at her proximity and Ada could tell I had seen the signal and would come. She turned quickly away. Even as I held Dorothy's hand I sent my heart over to Ada, for her to hold in her lap. I couldn't help it. I wished my head was there.

—

Charley Torlesse sailed away the next day with Captain Arthur Wakefield and his surveyors to Kāpiti Island. I worried terribly to see him go, though Charles Heaphy was of the party and promised to look out for him. He seemed so young and so promising, such a vulnerable boy to send to the den of the old cannibal Te Rauparaha.

"Why do you go on, so?" asked Jerningham, when I questioned him on the deal. We'd met on the grassy slope below the colonel's house—Government House, as we still called it, somewhat ironically now the governor had spurned us. Jerningham tutted at me in his annoying way, as if I was the one with questionable morals. "We bought Golden Bay from Te Rauparaha in '39, long before the government got involved. Uncle Arthur is doing absolutely the right thing—he's meeting the chief, he'll give him presents, he'll confirm the sale before witnesses."

"Presents! Call them bribes, Jerningham. I don't know where this talk of presents comes from."

"It's Māori custom to give gifts."

"Guns?"

"Well you won't get far with a bag of Bibles."

"How do you know they even owned title to the land you say you purchased? Look at how complicated things have become here."

We paused at the beach to watch an overloaded raft coming in, with stone for Baron Von Alzdorf's new hotel. Men tripped and cursed in the shallows as they grappled with ropes, precariously balancing the raft against the harbour swell. We continued walking.

"Well, there's an interesting thing about this particular sale of land. There may have been a whaler with a claim. A man called Blenkinsop had a deed that clearly showed purchase with tracings of all the facial tattoos of the chiefs and their marks. He paid with a cannon, though God knows who he stole that from. We traced his widow, a Māori woman—and you understand 'widow' is rather a loose term—but we found her, annulled her claim and signed an agreement, with lots of gifts of course, and bought the land from her. And!" he continued, lifting his hand as I began to interrupt. "And if the tribe that Te Rauparaha *says* he conquered starts bouncing, we bought the land a third time, off the local tribe. We bought Golden Bay thrice over before Hobson got his hat down over his silly ears."

I'd heard parts of this story before. What Jerningham neglected to mention was that Hobson was forming a court to test the validity of all Company purchases made before his Land Proclamation, and the Te Rauparaha deal would certainly be under scrutiny. The court could well rule against us.

"Isn't it safer to wait for Hobson's approval? For the Land Claims Court to approve Golden Bay for Nelson?"

"We don't have time. Anyway, we don't have Hobson's *dis*approval. He'll come around, he can't fight us forever. We have colonies in Wellington, Wanganui, New Plymouth and soon a thousand settlers in Nelson. We're too big for him."

"Jerningham, your arrogance astounds me! Hobson is the Queen's governor. You're too big for the Queen now, are you?"

He laughed and nudged me with his shoulder. "God bless Her Majesty. Imagine if she came to visit! I'd take her to the hot pools. You know, around Lake Taupō they have steaming pools, water heated by vents from the centre of the earth? I'm going exploring next month. You should join me."

"The colonel getting you out of the way again?"

"I don't care. I'm sick of it here, all the nay-saying and negativity. Seriously, Lugg, come with me! The weather will be delicious, we'll paddle and trek inland, we'll find places no white man has been before. There's a little bit of something in you still calling out for an adventure, surely? Yes! I knew it! Come with me."

And because the sun shone and Dorothy was happy in her garden and Ada was waiting for me and I was still young and strong and healthy, with a yearning for adventure, and despite everything I still enjoyed Jerningham's company, I said, "Yes. I might. All right. I'll think about it. Well. Yes. Perhaps I will come."

———

Ada was upstairs, curled naked in the shaft of sunlight that came in through the little box room window and pooled gold on the bedspread laid out on the floor. She stretched out long and reached the curve of her arms above her head and her little bubbies rose up off her chest. She rolled onto her side to enhance the swell of her hip and the curve of her young waist and to show me her firm white bottom. It was beautifully staged, she had heard my key in the back door and positioned herself for me.

I had meant to talk. The sight of her clenched tears when we last were here had hung around my neck for a month, a tight collar that I needed to loosen. Not break, I didn't think I could bear that, but loosen.

"Take your clothes off, Arthur. Lie in the sun with me."

"Ada …"

"I haven't got much time, my love. Come and put your hands on me. Here, come here. It's been a long month."

And she rolled onto her front and looked over her shoulder at me, her dark frizzy hair unbound and curly, wild as the springy fern of the undergrowth. As I hesitated, she lifted her hips, raising her bottom towards me in an invitation and I accepted in an instant, not bothering to undress, taking her on her hands and knees with my rough clothes chaffing against her white skin, my trouser buttons down at my knees, scratching, my good hand cupping her breast to bend her back so I could bury my face in her neck. She responded with calls of pleasure like the deep-throated birds in the bush.

And after, as we lay quietly in the sun and she tucked her head onto my out-flung arm, I couldn't find the words I needed to say.

The afternoon drifted across the window, the golden sunlight falling off our bodies. She broke the silence.

"My husband ..." but she stopped. She'd said the word softly, almost amorously, and I felt a constriction in my chest.

"You can tell me about him, Ada. Perhaps we should discuss things."

"No, no. You misunderstand, Arthur. In my mind, when I say my husband, it's you. You are my husband. I married someone else, but I was already promised to you."

I lifted onto my elbow, so I could see her face. "What do you mean, Ada?"

"We were betrothed on the ship," she said. "I promised myself to you."

"Ada, are you here with me because you consider yourself bound to me in some way? Because I assure you—"

"Don't let's talk about it. The sun's gone and I have things to do this afternoon and I haven't started on the house. You'd better get back to your office."

She pushed me gently, disentangled her legs from mine, and rolled away.

"It's a risky thing we do here, Ada. One day your brother will come to town early. You would be absolutely disgraced. And he'd shoot me, you know."

"Oh, no. No, he wouldn't do that. He has no right."

"Well, Ada, actually—"

"What else can we do?" She spoke a little sharply now.

"If I am making you unhappy in any way …" But it was always Ada who bent the flax leaves to invite me to her. Always Ada who called me. And I always came.

She'd been married over a year now. For much of that time we had been meeting. It occurred to me then, though it should probably have occurred to me before, that if she became with child she would have no way of knowing if it was mine or Bently's.

"Do you love John Bently?" I asked.

"Get up, Arthur, come on. Help me with my laces."

But I didn't move. She hadn't answered my question. I watched her dress, laces strung loosely without help, and tried again.

"I've heard nothing but good of Mr Bently," I said. "They say he is a fine man. Do you love him, Ada? Does he make you happy?"

I didn't want to know any details about Mr Bently, I didn't want an image of him and Ada ever in my mind. But I wanted to know Ada was with me because she loved me and chose me, rather than because she disliked him. Ada, who had everything, still wanted me.

"Mr Bently does not step inside this room. Nor does Dorothy. This room is our home, Arthur."

She pulled on her shoes and left me, scooping her hair into a ribbon. I heard her in the bedroom opposite, opening the window and shaking the pillows. I dressed and waited for a while, but she went downstairs without coming back. I hoped she wasn't standing by the door crying again.

I found her in the drawing room, primly arranging cut flowers in a vase.

"I'm going away for a while," I told her. "Jerningham has some business in the interior and needs me."

"I see. Well, good luck, then, Arthur."

Was that goodbye? I never was sure.

TO TAUPŌ

JERNINGHAM PLANNED our trip to Taupō for early November, when the weather grew more stable. Dorothy didn't like the idea of our going off together but I prevailed. She had friends around her now, and a house and garden to maintain. I did feel guilty leaving her, but we had years of domesticity ahead of us and adventures weren't offered to me every day.

Charles Heaphy was back from Nelson for a few days before we left. He was being sent to England in an ambassadorial role with his paintings and journals. The dear man was an inspired choice, eloquent and unassuming—a reassuring companion to encourage spare sons of the gentry to step aboard a New Zealand Company ship, clutching a deed of sale for colonial land.

I gathered with Charles and friends in the colonel's house on the eve of his departure to wish him godspeed, and to view his pleasing watercolours. He spread out painted landscapes of the Nelson expedition's three ships at harbour, the beginnings of settlement and other peaceful colonial scenes.

"These are splendid, Heaphy. The barracks look solid and tents white and welcoming. The grass appears fit for grazing all the way along the coast. Well done. Clear of bush, is it, around the settlement area?" The colonel was more interested in the promotion of the place than the place itself.

"It's tussock grass mostly, up to the Moutere hills in the background here, Colonel. They are bush-covered. Behind them are the Tasman Mountains. Snow all year on the peaks."

Charles's voice was wistful and I sensed his desire. He would far prefer to be crossing the mountains than the ocean.

"The harbour's rather small," said Jerningham. "Is that the full extent of it?"

"Unfortunately it's the best we have. Astrolabe is a good roadstead across the bay, but it lacks the required flat land and there are many Māori at Kaiteriteri."

"Where's the farm land?" asked Jerningham.

"The colonel has my report."

"Yes, Heaphy, but I'm asking you."

"There are about sixty thousand acres in Waimea. That's here, south of the proposed settlement."

"It's not enough."

"Mr Tuckett is surveying further afield."

"What about the Māori?"

"The colonel has Captain Wakefield's report."

"Oh, come on, Heaphy!"

The colonel answered for him. "Arty reports a successful kōrero at Kaiteriteri. A little bit of bluster—the usual—complaints that Te Rauparaha had no right to sell and so forth. But he soothed them with gifts."

Jerningham looked at me with a smile on his face. "Lugg doesn't approve of all these gifts, Uncle."

"I don't think it matters what Lugg thinks," said the colonel. "But we can't give them money, don't you see, Lugg? The law now forbids it. A small present to a native soothes the path of a knotty problem."

"There are missionaries in Cloudy Bay and up in the hills," Charles said. "They've told their Māori to keep away from us, told them all colonists are devils. But, of course, the natives can't stay away. We gave one a spade and he's been very industrious, digging a garden for the missionary in a week. And yet, we are still devils. Apparently God will smite them down if they fraternise with us."

"But not when we give them spades."

"The Māori want to live amongst us and have tools and wooden houses and proper clothes."

"They make good workers. Just bring them to town." This was Jerningham.

"It's not workers we need," said Charles. "Captain Wakefield stressed that I am to report we need settlers not labourers. Too many of our land owners are absent."

I noticed his tact in avoiding the word "speculators", but his meaning was clear. Many owners had no intention of immigrating and investing in the local economy. Without landed settlers there was no one to employ the labourers and the cost of their employment fell directly on the Company.

Charles was billeted with me for the night, and we walked up the hill in the evening, companionable as always. Since his last visit, the shacks on the waterfront had been replaced by timber buildings and stones laid on the quay. We passed a man with broom and bucket on his evening round clearing shit off the street.

"Why are you going off with Jerningham?" he asked.

"Someone needs to keep him honest. I know you don't approve."

Charles shook his head. "All adventure and no responsibility."

"Some of us don't have the skill to paddle up a river and come back with a full cartography of the region. Sometimes just the paddle is adventure enough."

I didn't like his disappointed look. I think Charles saw in me a man less ordinary than I was.

"I'll take a chess set," I promised. "I'll teach my Māori friends how to play."

"Good idea," he said.

"And my watercolours. I'll bring paints and brushes as gifts for Para and Kuru."

This seemed to mollify him. "Civilisation by stealth," he suggested.

"You'll be back?" His long journey around the world suddenly worried me.

Charles smiled. "As soon as I can, Arthur. I'd like to return to Nelson. It's full of opportunity and the society is … well … it feels more honest there than here. Captain Arthur Wakefield is an easy man to like. Come and visit when I get back—it's spectacular country. We can do some paintings together."

"I'd like that. Perhaps I'll bring Dorothy."

He left the next day beneath taut white sails, with his neat journals and soft pictures of an idyllic landscape under a gentle sun, while Jerningham and I went north, through driving rain and deep mud, into the harsh tangled landscape of the interior.

—

We were to journey upriver from Wanganui in several light waka—Jerningham effortlessly securing loyal guides from among his pool of attendants. Para and his men from the Patutokotoko tribe joined us, they were allies of the Taupō Māori, which seemed a good thing as we headed east. Also in the party were members of Chief Kuru's family, who were travelling inland to meet him. Jerningham was experienced by now in this world; during our few days in town he procured and packed large quantities of arms and powder, pipes, tobacco, farming implements, fish hooks, buttons and many sacks of clothing.

In town we paused to watch the thatching of the police and magistrate's office, which was a substantial wooden structure not far from Whare Wikitoria. As far as I knew, Jerningham had done no official work there. He shouted up greetings to the men on the roof but didn't intend going inside. The building was surrounded by the tall posts used by the Māori settlements. They were rammed into the ground, tied with flax and cut off at differing lengths, native style. I thought a neat picket fence would have made a better show of British order.

At the river we handed our knapsacks to be stowed in the waka, along with bundles of clothing and baskets of food. Beneath were long wooden crates.

"If we're trading," said Jerningham, "let's make a difference. Fill your pockets with beads for the children, certainly, but civilisation begins with warm trousers."

"But the guns? Are they necessary? They will turn them on us eventually, you know."

"I hope it never comes to that. And really, Lugg, most Māori are lousy shots. They do less damage with guns than with their damn tomahawks. And I, for one, would rather be shot clean through the heart from a distance than have a blade hacked into my head, a savage's breath on my cheek."

"How foolish of me," I said. "I didn't realise that with your guns you're merely fulfilling the Company's commitment to promote civilisation."

"Just load the waka—there's a good man. Leave the diplomacy to me."

Again, we entered the other world that was life on the river. My breath slowed. My eyes relaxed and I noticed details in the bush that escaped me on foot or horseback: exotic plants, fan-leafed or spiky, scratchy grey scrub and ferns of such pure pale green that I imagined, if I ate them, I would melt through the soft debris of vegetation into the rich, dark soil.

The river was brown, or green, or charcoal grey, depending on how the light hit the silt it carried down from the hills. Sometimes I could see a clear inch below the water, a kind of glassy transparent cover over the mysterious opaque liquid in motion below. There was a sheen on the surface. In the sunlight, the reflections could be extraordinary.

Para had kept a place for me in his waka, and though Jerningham grumbled that he should really split us up "because of all the tribal nonsense" the Māori would put in my head, he gave way, saying he didn't want to ride with me anyway.

The men paddled with seemingly little effort against the current. The river was sluggish, and the overcast, humid days passed in long stretches of rhythmic movement as the strong arms of the natives powered us forward through the wide, curving reaches of the lower river.

As we went inland the pace changed and we mounted the easy rapids, enjoying the occasional clamber over the rocks as a chance to stretch our legs. We camped with small communities, ate food baked in earth ovens and left gifts of fish from the coast. Jerningham gave the river people twists of sugar too, and boiled sweets, and we laughed to see their faces amazed by the bright taste, beyond anything they had experienced in nature. We passed a ruined village where a Taupō war party led by Chief Heuheu—a man Jerningham intended to visit—had torched the pā and killed the people. There were large fire pits strewn with bones as long as a man's leg and, at one site, a pile of human skulls appeared to have tumbled from the bowel of a hollow tree.

"Cannibals?" I asked Para, and he replied in great detail, with graphic gestures and fast, complicated vocabulary, most of which I was glad to lose in translation.

"Bodies decompose slowly in this place," Jerningham said. "There are few animals to carry them away. They're left for the birds to pick clean."

We returned to our waka and paddled away from the empty, steep-sided valley.

Once I might have felt a disgust at the sight of human remains left to rot, but the idea of birds picking the flesh from dead bones was no more shocking to me than feeding the worms as we did with our burial rites in Europe. I didn't believe the Christian dead had any better chance of an afterlife than anyone else. I knew natives here would exhume, pick over and re-inter their dead. The missionaries tried to stop the practice but it seemed the Māori had a more satisfactory relationship with their ancestors that we did. They didn't whip themselves with the sins of their fathers but carried their ancestors with them, talked to them, consulted them. What right had a missionary to tell them that was wrong?

"Tell me about your ancestors," I said to Para. "Have you always lived on the river?" We were paddling sluggishly now between bush-covered hills, everyone sleepy in the afternoon sun. The riverbanks were littered with white logs, picked clean and washed up like so many bones.

He pushed his paddle in and pulled it out twice before putting it across his knees and rolling his head to look at me. I enjoyed looking at Para. He had a face for a sculptor, with full curved lips and wide nostrils below a flat nose, over which curled the spiral of his tattoo. Sometimes, like he did now, he would tilt his head back and open his eyes wide to show me the whites. I didn't know what was expected in return other than to smile, and he would flare his eyes further and then laugh at my inadequate Pākehā response to his challenge.

"Not for English," he said. I was unsure whether he meant the stories were not for an Englishman, or couldn't be told in the English language. I tried in my hesitant Māori to ask when he'd come here and from where.

"Īnahea koe i tae mai?"

"Before," he replied.

"I haere mai koe nō hea?"

"Ah!" He seemed to get my drift. "Many fathers, long journey."

I ran out of vocabulary and Para returned to his paddling.

I thought the conversation ended there, but in the evening, in a small settlement of Kuru's relatives above a high flood bank, Para called me over to him and we settled on woven mats under a canvas awning. We'd eaten well on vegetables and eel and waited peacefully now for stories and songs, the fire rising as the light fell.

"Whakapapa," Para said.

Jerningham sat alongside the chief in the ring of men. He passed around tobacco, we lit our pipes from the fire and, carefully and respectfully, Jerningham translated the chief's story of his people. When he lost the words we simply absorbed what we could through Para's rhythmic voice and expressive face. I was taken back into the lives of his ancestors as they arrived in their great waka from an island across the sea, and walked over the land to find a place to call their home. Men and women lived in a world with gods and monsters, they seemed both living and dead, long buried and yet still breathing.

Para told legends of hardships and battles and courage, and of people who found spirits—great taniwha—in the river and tamed them. It was a story well told, and all around us the men nodded and smiled, flared their eyes and frowned, walking in their minds with their ancestors over the land.

I slept that night with the sound the river loud in my ears and had strange dreams of floating downstream. The river got wider and wider until it reached the sea where it merged with a powerful incoming tide. I walked along where the water mixed and was diluted—neither fresh nor salt—and all along the shore a new growth pushed up, sprouting out of the mud.

—

We stopped next at a missionary village. It was a haven of calm between towering hills of unruly bush where the former chief, now turned mihanere, guided his people in an extreme interpretation of Christian doctrine.

Jerningham, with his boisterous charm, was immediately in trouble. There was it seemed a rule of silence in the village, no jokes or laughter permitted, no singing or friendly chatter allowed. Even the inquisitive children were quiet, held back by the pastor's raised hand from running to greet the waka that pulled onto their beach. Jerningham had rushed forward with outstretched hands expecting the usual crowding and touching, but the one man who laughed in return had been severely reprimanded by the chief.

"Laugh ye not!" he called, his sonorous voice silencing his disciples, who gathered in rows outside the upright posts of the pā boundary. "For laughter is the way to sin."

He welcomed us formally with many quotes from the New Testament, and these he continued to regurgitate all afternoon as he showed us around his orderly gardens and spotlessly clean pā. His people were all at work or study and appeared unnaturally suppressed, with none of the usual joie de vivre of their race, their liveliness ripped away and replaced with the stern demeanour of the mihanere. For all their good behaviour and wholesome work, their respectable European clothing and basic trappings of civilisation, I found it a depressing place, a village neither one thing nor the other. They had taken the word of God but missed the point.

"God wants you to laugh," I whispered to one of the little boys as he came closer to stare at me, and his eyes opened wide in horror, whether at the shock of a white man speaking directly to him or my sacrilegious words, I don't know.

We were not invited to share a meal and chose to camp away from the mission, by the river. All those suppressed souls created a tightness in my chest I found hard to shake.

"This is a terrible village," I said to Jerningham.

"I know," he said. "No grog shop."

We rose before dawn. The men uncoiled from sleep and shook light dew from the blankets, and with a fine early mist brushing the river we pushed the waka off the beach. Para led the party around a sweeping bend to wait for Jerningham, who had gone alone to the pā to thank the missionary for his hospitality.

He was some time coming to join us and when he did arrive his expression was black.

He gave Para a shove. "Go on, out!" he said. We had been playing a game of point and tell, where Para would point to an object: a paddle, an ear, a tree, and if I couldn't tell him the Māori word he would hit my arm with the flat of his paddle. He was enjoying the game more than I was, and I was relieved Jerningham returned. "Other canoe, you. I need to talk to Lugg."

And he shoved the waka off violently into the water, wading alongside before flinging himself aboard, his trousers wet to the thigh.

"Paddle!" he commanded to the men around us and they pulled fast away from the gardens and open land that belonged to the mission to where the banks closed in, the river quickened and vegetation crowded forward with roots and branches stretching out over the water.

The mist lifted in patches. I saw glimpses of blue sky in the strip between the banks above but it was slow in coming and the light was glittery, flickering through a soft gauze. I would have enjoyed watching the paddles sink in the soft sheen of the silvery water had I not the heavy presence of Jerningham beside me. He didn't speak. Driven by our companion's sour mood, the men pulled hard against the flow and we left the other waka behind.

We broke at a stretch of white water. The sun was sharp overhead now, forming deep shadows under the cliffs. A stream fell tumbling out of the bank opposite with a rattle and splash, fed from a tall waterfall inside a steep gully where ferns turned from black to blinding green as the light struck. Birds darted in and out from the trees, glossy and dark with a burnt saddle across their backs and bright wattle of dribbled orange from their beaks. They were clamorous, with cries of *tira-ti, tira-ki-ki*, squabbling and chattering. These were the tīraweke for which Jerningham was named. He wasn't chattering today.

We rested on a wide flat stone on the south bank, the sun burning my cheeks and steaming the water from Jerningham's duck-cloth trousers, while the Māori poled and pulled the waka and supplies up a safe passage through the rapids.

"This morning I was chastised by a native," Jerningham said, breaking the long silence. He took some loose pebbles from a smooth gouge in the rock and threw them hard at a log wedged in the current. He missed. "That brown-skinned hut-dweller warned me about my godless ways in front of his entire congregation. He goes too far. He may wear trousers and hold a Bible, but I will not take instruction in morals from a native convert. He says my life does not follow the path of righteousness and he has heard of my many, many sins."

"I see." I scooped up a stone and threw. It flicked off my wooden thumb and hit the log with a satisfying clunk. "He does have a point. You do have many, many sins. Perhaps he has been to Wanganui?"

"Oh, Wanganui! Why hang me with Wanganui?" He threw again and again, the pebbles splashing right and left of the log. "If the place is the den of debauchery portrayed it is hardly my fault. When things go well it is always the work of the industrious settlers and when things go ill somehow the blame always lies at my door. As if I have any control whatsoever over the degenerates who roll ashore from Australia, or make the trek from Wellington after failing to find success there! I am not responsible for the corruption of Wanganui. What influence do I have?"

I thought of Whare Wikitoria and his retinue of attendants, the beacon of depravity in the middle of the town where Jerningham was king. I said nothing.

"You know, I am in such a difficult position here. I'm not just talking about that rat-arsed, shit-coloured missionary wagging his finger at me! My uncle expects so much of me—God knows he writes to my father in a very critical way about all my shortcomings. What do they want? It seems I can do nothing right. My appointment as magistrate didn't please him, but I have no formal position within the Company. How am I supposed to gain any influence if all I get is secretarial work?"

"What sort of influence do you want?" I asked. "I wasn't aware you had political ambitions. Aren't you planning to go home and work for your father? I mean eventually, after our larking around here is over?"

"Certainly not! My fortunes lie here. You may be larking,

Lugg, but I am learning—and yes, I do have political ambitions. I do. But my uncle isn't helping at all. I don't think he wants me to succeed. He's a bitter man. It's his peevish little way of getting back at my father."

"I'm sure the colonel is very fond of you."

"Don't be absurd. He hates me. It was my father who took him to prison, you know. Oh, don't look so coy, you read the press. Uncle William was an accomplice to the business with Ellen Turner, dragged into the mire by Father. And his wife died while he was locked away. I say 'wife'. Others might not. He has a daughter, you know, born while he was locked away. That would take a bit of forgiving. Yet he worships my father, of course. He would never criticise *him* and he knew the risk they took when they played their little trick, but he will get his revenge through me. I see it now."

Played their little trick. It was an interesting description. Jerningham may have been told that phrase as a child to soften the impact of the prison visits, but surely as a man he knew the crime that had jailed his father and uncle was the abduction of a minor.

He sat on the rock with long-limbed boyishness, scrabbling for stones to throw, imitating a childhood a world away from Newgate Prison. Perhaps his uncle's obvious dislike of him did stem from this boy, his brother's son, who was very much alive and full of adventurous spirit, while the colonel had no son. No boy to run around the world and find such obvious pleasure in being alive.

"What do you think, Lugg? Of my political aspirations?" He edged forward and kicked at a wedge of stick, slamming it until it cracked free and fell into the water.

"What?" I said. "Oh, I don't know. I think it will be many years before New Zealand manages anything remotely resembling a political system. What do you want to be political about? It's all so damn wild still."

"I'll civilise the Māori but let them keep their culture. We don't need to suppress them. We can live together."

"How marvellous."

I threw another few stones into the brown water, but they all missed the target.

The waka following us appeared, and one after another from around the steep banks downstream, bare-chested warriors paddled out of the bush and posed like a postcard advertising an adventure story.

"This country needs people who understand what is here, before we layer ourselves like a blanket on top of the natives and smother an entire race to death. The missionaries are doing terrible things with their God-coated gifts and suppressions. I'm not larking about. Do you see that? I'm serious now, Lugg."

I believed him. Or I believed he meant what he said now, in this situation, with these river people. He was a different man in town. He had a habit of inconsistency.

"If you are seriously considering politics, you need to be careful with your reputation. Stop giving them rope with which to hang you."

"Oh, but I am careful," he said casually, the seriousness thrown away like a stone from his hand. "I hide my indiscretions very well. My uncle and the worthies know nothing of what I do outside of Company business. And what they don't know never happened."

That expression pulled me up sharply. Dorothy had said that, almost exactly those same words. *What you don't know didn't happen.* It was a horrible, dishonest phrase. I hadn't liked it from her lips and I didn't like it from Jerningham. I also didn't like the unlikely coincidence of the shared turn of phrase.

A wind chilled my back as the men paddled in and Jerningham sprang to his feet to pull them ashore. He caught one of Kuru's young nephews, all gangly limbs and a gap-toothed smile, as he leapt from the waka into his arms.

"Ka piki tāua i te rākau!" cried the boy and pointed to a heavy-limbed rātā tree, half fallen from the bank. It curved up and out over the water like the ruined arch of a great bridge, the whorls of broken branches worn smooth as marble, nature's carved gargoyles.

Jerningham laughed heartily, discarded his boots and jacket on the stones and raced the boy up the bank. They laid their hands on the angled trunk to look up in awe through the parasitic vegetation that grew from the tree's decomposing limbs.

The boy went first, a lift from behind sending him scampering fast up and along with the dexterity of youth, while Jerningham followed more cautiously, his pale feet gripping the texture of the bark and his hands seeking holds overhead. The Māori below clapped and called encouragement as the climbers appeared through the verdant growth out over the water. Legs astride, they edged along a knotted branch, standing to shimmy around a tangle of debris deposited some twenty feet in the air, evidence of the power of a previous flood.

Kuru's boy crouched and called an impressive cry—his voice was not yet broken but already it had the note of a young warrior. He leapt, spread star-shaped, then tucked roundly to plunge into the murky water with the splash of a boulder. Jerningham, cheered on by the natives below and with only a second's pause, shouted his war cry and followed suit. He fell as the boy had, curled up like a cannonball.

After the splash there was quiet, and then he shot back up into the daylight, with the river streaming from his hair and beard and a look of such exhilaration on his face I almost cried out with envy.

"You! You!" Kuru called out, turning to me; the Pākehā

friend who had yet to prove his courage. "You next!" The men on the beach turned to me and cheered me on.

But I shook my head, shutting my ears to the disappointed clacking of the natives. I wasn't a tree climber. Besides, I couldn't swim.

After that the weather turned, spring took a step backwards into wintery rain and my joy of adventure began to falter. Our constant paddlers felt neither rain nor cold and Jerningham, in a separate waka to avoid my falling mood, seemed in typical high spirits, teaching sea shanties and learning Māori songs. No one but me seemed to be worried that everything was wet, and we could get sick. I was miserably uncomfortable and felt a rawness beginning to scratch the back of my throat. My thumb stump ached with the damp, so I didn't paddle. I sat hunched under my inadequate adventurer's hat as water pooled around me and soaked through my jacket to my skin.

The nights we camped out were sodden, the wax on our tent rubbed away so rain seeped through to join the condensation inside and ran into our blankets. My skin felt constantly clammy and damp. Jerningham told me I complained too much, and he went to sleep out with the Māori under their bivouac.

One afternoon, in a stretch between towering cliffs, we climbed supplejack ladders through ferns and moss to a native village, a slippery and dangerous exploit for a man with one thumb. There we rested for a few days, hanging our gear in front of the fires to dry while Para went on to scout the river ahead.

"How do you do?" the villagers called to me in impeccably polite English as they rushed forward several times a day to shake my hand energetically, marvel at my stubble of blond beard and touch the blisters that had formed and broken on my sunburned skin. Some of the men had been down the river and claimed to recognise me; they said we had drunk together in Wanganui, but I didn't know them. They mistook me for another white man.

Our hosts fed us from their earth ovens and we ate with our fingers straight from the steaming flax baskets: kūmara and pounded fern root sticky with grease from kererū birds, flaked salted pork and slimy eel with watercress. We ate beyond capacity, and afterwards Jerningham passed spirits around. I witnessed both men and women take their first sip of alcohol and saw the twisted, sour expression it produced on their faces as they laughed and pretended to enjoy the fiery, foreign taste.

"The missionaries haven't got hold here, yet," said Jerningham as he smiled indulgently at the gathering of excited men who were playing games now, wrestling and mock fighting and posturing as they challenged each other to feats of strength. "They still own their own souls and are proud to be fierce and strong. But it won't be long before our Bible-bearing brothers tame them into passivity. They'll all be miserable as missionaries in a few years, mark me."

Although we were two hundred feet up a cliff face there were no barriers. Native children wandered to the edge and looked over as the traffic passed, heavily laden, up and down the rickety ladders.

"Kei taka tētahi tangata?" I asked a barefoot boy as I gently led him back from the edge. *Does anyone fall?*

"I ētahi wa!" he replied, his face lighting up. "Āe, ka kaha taka ētahi. Tokorua o ngā kuia i taka, i whara rāua." I loosely translated this as: *It happens all the time and two elderly women fell and were hurt.*

The splatter action the boy made with his hands was decidedly unpleasant. He ran away laughing.

These were Te Āti Awa people, related to Kuru and more distantly to Te Puni in Pito-one, and they were generous with us and plied us with gifts. Twice women came to my room at night, lowering rugs from their naked shoulders and blinking soft brown eyes. I sent them away with some small token, but I heard through the wall that Jerningham had no such scruples.

"Why can't you keep your trousers on?" I rebuked him. "There will be a tribe of little Jerninghams up and down the river."

"What a marvellous pedigree! My intelligence and Ātaahua's beauty."

"They will be half-caste bastards. Why assume the village will welcome them?"

"If you're writing a report for my uncle you should add that she sings a Māori verse before she sucks my cock, and her cunny tastes of those shiny river fish from the rapids. You know the ones, Lugg, you've eaten them. Very savoury, soft flesh tasting of herbs and salt. Lovely."

"You are debauched."

But he just waved his hand at me and went off in search of entertainment. His beard was long enough again to stick feathers in, and he'd taken to going barefoot and rolling his trousers. It was a stupid affectation and irritated me. It was cold and there was nothing wrong with his shoes.

I was sick when we continued, my throat was raw, I had a thumping head and pain in my bones. My thumb stump throbbed so I cradled my hand, not paddling, unable to get warm. Jerningham had gone ahead to meet Para, leaving me behind with the baggage and companions who couldn't make sense of me. I had no obvious dents, nor was I spurting blood, and the Māori didn't seem to recognise my illness. Perhaps general malaise was a European trait. The rain came in drifts and slopped at my feet and I became another piece of baggage to be carried ashore and placed in my tent in the evening, fed and returned to the waka the next morning.

We had lost the impatient Jerningham, who had taken a few porters up the Manganui tributary and overland towards the mountains ahead, though Para returned to guide us and we followed, encumbered by the increasing rapids and the large quantity of goods we carried. In my miserable state I was glad of a break from Jerningham's incessant energy and I dropped the pretence of intrepid explorer, dragging myself pitifully along, thinking of home and Dorothy and my warm bed. If there had been transport returning downstream I would have happily abandoned the expedition.

But on the third day out from the cliff-top pā the sun and the warmth returned, and I forced myself into happier spirits to look around me. The tributary was of a different character to the Wanganui, the water clear and fast, and we paddled under steep-sided gorges past foaming waterfalls dropping from cliffs. The brooding trees were replaced by regrowth of pale fern that the men dug up to bake the crushed roots. We ate them mixed with young eels that had a sour smell of dark earth and smoke.

Without Jerningham to push us on we rested often and stopped early, once at an abandoned pā where the mud and straw walls of the huts had crumbled fast into dust, and little remained but small brown lizards that flicked through the ruins. It seemed a whole village could disappear in months without trace, nothing remaining in metal or stone or clay for an archaeologist to read. I took my gun along the river and re-established my favour with the men by shooting several whio—small native ducks—and a couple of fat red-beaked pūkeko that looked like shining blue chickens on storks' legs but my companions told me tasted like mud.

There was pūhā growing wild all along the banks, a dark green leaf like sow thistle but without the bitterness. Our cook threw this in with every meal and I came to enjoy the fresh, sharp taste. I would ask Dorothy to add it to her garden.

We left the waka to walk overland with our burdens. For two days my legs burned with fatigue but my strength came back as we scrabbled through the lush forest, barren tussock tableland and swamps, until one morning the cloud lifted from our campsite and we stood before mountains of such dramatic beauty that all the pain of the travel fell to insignificance.

We were at the foot of Ruapehu, and I was astonished I had not felt the weight of it as we drew closer, that this wall of mountain could have been hidden for days behind something as ephemeral as a cloud. It rose on a wide, dark base, sprawled across the horizon from south to north, with snowy caps jagged against the blue sky. Little puffs of cloud drifted across the lower slopes. I had never been close to a mountain before. It was magnificent.

Para put his hand on my shoulder and introduced me proudly. It felt quite natural to be introduced to a mountain. Para te tai Tonga was the tallest peak of Ruapehu. North of this mountain was the smooth, symmetrical cone of Ngāuruhoe and, beyond that, the giant's smash of white-topped rubble that was Tongariro.

We walked north and east around the mountains for a couple more days, the porters resting frequently and struggling through swampy ground, crossing another large river, the Whakapapa, with the help of ropes braided from vines.

While I stumbled with my footing and complained of the soaking, Kuru's family, the women wrapped in their bundles with children tied on one side, walked into the water and out the far bank without pause. One child was swept away and retrieved, happily enough, from a rock above a tumbling fall.

After a long march as the light was failing, Para found, by some instinct, a stony path through the wetland. Every mile or so after that our men let off a volley until, just as the porters had found a dry patch of ground and put down their burdens for the night, there were answering shots that bounced around, echoing off a lake ahead. A party came running through the fern, whooping and laughing as they swept down on us with their arms outstretched, greeting their friends and cousins from the coast, pressing noses and crying their tangi and lifting our possessions to carry us all to the pā below the shapely Mount Pīhanga.

I felt a great unburdening when I came upon Jerningham. He sat in his battered hat and mud-splattered jacket, chatting with a near-naked Māori man. Despite the differences in their status and attire they looked remarkably similar, both lean and straight-postured with faces animated in the fire's glow. They were drawing sticks across the ground in what seemed to be a geography lesson, though I was unsure who was teaching whom.

I reported an uneventful journey, the possessions safely conveyed, and, with relief, passed leadership of the expedition back into Jerningham's far more capable hands.

—

Over the weeks that followed, Jerningham was everywhere, visiting chiefs, giving gifts, exploring the mountains and marvelling at the steaming pipes that came from inside the earth and hissed from the crevices.

In the evenings we walked to where water bubbled from under the sandy ground and merged with the cool water of a stream. This was irresistible to Jerningham, who stripped naked amidst a mass of vapour and lowered himself into a hot pool, the whiteness of his privates causing great amusement.

"Come on, Lugg, don't be shy. Yours won't be the first white cock they've seen, though obviously it'll be the smallest."

"I'll keep my clothes on, thank you," I said, though I did remove my boots and roll my trousers to rest my pasty feet in the sulphuric water. I am not a believer in the hocus pocus of the healing properties of water, but within minutes I was soothed and lulled into a peaceful repose beyond all expectation.

"Do you feel the ancient magic warming your bones?" asked Jerningham through the steam, liquid in his voice.

"Magic? No," I said. Jerningham was on one of his native fancies. But I did feel a deep and utterly satisfying relaxation.

The women arrived and stripped naked without shame. They sat with the men in the water or on the rocks in the steam, and I found myself with no alternative but to regard the curve of their bodies and their warm, honey-brown skin. Their muscles moved fluidly beneath the surface as the heat claimed them and they let go of all tension of movement and *doing*. These were strong women at rest, relaxed. I thought with wonder at how far I had journeyed from my home in Somerset to arrive in this exotic place.

As the evening cooled the steam rose in the darkness, hiding the bathers across the pool.

"Beautiful, aren't they? And free of all the nonsense about sin. You can have one if you want while you are here, Lugg, and no one will ever know. I certainly won't report you."

There was a woman on the rock behind him now, her legs dangling in the water, and he let his head fall back into her naked lap as she rubbed his shoulders and sang quietly to him.

He turned his head, his long, thick hair rubbing against her pubis, and gave me a lingering look through slanted eyes. "You want one, don't you? You are a man, and lust is common to us all. It's not a sin here. Oh, it's a pleasure. You have no idea what they can do."

I realised then, how far Jerningham had fallen into depravity; his sensual promiscuity leading him to create a new world with reconstructed morals. I stepped away, retrieved my boots and went away down the dark track.

———

We stayed a month in the region while Jerningham made friends, ingratiating himself with the prominent Ngāti Pehi Chief Heu Heu, and handing out his largesse like a visiting prince. We were not the only white men prospecting in the region: traders and missionaries passed through with their hidden ambitions, circling us like bristling dogs.

I climbed Mount Tīhia with our native companions, to where the great Lake Taupō filled the view, the far side just visible across a vast expanse of windswept water, dark grey and moody as the mountains behind us. There were pā all around the lake's edge and we visited many, our waka bobbing among the volcanic pumice stones that floated on the water. We were treated graciously everywhere and sat at many fires listening to stories of turbulent mountains that belched smoke and rock, and the rivers of liquid fire that flowed from the deep crevasses in the volatile land.

The natives entwined all this physical activity of the earth into ancestral stories, earnestly explaining their chiefs' descent from physical objects, and I grew to understand this belief as a leap of faith, in much the same way we believed our Queen was appointed by God. Their mountains contained spirits who danced, grew angry, loved, married and fought. One mountain, the classically shaped Taranaki north of Wanganui, had even picked up his skirts and moved to the coast in a pique of unrequited love, gouging the river as he passed through the land. Our lake, Rotoaira, was visible proof of his uprooting. Jerningham filled his journals with these narratives.

One idle afternoon Jerningham and I followed a trail from the settlement past a swampy flax grove and up Mount Pīhanga, expecting a good view of the distant Lake Taupō. We discovered instead, tucked in a crater in the mountain's top, a heart-shaped lake of extraordinary beauty. It was shallow and full of volcanic dust that threw sparkles from beneath the surface. The track wound through the bush to the water's edge.

"What would Dieffenbach make of all this?" I asked Jerningham as we sat on the beach to rest our legs, the chatty pīwakawaka birds fanning their tails at us. "All these stories of moving mountains and monster taniwha beating channels in rivers and lakes."

"He loves all this stuff," said Jerningham. "Talking mountains and gods and ancestor worship. He's more than happy to find science in myth. He thinks the Māori are a magnificent race and need protection from us. He's gone back to England now, you know, shipped out a few weeks ago, with his journals and records and observations. I don't imagine he'll paint us in a particularly good light." Jerningham was playing with the quartz sand, forming collapsing peaks on his knees. It had small grains of black and white and transparent glass and it looked precious. "He was here in Taupō exploring recently, and rather stupidly travelling with one of Hobson's men who was trying to buy up land from Chief Heu Heu. Without success, of course. He is not selling."

I was surprised at his news. "That puts Dieffenbach in a compromising position. He often told me our fundamental difference is that colonials work as individuals while the Māori think as a collective, and he was very keen on the

Māori keeping their tribal lands. Why would he travel with a land purchaser?"

Jerningham scooped handfuls of sand and let them fall, blowing them in an arc. They caught the light and sparkled. "He quarrelled with old Wide-awake," he said, "so perhaps he needed a new sponsor to fund his travels? My uncle never liked him. Too German. So he found another arrangement but Heu Heu would have nothing to do with them and sent them packing, and now the old chief's very suspicious of me. You should have heard the lecture I got about his sacred mountain and his unyielding right arm."

"Should he be suspicious? Why are you here if not to scout for land?"

Jerningham rolled his eyes and gave me one of his dramatic sighs. "Not you, too! I am not on Company business. I'm here because I'm curious. About everything. About the people and their mountains and stories and history and their way of life. How can we protect what we don't understand?"

He liked to paint himself in this light. Jerningham the defender. Jerningham the compassionate. He swam naked as a native in their rivers and listened to their language at the fireside, took part in their dances and learned the warlike haka, but during the day his eyes were everywhere, and he recorded in his journals where there was flat land for grazing and flax swamps for harvest. He made many friends but I wondered whether they, too, were for future exploitation. Any promises he gave would prove hollow if the men who followed decided they had no obligation to be bound by them.

When the last of his toys was exhausted; when the rolls of calico and blankets, tins of tea and sugar had been spent; when the cases of paper and pencils, boots and clothes and lamps and baked legs of ham were gone, we said our farewells to our new friends, leaving them with a final pouch of tobacco. Jerningham and Para paddled light and fast downstream, back to Wanganui.

I left Jerningham there with his business and friends. On my way home, I fell in with Mein Smith for a week or so surveying the Manawatū district. It was mid-summer now, the days running over with glorious, calm weather. I could have stayed longer but my thoughts turned to Dorothy, and so I accepted a horse and the company of Mein Smith's assistant surveyor, Mr Kettle, and rode overland back to Wellington, optimistic that with all the talking and listening, all the shared stories and songs and, yes, even the dancing, we could build decent lives in harmony with our natives, in a colony of which we could be proud.

FATHERHOOD
AND LAND COURT

WHEN I RETURNED HOME, not only was there a fourth pier in the harbour and four new houses along our road, but Dorothy had a belly on her.

"Four months," she said.

"How do you feel?"

"Oh, Arthur, I feel fine. Strong."

I wrapped my arms around her and cradled her head on my shoulder. I began to tell her how sorry I felt at being so long away on my travels, but she shushed me and told me I looked well on it.

I found Te Puni in our garden with Mr Ingestre, directing three energetic Māori boys who were filling a trench with cleared stones.

"Mr Ingestre is teaching me about proper drainage," Dorothy said. "And Te Puni is making the boys learn for his gardens at Pito-one."

Te Puni rushed over to shake my hand, reassuring himself that still, I was alive. "Aue—the drowned man is back!"

I took his warm hand in both of mine. "Kia ora, Te Puni. Kei te pēhea koe?"

"Kei te pai, eh. Kei te pai." His eyes rounded at my improved accent.

Dorothy had achieved a bountiful garden of summer

vegetables. I'd left bare earth and little seedlings sitting on our windowsills, and now the patch behind the house was vivid with green, a cottage garden as pretty as any in England. Lettuces, radishes and leeks stood in long neat rows, swathes of sweet-smelling flowering herbs at each end.

"For the insects," said Dorothy.

I brushed my hand over a patch of mint and the aroma broke powerfully enough to taste. There were climbing beans and peas as well, and a large raised bed of early-flowering potatoes. Other root vegetables, too, some of which I recognised from the Māori plantations but couldn't name. Baby fruit trees, fluttering with insects, formed a wall along the south fence, looking north to the bright sun. I told Dorothy about the pūhā rather hesitantly, thinking she would prefer English crops, but she agreed immediately and asked one of the boys to find some for her.

Te Puni, always tactile, put his hands on my arms and rubbed me in a friendly manner and then apologised that they had eaten the strawberries that morning. There had been only one each. But he twinkled and smiled, and I was inordinately proud of Dorothy for bringing him this pleasure.

The garden was awash with the high-pitched drone of the cicada. At first I found it excruciatingly noisy but soon it became the background sound to the bees, punctuated by a gang of noisy tūī whistling and cackling in the flax clumps along the border.

Lucy brought us out a jug of lemon water and put it on a new table. Te Puni wouldn't let his boys join us, but allowed them a cup of water and sent them away to sit on tree stumps.

"The table came from the wreck of the *Jewess*," Dorothy said, smoothing a colourful cloth over the wooden surface. "It was water damaged and no one wanted it, but it's rosewood. I thought it would do very well for the garden."

I went to bed early in the evening, exhausted from my travels, but woke when Dorothy joined me. I took her in my arms carefully, gently, asking all the while, "Is this all right? Will the baby know? Can I go deeper?" And she whispered, "Yes, yes, it is all right," until I quietly abandoned myself in her, lost in images of shiny brown limbs and naked breasts wrapped in steam. My bed had never felt softer and I slept well into the morning.

I went to the office around noon, but the colonel, after hearing the report of my travels, had no work for me. He was tied up with the recent arrival of his daughter Emily, from whom he had been estranged for years. I was pleased for him. A young woman about the place would do him good. It occurred to me that he was lonely.

Mr Hanson, now Crown Prosecutor, had commandeered the little room I shared with Jerningham and was in a meeting with the door firmly closed, and the colonel declared he would work from home for the rest of the week.

"I can't work with him there, you know," he muttered as he collected his papers together. "Hanson. Pompous ass."

He spoke as if he were growing tired of the pressure of public life, but perhaps he wanted to be closer to his daughter.

"You take some time off, Lugg, and enjoy the company of that pretty wife of yours. I don't understand why you would go traipsing around the country with Jerningham when you should be home building a family. And I do want you to start work on your country section. Get some men to clear it at least, before the end of the summer."

I did as he suggested. I spent time with Dorothy and kept her well fed and rested as her belly grew. I looked over my country land to keep up the pretence that I was a potential farmer rather than a mere speculator, and I had Mr Kettle do a survey, but I had little desire to clear and farm it and no financial need, yet, to sell.

Kettle discovered I had a gully filled with a valuable flax, which I organised to have harvested and sold to an American trader for a good price. I cleared the area and scattered grass seed with the thought of fencing it and bringing in a few sheep, but the birds took the seed and, without the flax to hold it, the whole bank slipped down the hillside, leaving a muddy gash. I walked away rather ashamed. Perhaps the flax would grow back eventually.

The summer stretched out and Dorothy spent it in the garden. I was often there with her as she grew less able to bend down. When our Lucy asked if she could keep hens, we picked up a gross and she managed them well. She learned to cook an excellent chicken broth.

In the autumn I took on some bookkeeping work for Dr Evans, and helped Captain Chaffers establish a filing system for the maritime office.

The first Nelson settlers had arrived on the *Fifeshire* in February to much celebration. It was followed by the *Lloyds*, a ship that had us all scandalised and provoked a scathing report from Captain Wakefield. He described the ship as a floating brothel with the master at the head of it, which had suffered the appalling loss of sixty-five children during the journey through the carelessness of the surgeon.

It was a damning indictment on the New Zealand Company. The colonel offered me the job of interviewing the landed settlers in Nelson, but I turned this down. I'd take no part in any attempt to bounce the tragedy away. The blame lay squarely with Edward Gibbon Wakefield and his poor selection of staff in England.

The *Martha Ridgeway* arrived in Wellington, her second trip to the colony, with more immigrants on their way to Captain Wakefield in Nelson. In 1840 she'd carried smallpox and the passengers were quarantined on arrival, but this trip brought hardy immigrants from Liverpool and a better welcome. Jerningham, back from Wanganui with a quick stop to greet his cousin Emily, leapt aboard to cross Cook's Strait and visit Charley in Nelson.

"Come with me, Lugg!"

But this time I had no desire to go adventuring. I had responsibilities.

———

I became a father in June, with Dr Dorset presiding in the bedroom, and Sam Revans filling my glass with brandy below and standing godfather to our daughter. We christened her Alexandria, for Dorothy's mother, and because such a delicate little thing deserved a pretty name. Dorothy held Alexandria close, nursed her and rose for her in the night, and only gave her up to Lucy when she was desperate for sleep.

The baby was placed in my arms occasionally, when I was sitting in front of the fire in my armchair, but the little thing was so well swaddled I found it hard to get a sense of her. I touched her downy pink skin with the tip of my finger, watched carefully by Dorothy as if she were afraid I would be clumsy and damage her. Then she would claim the baby back, as if aching with the pain of being apart.

I wrote an announcement to my father and took it to the shipping office. Alexandria wasn't his first grandchild, my brother had given him twin boys the previous year, but I wrote a proud letter and was probably looking well satisfied with myself when I met Ada collecting her mail.

I gave her my news.

Ada had grown thin since I had last seen her. The small groove in her collarbone I had so often traced with my tongue was now a long chiselled sweep. I had become used to soft, full women. Ada looked sharp. "I am pleased for you, Arthur, congratulations."

"And you, Ada, how are you?" Her eyes were glassy and I had never seen her look so unhappy.

"We have had no such luck, you know," she said quietly. Together, Ada and I turned away from the bustle of the post room and the chatter at the counter and looked out of the window, across the thick mist that hung on the harbour. There was a crack in the glass. "And of course I am no fool. I know the fault must lie with me. Your news now is proof of that."

"Ada ..."

"Well. It's a fact." Her voice was low and controlled and she looked out into the mist as if the black sticks crawling across the flat grey water were rowing in with her mail, and she would wait without moving until they arrived. "I don't mean to dampen your joy, Arthur. I really am very happy for you." She took a breath. "And Dorothy. Please give her my best."

"Thank you."

"Do you miss me, Arthur?"

I hadn't. Until that moment, Ada had settled into my past. I had other images in my mind now and I'd hardly thought about her over the summer when I was travelling, or for the last months as my baby grew inside Dorothy and was birthed. It didn't occur to me anymore to walk past Malloy's house on a Friday to see which way the flax fell.

I started to reply but there were no words that made sense; she was wild country and I had come home now, to domesticity. In profile, her face had a tragic aspect, her lips stretched long, and the skin over her cheeks was pale and tight. There was a map of fine lines on her neck, and I thought of the times I had followed those ley lines down across her landscape and into the interior of her. I steadied my breathing.

"John throws himself into his work. He's an observer in the Land Court now, all this complicated business of who owns what and what has been paid for. He's back and forward to Nelson to visit Captain Wakefield over all these disputes about a valley they want to survey. He talks of nothing else." She sighed. "I am so tired of the whole jolly thing."

"You don't look well."

She turned and gave me a grateful smile then, surprised someone had noticed her. But her words were chilling. "I don't know that I am. I find it hard to be happy. I want what Dorothy has."

"Ada," I said gently. "A baby is in God's hands."

"Not a baby. You. I want you. It's always been you. There can never be anyone else."

She turned slightly and I, too, moved and our hands touched in promise and fell apart as we went back to the counter to collect our mail.

Obligation, friendship, love, lust. I felt all these for Ada, along with the choking sadness that came from knowing that she was not my wife and I could never be allowed to make her happy.

—

Jerningham was called back to town to give evidence to Hobson's Land Claims Court presided over by William Spain, which had settled into Wellington with the ponderous authority of a slow-moving turtle.

Spain had a shining bald head, casually trimmed brows and beard, and a cheerful expression, as if happy to engage a man in light banter. This was misleading. Spain didn't banter. Behind the jolly face was a fastidious inner mind that concentrated on the work at hand.

He came to undertake an examination of every land purchase by the New Zealand Company and to hear all claims and counter claims. Each witness had as much time as required on the stand for the court's methodical interrogation. Jerningham's expectation of a swift and predetermined settlement was smothered under the weight of political pedantry.

Spain was accompanied by George Clarke Jr, a surprising appointment for the sub-protector of aborigines as the lad was not yet nineteen and also expected to act in the capacity of interpreter. He was the son of the despised missionary who had previously accompanied Hobson and, as such, the butt of much hostility by settlers.

"This is nonsense!" roared Jerningham in the public bar of Dicky Barrett's hotel. "How can the boy both interpret *and* fulfil his duty as protector, without bias? Someone give this child a lesson in the meaning of 'conflict of interest' and for God's sake take him a razor to wipe that chicken fluff off his face!"

A rivalry had sprung up between the two young men, and outside of the courtroom their mutual loathing became a public spat. Sarcastic comments flicked between them, two fighting tom cats with their claws out. Jerningham said that Clarke was a lad with his tail-coat on for the first time, poorly educated and incapable. To which Clarke replied Jerningham was an eccentric wastrel, sarcastic and bitter. He said he exhibited a strain of rowdyism, which had us all laughing. It was true, of course.

After church, with a dozen settlers as his audience, Jerningham loudly suggested to the reverend that Clarke should join the boys' choir as his voice had yet to break. Clarke raised his head imperiously high above his thin shoulders but the effect was lost as his child's voice broke into a man's register. "You may mock me, but you walk with sin as your constant shadow."

Laughter followed his red face through the church gates.

But the damage to the Company, inexorably, was presented not by these bickering youngsters but by our own turncoat, Hanson, who petitioned the Company's arrangement of providing tenths of land for the Māori through random sections that took no account of their traditional gardens and pā.

"Traditional?" cried Jerningham, interrupting the court. "Do you think so, Mr Hanson? Ancestral land handed down from father to son from times immemorial, is it?"

William Spain's eyes narrowed, but he allowed the challenge to continue.

"These iwi came from Taranaki less than eight years ago. Existing sites, yes. Traditional, no. Mr Spain, do you see how Mr Hanson twists his words? Our Māori friends will be badly served for the future if Mr Hanson corrals them together into ghettos in the town. If the natives live among us, the value of their land rises in line with our own. Our prosperity becomes their prosperity."

Spain waved at Jerningham to sit and continued with Hanson. They debated the meaning of the word "purchase".

"To the Māori 'purchase' means, at most, the right to settle on the same terms as the existing Māori owners. To share the land and to maintain it unchanged for the future," explained Hanson to Spain, at which Jerningham again leapt to his feet and objected.

"Mr Hanson has little knowledge of Māori custom and no skills as a translator. He is prejudiced by the twisted interpretation of these *missionaries*." He spat the word at Clarke.

Spain slapped his hand on the desk and tipped his

shining head forward to glower at Jerningham. "You will be silent until given the floor, Mr Wakefield, or I will hold you in contempt of this court."

The colonel, too, was brow-beaten by the indefatigable Spain. After calling Jerningham, Dr Dorset and Te Puni as witnesses to the original purchase, Spain wanted more evidence, but the colonel had no more witnesses to bring. Spain demanded proof both of Māori right and Māori intent to sell the land, and this the colonel was unable to provide.

"Which law are we following today, Mr Spain?" the colonel asked one morning, at the end of a long week of battling. "British law of 1841? Our various interpretations of the laws of the Confederation of Chiefs of 1839? Or young Mr Clarke's personal interpretation of tribal law, as he sees fit to share with us from his deep wisdom and experience of colonial diplomacy? Hmmm? Which is it today?"

That morning Hanson called Chief Wī Tako to the stand. The Māori stood soberly before the court in a tailored English suit with a startlingly white front and formal bow tie. He held a top hat in his hand and his hair was parted and glistened with pomade, framing the chiselled tattoos that rose from between his brows and circled his cheeks and chin. He bowed politely to the court with a dignity that had nothing to do with his fine clothes.

"He looks impressive," I said under my breath to Jerningham.

"He didn't look like that in '39," Jerningham snarled.

Wī Tako's evidence was clear and compelling and William Spain hung on the details. Yes, he had accepted gifts from Colonel Wakefield when he had arrived with his small group of men on the *Tory*, and he had agreed that the white men could live among them. This is what he agreed. He had not agreed to give up his land. Absolutely not.

Colonel Wakefield walked out.

Both men could see only the one truth, which they iterated clearly and authoritatively in their own language, convinced that there was no need for compromise or compensation because justice should and must be on their side. I didn't envy William Spain, his usual sanguine expression turned melancholic as he watched the door slam behind the colonel. He rubbed his tired eyes. There was no justice that could satisfy this court, and this was only the beginning.

BOWLER AND BETRAYAL

GOVERNOR HOBSON died in September of 1842, and Willoughby Shortland was appointed to hold the country until a new governor was appointed. It made little difference to us in Wellington. There was no mourning. As Jerningham said before he disappeared up to Wanganui again, one pompous ass bankrupting the country in Auckland was as good as another. It seemed a sad end to a difficult life.

The colonel eventually, after months of delay and tactical manipulation, came around to some kind of agreement with Spain at the Land Court. It appeared there was nothing on this earth that could not be bought and sold, it was just a matter of price. Captain Wakefield was called from Nelson for consultation, and missives were despatched to Ernest Gibbon Wakefield over the sea but, eventually, the New Zealand Company was obliged to reach deep into the coffers to distribute gold in large quantities to all claimants, which appeared to satisfy the Māori and the crown, though many of us could not understand how this purchase differed from any that had gone before.

I invited Mein Smith, Revans and Captain Arthur Wakefield to Sunday dinner. We arranged a cook for the occasion, who turned on a splendid leg of mutton, and Dorothy presented us with a colourful array of vegetables from her garden.

"Does this agreement mean your land in Nelson is now guaranteed, Captain?" I asked. The whole settlement process was so haphazard and confusing I had lost track of what had been compensated and what lost.

"Mostly, yes, I think so. Unfortunately, Te Rauparaha is still challenging some papers with his mark on them." Captain Wakefield helped himself to a serving of beans and complimented Dorothy kindly on her produce. "Marvellous, Mrs Lugg. We should get you over to Nelson to show them how it's done!" He turned back to the men, the dip of a frown between his brows. "There's a valley in the east that might provide the space we need for our country sections, which Te Rauparaha now insists was not included in the original purchase. Beans, Sam?"

"No, but I'd be partial to another helping of those potatoes, Mrs Lugg, if I may?"

"Good land, is it?" asked Mein Smith.

"We don't have a proper idea of what's there yet—it needs surveying. It's empty wasteland, but flat and with good access from the coast. Wairau Valley."

"Oh, yes," said Mein Smith. "I think it was part of the agreement. I know the place. Flood prone, perhaps? Best to have a good look before you get the courts involved—it may not be suitable."

I didn't know the area. I asked after the young surveyors. Dorothy, who had taken the men's compliments shyly without speaking, looked up at that.

"How is Charley Torlesse getting along?" she asked. "We enjoyed his company when he visited us here. Is he finding his feet?"

"He is indeed, Mrs Lugg," said Captain Wakefield. "I shall tell him you were asking after him."

It was the only conversation Dorothy initiated during the meal and she blushed when she spoke. All three men smiled indulgently. My quiet wife with her reserved manners was turning into a charmer.

We had poured the port when we learned that Mein Smith had been dismissed from his survey in Manawatū.

"The colonel has appointed Samuel Brees to replace me, with immediate effect," he said. "I've disappointed him yet again with my inflexible morals. I'm sorry, Arthur—" this to the captain, "—your brother is a fine man in many regards, but we do not always see eye to eye on how things should be done. I draw the line at surveying where land ownership is not confirmed."

I was not particularly surprised at his dismissal. The colonel and Mein Smith had been coming to this pass for years.

"I have a commission, though, to explore the east coast of Middle Island, Banks Peninsula area. There's a possibility of a further colony, don't you know? I will leave the family here and take to sea again. I'd be grateful, Mrs Lugg, if you would drop in on my wife occasionally. She is very fond of your little baby and I dare say she'd enjoy the company."

Dorothy signalled to Lucy to remove the plates. "Of course, Mr Smith. I'd be delighted to call." Her happiness at being included and considered useful was clear on her face.

—

October came with blustery gales. Mein Smith went south, Captain Arthur Wakefield returned to Nelson and Revans was busy with his timber and a new enterprise he was chasing around the coast in the Wairarapa. Charles Heaphy returned from England, as he promised he would, but went directly to Nelson to explore the mountains he loved so much, and we didn't see him.

Jerningham stayed in Wanganui and took up his old ways. News from that quarter always included some tale or other of debauchery and recklessness. In a peevish fit he ordered Whare Wikitoria be dismantled. The combative stance of the Māori over land had led him, he said, to declare that they had broken faith with him and he would no longer grace them with his presence. Although the house had been used for ill purposes, it was beautifully built and the rafters carved from a magnificent tōtara tree. Such trees held a history and a story to the Māori. Jerningham, of all people, knew the offence this would cause, but he had his boys level the place and then complained to everyone of the slippery hearts of his erstwhile friends.

Towards the end of the summer Jerningham wrote to me, asking me to meet him at Waikanae, at Reverend Hadfield's mission. I rode over the newly widened Porirua Road without difficulty, more for the pleasure of seeing Hadfield than in response to Jerningham's summons.

"You're to go to the island," Hadfield told me, after I had been formally welcomed and touched by a hundred hands. I was deft now at dispensing trinkets and sweets and able to converse, albeit superficially, in Māori. "Jerningham has an appointment with Te Rauparaha tomorrow and wants an honest witness. Something about the Nelson business and the deal for the Wairau Valley. I expect him this evening."

"I won't go to Kāpiti," I told him. I had a fear of that place, the long dark island on the horizon and the unpredictable warrior chief who walked there. "I have no aspiration to meet Te Rauparaha or to go into his den."

We walked to the beach as the sun went down, with a bright fire lit as a beacon for the travellers, and waited for Jerningham to appear. There was no sunset as there had been no cloud, and the light dropped out of the sky as the sand and sea faded to grey.

It was around the end of March and the ground was still full of summer: the thick dry beach grasses smelled of salt and the waft of early decay came from vegetation at the river mouth. This coast didn't suffer from ill winds like Wellington and the heat remained in hollows of the dunes with the warmth of recently extinguished fires. The tribes were at peace still, perhaps the longest stretch of comparatively easy living the coast had ever known. All was well under Hadfield's pastoral care.

Over the crash and drag of waves on sand eventually came other splashes with a different rhythm, and from the north two long waka appeared through the dusk and turned into the waves. Jerningham made his flamboyant entrance, riding tall on the carved prow above foaming breakers. He was dressed in a Māori korowai, a cloak of flax and feathers. He leapt ashore in the pause between crash and undertow and, with his band of companions, dragged the waka onto the beach.

"Lugg!" he called, his voice a clear note above the smash of the waves and scrape of the sand. "Good man! Stand back out of the way there or the boys will run over your feet. Good evening, Reverend!" He immediately turned to his men and called instructions, there were sacks of goods and a large leg of ham to carry to the mission before they could disperse to find their relatives.

Jerningham stayed on the shore until the last of the men had gone, resisting Hadfield's invitation to go up. He seemed excited about something as he chivvied his men and then shooed them away.

"Have you seen it?" he asked, when we three were alone— Hadfield, Jerningham and myself. He was looking up at the clear night sky. The stars were bright overhead. He pointed to the south-west where the sky was now a gunmetal blue-grey, the last of the light dragged down under the horizon.

Once I focused on where he pointed, I could see it: a ball from which came a long stoke of light, extending upwards and spreading across the low stars on a northward trail above the island, a pale, luminous light that faded into the sky like the edge of a brush run dry of ink.

As the darkness deepened I recognised it as a comet. It was a spectacular thing, a beautiful phenomenon.

"They used to think a comet signified the end of the world," said Hadfield. "Or bad harvests, or plagues."

"Bodinus taught that it was the soul of an illustrious man sweeping across the heavens," said Jerningham. "I heard the story as a child, that comets were guardian angels watching over us. We can use this with Te Rauparaha, tell him it is an omen for peace."

"Are the Māori superstitious about comets?" I asked Hadfield, but he didn't know.

We walked through the sharp beach grasses to the mission, where people were gathered, watching the sky.

"He aha te mea?" they asked. What is it? I heard the word—atua. Spirit. We watched for an hour as the comet moved down the sky. It was startlingly bright in the clear night.

"He has gone," one of the elders said, as the earth turned her shoulder on that part of the sky.

"He has gone to rest," said Jerningham. "He will be back tomorrow."

The old man looked at Jerningham in disbelief. As if this white man could call the stars into the sky.

—

Against my better judgement, I went with Jerningham to Kāpiti Island. Perhaps it was the excitement of the comet, wild and flaming in the heavens. To me it seemed it could only be a brilliant portent, making me brave. Or perhaps it was just Jerningham, who always seemed able to goad me into accepting an adventure.

As we packed our gear he mentioned he had another job lined up for me. He needed me to accompany a man called Mr Bowler to New Plymouth. Recently arrived in Wellington and a friend of the family, the colonel wanted Jerningham to show him around but he was tied up with upcoming business in Wellington. I knew the New Plymouth settlers as well as he did. Would I mind? A couple of weeks, next month, up and back to settle him in?

"Who is he, this Mr Bowler?" I asked, and Jerningham replied that he was no one of particular importance, someone his father knew, starting a new life in New Zealand.

"What happened to his old life?" I asked.

"Oh, I don't know! Do you want a trip to New Plymouth or not?"

I agreed. I saw no reason not to, and it was an opportunity to see the progress of our fellow colony.

We were rowed out into the sea from Waikanae in a boat that came from the island. The whalers on board were rough and coarsely spoken, but I knew better now than to put myself above them and I shook their scarred hands as I climbed aboard and let them examine the workmanship of my wooden thumb. They were steady, competent rowers, and I wished we had their like in Wellington. We pulled into a little islet off the main island where there were fishing and whaling vessels, a large sealing boat and a crowd of twenty or so native men gathered on the shore.

"There's trouble for us here, potentially," Jerningham said. "That sealer, I think, has brought a delegation from Otago in the south including a Ngāi Tahu chief. They've been at war with Te Rauparaha for years, but the tribes now may form an allegiance, which will change the balance of power all across the country. I expect Rauparaha to be cocky today. You stay in the background, Lugg. It's enough that you witness a meeting taking place. Don't engage."

We stood respectfully aside on the beach as a contingent of Māori men walked past us into the water and lifted a man from their midst into a row-boat. His face was so covered by tattoos there was nothing recognisable beneath, the blue ink a mask. One eye was sewn shut over an old wound and pockmarked cheeks sagged on his skull, though his lips pulled back tightly in a grimace. He wore a dirty mat and a black tail-coat, and on his tangled hair was an old dragoon helmet.

"The whalers call him Jacky White," whispered Jerningham. "On account of his blue face. That'll be him, Chief Karetai, an extraordinary man. I do believe he's grinning. His day has gone well. That's not good for any future colony in the south."

There were a dozen men remaining on the beach. They looked strong and young and terrible, muscular bodies wrapped in flax skirts. From behind them came two leaders to greet us. I knew at once from their swagger that this was Te Rauparaha and his nephew, Te Rangihaeata.

The older man was small and monkey-faced, with a hooked nose, full facial tattoo and an overbite of long yellow teeth. He wore a captain's jacket over baggy trousers and a peaked cap, shiny with grease. I tried to judge his expression but his eyes drooped down and the eyelids overhung so low I couldn't see their light. He stood with the same stately posture of Te Puni but, where Te Puni held on to his pride, Te Rauparaha radiated his mana forward, sending out heat from his fire. He came distrustfully towards us and put his head up. I could see his eyes now, flickering to and past me—I obviously constituted no threat—to scan the men behind. Finally, he nodded to Jerningham, who stepped forward to press noses.

And then I was presented to Te Rauparaha, there on the beach. I bent my head, so he could push his nose against mine, and I mingled my breath with the cannibal's. His hand, when I shook it, was dry and thin, a brown claw. I thought I had got away without being much noticed, an unimportant travelling companion of Jerningham's, but when I pulled back he had his fierce eyes locked on my face and I knew I had been seen.

Next to Te Rauparaha, Rangihaeata was a giant of a man, swarthy and handsome, his hair elaborately curled and tied with feathers. His lips pulled back and he tipped his head as he greeted Jerningham. He spoke in a Māori slang I didn't understand but I recognised the insolent tone. His tattoos drove down in thick channels to the centre of his brow, so that he appeared to wear a constant, ferocious scowl.

He eyed Jerningham up and down, threw out more words and waved an arm forward threateningly, but Jerningham held his ground and his smile. I felt dizzy and unsteady at the thought of his turning on me, but Rangihaeata showed no interest in me at all. He shouted some insult in a bouncing voice and stomped a few paces away up the beach.

"You will forgive my nephew." Te Rauparaha's voice was reedy. He sounded like an old man to be pitied, and yet I knew I stood before one of the greatest orators of the Māori world.

It was Jerningham's reaction that chilled me. He spoke to the old chief in his language, some quip about Rangihaeata's manners needing improving, but it wasn't the words that sent the creeping dread through me. Jerningham's voice had risen in pitch, as if he spoke with a man he feared. It was a tone I'd never heard from him before.

They walked away up the beach, Jerningham and the cloaked chief. Te Rauparaha was shouting in English like a man coached in an argument and I wondered if the switch was for our benefit, the witnesses. "Will you chase us from our land? Does Wide-awake mean to take it all?"

Jerningham bantered something back in Māori, his language fast and fluent and said with an unconvincing laugh. Rangihaeata ran up and down around them, swearing and swaying like a drunk man, until the diminutive chief turned on him and shouted for him to go away, which, to my relief, he did, weaving unsteadily through the trees.

I remained with the whalers, but even from a distance I could see Jerningham was forcing nonchalance. He sat on the stones, stretched his legs out and prepared a pipe, passing it to Te Rauparaha, who eventually stopped his outburst and sat with him. All the men on the beach followed suit.

"Do ye know what Te Rauparaha did to that old man's tribe back in the day?" The whaler who had admired my thumb sat on the sand next to me, resting his back against a driftwood log, and jabbed a finger towards the ship with the departing delegation. I could see the blue-faced chief was on board and looking back to the shore as his men set the sails.

"The Ngāi Tahu?" I said. "No, I hadn't heard of them before today."

The sailor laughed. "Och no, they'll not tell ye that, the New Zealand Company, before they take your money and send ye here. It's a story that will haunt your sleep."

"I suspect you are going to tell me."

"Aye. I will. And ye'd better tell your master Wakefield to walk with care. He's a beast, Te Rauparaha, when he's riled, and he's riled over land in Wairau." His accent was hard Scottish—Glaswegian or somewhere else on the west coast—and the rolled "r" of the chief's name gave it a depth and colour I didn't like.

I watched the discussion across the beach. Jerningham, sprawled back on his elbow, was chatting with the chief, who was not relaxed, his head snapping around at anything that moved, jerkily pulling smoke from the pipe.

"Before I came out—1830 it were or '31—it was the usual haver, back and forward between the tribes. *I'll crush ye and all your descendants, I'll slit your belly with a shark's tooth*, that sort of thing. And then he, Te Rauparaha, went rampaging down south and it was a massacre. Ye'd not stomach the detail if I were to tell ye. Women and bairns too. He decorates his canoes with body parts, ye'll know the tales."

"He ate them, too, I'll warrant," I said.

"Aye," he said, "and worse. He dug up an elderly aunt of some chief, recently buried. He washed her body in the stream outside the chief's house. Then he cooked and ate her."

My stomach flipped. I looked away over the pretty blue sea to calm my guts. But there was more.

"The next season he went back. Och, he's a lying, treacherous bastard, for sure." The man lowered his voice now, taking no risk of being overheard. "Ye'll know about Captain Stewart? He's a bad one. Rauparaha promised him a cargo of flax if he'd transport warriors to Akaroa, down on Banks Peninsula. There was a chief called Maiharanui who'd given him bad words, and Te Rauparaha wanted his utu, you know they seek revenge for the slightest insult. So they sailed south on Stewart's ship and when they got to Akaroa, Rauparaha hid with all his men below deck. Stewart called Maiharanui on board the ship. 'You have some flax for me? I can pay you in muskets, you want muskets? You go down below, chiefy, and see the muskets.'"

I could imagine the scene. The chief descending the ladder into the hold where his wide-eyed enemy waited.

"Maiharanui had his lassie with him. She was, oh, maybe ten or eleven. A wee bairn she was. So down she went, into the hold, with her da. The wife came on board, aye, she went down to find her man. And then another chief came on board, and another one. And their men followed, to see the ship, to meet the captain and the crew, and one by one they went down into the hold. They had quite a human cargo by the end of the day and they kept them alive in chains and tortured them for six weeks. Oh, all except the little girl. Rauparaha didn't get her."

My ears were cold on the inside. It was a warm morning, but I tried to freeze out this man talking and talking.

"Her father strangled her to death with his bare hands. Strangled his own bairn."

"Stop talking now."

"That was before Rauparaha burned his eyes out. I don't know how the wife died, but they ate her in front of him, though I suppose he couldn't see it by then, so that was a blessing, eh? The smell must have been horrific. And the sound of men eating his wife. Then they slit Te Maiharanui's throat and all gathered around to gulp down his blood."

Jerningham! What was he doing with this cruel and dangerous man, sitting on the sand as if in friendship. He was making gestures now, pointing into the sky and trailing his hand across, talking about the comet, and Te Rauparaha was listening closely, his entourage crowding in, hanging on his words, listening to the Englishman's predictions. They were suspicious and in awe, undecided if Jerningham was a god or a devil. These were dangerous, unpredictable men, vicious beyond imagining and he juggled with death even being here, on this island. At any minute the old cannibal could light the fires in which to cook his enemies.

I wanted to be away from that beach. It was not my place.

I closed my eyes to the scene of the natives gathered around Jerningham, and my ears to the horrors of the whaler's talk and imagined myself far away. I had no other defence. If I couldn't see them, perhaps I wasn't there.

I was still sick and shaking when we crossed back to the mainland. Jerningham was rattled and in no mood to talk.

I asked if he had told them the comet portended peace and he snarled that Rauparaha said it was a sign of death. It was one thing hearing fireside stories of these cruel and violent men, quite another to put yourself deliberately in their path. I pleaded a headache to Hadfield at the mission and wrapped my blanket around me in the communal sleeping house, feigning sleep when they came to rouse me for the evening meal.

"I'll follow you to Wellington in a few days," called Jerningham as I went to leave early the next morning. "Don't forget Mr Bowler, will you? In a couple of weeks. I'll arrange everything."

—

"I don't want you to go to New Plymouth with this Mr Bowler."

We had finished breakfast, Dorothy had Alexandria on her lap and the baby was playing with the stuff of her shawl, fingering the table cloth, little fingers reaching everywhere. My wife seemed angrier than necessary. I had agreed now I was a father I would not go adventuring any more, but this was a quick trip up and down the coast and it was Company business, not a pleasure jaunt.

"I do it as a favour for Jerningham. He's busy and I know the New Plymouth settlers. He's asked me as a friend."

"You think he's your friend?" she said. "Jerningham? He is not to be trusted, Arthur. Oh, believe me, he is not."

"What is the problem, Dorothy? Why this hostility?"

"Have you even met Mr Bowler? Do you know who he is?"

"He's a friend of the Wakefields from London. They are helping him settle here. It's really no—"

"A friend of the Wakefields?"

"Don't question me, Dorothy," I said. "I have a job and

I'm going to do it. Yes, he's a friend of Colonel Wakefield's and I'm taking him to New Plymouth to introduce him."

Dorothy peeled the baby's fingers from her face impatiently and held them tightly in her fist. She reached for her teacup but her fingers were shaking. It clattered as she dropped it back onto the saucer.

"Oh, Arthur! He *is* a Wakefield. He is the colonel's brother. His real name is Daniel Wakefield. He is on the run from his wife and creditors."

"How do you know this?"

"Mr Revans told me. It's the truth, Arthur. Daniel Wakefield is disgraced, a drunken gambler. He infected his wife with a dirty disease and he has left her bankrupt and come here to hide under a false name. They are horrible people. And now they implicate you in their nasty scandal."

"Revans told you? Why would he take you into his confidence?"

Dorothy shrugged. The baby, suddenly still, turned to stare at me with her big eyes. What didn't I know?

"Why would he?" I asked again. "When does Revans ever talk to you?"

"When you are away. You told him to drop in and look after me. And he does, Arthur, he keeps me company— oh don't be silly—he behaves entirely respectably! He comes for dinner and we talk about gardening and politics, everything, really."

"Revans comes here? When I am away?"

She lifted an eyebrow to me, as if to say *why not?*

The idea of my gruff, intelligent friend enjoying dinner conversation with my wife was absurd. On the other hand Revans had always treated Dorothy with consideration and respect, and he was the godfather of our child. I found Dorothy's quiet company soothing sometimes—perhaps lonely Revans did too.

"Like a father, Arthur. He's fond of Alexandria and he is kind to me."

"This is true, then? Revans told you Mr Bowler is Colonel Wakefield's brother, Daniel?"

"Yes. They're hiding him here. Jerningham is using you to introduce a criminal to society. It's despicable."

The bastard. He had me running up to Kāpiti and to that stinking island so he could discharge a dirty job to me. He'd looked me in the eyes and lied to me. Deliberately. And I had discovered his deviousness through my wife. How galling. Dorothy, who sat with her pretty lace collar and her baby and her white skin, all these years her intuitive dislike of Jerningham had been right and all the times I had defended him made me the fool.

I pushed my chair back and the china jumped. I stood up. I wanted to say something to Dorothy: that she was right to tell me about Bowler, that Jerningham *was* despicable, that I would run no more errands for him. But she sat with her eyes down as if afraid of me and I turned my back on her timidity. I would not give her the satisfaction of an apology. I wanted satisfaction from Jerningham.

With a clenched jaw I went into town.

—

Jerningham was alone in the office and sitting at the colonel's desk. "Lugg! I was about to take a break from this nonsense. The Southern Cross, dear boy, is a favourite of mine these days. We'll have a quick after-breakfast brandy and make plans for your trip. Mr Bowler will join us."

"No."

He was so smooth, so sure of me. Was I such an easy man to implicate in scandal? As I approached the desk he quickly covered the documents in front of him. The letters of introduction, perhaps.

"No," I said. "I will not go anywhere with you or with Mr Bowler. You are contemptible, Jerningham."

He looked up sharply with that way he had, his narrowed eyes as if the rest of the world had disappeared. "How so?"

"I've just had a very distressing conversation with my wife."

His whole countenance shifted then, as alert as when he switched from drunk to sober in a blink, but this time he wasn't drunk. He heard me. I was a war cry in the hills. I slammed my hands on the desk and leaned over to him.

"Dorothy told me your dirty secret. Why do I obtain this knowledge from my *wife*? You are dishonourable, sir, to taint me so. For how long do you think I should remain a fool?"

And once again, as he had in Whare Wikitoria in Wanganui, Jerningham lowered his head in abject submissiveness. He clutched his hands together as though in prayer. He could clean up his family's mess himself.

"Does it amuse you to prey on my naïvety?" I asked. "Do you think so little of my honour? Do you think you can dispose of your sinner by passing the responsibility to me? How dare you, Jerningham. How *dare* you!"

"Arthur. Please believe me. This has hung over me. I am not proud of it. It was very wrong, but 'dispose' is the wrong word, and there are so many times when I have wanted to beg your forgiveness, but you know, this was not my secret to tell."

"Yet you would disgrace me with it."

"I hope not." He looked up then. God had given the bastard clear eyes in a guileless face. "I hope you are not disgraced. Please forgive me. It would have been better if I had told you at the beginning, I know that. But some things are so very hard to say." His breath left him, his eyes shifted and he looked deflated, smaller. His shoulders rounded and he put his head down. "It was once, Arthur. Just the once. And then you married her and I have never looked at her again."

There was a tick in the corner of my eye. It flicked once, then again. The sounds of his words ran across the top of my brain and joined somewhere in my head, where noise becomes words and words become meaning and the pain began. He looked up then and realised what he had done.

His mouth formed into an O for a second and then shut abruptly and I saw the Adam's apple in his throat go up and down, the sin from the world's beginning lodged in his throat.

So it was true. Words and pictures jumped and twisted behind pain in my eyes and they formed a familiar story.

I had let it go. Dismissed it. I had accepted that the tension between Jerningham and Dorothy was caused by his knowledge of her debasement with the scoundrel on the boat. The stiltedness when they met was his restraint at her embarrassment.

But there had been no restraint. At some time, between Dorothy coming ashore in distress and our marriage, Jerningham had fucked her. Just the once. As if just the once was forgivable. Not twice. Just the once. And since then, both of them, *both of them*, had lived with the frisson that one or the other might tell. Every time they met, that tight intimacy must have pulled and pulled. How horribly thrilling for them to keep such a secret from me.

The pain ripped through my head now, with unbearable violence. It had all been a lie, right from the beginning. She had lied to me. Jerningham had lied to me. My life with Dorothy was entirely a fabrication; she had never fallen in love with me at all. My whole life in the colony was a construction designed by Jerningham. He had used Dorothy, after she had already suffered such violation, and then pushed her onto me. I knew it now, all the hints, the chance meetings, my *nurse*. I mopped up his discarded woman and I was the biggest fool that ever walked this rotting earth.

His voice was quiet. He was watching me. "Oh my God, Arthur. You didn't know. She hadn't told you. What have I done?"

I walked out. It was cleaner that way.

"Lugg!"

I walked out on Jerningham. I walked out on Dorothy and the child.

I left a note for Revans, shed my sullied self on the beach and called to a dinghy pulling out on the water. There was a ship weighing anchor and I climbed aboard.

We were at sail before I made my presence known to the captain. He was only going to Nelson, but I didn't care. Sydney would have been better but Nelson, at least, was away. The ship's wake slipped behind me like slime and I turned my back on Wellington and its people. I couldn't bear to be near any of them.

NELSON

PORT SIDE, between the aft steps to the quarter deck and the ship's rail, lay a pocket of space, an unpleasant place where the wind gusted in sharp rips, stinging my eyes with its tears. I braced myself and faced the cold south, away from the coastal view and whatever winter warmth was to be found in the midday sun. There were dolphins in the bow wave and I could hear the delighted cries of other passengers flying away on the westerly wind.

The sound of trampling and crying of penned animals came from below decks, and the reek of urine, flesh and mud melted into a foul bile in my throat, though if I paused and concentrated, in reality there was no smell from the animals at all. I took a deep breath and there was only cleanliness and salt. The smell of shit and guts was inside me.

I remembered Jerningham's heroics during the storm on this same water, on the ill-fated journey back from Wanganui the first time. I thought I had known how to hate him then, but he had turned me around with an extraordinary act. We had been falling down a wave the size of a small hill, clinging to the braces with the strength of every prayer we could muster, when Jerningham had let go and dropped down the length of the steeply sloping deck, looking like a lost man. He threw out an arm and hooked the rigging, reaching out to wrap himself across my friend

Aata, who dangled half into the sea. When we smashed into the bottom of the water hill, with the strength of ten men he used the momentum of the wave to scoop the boy back from the brink and with fast, controlled movements, he lashed them both to the rigging. For hours we were punished by the storm and I saw Jerningham speaking to the boy as if no rain slashed across their faces, as if this was a jaunt and they should laugh into the wind and trust this storm would pass.

We held on, Aata survived, the storm passed.

I blinked Jerningham away. Now, in my loneliness, Ada was there. Not naked and wanton on the rug in the sun at Malloy's house, but as she had been on the rolling *Aurora*, buttoned up and seriously spoken, earnest in her desire to be part of this better life we were going to create. We had walked back and forward across nautical miles, making plans to change the world together. Ada declared our marriage would unite her imagination and my common sense, and what a wonderful union it would be! We would bring good principles to the colony and allow freedom to grow from generous hearts. She ardently believed in Ernest Gibbon Wakefield's colonial system and his nostalgic dream. Our settlements would recreate England as it was before the upheavals of industry drove our country peasants to city slums. We would give the working class education and skills, so they could contribute to their own future. "People need to have control over their lives, Arthur," she had said.

Indeed, Ada.

Within a year all that was forgotten and she had handed control of her life to Bently, the godson of a Wakefield. And that was Jerningham's doing, too, of course. I have no doubt it was Jerningham who spread rumours that Dorothy was more to me than my nurse, so Ada would despise and reject me. Malloy would never have come looking for me that night when Dorothy happened to be waiting in my darkened room, if Jerningham had not sent him.

How much simpler, better, my life would have been if I had never met Jerningham, if Ada and I had been allowed to marry properly, in law, rather than living this absurd fantasy where we were married only in a box room, on Fridays, when her brother and his wife were in the country.

Middle Island was visible as a series of lines, blue on blue above a misty sea, each hill and mountain getting progressively lighter to the snowy peaks. We journeyed north towards Kāpiti Island with a fair wind in our sails and, broadside to the swell, rolled alarmingly through the troughs that marched across the narrow strip of water between the islands.

Once past the Wellington heads most passengers had gone below, but I was sick and wretched and preferred to stay above, drenched with spray and eyes stinging. I shed tears to clear the salt. As was my habit on board after the storm experience, I had looped a standing rope around my arm but annoyingly now it had become tangled and my unmanned right hand could not pull the rope apart where it crossed. It was not the first time I had discovered that fingers without a thumb could not untie a knot. As I pulled, the knot drew tighter. I was about to bring my teeth into play when a shadow fell across me.

"Mr Lugg. This is a surprise, I didn't see you on the passenger list."

Ada's husband was at my side holding out his hand, which of course I couldn't shake. I looked at him bleakly. God had a cruel sense of humour. There was no man less welcome to me than John Bently.

He had lost the sleek, self-important glow of the newly arrived and had turned into a colonial like the rest of us, with an often-brushed jacket, and boots that would go extra miles before being replaced.

"Oh, you're tangled! Excuse me. May I help?"

"All's well, sir. Please do not trouble yourself." I turned away from him, but my arm remained caught.

He didn't touch it, but looked at me quizzically.

Bently was taller than me, broader, but we shared the same fair colouring and mild-featured, complacent English look. He might have been my older more handsome brother. I wondered that I had not noticed this before. Is that what had attracted Ada to him? Or perhaps she wasn't looking at his likeness at all but noticing, instead, his considerable wealth and superior position. I wished he would leave.

But, instead, Malloy leaned his arms on the railings and looked across to the sculptured mountains of the Sounds and the light bounced from water to flicker over his gentlemanly face. He seemed content to watch the seagulls swooping low across the sea.

We lurched and I twisted my arm as I steadied myself, tied like a leashed dog while Bently graciously ignored me. I picked at the knot again with my fingers but could get no grip.

"Look, Bently, would you mind?"

I was the fool, with my crippled hand flapping and tangled in a rope like a punished dog. Yet, Ada loves me, I thought. She chose me.

I was still while Bently obligingly dug in his thumbs to part the wet rope so my arm could slide out.

He made no conversation, for which I was grateful, and when I was free he merely stepped well back as I squeezed past him to escape our confinement and went below.

—

A pilot took us into Nelson Haven, past the dismantled wreck of the *Fifeshire*, wrapped on the large lump of rock in the harbour entrance. It seemed typical of the colony that an otherwise perfect harbour was marred by such a thorn. Every harbour had its rock. We moored and were rowed ashore in a cool rain and the evening closed in.

I stood on the beach. A freshly painted white picket fence ran along the shoreline for no reason, not appearing to separate anything from anywhere, but it was a welcome sign of civilisation nonetheless. There was little else. A good road wound along the shore to the left, past a cluster of wooden buildings, and to the right a dirt track went steeply up the hill. Tents and loosely built sheds cut into a ledge on the sloping shore. In the year and a half Nelson had been in existence, it didn't have much to show for itself. Firelight glowed from the windows of small huts on the bank.

I hadn't much in mind other than to find a billet for the night, and some drink, but I seemed incapable of making either come to pass. I was wet, with no change of clothing and no money other than a few pounds in my pocket and some coins. I hesitated on the grey sand as passengers from the ship came ashore, loading their possessions into hand-carts or hefting them onto their backs, and walked on past me. Barges pushed off the shore to retrieve the ship's animals.

"Mr Lugg, come on, you don't seem yourself. I have a cart, let's start at Captain Wakefield's house and see what is to be done."

It was Bently again.

I was cold now and shivering in the dark, and I looked around as a couple of elderly porters carried Bently's boxes along the path to load onto a two-wheeled open cart, harnessed to a strong black horse. She was glossy and groomed, with lines too good to be hitched and working. Jerningham would like that horse, I thought, and there he was again, at the edge of my mind, always stepping in when I wished to God he would fall into a deep hole.

And so I found myself being led along the path by my lover's husband, as if we were companions and going to the same destination.

"No bags?" He didn't wait for an answer but threw in his hand luggage and pushed back some bundles so we could sit at the rear. Bently accepted a leg up from his man to perch on the tray. "You don't want to walk up the hill—it's a climb and slippery and there's no light. Will you come?" He indicated the place beside him on the cart.

I looked up the hill and could make out a thin white house in a cleared patch with native trees on one side and a new orchard on the other. There was smoke coming from the chimney and it looked a pleasant place.

"I'll stay with Heaphy," I said, but Bently shook his head.

"Mr Heaphy is not here," he said. "He has a place in Motueka, but he's away on an expedition looking for flat land over the western hills. He's not expected back until the end of the month at the earliest, though more likely it will be June." I could see his forehead wrinkle, though his voice was even and calm. "Come up, Mr Lugg. You seem in some confusion. Sure, we can billet you for the night and you can be off on your business in the morning."

It seemed easier to go with him than not. His man gave me a hoist up. Bently didn't hold out a hand to me and made no attempt to talk as the horse was led up the deserted path.

"I've left my wife," I told him, breaking the silence.

"I see."

"She deceived me."

"I'm sorry to hear it."

"You are lucky to be happily married, Bently."

"I know it."

And maybe he did. He was such a thoroughly good man. I imagined he had done nothing to be ashamed of in his entire life. I clenched my teeth. I was feeling unwise and I needed to hold my tongue.

Captain Wakefield was surprised to see me arrive, bagless and bedraggled, with his godson.

"Mr Lugg needs a dose of your kind care, Wakey. Can we offer him a change of clothing, a glass of wine and a bed?"

I was embarrassed at their attentiveness, as if I were an invalid or a child. Or worse, as if I were a man so old I had taken leave of my senses.

"Here, do come in, come by the fire. There's a rug and a blanket on the settee. It's quite comfortable. No pillow, I'm afraid, we are rather frugal. Have a glass, Mr Lugg, there's a nightshirt and if you leave your wet things we can dry them by the fire for the morning."

"I am afraid I have been rather foolish," I said to the attentive Bently as I drained the wine and the captain's man pulled my boots from my feet.

"Have a good night's sleep, Mr Lugg. We'll talk in the morning."

I looked at his honest face and thought of Ada and utterly despised myself.

—

"You say you've left your wife," said Captain Wakefield after we had breakfasted and ascertained that I had nowhere pressing to be. We stood at his window overlooking the rain. Below was the harbour—a slipway of water between some sandbars and the beach. It was flimsier and backed by steeper hills than in Charles's watercolour. There was a collection of ships moored out, not wanting to risk going the way of the *Fifeshire* on Arrow Rock.

Bently was out on an errand.

"I have, Captain. I discovered she has not been absolutely truthful with me. I regret to say that Jerningham has also betrayed my trust. I can only say, right now, that I wish never to see either, ever again."

"Jerningham is involved? Mr Lugg, that is most upsetting news. Is it a scandal that is all over town?"

It seemed a strange question to ask. "I think not."

"Well. Hmm. Well. Jerningham's morals are … a growing cause for concern. Standards are important in a new settlement, to set the tone. A holiday here, in Nelson, is it, Mr Lugg? Business trip? It is difficult to see how one can leave one's wife."

"It seems a simple matter. I left. I am not on holiday or business, and the moral standard of the settlement is rather why I have come away."

"You have made arrangements for your wife before you left? Good heavens, you have a child, I remember. You cannot just abandon your wife and child, Mr Lugg."

"I have asked Mr Revans to act for me."

"When do you intend returning to Wellington?"

"I am not sure I do intend to return."

"Not return?"

"It is a common thing for a man to live away from his wife. Of course, I will ensure she is provided for, financially."

I could see a group of men mounting the steep path from the beach and I recognised the police magistrate. He'd been christened Henry "Nose-end" Thompson during a brief post in Wellington, for his inability to see anything beyond the end of his own nose. He hadn't been liked, believing himself rather grand until Revans put him right. I pitied Captain Wakefield being lumbered with such a man.

And there was Jerningham in my thoughts again. This same Thompson had tried to handcuff him in Thorndon when he had ridden his horse through a shop for a dare, creating mayhem. "My good man, I will pay for the damages!" Jerningham had cried amid the applause of his attendant young bucks. "Tell him who I am, Lugg," and he had ridden off, leaving me to explain to Thompson about the exceptions to the rules that applied in town. I can't imagine why I had thought it funny at the time.

But it seemed Thompson had no memory for names or faces and I retired to a corner, unnoticed, while the men held their meeting. It was a small house and there was nowhere else to go.

And so I learned that Te Rauparaha had been in Nelson with his twitchy nephew, Rangihaeata, disputing land, demanding compensation for stolen land, threatening retribution. They should have been behind bars for the sins they had committed. Captain Wakefield explained to his men that the chiefs had returned to Spain's Land Court in Porirua but would find no success there; he reiterated his belief that the settlers of Nelson had nothing to fear, that the land they occupied had been fairly bought.

"They are back though, Captain," said Thompson. "The chiefs have landed at Cloudy Bay and are gathering in the Wairau Valley."

"Well, we have no authority stop them," said Captain Wakefield. "The courts are still investigating the Wairau. There is no doubt it will fall to us, but we must go through due process."

"We should send a force to chase them off."

"We are not invaders, Thompson. Anyway, look, we don't even know how much land is there and the quality of it. No one is taking possession, yet. Let the surveyors do their jobs, and the courts, and meantime Te Rauparaha is free to walk the hills if that is his pleasure."

Another man, a surveyor, said, "I'm taking supplies to

the Wairau tomorrow, wind willing. I'll check that our men are not being harassed and report back next week."

When the rain stopped I excused myself and went down the hill to the harbour. A flat sky floated above the pale sea, over which sheets of rain walked in shadows. Across the bay, the charcoal mountains seemed far away, soaring high, tipped with white, and I knew that was where Charles would be, compelled to explore and sketch and discover. I was glad his journey took him west and away from the gathering of chiefs.

I followed Haven Road with the waterfront on my left and dense bush on the steep hill to the right. Charles's painting of open landscape, I realised, must have been painted from the site of Captain Wakefield's house with much artistic licence; a narrow viewpoint with a shallower perspective, much kinder than the reality.

Around the corner was a bank of grey mud and the valley opened out. There the settlement looked healthier, a good cluster of wooden buildings along a grandly named Trafalgar Street and some semblance of commercial activity taking people out into the town. I asked where the surveyors were quartered and was directed to a rise at the road's end where the barracks perched, looking northwards over the town.

I was looking for my young friend Charley Torlesse, but he wasn't there. "Charley's up at Heaphy's hut," a man told me, pointing into the scrub behind the settlement to where a few huts were scattered on the hillside. "He's packing supplies. We're off to join his survey tomorrow."

Charley was alarmed to see me. It appeared my expression was frightful.

"What is it?" he cried, as if he expected the sky had fallen on Wellington and I had swum the strait to bring the news.

I told him I'd had a disagreement with Jerningham and was looking for somewhere quiet, away from home for a while. He looked confused, remembering Jerningham and me as the best of friends.

I looked around Charles's wooden hut. It was miserably small and smelled of disuse. There was a shelf bed with a thin mattress, a fireplace and neatly stacked wood. A table and chair. A surveyor's cabinet, from which Charley was extracting sheets of paper and rolling them into a leather tube. Some books. I was pleased to see there were a couple of thick blankets folded on a drying rack. Charles was getting soft.

"Is no one using this hut?"

"I don't think so, Mr Lugg. Mr Heaphy usually stays at his farm, he doesn't come to town much. Are you all right? If I may say, you look not your usual self."

"Don't you worry about me, Charley. Would you give Heaphy a message? I'm going to camp down in his hut for a bit. He'll understand."

"I don't know that I have the authority to give you his key."

"Of course you do. I'll write him a note."

Charley fidgeted uncomfortably with his bag of supplies while I wrote a quick note, but he took it and gave me the padlock key. It must have occurred to him I could as easily break the door and come in.

"Mr Lugg. I don't mean to be presumptuous, but is there anything I can do for you? Do you have bags to retrieve? A message to send, perhaps?"

"Thank you, no. I am perfectly content here. Send my regards to Heaphy."

And there I stayed alone for over a week, snug in the hut while outside it rained, reading Charles's books and thinking of nothing, eating his few dried supplies and burning his wood until a sharp earthquake jolted me awake in the afternoon, and I went down into the settlement to hear the news. Comets and fires and earthquakes—New Zealand was a restless place—but the people of Nelson were already back about their business.

"There's no damage, no harm done," a plump woman was saying at a roadside shop. She looked me up and down, a stranger in town. I imagined by now I looked like a wretched stray, with a half-scratch of a beard and crumpled suit. "No need to worry, my love, you are perfectly safe, it's just the earth having a stretch."

I spent some pennies on the handful of liquorice jujubes she held out to me, but they were nasty and tart and I spat them out.

As I walked aimlessly along the streets, there, again, was the unshakeable Bently. He seemed relieved to see me.

"Mr Lugg, what a relief," he said. "We have been very worried about you. The captain sent searches out, you know, following all the trails out of town. And yet here you are."

"Indeed."

We regarded each other for a while and I wished him gone.

"You are hostile to me. What is the cause of this? I hope I have done you no wrong."

He was a blind man not to see the shame in my eyes. I looked at Ada's fortunate husband but found I couldn't hate him. I felt a sharp twinge in the place where tears form and blinked away my self-disgust.

He had no reason to be kind to me and yet he took me into the building next door, into the dining room of a small hotel, and sat me down.

"I'm going to get you something to eat, Mr Lugg. And then perhaps you might walk up to the barracks with me."

He signalled the proprietor for two meals and sat opposite.

"Why the barracks?"

"Captain Wakefield is there."

"Does he want to see me?"

"Mr Lugg, you have been lost for a week. He has been concerned for your safety."

"I have been staying up at Charles Heaphy's hut," I said. "We are old friends. Even without him there I find a certain peacefulness remains."

Bently gave a slight smile.

When the meals arrived I found I wasn't particularly hungry, though I'd eaten no more than boiled beans and damper for the best part of a week. The meat stank and had a rancid, gamey tang.

"What is it?"

"Probably goat, I'm afraid," said Bently. "We don't have much selection here."

"Do you like Nelson?" I said. I felt my antipathy to this man was churlish. He was not to blame for my dishonourable relationship with him.

"Very much so. I've been coming regularly since the foundation and eventually, perhaps, would consider making a life here. I feel a certain possessiveness about the place. Probably you feel that for Wellington."

"No."

He picked at the potatoes for a while, the ones that weren't touched by gravy. He tried a bit of meat and his mouth turned down. I couldn't manage it at all.

"Well. If you're not going to eat, shall we go? The barracks are on the way back to Mr Heaphy's place."

Captain Wakefield was in the middle of a meeting with Thompson, the surveyor Cotterell and some citizens. They were setting weapons out, a rusty cutlass, a few muskets, a fowling piece and a line of small pistols. He seemed relieved to see me alive and I hung my head.

He gave Bently a quick nod. "Perhaps the hotel?" Captain Wakefield said, and Bently disappeared.

Captain Wakefield was a kind man and a friend. He took my shoulders and gave me a gentle shake, his face creased with anxiety. I apologised for the bother I had caused him, ashamed that soldiers had been sent to search for me, causing unnecessary trouble to the already troubled man.

Thompson, with his arms folded, looked me over as if sizing me up for a suit. He focused on my hand. "What's wrong with your thumb?"

I gave the wood a sharp *tap-tap*. "It's not."

He looked at me stupidly.

"Not a thumb," I explained. "It's wood."

"Can you fire a pistol?"

"Certainly." I had practised regularly since the Wanganui days.

"I don't think so, Mr Thompson," said Captain Wakefield. "Mr Lugg is not a resident of Nelson."

"Captain Wakefield, I remind you that we need a show of arms. A show, I say. We cannot give Te Rauparaha a piece of paper and put him under arrest without some semblance of authority backed by arms. We need every man who can hold a pistol and most of our men are out over the ranges."

"What's this?" I asked. "Are you going to arrest Te Rauparaha?"

"He has burned down the surveyors' huts in Wairau Valley," said Captain Wakefield. "Mr Tuckett informs us he escorted the surveyors out like a damned landlord, but he burned our property and we will punish him for that."

"Mr Tuckett has asked for at least twenty-five armed men," said Thompson. "Therefore, I need you, Mr Lugg.

If you can fire a pistol I will make you a special constable here and now, and you can sail with us tomorrow and teach those travelling savages a lesson."

"I will," I said. Why not? I would become a constable and help put Te Rauparaha and his warrior nephew behind bars. That would be a good day's work. I hadn't done one in a while.

The captain eyed me dubiously. "Are you sure? You do not seem in the right frame of mind to make such a decision and, if I may say so, you look rather frail. We intend not to engage, we are a superior force, but there is always a possibility of conflict. You'll need your wits and your strength about you."

"I am with you. Magistrate Thompson, sign me up."

"Look, Mr Lugg," said the captain. "That's noble of you and shows a good spirit. But before we sign anything, I need you to attend a meeting at the Whakatū Hotel in town. Go on, there's a good man. Then, if you are still willing, come back and we'll sign you on and issue your arms. Off you go."

A meeting? Captain Wakefield opened the door for me and nudged me out in the direction of the town. Was it Bently? Surely if he'd wanted to challenge me, he would not have brought me dinner. I knew no one else in Nelson, a few settlers, perhaps, who had crossed the strait. It wasn't until the landlord showed me in that I thought of Jerningham.

—

It was Dorothy who stood in the little drawing room in front of a jewel-bright fire, with plump Alexandria on her hip, such a scene of domestic goodness that they didn't look real.

This whole week I had sent them from my mind. What I had lost. What I had never had. My thoughts were blocked by Bently and Ada and I couldn't get past them. Jerningham laughed from the corner of my eyes, crying: *Look at you! Throwing stones from your glass house!*

I had read and read the entire week so as to distract myself. Charles's books on naval timber and shipbuilding. *The Principles of Geology*. Physical sciences. Pirates and mutinies and the *Bounty*. Dickens. Anything on the shelf that would put my mind in another place and keep my thoughts divorced from my circumstances.

I hadn't made further plans or considered Dorothy and the baby. There was pain. So the scene surprised me. My wife and child at the hearth.

She was graceful, and shone with good health. She looked so much like an honest woman. There was a roundness to her and the thought that she might again be with child impaired any logic remaining to me. With Alexandria she wore a changed expression, there was no sulkiness anymore. She had someone to give her love to now, and the baby looked at her with trusting blue eyes.

Dorothy's lips parted in a cry when I entered looking woeful and disbelief swept across her face.

"Arthur, you look terrible. My dear. Please, come home."

The landlord closed the door behind me and Dorothy hesitantly came forward, gently placing little Alexandria against my chest, folding my arms around and under the baby who was uncovered really for the first time to me, round-cheeked, chubby with wispy dark curls and smelling of soap. She held her head back and blinked with heavy lids.

Her skin was porcelain pale without blemish and her lashes ridiculously long and black; her gaze was steady and sweet. My daughter's lids dropped again. Mine with them.

Dorothy was making a nest on the couch, a little berth with cushions.

"Will you put her down, Arthur? I think she is ready for a sleep, don't you?"

I didn't know. It took me a while to release her. I laid my daughter down on the cushions reluctantly, not wanting to lose her warmth. She instantly put her thumb in her mouth, sucked, and rolled onto her side, eyes drooping, drooping, sucking on her thumb. I watched her fall asleep and felt my heartbeat slow.

There were small armchairs on either side of the hearth. Dorothy put a log on the fire before sitting down. That was my job, to put wood on the fire.

I sat in my crumpled suit and grey shirt with a dirty collar, unshaven and unwashed, while Dorothy folded her beautiful white hands on her lap. She didn't rub them anymore.

She was a good woman. Jerningham was a liar.

"Yes, he did. We did."

I hadn't realised I had asked the question. What had I said?

"I gave myself to him, Arthur."

There is a gap in time that exists when your mind has gone on a journey somewhere, through a forest, following a light that flickers brightly a long way in the distance, and then suddenly it disappears and for a moment you are in absolute darkness. That's the gap. And then you turn around and realise you have gone nowhere at all, but terrible things have happened while you've been away. In the gap.

I closed my eyes on her. I put my hands over my ears. I think I shook my head slowly back and forwards. She reached over and took my hands away, and when I opened my eyes she was kneeling at my feet. Her look wasn't apologetic, or pleading, or the sulk of the disbelieved. It was a look scrubbed bare.

"Arthur, my love, I think you are going to leave me. But I won't let you go until I have been truthful and final. Will you grant me that?"

Truthful and final? What did that mean? Was there such a thing as final truth, or did we all deceive each other constantly from cradle to grave? And wasn't it better not to know, when there was no going back to change the things we wish we hadn't done?

"Once you asked me to tell you everything, but you wouldn't hear me. If you leave me now, there will always be something over your shoulder that you don't understand. It will fill up the spaces in your head with wool for the rest of your life. I want you to judge me. I put myself at your mercy."

She dropped her eyes then, looking for words. I knew I was going to have to hear them. The muscles in my legs twitched to propel me up and away, but I waited as the minutes passed and I saw how she struggled. I didn't think she was struggling to make up a palatable story, something that would reflect well on her and convince me to forgive her. She had the aspect of a woman who was praying to God for courage and truth. She looked sometimes at me, sometimes away over my shoulder to the past.

The baby stirred on the couch, a loud half breath until she found her thumb again, sucked and was silent.

"You know I came to the colony alone. The Māori carried me through the waves. I've told you how it was."

Dorothy, abandoned by the Peabodys and that man, had been carried by natives who, despite her fears, had carefully and respectfully placed her on shore. I felt pity but I knew my face was curdling with the shame of it.

"Colonel Wakefield had brought the ship into harbour because we had lost our captain. I don't know what Mr Peabody told him, but the colonel sent me ashore with a letter to Jerningham, telling him to find me a billet. I let him know of my circumstances, that I had been left and had no money and no one to look out for me, and needed shelter and work. 'And a husband, too, I should think,' he said to me. He said it kindly, Arthur. It was the first kind thing anyone had said to me for … I don't know. For years, perhaps. He said he was sorry for my misfortune and would do what he could to help me. He put his hand on my hair. He let me sit in his office and ordered a plate of victuals and beer while he organised the Barrows to take me in. He paid them, Arthur. He brought blankets and issued the family with a large tent, because of me. He kissed my hand and I thought … it doesn't matter what I thought …"

Once again I was walking in Dorothy's shoes, in her life before she knew me, vulnerable and lost on the wrong side of a lonely world. I felt her reluctance to talk now, what it cost her. Her voice was tight and small. But, as before, when she opened a crack I wanted to push inside and know it all.

"Yes, it does, Dorothy. It matters very much what you thought. You are telling me the truth."

She pushed her lips together and her eyes were shiny. Dorothy wasn't given to crying and I didn't want to see it. I nodded at her, impatient for her to get to the part where she let Jerningham seduce her. She was right, there was wool in my head that filled all the gaps and I wanted it cleared so I could think.

"I don't know how a man looks when he is in love. I don't think you love me, do you, Arthur? I've never seen a look on your face to suggest it. He stood a bit too close, not enough to make me uncomfortable, just enough for me to notice that his eyes didn't blink when they looked at me and it felt like he was trying to draw something out from inside of me.

"When he told me to come back to his hut later, perhaps I knew what he wanted, but he wasn't like other men, leery and hot-faced. He was different. I thought he was a good man. What if he fell in love with me? I was ruined, Arthur, it was just a matter of time, I knew I had a baby growing. Only just, but I knew. And if you are cast out from the end of the earth, where is there to go?"

"I'm listening."

"I was so stupid. When he said he would arrange a husband for me, I thought he was talking about himself. I thought he might marry me, and I wouldn't be left alone."

Marry her? Jerningham? Why would she possibly think that?

"Did he tell you he would marry you?"

Her answer to this was vitally important. I needed to know what kind of a monster Jerningham was, how cruelly he had deceived her. She was looking over my shoulder again as if she hadn't heard.

"I asked you a question, Dorothy. Did he say if you did this thing with him, that he would marry you?"

She gave me a dismissive gesture with her hand, exactly the way Jerningham would have done. "What difference does it make?"

"I will shoot him. If he offered marriage, seduced and then left you, I will take the first ship to Wellington and I will shoot him in the head."

Her head moved, I wasn't sure if in a shake or a nod.

"Did he offer marriage, Dorothy?"

"No," she said, abruptly. "It was my fault. Entirely mine. I encouraged him. I had been brought so low by then, the humiliation was deserved. Later I went to tell him he put a baby on me but he knew I was trying to trap him, for by then he had heard the stories about Mr Peabody. Instead, he arranged a meeting with you, and the colonel sent me to nurse you and I was so ashamed. You were a good man and so kind to me and they wanted me to trap you like that. I couldn't do it. Then I lost the baby and lost you. But you came back for me."

For a long time we stayed there like that, me in the chair and her at my feet. The light faded outside and the room lost colour, grey cold coming in from the window across the room towards our fire. I sensed that Dorothy was waiting for me. To leave, to tell her to go, to start making arrangements for what happened next.

She was a stone in my hand, poised.

"What do you want to do, Dorothy?"

I was giving her a way back. That was why she had come. It was up to her now, to ask for what she wanted. I couldn't make the decision, but I wanted to go back and I wanted my life with Dorothy and our baby. Babies, perhaps. What she had done didn't shock me, not really. I'd come to realise that a slight tap on the fragile shell of a woman will expose her vulnerability and helplessness, her lack of choices.

"Are you with child?" I asked on impulse, and she nodded.

There was no smile. She was holding back.

"What is it?"

She had something more to say and it looked bitter in her mouth.

"I want you to give up Ada Bently."

Ada's name was shocking on Dorothy's lips.

So, there it was. She knew about Ada. Perhaps she had always known about Ada. I hung my head, heavy with the weight of the last two years. Of course.

It was time for my confession, now, but I had nothing to say, no defence. It was inexcusable.

Strangely, then, the earth jumped and did another little shake, sharp enough to make the ornaments rattle on the mantelpiece. I reached for Dorothy's hand as she started up in fright.

"No need to worry, my love, you are perfectly safe. It's just the earth having a stretch." The words the shopkeeper had said to me earlier, a platitude that smoothed the way through the unknown.

Dorothy told me quietly then that she had always known about Ada—Sam Revans had told her. Not in so many words, but he had sought her out before our marriage and said she should be aware that my heart was elsewhere. He had told her she could do better.

"Revans said that? Before he stood witness at our wedding? Why would he do such a thing?"

"It was the truth. He sets a high regard for truth."

I knew it. I loved Sam for it. Perhaps it was something I could learn from him. "You never said anything."

"By then I loved you, Arthur," said Dorothy. "I thought you would give her up. But you didn't. You came home some days with your little secret smile, and her smell on your skin, and occasionally I found a strand of her long curly hair caught on your button or seam of your clothing. You brought her home."

"Forgive me."

"I will invite Mrs Bently for tea and I will wait in the garden while you say goodbye. Then we will forgive each other."

I drew her to me and reached hesitantly to touch her shining dark hair. It felt so soft under my rough hand. She turned her head into my palm and closed her eyes, her lashes long and dark against white skin, and I felt the same sense of peace then, as when holding our daughter asleep in my arms. I kissed Dorothy on the forehead and her eyelashes fluttered against my chin like a new life beginning. She covered my hand with her own, sealing in a promise.

WAIRAU

THERE WAS a ship crossing to Wellington and I put Dorothy and Alexandria on it.

We had spent a gentle night, being honest with each other, talking in a way that had not seemed possible in the past. I explained, as best I could, about how Ada and I had made our secret engagement on the *Aurora* and the misunderstanding that made her marry Bently.

It occurred to me, as I spoke, that Ada was waiting for me to set her free, as if I held a kind of sovereignty over her and needed to give her up before Bently could truly possess her. A woman could not be owned by two men, and God knows I had done nothing to make her happy.

I made my promise to Dorothy to give up Ada. Then I took her face in my hands and told her I loved her. I couldn't recall telling her so before.

We rose early and dressed Alexandria warmly for the voyage.

I felt a sense of obligation to Captain Wakefield and was determined to honour my commitment to him. I agreed with Dorothy that I would fulfil my duty and go to the Wairau and see if I could get a vessel directly home from Cloudy Bay. I would sleep better if I witnessed the arrest of Te Rauparaha. Then, as soon as possible, we determined to leave Wellington behind and move to Nelson, under

Captain Wakefield's gentle rule, away from the colonel and Jerningham and the bitterness they inspired. We planned to build a shop in the growing town and become merchants. I had no love for my land in Porirua, no wish to play at being a gentleman farmer. As soon as Dorothy suggested a shop I felt absolutely sure it was the right thing to do. I liked bookkeeping. It seemed I was good at it. And Dorothy had a love of furniture and antiques.

We walked along the shore to the boats, me with Alexandria tucked into my jacket and her little mitten-less fingers pulling at my hair. I kissed my wife, helped her into the row-boat and handed our baby into her arms.

"I'll be no more than a week," I told her. "Get Lucy to start packing."

"We'll take the table, the outside one, from the *Jewess*."

"Yes, of course."

They were rowing away from the shore now, boats ahead already loading passengers to the ship.

"But not the dining table—let's sell that."

"Really? Well, yes, all right."

"I'll divide the strawberry plant for Te Puni."

"We can plant it in his garden before we leave."

"Oh, yes, Arthur, let's! And one for the Mein Smiths, and for Mr Ingestre."

I waved as they drew away. "But don't give too many away," I called. "I love strawberries!"

"Take care, Arthur." She blew me a kiss.

That afternoon I was issued with a small pistol and a rifle. The rifle had a jammed cartridge and I didn't know how to fire one anyway, but it looked impressive and, as Thompson said, it was all about the show.

—

Mr Spain you have heard the Pākehā's story—not mine.
Listen I will tell you how it all began …

Rangihaeata persisted in going to Wairau, which we
did. We told the surveyors not to work any more and
go away; that we would not allow them to do anything
more till we were paid for our land but they took no
notice of us.

We went again to their stations and told them to take
their things out of the house. They would not—but we
did, and put them in their boat, burnt the house and
took the white people to the entrance of the river and left
them at the Pā.

We went up to the river to a creek Tua Marina and
were there clearing the land for potatoes when I saw
the Victoria laying off the mouth of the Wairau.
Next morning when we had done eating, some of my
men said there were Pākehā coming towards us. We
assembled men, women, and children on the bank of the
river to see and hear what the Pākehā wanted. They all
got on the brow of a fern hill and stood.

Then part of them came to the bank of the river and
called for a canoe which was given them. Mr Thompson,
Capt. Wakefield, Capt. England, Mr Cotterill,
Mr Tuckett, Brook the interpreter, the Constable and
others came over to us.

I told him [Thompson] I burnt nothing of theirs; it was
my own; the grass and wood that grew on my land! And
I would not go with him. It would be good to talk of the
matter there—what odds if it did occupy two or three
days—I would let them have the land when they paid
me for it.

*He [Thompson] would not listen to me he turned away
to the constable and got handcuffs, and then came to me
taking me by the hand. When I found what he wanted
I snatched my hand away from his. He got very angry
and said if I did not come he would fire on us. I said
don't be foolish we don't want to fight …*

*Puaha (Rawiri) rose with a testament in his hand
saying to the Pākehā: "Don't fire on us; we are
Christians and do not want to fight."*

*When the Pākehā got to the top of the hill they waved a
white handkerchief to make peace. I could not get up the
hill fast—the young men ran before me, shooting and
cutting down Pākehā as they ran away. I called to them
to spare the gentlemen, but Rangihaeata coming up
behind me at the time said "Why save them—they have
shot your daughter." When I heard that my voice failed
me. Rangihaeata got up the hill and all the Pākehā were
killed.*

TE RAUPARAHA'S ACCOUNT OF THE WAIRAU AFFRAY, DELIVERED ON
1 JULY 1843 BEFORE LAND CLAIMS COMMISSIONER WILLIAM SPAIN.

—

I dropped my pistol when I was shot. My hands clutched
my thigh and it felt sticky and raw.

"Fix bayonets!" came the shout from the front. But
it seemed no one obeyed and our men ran backwards,
shooting wildly over their shoulders as they fled.

The captain shouted, "For God's sake, men, stand firm,"
but they were not soldiers, just ordinary men with ordinary
courage that failed them.

I staggered to the side, my leg gave way and I slid fast
downhill, burning my face against the rough fern and

screaming at the pain that tore from the open flesh on my leg. Blood splattered into the air on collision with a rock and I lay dazed, face up on the bumpy ground. The cracks of muskets and shouts of the men ripped around me, but I looked through the lacy fern to the pale wheeling sky and felt far away. The pain came and went but I didn't feel it especially, though my body jarred and clenched. It was something happening outside of me.

I watched the clouds and listened to the fighting on the hillside above me. It went on for a long time, the shouting and shooting.

How had it come to this?

Captain Wakefield had crossed the stream with Thompson, the surveyor and some others, all holding back their coats to the gathering of natives to show they were unarmed. Te Rauparaha had stepped forward and I saw him hold out his hand to Thompson, but the magistrate batted it away. They began to argue. Of course they'd argued. Had Thompson expected the cannibal to submit to being shackled by the cuffs he dangled? Captain Wakefield knew it, but he let Thompson take charge. "We'll be mocked if we turn back without teaching the savages a lesson," Thompson had said, when the captain had voiced his reservations earlier in the day.

There were about forty of us left on the hill then, untrained labourers mostly, and volunteers like me, who were not making a good job of it. Over a hundred Māori made a fine display with their intimidating, stalking dance, their tongues extended and eyes wide with passion. The strong women stood with their men, hands swinging and flicking in the way they did. This was a greeting. I had seen flickering hands often lifted with a song. But Nose-end Thompson would only see hands twitching to be put to some barbaric use.

Come back quickly, I urged under my breath. You know this is lost. Parley fast and come back over the river. Don't engage. Te Rauparaha is not a normal man. He will punish your foolish bullishness and bluster.

Te Rauparaha's parley ground was no place for arrogant Nose-end and gentle Arthur Wakefield.

I could hear Thompson shouting as he waved his handcuffs, towering over the diminutive Māori, and I thought, what a fool. I remembered how on the island Jerningham had sat himself down on the ground in front of the chief, unconcerned by the surrounding natives. He had peacefully lit his pipe and talked to them in their own language, showing that he saw their strength and was unimpressed, as if he held a power beyond anything they could see.

Rangihaeata came dancing out of the trees. He held a tomahawk in his hands, which he twirled and twirled as he lifted his bare feet high and stepped carefully, feeling the ground, the ball of each foot tasting the soil and sucking up power from the earth below. He called out taunts and insults, shouting to Thompson to get off his land, telling him that he would eat him. That he would eat them all.

I don't know what the translator said into Thompson's ear, but Thompson called for his men to advance and the Māori picked up their muskets.

A shot rang out, changing everything.

With no one to tell us what to do, some men rushed forward down the bank to cover the party retreating over the river, firing volleys down on the Māori below, while others fell back, out of the line of fire, waiting for the return of Thompson and Captain Wakefield. I stood between, on the prow of the rise, thinking how Jerningham called me the invisible man, and hoping it would help me now. But they shot me and I fell.

After a long time of drifting clouds and the sound of distant clamour, the rushing about stopped and the last of the footfalls died away through the bush. My leg throbbed. I came back into myself to find I had not bled to death, but neither had the pain lessened.

By twisting and prodding I ascertained a large chunk of the side of my thigh had been ripped away and the skin flapped back to leave a bloody steak peppered with dirt, dried fern sticking out of the flesh like so many little bony fingers. I knew I needed to tie it, and I struggled for a long time with my clumsy hands to try to rip the edge of my shirt to no avail.

I forced myself up against the rock, stripped off my jacket and pushed my head above the fern. Stunted trees. Scrub. A bird soared high against the blue sky at the top of the rise. Nothing else moved. I removed my shirt and tied it around the bloody mess as tightly as I could, all the while engulfed by dizziness. It was a flesh wound only. The bullet had passed by. I took several deep breaths and pulled myself up.

I edged past the rock and fell a foot or so to a path below, with no idea where to go or what to do, frightened to be on my own. I slipped back into the fern at the top of the rise, teeth clenched against the pain and silently, silently, I crept away.

A white handkerchief hung tattered on a scrappy mānuka tree and I drew towards it, thinking it would be a good thing, to have a white flag. I almost stepped onto Mr Cotterell, the surveyor. I recognised the flapping boot sole that had come adrift that morning. "What a nuisance!" he'd complained to me as he tied it with string. "But we have two cobblers now in Nelson, Mr Lugg, and if I may, I'll ask you to take my boot with you for mending, one of the boys can bring it back. I expect to stay in the valley after this affair is over."

His legs were tipped up over a tree root and arms flung wide, as if he had spread them to prevent himself from falling. His head, from behind, was cleaved in two.

I fell, dragging my weight down the mānuka, pushing away so I didn't collapse onto the dead surveyor. I covered my head, imagining my puny arms could protect me from the violence of men. I couldn't tell if he had been killed an hour or a minute ago, or if his murderer was still within deadly reach and watching me, biding his time.

Face down, I slithered down the ridge under the cover of the fern and bush, until my way was barred by a circle of dense foliage. Below I heard Māori voices and then, quite clearly, Captain Wakefield's cry for *Kati! Peace!* and a dreadful sound like a tree splitting, followed by the thump of a falling body.

"Desist, I say!" cried the captain, and there was another terrible crunch and a fall and a wailing from many men.

I heard Te Rauparaha calling out and Rangihaeata shouting over him, screaming in his foul language that they were chiefs and they would kill all the Pākehā chiefs and he, Rangihaeata, would claim utu now for the death of the woman, all the deaths in the past and all the deaths they would face in the future at the hands of the Pākehā.

The trees were split asunder and fell to the ground. The men shouted in fear and I lay still and invisible in the fern until the Māori finished their terrible work and went away, and only then I climbed down through the trees, but there was nobody left alive.

The men lay discarded and bloody, crumpled as if dropped from a great height. I recognised Thompson by his jacket. His face was cut away, nose-end and all, as if he had turned into a blow intended for his skull. The men had raised their arms in fear and protection. All except the captain. I found my friend, Arthur Wakefield, with his jacket pulled down from his shoulders to bind his arms and his gentle face hacked about in a dozen deep wedges. One eye remained, clear blue and open. I closed the fragile thing with shaking fingertips and bowed down, kissed his battered forehead and laid my hands on him. I said a prayer to a god I no longer knew. Then I fled.

—

For three days I hid in the bush towards the coast, pulling turnip-tops and pūhā and eating them raw. I had seen our brig depart for Wellington, far out to sea by the time I surfaced, and I knew an English force would soon return. I bathed my wounded leg, washing away the pain in an icy stream, fearing infection.

From a safe distance, I looked over the land towards the hill where the fallen men lay, watching for the return of the Māori. I had seen them in the valley below, burying their own dead, and knew if they came back I could not allow them to dig a pit, light the fire and put Captain Wakefield in their oven. I found a heavy wooden club and decided to strike down Te Rauparaha first and take whatever consequences would follow. But it was a missionary who came up the hill, a sturdy man in black robes decked with a white bow. If ever I had need of a man of God it was on that hillside above the Wairau Valley. When he got close enough for me to see the beads of sweat on his high forehead, I stepped forward.

Others of our men came out of hiding to join him and, together, we collected the bodies of our twenty-two fallen and buried them in a patch of cleared fern above the river. Mr Ironside, the Wesleyan Minister, read the burial service for the Church of England and we stood around and wept. We tried to sing but no man amongst us could raise more than a whisper.

"Te Rauparaha and his party have returned to Kāpiti," said the minister. "He is preparing for war."

Our ship arrived next, with Dr Evans, Colonel Wakefield, Mr Spain, Dorset and others from Wellington. They had come to negotiate the release of Captain Wakefield and the prisoners, not knowing yet that there were no prisoners to release. It was Mr Ironside who gave the colonel the news that we had buried his brother and the others that morning.

I limped beside the colonel, in deep misery and stumbling often, up the narrow, irregular track to the grave. These ordinary men had suffered such indignity, slaughtered in captivity, but I told the colonel that I had heard his brother call for peace up until the end.

In a tent on the beach I had my leg washed, stitched and bandaged by the capable Dr Dorset, who muttered about the absurdity of sending a man without a thumb to shoot a pistol. The pain was dreadful. I was sick with grief and it seemed only right I carry physical evidence of the horrors I had witnessed and wear the scar of the battle on my body. There, Mr Spain and Dr Evans took my account, and that of the other witnesses who had escaped the massacre, while the colonel sat outside on a frail folding chair and looked up at the hills.

Dr Evans, pacing, said to me, "You know, Lugg, we should have seen this coming. Rangi warned us he would *pung-a-pung* Wide-awake if we took Wairau and, by God, we must *pung-a-pung* them right back. We must forget this antiquated nonsense about native justice and treat them as the savages they are. We must stop dancing around them negotiating for this and paying over and over again for same pieces of wasteland and put an end to the power of Rauparaha and his monstrous nephew. The colonel should have passed that message to his brother very clearly, and you should have gone to that valley in full force and fully armed. Whatever hell we bring down on them now won't bring those good men back." He sat heavily, then, on a bench with the other wounded men and put his face in his hands and cried. It was difficult to watch.

"I forwarded a letter from Cotterell to his mother last month," he said. "Now I shall have to write another." He wiped his eyes on the back of his hand. "We will repay this insult tenfold."

I lay back on the stretcher and closed my eyes. I heard the creak of the tent and the flap of the flags and the rattle of lost humanity that would no doubt shake up this country for generations. Overhead and far away a bellbird called his three clear notes, piping sweetly out of the evening sky.

There was nothing more to be done in Wairau. We transferred to the ship, a rising westerly filling the full white sails and pulling us sharply away from the valley. Under gathering clouds and across choppy waters, we returned with our terrible news to Wellington.

———

Dr Evans barely let Jerningham remove his hat before he had him in the Exchange for questioning. I was there, with Tuckett, who had also escaped Rangihaeata's massacre and had raised the alarm in Wellington. We were once again going through our testimonials in front of leading settlers when Jerningham rode into town.

"Where is my uncle?" he asked Evans.

"The colonel is overseeing the defences. We have a battery with two eighteen-pounders on Flagstaff Hill, some twenty cavalry, four hundred bayonets and a hundred rifle corps. Tell us what is happening up the coast—are they coming?" Dr Evan's voice was heavy with panic.

Jerningham had learned of the death of his uncle through a series of ripples that had spread from settlement to settlement and finally up the Wanganui River. Te Rauparaha had sent him a message, to meet at Ōtaki to talk. Was it war or peace?

Jerningham had many supporters among the Māori, and they promised warriors should he decide to rise up and fight Ngāti Toa and bring Te Rauparaha and Rangihaeata down. Kuru pledged to put nets over their heads and offer them up, and if he were killed then Jerningham would have two kin to revenge—an uncle and a Māori brother—and would be the stronger for it.

Dr Evans and all his men moved closer at this news. They had not counted on Māori support. Suddenly the value of Jerningham's alliances dawned on them. Men who had rebuked Jerningham and scoffed at his foray into the native world were now regarding the young wastrel with new respect.

Jerningham's face was pinched. He turned to the crowd with a cold look. "I told Kuru, that is not the way we do things. White men do not take revenge for the deaths of their relations. I told him we have laws and magistrates to punish such deeds and that the sin stops with the man who has committed the crime. Not his family. Not his whole tribe. Our retaliation will come with British law."

"Did your men pledge support or not?" This was from the Crown prosecutor Hanson, a man who had not addressed Jerningham directly for over a year.

Jerningham flushed. "They are not my men, Hanson. They have their own allegiances, their own battles to fight. If they want to bring Te Rauparaha down—and God knows the devil in me would whip them up—they do not do so for my uncle's sake, or for the sake of those good men killed at Wairau. They have their own scores to settle. Do not confuse their motives with our own."

"How did you leave them?" pressed Hanson.

Jerningham shook out his filthy hair and pushed it back off his face with trembling fingers. "There was a sudden and severe earthquake. I left them very disturbed and confused—they see the rocking earth as a sign. As do the gullible assembled here, hey? Who among us felt the ground quake and thought God spoke? Was He speaking to us? To them? To Rauparaha and his bloody followers? I am fast losing faith with your hocus pocus god! If he, indeed, watches over us, he took his eyes elsewhere when the tomahawks fell at Wairau." Jerningham locked eyes with Hanson. "The natives are preparing for war, whatever we say."

Hanson dropped his eyes first, scowling his dislike of Jerningham's brashness, and men shuffled their feet and muttered.

Mr Evans held up his hand, focused on Jerningham. "But you met Te Rauparaha at Ōtaki?"

"I went to Ōtaki with Te Ahu, and other chiefs from the Rangitikei area. They were very angry with Te Rauparaha for bringing the wrath of the Queen upon them. The chiefs will let us take the Ngāti Toa leaders captive. The chiefs want peace."

Jerningham looked more exhausted than I had ever seen him, even at the extremes of our adventures. Hollow. He persistently rubbed his hands through his wild hair. Someone put a mug of ale at his elbow and he gulped it down. "They were wailing that I had come to shoot the chiefs, to claim utu for my uncle," he said. "Rangihaeata is fortifying a pā on the river for a standoff, but Te Rauparaha has turned missionary. He converted on the day he returned from Wairau—purely so he could claim as allies missionary natives all the way up the coast. He goes to chapel, and yet his wives and slave women wear the rings and clothes of the murdered men."

"Spain has been there already, you know, and assured them that they will answer to the law," said Evans. "Did you speak with Hadfield?"

"Hadfield! He is doing his best to prevent a war, but is adamant it is of our own making. Even in private he said to me that poor Te Rauparaha was acting in self-defence, protecting his people and his land, claiming utu for his daughter according to their custom. Hadfield's sympathies lie with the Māori."

Jerningham lifted his head and he saw me then, in the jumble of men around him. I leaned on a crutch, my leg bandaged and strapped to a splint. He stepped forward and took my hand in both of his.

"I heard you were there at the end and you buried my uncle. I thank you, Mr Lugg. You are one of God's good men."

We locked eyes and I was back with him, pulled into his orbit, singled out in a crowd of men by Jerningham's grace. God knows he was easier to hate when he was out of my sight. Dr Evans tugged him by the arm, breaking the connection, and I stepped back.

"What of Te Rauparaha?" Evans asked.

Jerningham rubbed his brow, bringing his concentration back, giving it to the man in front of him. "He offered to shake my hand, but I wouldn't have it," he said, his voice flat, devoid of it's usual bounce, the voice of grief. "Rauparaha gave one of his great orations, calling all his people to recognise his mana and his chiefly authority and his exploits. He told me our wahine has no authority over him."

"Wahine?"

"It means woman. He was referring to our Queen Victoria, Dr Evans. You know they have few words in their language, and one word must stand for many meanings depending on the way it is said. The way he said it was utterly objectionable. I then asked if he had not signed a treaty and he replied, 'What of it? They gave me a blanket for it. Give me another blanket and I will sign it again tomorrow. What is there in writing? I am Rauparaha. I am the king of this land! I have lived as a king, I will fight as a king and I will die as a king.' And then he told me, 'Send me your queen and I will eat her, ship and all.'"

The Exchange fell silent and I looked around at the gathered men. Good men, for the most part, decent. Confusion crumpled their expressions and they blinked hesitantly, scanning from face to face, hoping someone would step up and fix things. Like me, they couldn't understand how we had come to this pass. How, for all our good intentions, we had managed to provoke war with the natives within four years of our arrival. No one had wanted that.

For all my friendship and respect for Captain Wakefield, I acknowledged that he hadn't shown leadership when it was needed, nor pulled back from a confrontation he didn't understand. He should have met with Te Rauparaha, as Jerningham would have done, smoked a pipe with him and kept talking until a solution appeared.

But then a powerful memory almost overwhelmed me and I thought back to the fierceness with which I wanted to witness Te Rauparaha's punishment and see him put out of the way. I lowered my eyes and I knew that I, too, had gone to the Wairau desperate to provoke an excuse to have him shot, to keep us safe from him. When it came to it, all men knew that war was more powerful than diplomacy. It was ever thus, we were all of us guilty, and no one in the room should have expected otherwise.

AFTERMATH

IN THE END, nothing was done. The government brig arrived in Wellington and disbanded the civilian armed corps, and the bluster of Te Rauparaha and his followers blew over. It wasn't diplomacy that had prevented immediate war, but the pusillanimity of Captain FitzRoy, the newly appointed governor. After investigation, he decided no action would be taken against the Māori for the deaths at Wairau. No action! Some saw it as a decision of humanity and forbearance, others as weakness and cowardice. The Māori simply could not understand why we took no revenge. Where was the power of our Queen?

Jerningham could not accept the verdict and had several turbulent encounters with both Te Rauparaha and Rangihaeata as he travelled through their lands up the coast. He was charged by his rival, Mr Clarke Jr, with inciting trouble and anti-native sentiment and he reacted bitterly.

"These men are our equals, and should be held to account," he said. "With your patronising forgiveness and separate laws you would enslave them. You see them as a collective to be managed, all good, or all evil, all constantly and forever in need of your teaching and compassion. But a missionary will never invite a Māori to his table as a friend, so how can you understand the heart of these brothers? If a brother commits murder, he must be held responsible. To do otherwise is condescension beyond belief."

Jerningham was incensed with the loss of his uncle and his own powerlessness in the face of the Kāpiti chiefs. I rarely saw him, and never alone. I passed him once outside the newspaper office where he was arguing with Wī Tako— an angry, shouting argument rather than his usual disdain that used to rile the Māori so effectively. His movements were agitated and Wī Tako was looking at him as if he were mad. I let Jerningham see my back as I turned away to cross the road.

In print, Jerningham was no less rowdy. He filled the *Gazette* with vindictive, highly personal criticisms against government officials—unsigned, but such pointed bitterness and frustration was hardly anonymous. He wrote and he ranted. Revans told me Jerningham drank himself to wretchedness most nights, but I said he could die in his own vomit for all I cared.

Meanwhile Dorothy and I made our preparations to move. We sold our country land at a loss, and our town house at a good profit to settlers coming down from the coast seeking protection against the gathering storm of Te Rauparaha. Nelson had become a fortified town after Wairau and was abandoned by many settlers, but both Dorothy and I felt committed to returning, to help rebuild the town that Captain Wakefield had founded and for which he had died. Revans invited me for a drink before we left and we sat in the bar at Barrett's at our usual table, where he and Jerningham, Heaphy, Chaffers, Mein Smith and our other adventurer friends had passed the hours, but no one came to join us, and even Revans wasn't lining up the drinks in advance anymore.

We savoured a good bottle of French wine that smelled of Europe, full of dry continental heat. Revans pushed a newspaper across the table to me, the *Sydney Herald*, and tapped an article with a quiet nod. I read.

Murdered in his Bed

Mr Adolphus Peabody, formerly of Mayfair, London, has been found stabbed through the heart in his home in the Sydney suburb of Parramatta. A week previously his wife and two children abandoned the colony and returned to England on the Rose Laughley. *Mr Peabody's manservant, known as Scotch, has been arrested, awaiting trial.*

"I assume this is the Peabody that did your Dorothy such harm?" said Revans with his eyebrows pulled in tightly. "I am so glad the man is dead."

He left the paper with me and went out into the night, still sober.

Revans and Mein Smith had bought their much-discussed farm in the Wairarapa, and both men were easier with themselves with their backs to town, facing a challenge independent of the Company.

I hid the newspaper and wondered how to tell Dorothy. My instinct was to let sleeping dogs lie, but after a week or so I realised I had no right to hold back the news. I sat her down and showed her the paper, as Revans had showed me. She read the article and there was a bitter set to her jaw. She blinked as she laid down the paper and pushed it away.

"Is it a relief?" I asked. I took her hands in mine and rubbed my good thumb over her knuckles.

"A relief?"

"That the man got his just deserts. Utu," I said. Dorothy knew the word. I had spoken of it in regard to Wairau.

"No, she said. "It has nothing to do with me. I don't think about it. It never happened."

We had a different way of dealing with things, Dorothy and I. Happiness was a slippery thing and who was to say that the way she buried things would not, in time, allow the past to decay into insubstantial dust? Either way, Peabody was a dead dog now. We never mentioned him again, and Dorothy became happier. Even I learned to look forward. Some indefinable shadow seemed to drop away from us both.

———

As Dorothy had said she would, she invited Ada to our house for tea. She arrived with her sister-in-law, Catherine Malloy, and after some small talk, Dorothy took Catherine out to look at her garden. Dorothy was round-bellied and nearing her time, Alexandria playful at her feet.

I heard the *click-clack* of the little picket gate as they walked down the path in the sunshine and we were left standing by the window, Ada and I, in no doubt of why we remained alone together.

Ada's hair was tightly packed away under her bonnet, but her face had the same intelligent, dear look that had so enticed me on our journey. She was still thoughtful and a little bit sad, but the rawness had gone and I no longer felt her emotions belonged to me.

"She's lovely, Arthur, your Dorothy. I'm sorry we never got to be friends. She looks so … I don't know … uncomplicated. Honest. A woman who has followed a straight moral path all her life." She paused and nodded gently. I realised I was copying her nod, and we smiled at each other. "She is your wife, and I belong to John. We were misguided in what we did. We wronged two good people. I am truly sorry for my part in it."

I felt no frisson, standing close to her. The physical excitement had entirely gone. The thrill of secrecy had been essential to our relationship, and without it we were easier, standing side by side as two comfortable old friends.

"Will you tell Bently?"

"Oh, no. I can't. Not now. He is deeply depressed after the death of Wakey. They were very close. He should have been with you, you know, on your mission, but Wakey had asked him to stay and see to the American ship that had arrived—something trivial, documents to sign. John blames himself horribly that he wasn't with you at Wairau, as if he could have done anything to protect him …" Her voice trailed off and we looked through the window for a while in silence.

I gave her a half bow, took her hand and squeezed it gently. It seemed, after all, there was nothing more we needed to say. Life had jumped ahead of all those unfinished conversations and they had entirely lost their point. "Shall we join them in the garden?"

Lucy brought boxes from the lean-to, and Dorothy, in her favourite gardening gloves and bending carefully, was packing a box of plants for Catherine's Karori garden.

At the visit's end, Dorothy watched me say goodbye to Ada, and we all knew the affair was over.

Later, Te Puni came by and stayed for dinner, telling fanciful stories to Lucy about fishing me out of the harbour the way Māui hooked the fish out of the sea. "Before I pull Mr Lugg from the sea, there come a man," Te Puni said, "a great man, we call him a god or spirit chief. One morning he go fishing in his war canoe and he hook a fish so large it pull and fight and tug the line."

His voice faded to the background as he wove the story with his hands, with gestures and dancing, and his clever, expressive face—the battle with the fish, the looks of wonder from the other fishermen, the final rising of the great fish-shaped land out of the sea and the bashing of the fish to form the mountains and plains. "Then a great lizard comes, and he breathe on the land ..."

Lucy was no longer afraid of the chief, and Dorothy and I watched as the girl mirrored Te Puni's expressions and clapped her hands with every surprise.

He was about to leave when Dorothy's pains started.

Our baby, a son, was born early in the morning. Te Puni waited through the night with me and when Dorothy received us, we asked him to stand as godfather. The fact that the chief was not christened and had gods of his own didn't matter to either of us.

We called our boy Arthur, not for me but for Captain Arthur Wakefield.

Arthur Te Puni Lugg.

Alexandria snuggled in with Dorothy and laid her sweet hand on her brother's head, and I hoped our boy would grow up with his sister's gentleness and his mother's kindness. I wished for him the grace of his godfather, and hoped Lucy's engaging curiosity would teach him the wonder of the world. And I wished for him, every day, the happiness that I felt then, surrounded by the people I loved.

—

Humiliation came to Jerningham at the hand of Governor FitzRoy, and he was sent home to England in utter disgrace.

Revans brought me the news on his first visit to our new home in Nelson. He arrived on the mail-boat and stumped up the hill looking like an ogre from a fairy tale in his big boots and a baggy coat. But he won over Alexandria immediately with pockets full of toys and a jack-in-a-box under his hat.

He took the perch at the old *Jewess* table near the end of the verandah and presented Dorothy with a chess set. They played, a skill he'd apparently taught her while I had been adventuring. On the second game he let her win and she chastised him. "How very silly, Mr Revans, to let a bishop decide the game. I'll leave you with Arthur while I check on the baby."

"Those bothersome bishops," said Revans.

I filled our pipes and we sat gazing out across the blue waters of Blind Bay.

"I had no idea she could play chess."

"She plays an intelligent game. Quietly defensive and then—bam! Good timing."

"You were telling me about Jerningham."

"Yes, it all got rather nasty," he said, tilting his head back and blowing away a long line of smoke. "He was publicly reprimanded in a most censorious way. Called an enemy to the government and to the missionaries. To religion, in fact. He was accused by the governor himself of childish bravado with the natives, inciting hatred and animosity, and all sorts of indiscretions."

"Good heavens."

"He was struck off as a magistrate. Which, we probably all agree, is a good thing for the fine people of Wanganui."

"But FitzRoy has no authority to expel him, surely?"

"Ah, no," said Revans. "It was the colonel who sent him off in the end. Finally, he had had enough. He packed Jerningham back home to his father."

"He's gone?"

"This last week. It's the end of an era, my friend. Extraordinary, difficult times. It is unsurprising we seem to have got it all wrong." He sighed and rubbed his hands briskly, as if to say, that's it, on with it! But then he paused, reflective. "It is very sad, you know. Jerningham is one of the few with a deep, intuitive understanding of New Zealand. He grasped the complexities of this place in a way that those buffoons in government never will. Another example of God's cruel humour, to waste such remarkable intelligence on a drunken scrote."

"Is it the last we will see of him?"

"Oh, he'll be back. He still thinks he owns the place."

We forgot about Jerningham then, as Dorothy came out to join us with a tray of lemon water and some sweet biscuits of Lucy's, which Revans praised heartily although they crumbled and fell apart, leaving a glitter of sugar down his suit. He smiled fondly as Dorothy served him, and with surprisingly elegant grace he reached for her hand and kissed it. "You are a veritable jewel in my desolate world, Mrs Lugg. God bless you."

We talked some more and then sat in quiet friendship as the sun set over the mountains, and later Lucy came with a candle and called us in for supper.

—

It was thirty-five years before I would see Jerningham again. He called to me from the side of the road.

"I don't suppose, sir, you could help me out?"

I was in Christchurch and had spent the morning at an auction, bidding for a wedding gift for our youngest, Caroline. She had married a man with land and they required furniture for their farmhouse. I wasn't used to the city nor the beggars in the street.

I fumbled for a coin in my pocket as memories from days long past tumbled from the depths to stand before me. There was something in the light from the pearly sky, the smell of the road and the voice of the man. I looked at him carefully. Hatless, with lank greying hair catching in dark brows and a moustache falling into the unkempt growth on his chin, he peered up. In his wary eyes, I recognised him.

He had been back in the country for some time, of course, with a chequered career in Christchurch politics and a failed marriage, but Dorothy and I had been living away from all that. We had our family and our business in Nelson and didn't travel, content to stay on the outside. We didn't reminisce over our Wellington days. It had been a long time since news of Jerningham had given me any particular wrench.

"Just a shilling or two would help. I seem to have mislaid my wallet."

"Jerningham?"

He appeared not to recognise me. I handed him some coins which he took and counted carefully, something I had never seen him do before.

"There's not another shilling in there, is there, my man?"

"Do you not know me, old friend?" I asked.

I was distressed to see him brought so low. It wasn't the dirty clothes, for on our travels we'd slept rough for weeks and many times he'd walked unshaven out of the bush. It wasn't even the begging, as he'd always borrowed money shamelessly and never paid it back. It was the way he ducked his head between hunched shoulders in the manner of a subservient dog that broke me. I could feel no animosity for him now.

"Come," I said. "Let me buy you dinner."

He lifted his shaggy head to me then and his chin went out. He couldn't name me, but he knew there was something wrong with the order of things. For a moment I thought he would throw his head back and laugh.

He followed me willingly enough to a nearby hotel and had a glass of wine on the table before I had seen him signal the proprietor.

I ordered roast beef and a carafe of local red from the cask. After two quick glasses he looked more like his old self. The street still clung to him like an odour of mushrooms but the arrogance was back.

"You're looking fat, Lugg," he said.

That made me smile. "I'm glad to find you," I said, and it was true.

Both after and before Jerningham, every other adventure in my life had been tame. Nothing matched those years, fresh in the new land and extravagantly reckless, travelling up unchartered rivers with Māori in their war canoes, pistol shooting and riding through wilderness, drinking until we were blind. He had given me an intrepid youth to look back on and I was glad of it.

"I'm writing again, you know," he told me, though I hadn't asked why he found himself begging on the roadside. "I have a book commissioned by the government I am working on. But my immediate circumstances are such …" He waved his hand dismissively, a gesture I knew so well.

He asked no questions of me. He had my name now but not my substance. He seemed to have lost the details of days so long ago they were less real to him that the fictions he had written in his best-selling books. I imagined he had forgotten Dorothy, hundreds of women and barrels of wine ago. Tīraweke was no longer the chattering bird with bright inquisitive eyes and fast movements. He drank in gulps, and when the dinner arrived he shovelled meat into his bony body and the gravy dripped onto his dirty shirt.

His father had immigrated to New Zealand, but both Edward Gibbon and the colonel were long dead. Other uncles had arrived and died, the notorious Daniel and a belligerent Uncle Felix. His cousin Charley Torlesse had been invalided home before an early death, a sad end to my fine young friend. Jerningham was the last man standing.

He wasn't listening to me, but I told him about my life. Eight healthy children, all married now. Grandchildren too. An import business I ran with my wife—antiques and furniture mostly from the East.

"Dorothy has an eye for quality," I told him, but at her name he didn't pause, just went on lifting his fork from plate to hungry mouth.

Once, Bently had found me hungry on the road in Nelson and had taken me in for a meal. I never thanked him. After Ada had come for tea, I saw neither of them again. Bently had been distraught at his godfather's death. There was nothing to keep him in New Zealand and they had left a few months later for Valparaiso, Ada growing with child. We heard she gave birth to twins on the boat and I was pleased for her.

"I still walk the hills with Charles Heaphy, whenever our paths cross," I said to Jerningham now, and he looked up at that.

"You know Heaphy?"

"You remember we were together in Wellington?"

He shrugged. I was only important as coin for dinner.

When the food and the wine were gone, I refused to buy another carafe. "That's it, Jerningham. I'm going home to my family."

He pushed his chair back and held his hand across the table to me. When I took it, for the first time he noticed my artificial thumb and tilted my hand towards him. It wasn't his original gift, the wooden one, but an updated version of silver and leather. My eyes, rheumy now with age and use, filled fast. I saw his face shift and quiver, but it was in vain. He searched for something he couldn't find, a memory that had turned to dust and crumbled away so only the faintest outline remained.

Finally, he took his hand away and rubbed his eyes. Then, with the refreshed vigour of a watered man, he pushed his fingers through his hair, straightened his shoulders, lifted his chin so he looked almost sober and sauntered out into the street.

I was in my office a month or so later when I read in the newspaper that Edward Jerningham Wakefield had been taken unconscious to the Ashburton Almshouse. He had no papers with him and had died unrecognised and alone. A cousin eventually came to find him, but by then he'd been buried in a pauper's grave.

I took the afternoon off and went home to Dorothy. It was Easter; the children had recently left after a weekend of noisy family life. Dorothy was working in her garden, under the fruit trees, with her leather gloves on. I kissed her and gave her the sad news.

Long after she returned to her pruning I remained, looking over my world and thinking back to those chaotic Wellington days and Jerningham's reckless influence on us all. Wondering how possibly to make sense of a man like that.

AUTHOR'S NOTE

Jerningham is a fictionalised account of the early colonial settlement of Wellington. Many of the characters, including Jerningham himself, are real, and while I have given these characters actions and words from my imagination I have tried to be true to their characters, as much as one can, drawing from journals, letters and contemporaneous reports. Events are similarly fictionalised to make a story, but for major events, like the Wairau Affray, I have pulled together a possible sequence of actions from many reports. The dates of historical events are accurate.

My narrator, Arthur Lugg, is imaginary, as is his wife, Dorothy.

To avoid confusion I have mostly adopted modern spellings and used macrons for Māori words, although have kept some colonialisms for authenticity, such as Cook's Strait, Pito-one and Wanganui. "Maoris" appears in dialogue. For names of iwi and hapū, when in doubt I have defaulted to Jerningham's usage in his journals.

Please know that the attitudes to race, culture, gender and class in this novel are not designed to offend or provoke, but to illustrate the common perspective among 1840s colonials. They weren't bad people; this is what they knew. I wish I could have had a feisty heroine and woke bloke. But, above all, I have aimed for authenticity.

ACKNOWLEDGEMENTS

Unfathomable thanks to Paul, for his belief, support and patience over the last years as Jerningham moved in and joined us every night at the dinner table. And to David, Annie and Guy, best kids in the world, for the conversations and banter and the lovely friends they keep bringing home.

For teaching me the craft of writing I owe Mandy Hager a huge debt, and for her Whitlits class of 2018, with whom I workshopped and laughed and learned how to be an author. I discovered so much that year at Whitireia, more than just how to put words on a page. Thanks to Helen and Omara for the music and friendship.

Mary McCallum of The Cuba Press is a kind and generous editor, dead smart. Many thanks to her, Paul Stewart, Roger Whelan and designer Sarah Bolland—I'm so proud to work with this creative team—and to Carrie Wainwright, for checking my te reo. Also big thanks to Wakefields Digital in Wellington for support in printing the book. Rakai Karaitiana, it's a hell of a cover. You captured the essence of Tīraweke and the surreality of colonialism and I am awed and delighted.

I'd like to acknowledge the support of librarians and curators in the Museum of New Zealand Te Papa Tongarewa, the National Library of New Zealand Te Puna

Mātauranga o Aotearoa, Nelson Provincial Museum Pupuri Taonga O Te Tai Ao and Puke Ariki in New Plymouth. The New Zealand Society of Authors continues to guide me through the complexities of the book trade in 2020 and has given me new friends, for which I am very grateful.

To the *Spirit of New Zealand* captains, Gerard Prendeville and Nic Charrington, and their wonderful crews, thanks for sharing your knowledge of the sea and the history and workings of tall ships and for giving me hands-on experience of what it means to sail "close enough to throw a biscuit" on a reef. I feel closer to the 1840s up the rigging than anywhere else.

And finally to Wellington, where I grew up not knowing any of this story. The Wakefields were scoundrels, but they founded a wonderful city. You can't beat it on any day.

PHOTO: ANNA WARD

ABOUT THE AUTHOR

CRISTINA SANDERS grew up in the family's Gateway Bookshop in Wellington, where all books were tested on children. She went on to work for some years in book marketing and publishing both in New Zealand and London, and has recently begun writing novels.

Her young adult manuscript, *Displaced*, inspired by her family's immigration from Norway in the 1870s, won the 2020 Storylines Tessa Duder Award. *Jerningham* is her first novel for adults.

Cristina lives in Hawke's Bay with her family, where she runs on the hills and, whenever she can, sails away on tall ships.

www.cristinasanders.me